Praise for The Memory Thief

"Dazzlingly original and as haunting as a dream, Emily Colin's mesmerizing debut explores the way memory, love, and great loss bind our lives together in ways we might never expect. From its audacious opening to its knockout last pages, I was enthralled."

—CAROLINE LEAVITT, *New York Times* bestselling author of *Cruel Beautiful World*

"In *The Memory Thief*, love itself is a character, able to transcend all natural boundaries to find its way home, or learn to let go. Emily Colin writes about loss with heartbreaking conviction, and yet there is a knowing sweetness at the core of this richly emotional tale. Here is a lovely, self-assured debut from a writer to watch."

—JOSHILYN JACKSON, *New York Times* bestselling author of *The Opposite of Everyone*

"This absorbing first effort brings to mind the mountaineers of a Jon Krakauer read, the tenderness of a Nicholas Sparks novel, and the enduring love story of Charles Martin's *The Mountain Between Us*, all sprinkled with a heady dose of passion. Colin is an author to watch and savor." —*Booklist*

BY EMILY COLIN

The Memory Thief

The Dream Keeper's Daughter

The
Dream Keeper's
Daughter

The
Dream Keeper's
Daughter

a novel

EMILY COLIN

BALLANTINE BOOKS

NEW YORK

Copyright © 2017 by Emily Colin

Published in the United States by Ballantine Books, an imprint of Random House,
a division of Penguin Random House LLC, New York.

BALLANTINE and the HOUSE colophon are registered trademarks of
Penguin Random House LLC.

ISBN 978-1-101-88431-7
Ebook ISBN 978-1-101-88433-1

Printed in the United States of America on acid-free paper

randomhousebooks.com

2 4 6 8 9 7 5 3 1

Title page illustration: © iStockphoto.com/embra

First Edition

Book design by Jo Anne Metsch

This book is for the justice warriors. For those who fight for what they believe in, to give voice to the voiceless and agency to the oppressed, though the battle is long and the rewards may be long in coming.

This book is for the voiceless and the oppressed. Your thoughts and words matter, though it may often seem otherwise. You matter. Don't let anyone convince you otherwise. You hold in your hearts the power to change the world.

This book is for the heroes whose lives are dedicated to a cause greater than themselves, who work long hours for little money and sometimes for no money at all. There is always more work to be done. There is never enough time. Because you would never sing your own praises, I'll sing them for you. The world is a better place with you in it.

And finally, this book is for the artists—the writers and musicians, the painters and playwrights. Now, more than ever, we need you. Accept nothing. Make us uncomfortable. Keep us curious. Show us the truth. See us home.

The
Dream Keeper's Daughter

Isabel

I am on my knees, the sun beating on my back and dirt from long-dead bones sifting through my gloved fingers, when my cellphone rings.

Focused as I am on the dig, the phone's shrill summons startles me. I jolt upright and lose my balance, falling on my butt and sending a cloud of dirt into the air. Behind me, I hear Jake, one of my graduate students, let out what can only be described as a guffaw. I swivel to glare at him and he smothers it into a cough, looking abashed. Color creeps up his cheeks, already reddened from the sun and wind.

I assume the phone call will be from my supervisor, back at the College of Charleston. Or from my dad, who keeps Finn, my seven-year-old daughter, when I do fieldwork. Squinting to make out the number, I try to suppress the instinctive, icy panic I feel whenever the phone rings: *It's the school. Finn is gone. She was on the playground at recess and now they can't find her anywhere, it's like she vanished into thin air.*

It's not useful to react this way, I admonish myself. It's not productive. But I can't help it. For all my years of mixed martial arts training and a black belt in judo, I still don't feel like the world is a safe place, a place where people stay.

Then I see who's calling me, and I forget Jake, forget Finn, forget everything but the three innocuous little letters that have appeared on my screen.

Max.

The phone rings again, but my hands are shaking so badly that it takes what feels like forever to get my gloves off, and then two tries before I can answer the call. My heart beats in triple time as I press the phone to my ear. "Hello?" I say, and then, when there's no response, "Max? Is that you?"

There is silence on the other end of the line, and then, as if coming from the end of a long, long tunnel, laced with static, a voice I thought I'd never hear again: "Isabel."

All he says is my name—but it's Max, there's no doubt in my mind. In the six years we knew each other, I heard Max say my name innumerable times, in a thousand different ways. Hollering at me from the woods that linked our houses, eager for me to come outside. Trying to get my attention as we lay next to each other in the tree house he'd built, paging through old *National Geographic*s. In wonder, the first time he kissed me, his fingers light on my face. And later, when we made Finn, as if those three syllables were a sacrament, a holy word that held more meaning than "I love you." I would know Max's voice anywhere.

The thing is, I haven't heard it since before Finn was born.

My fingers are suddenly nerveless, and the pick I'm holding thumps into the dirt. "Oh my God, Max," I say. "Where are you?"

Silence on the other end of the line, and then he says my name again, his voice limned with desperation. "Isabel," he says, and then there is static. In frustration, I press the phone harder against my ear, trying to make out the words. But I can't understand a damn thing. Then his voice comes clear again: "Keep her safe."

"Max, I can hardly hear you. Keep who safe? Tell me where you are," I say, but it's too late. I'm talking to an empty line.

I try to call back, but all I hear is the message I've gotten for the past seven years: *The number you've dialed has been disconnected or is no longer in service.* I call over and over, but the result is the same.

Gradually I become aware that I am still kneeling in the dirt, tears spilling down my face, in the middle of an archaeological dig I am supposed to be overseeing. One by one, the blurry faces of my grad students swim into view. Jake is staring at me, puzzled and alarmed.

Dizzy, half-blind, I get to my feet. "Excuse me," I mumble. And then I do something I've never done before, not in five years of graduate school and two years of teaching.

I walk right off the dig.

Isabel

I can hear Jake's steps behind me, crunching on gravel, can hear him calling my name, wanting to know what's wrong. But how can I possibly explain?

I make myself turn and lift a hand in reassurance, hoping my sunglasses hide the tears that sting my eyes, unbidden. I hear my voice, impossibly even, say that everything is all right, I just need a few minutes alone. That he is in charge until I get back.

Even through the haze that clouds my vision, I can tell Jake is unconvinced, so I attempt a smile. Apparently this is less than successful, because he winces. His mouth opens, but before he poses a question I have no idea how to answer, I fumble in my pocket for the keys to the van and manage to open the door. Moving as if in a dream, I settle behind the wheel and shut the door between us with a vague feeling of regret. This is not how a supervisor ought to behave, but right now I can't muster the energy to care.

Hands trembling, I back the van out of the site and pull onto the road, ignoring the bone-rattling thump that ensues when one of the wheels sinks into a pothole. The last thing I see is Jake standing at the edge of the parking lot, hands shoved in the pockets of his khaki shorts, staring after me with a look of total bewilderment on his face.

I have no idea where I'm going, and after a few minutes it becomes clear to me that I really shouldn't be behind the wheel at all. I can hardly drive in a straight line, much less watch out for traffic. The fact that we are in Barbados, where people drive on what I still think of as the wrong side of the road, doesn't help. And so I pull over at the first place I see—Cutters Deli, a restaurant that proudly advertises itself as the purveyor of "#1 Rum Punch."

Harboring the vague notion that a drink will calm me down, I stagger out of the car. But as I make my way toward the porch, logic asserts itself. I can't get drunk—I'm working. What the hell am I thinking?

I look back at the car, then at the restaurant. The shaking has resumed, a head-to-toe trembling that makes my teeth clack together and my knees buckle. With the exception of the day my mother vanished—six years before I lost Max—I have never felt so alone.

In desperation, I imagine that my closest friend, Ryan, is here with me. I hear his deep voice telling me to focus. Concentrate. *If you're thinking,* his voice says, *you can't be feeling. Look around. Tell me what you see.*

"All right," I say aloud. I force myself to look at Cutters, to truly take in the bright yellow plaster of the exterior, the blue metal roof that gleams in the midday sun. My eyes travel over the patio, with its flagstones and round white tables surrounded by benches, where two families sit, chowing down on the restaurant's specialty—flying fish sandwiches. I can smell the seasoned batter the cook used to fry the fish, and rising above that, the tang of the hot pepper sauce Cutters is famous for using in their slaw.

Ryan's strategy is working. Heartened, I continue my inventory. The tree that shades the patio needs trimming, I note with commendable objectivity. The stones could benefit from a good power wash. And the paint on the broken trident—the symbol of the colony's break from England—next to the restaurant's name could really use a touch-up. Breath coming easier, I take in the words painted on the side of the building: *Cutters Bajan Deli,* large enough to cover the entire wall, and then smaller, *of Barbados*, just in case a hapless traveler has lost their way entirely. If Ryan were here, that would make him laugh.

"Okay, Ry," I whisper, taking a few steps closer to the building. "I'm okay."

I don't know if this is actually true, but at least I am capable of deciding what to do next. Leaning against the side of the restaurant, phone slick in my sweaty hands, I dial Max's number one more time. Again I hear the woman's dispassionate, automated voice. I have to fight the effort to throw the phone to the ground and stomp on it— after all, I reason, how will Max call me back if I don't have a phone?

The better question, of course, is this: How did he call me at all? And why now, after all this time?

I haven't seen or heard from Max for almost eight years. The day after I'd told him I was pregnant with Finn, he disappeared—less than fifty feet from where I was standing, while I screamed his name.

It's over ninety degrees outside, but I shiver in my tank top and shorts. That day—it feels like another lifetime—he'd asked me to meet him in the woods between our parents' houses. This was in no way an unusual request—we'd come upon each other for the very first time in those woods, when I was sixteen and he seventeen, and we'd been meeting there ever since. It was our retreat, a place where we could escape—he from the claustrophobic demands of his parents, I from the oppressive silence of an empty house, haunted by my workaholic, grieving father and the uneasy ghost of my mother.

We had made love for the first time there—had made Finn, five years later, on the sun-warmed boards of the tree house Max had built, high in the branches of one of the ancient oaks. It was spring break of my senior year at the University of South Carolina at Columbia, and I'd just come back from a volunteer dig in Greece, still glowing with the memory of it. I'd told Max every detail, like I'd told him so many stories over the years, and he'd listened, his eyes fixed on my face, running his hands through my hair, winding the curls around his fingers.

This is a far better memory than the day I lost him, and standing in the bright sunlight of a Barbados afternoon, I close my eyes, bringing it to life. The plaster wall is warm against my back, but I barely feel it. I breathe deeply, taking in the unmistakable scent of a South Carolina spring: the delicate fragrance of wisteria, winding inexorably around the trunk of the oak that held the tree house, the sweet tang of the strawberries Max had brought, fresh from his family's garden.

I must be in shock, that's all I can figure, because as much as it hurts to think of him like this—to remember a time when we were happy—I can't seem to help myself. Around me, life goes on—the restaurant door slamming shut, a waitress asking if she can bring anyone another drink—but these sounds retreat, dialed back as if someone has turned down the volume. Instead I hear the chirp of crickets and the call of frogs from the pond beyond the tree house's clearing. I see Max's gray eyes, intent on my brown ones, dark hair framing his face, the stubble that covers his cheekbones sparking blond in the fading light.

It had been weeks since we'd been together. I knew he wanted me—I could feel it in the tension of his body against mine, in the need, barely stifled, as he traced my shape, skimming his hand over my ribs to the swell of my hip and back again. Still, he let me tell him about the tombs and the dust, the exhilaration I'd felt when I touched a shard of pottery no one had seen for thousands of years, brushed the dirt from it, and lifted it from the earth. He let me talk the sun down as we lay face-to-face on the tree house floor, heads pillowed on the cushions we'd brought up long ago, wrapped in an unmistakable sense of peace. Until finally I ran out of words and he moved above me, blocking out the last of the light. *God, I've missed you*, he said. *Don't go away like that again, okay? Or better yet, take me with you.*

I laughed at that, my breath coming short at his touch on my bare skin. *On a dig? All those hours kneeling in the dirt, poking at things. You'd be bored to death.*

He raised his head then to look at me, one hand moving between my legs, fingers sliding inside me first in query, then in demand. *What do you think I do all day?* he asked, closing his mouth on my breast, slipping backward out of my grasp when I tried to pull him down to me. *Besides, I'd follow you anywhere. You know that.*

Come here, then. I tried to pull him closer, and he shook his head, laughing.

Not so fast, Isabel. I've been waiting for you for weeks. You can damn well wait a few more minutes.

Really? I said, and pushed him down onto the floorboards. His smile faded and his eyes fixed on me, hypnotized, as I knelt between his legs and took him in my mouth, bent on revenge.

All right, he said, pulling me on top of him. *You win.* He arched his hips, filling me, and we began to move, there in the gathering dusk.

I can still remember the feel of Max's hands, callused from years of working in gardens and greenhouses, settling on my hips. Can remember looking down at him, seeing the darkness that filled his eyes, his lips mouthing my name. And then him coming to his knees with me in his arms, my hair falling like a curtain to shelter us both, his mouth warm and urgent on my neck, my breasts. *Isabel,* he said, panting. *I don't have—you know. Oh, God, I can't stop.*

I dug my nails into his shoulders, pressing myself against him so I could feel him moving inside me, deep as if we were one flesh. *So don't,* I whispered, swept up by a wave of recklessness. And, covering his mouth with mine, I let the wave carry us both away.

That was how Finn came to be—a surprise but not an accident, the way I'd always thought of it. I'd known good and well that afternoon what might happen, and so had Max. The way we'd both figured it, it had just been a matter of *when.* Or at least that's what I'd always thought. Maybe Max had thought something else. Maybe he hadn't wanted her at all.

I open my eyes, breathing hard. Around me the world comes back into focus—the searing light, the hum of the restaurant's air conditioner, a sunburned couple walking up the steps to the porch.

The woman gives me a curious glance and then lengthens her stride in a sudden hurry to get inside. I look down at myself, realizing for the first time that I am covered in dirt and mud from the dig. My cutoff shorts are ripped from their encounter with an ancient piece of jagged metal.

Still, I can't bring myself to care. I can still feel Max's touch on my skin, gripping me hard enough to bruise, branding me. I can see myself standing in my father's kitchen eight weeks later, fingers splayed on the worn surface of the table, telling Max I am pregnant. Can see his face, eyes first wide with shock, then lit with what I could swear was joy. I remember him walking around the table and taking me by the shoulders, asking me if I was sure, lowering his face into my hair and wrapping his arms around me, saying that he loved me and everything would be okay. He would take care of us both.

And then I remember him dropping his arms and backing away, an odd look on his face. "I have to go," he'd said, which was true enough—he had work in twenty minutes. "Meet me at the tree house tomorrow? Noon? I have the day off."

"All right. But Max, what's the matter? Are you angry? Or is there . . ." I'd stopped, unwilling to articulate the ugly thought that had come to mind as soon as I'd seen that look on his face—that there was someone else. Five minutes before, I would have sworn that wasn't possible. Now I wasn't so sure.

"Of course I'm not angry. Everything's fine," he'd said, but I knew him well enough to tell when he was lying. I could see it in the way his eyes slid from mine, the way he shifted from foot to foot, as if he couldn't wait to get away from me.

That hurt more than anything else. Max had been the one who consoled me when my mother disappeared, who filled the hole she'd left in my heart. He'd held me when I cried for her, let me say the words my father refused to hear: *She's dead or she deserted us. Either way, she's not coming back.* Max had been there for me when my father sank into obsession, when he stopped coming to my parent-teacher conferences or even buying food. For six years, Max had been everything to me. Other than a brief period when I'd wanted space from our friendship—terrified that I was falling for him—we had been inseparable since the day we met in the woods. Even the four years I'd spent at Columbia, earning my degree while Max studied history at the College of Charleston and worked his way up the chain of a local gardening business, hadn't driven us apart—or so I'd believed.

"Max," I said again, mistrust clear in my voice, and he forced a smile.

"I'm happy, Isabel. Really, I am." He rested his palm on my belly with a gentleness I'd never felt from him before, and for a moment I let myself believe that it was true. I stood still under his touch, imagining the cluster of cells that was Finn, growing and changing even in this single moment, becoming a tiny person that one day I would hold in my arms. And then, with eerie premonition, I imagined raising that person alone.

"I'm glad," I said, and lifted my chin. "Because the way you're acting, it's pretty hard to tell."

His voice went soft, apologetic. "I'm a little overwhelmed, that's all. It's a lot to take in. And I . . . well, I need to tell you something."

Fear must have flashed across my face then, followed quickly by anger, because he shook his head, a rueful smile lifting his lips. "Nothing like that. Jesus. You think I'd have the balls to cheat on you, let alone the desire? Christ, you'd scalp me."

"What, then?" I didn't like the way my voice sounded, fearful and small.

"Tomorrow, all right? In the clearing. I'll tell you everything, I promise."

"Why not now?"

"Because I have to get to work. In fifteen minutes," he added, checking his watch. "Which isn't nearly long enough. Not to mention—well, never mind."

I stood there, taking in the worry in his gray eyes, trying to figure out what could be so awful. "Are you dying?" I asked, my voice cracking.

"What? Of course not." His lips twitched.

"Well, then—what?" I said, staring up at him in confusion.

For a moment I didn't think he was going to answer. Then he muttered, "I'm late anyway. The hell with it," and took my face in his hands, kissing me with a savage desperation that struck an icy chord of fear in my heart. "I love you," he said, the pressure of his fingers insistent against my skin. "You believe that, don't you?"

"Of course," I said, more alarmed than ever. "Max, what is it?"

He cradled my face between his palms. "I've always loved you," he said, brushing one last kiss across my lips and stepping away. "Always. Remember that, would you? No matter what."

I said I would. And I've kept my promise, despite everything.

He'd asked me to meet him that day, and I'd come—just in time to see him running into the trees that bordered the other side of the clearing, crashing through the brush. *Stop, Isabel*, he'd yelled when I gave chase. I hadn't listened, for all the good it had done me. But I'd gotten tangled in a briar bush—I'd never known those damn woods as well as he had—and by the time I'd freed myself, he was nowhere to be found. I'd followed the trail he'd left until I couldn't pick it up anymore. Had run all the way to the road, calling his name, then back to the clearing, with no sign of him. He was just—gone.

It's been years since I've let myself think of him like this, let myself remember what it was like to have him hold me, much less move inside me, calling my name. This phone call has ripped me wide open, and I force myself to take deep breaths. *Keep her safe*, he'd said. Fear ripples through me. Did he mean Finn?

This is an absurd thought. I'm sure of it. Max has never met his daughter. Besides, she's home with my dad, who has redeemed himself by being a grandfather extraordinaire. He would never allow anything to happen to her.

Still, the fear that's been with me since the day my mother

vanished—a low, simmering flame that burst into a conflagration when Max disappeared and only burned hotter when Finn was born—won't let me rest. *What if she's gone?* I think, clutching the phone in my hand. *What if it—whatever it is—got her too?*

I know I'm not being reasonable. Yes, Max and my mother vanished in the same approximate geographic area, six years apart. Yes, neither one was ever found. But despite the police's concerted efforts, they never discovered a connection between the two disappearances. A *coincidence*, they said. There is no bogeyman that rose up out of the ground and swallowed my mother and the father of my child. No incorporeal curse destined to strike her down like a doomed princess in a fairy tale. I know that to be true. But all the same, I am afraid.

I shouldn't have left her, I think, dialing my father's number. *What good is all my martial arts training if I'm in another country? I got complacent, I let down my guard. And now look what's happened. It's all my fault. I know better.*

My father's cell rings once, then again, and my heart flutters in my chest like a trapped bird, struggling to breach the bars of its cage. *Please,* I pray, even though organized religion has never been my thing. *Please let her be okay. Oh, God, please.*

Just when I've decided that the bogeyman has gotten him too, my father answers. "Hi, Isabel," he says, calm as can be. "How's it going?"

I am so relieved to hear his voice, for a second I can't even reply. Then, gripping the phone for all I'm worth, I blurt out, "Finn. Is Finn all right?"

"Finn?" my dad says, sounding puzzled. "She's fine. I just picked her up from school. It's the last day, you know. We were about to go down to the creek and see if we could catch some frogs for her terrarium."

My legs give way, and I slide down the wall until I'm sitting on the ground. "Thank God."

"Isabel?" my dad says. "What's the matter?"

My throat is bone dry, and at first all I can manage is a stammer. "I . . ."

"Are you okay?" my dad says, and now he sounds panicked. I make an effort to pull myself together.

"Yes," I say. "And no. Max called me."

There's a muffled sound, as if my father has put his hand over the speaker. Then I hear him yell to Finn, "Yes, it's your mom, sweetie. Of course you can talk to her, in a minute."

I can't make out Finn's reply, but I can hear her voice, sweet and high-pitched. Something in me relaxes at the sound of it, and my heart resumes its normal rhythm. I watch people walk by on their way to places unknown—an older woman pushing a baby carriage, her dark hair twisted up in a complex arrangement of braids; two teenage boys, shouting at a group of girls across the street—and feel the world settle back into place around me. *All right*, I think. *She's all right.*

"Isabel!" my father says, sharply enough that I realize this isn't the first time.

"What?" I ask, startled back into the present.

"I thought you said—but you couldn't have. Did you say . . . Max called you?"

"Oh. Yes, I said that. Because he did."

"What do you mean?" His voice is harsh, urgent. "Just one second, Finn. Hang on, love. Go check on the crickets we caught, would you? Make sure they haven't escaped."

I hear Finn murmur in acquiescence. Then my father says, "Okay. What do you mean Max called you?"

So I tell him everything that happened—which seems like precious little, to have disrupted my world the way it did. He's silent for a long minute. At last he says, "Sweetie, it couldn't have been him. How could it? You called back, and the line was disconnected. It had to be some kind of—I don't know, some sort of cosmic cyber-mistake."

"But he said my name," I say stubbornly. "It was his voice, Dad, I know it."

"Isabel, you said there was static. Maybe you just wanted it to be him so badly, you heard what you needed to hear."

"How can you say that?" I hiss, earning peculiar looks from passersby. "You of all people. How can you just discount this?"

My father sucks in his breath and I know I've hurt him. "Me of all people," he says. "Of all people, I know how much you want it to have been Max. All right, Isabel? I *know*. That's why I'm saying this, not to judge you, honey. Christ, I'm the last person who's got a leg to stand on in that department."

"Damn right." I only mean to think it, but from the sound my dad makes—like I've stabbed him—I know I've said it out loud. For a moment I consider apologizing—whatever my dad lacked when I was a teenager, he's more than made up for it with Finn—but then I change my mind. We've never talked about what happened after my mother disappeared, but there's a first time for everything.

"Isabel," my father says again, "I know I've hurt you. I know I can't ever fix it, even though I've tried my best with Finn. But please listen to me. Don't do to your daughter what I did to mine. Don't let the obsession devour you—because believe me, honey, it will if you let it."

"It was him," I say. "I know it was."

"Don't do this," my father begs.

"Let me talk to Finn," I say, getting to my feet.

"If you won't listen to me," my father says, "then maybe you'll listen to Ryan. Have you told him yet?"

"No. I called you first. I wanted to make sure Finn was okay."

"She's absolutely fine, Isabel. Look, here she is." The receiver changes hands, and then I hear Finn's voice, small but clear.

"Mama?"

"Hey, sweetie," I say, injecting cheer into my voice. "How was school?"

"It was good. Me and Grandpa helped Miss Evie with her

garden—you know, his new neighbor? She has *chickens*. And guess what? When we were there, the baby chicks hatched! There were *six* of them. Miss Evie said when they get a little older, I could take one home. Can we, Mama? Please?"

The sheer normalcy of our conversation makes me smile. I imagine her in her South Carolina Aquarium T-shirt, jeans with the hole in the knee, and rubber boots—her "frog-catching clothes"—her black hair in two messy pigtails that constitute my dad's best effort at little-girl hair care. I can see her clutching the phone in one grubby hand, her gray eyes—a legacy from her father—shining with an eagerness I've always found so hard to resist. "I don't know, monkey. We'll talk about it when I get back, okay?"

"Okay," Finn agrees reluctantly. "They're really cute. All fluffy and yellow."

"Yeah?" I straighten up and start walking to the car. Relief floods me. She sounds just like she always does. As long as I know Finn is all right, I can put one foot in front of the other. I can finish up my dig and go home—as long as she is all right. "Be a good girl," I tell her. "Listen to Grandpa, okay?"

"I'm always good," she says, affronted.

"Of course you are." I fumble with my keys and ease into the van, grimacing as my bare legs stick to the seat. "You and Grandpa are going to catch frogs, huh?"

"Yep. We have the net and the bucket and everything. But we won't *hurt* them. Just keep them for a couple of days, and then put them back again." Her voice is reproachful, as if I've insinuated that she and my father were poised to go on an amphibian-murdering spree.

"Sounds fun, baby. You be careful."

"Oh, Mama," Finn sighs. "Grandpa is a good babysitter. And you're coming back on Tuesday. Then you can look after me yourself."

She sounds so much like an exasperated teenager, I have to laugh. In the background I can hear my father rustling around, most likely gathering their frog-catching equipment. The sounds are homey, familiar, and I feel myself begin to relax bit by bit. I envision the house where I spent my teenage years, its high ceilings and dark wood floors, its back door that opens on the small expanse of grass where I used to sit and read, my back propped against the gnarled trunk of the magnolia tree. As if meditating, I walk myself across the lawn and down the path to the creek, a thin ribbon of water no more than two feet wide. I can hear the croak of the frogs, see the low sweep of dragonflies. Beyond the creek I can see the trees that mark the edge of the woods, the property that linked Max's home to mine. Step by step I make my way through the trees, feel the filtered sunlight bathe my face and the branches scratch my skin.

"Grandpa!" Finn scolds. "Not that one. It's way too small. The frogs will be all squashed. They need their space."

While they haggle over the size of the frogs' transport, I close my eyes and silently repeat my mantra — the one that's kept me going for the past eight years, through losing Max and a rocky pregnancy with Finn, through graduate school and twelve-hour workdays and countless training sessions at the dojo until every muscle in my body ached. *Don't worry, baby. I won't let anything happen to you.* It's as much a promise to Max as it is to myself and Finn, and I have kept it all these years without fail.

I could have sworn that I was repeating those ten words to myself, that they never passed my lips. But perhaps I am wrong, because Finn speaks again. Her tone is matter-of-fact, but the words send my heart racing all the same. "Silly Mama," she says. "Don't you know? It already has."

Max

The world is night, and in it I am falling.

In the darkness, I hold tight to memories of Isabel—not the last time I saw her, screaming my name as she tore after me through the trees, but the first time, six years ago. She'd been wandering in the woods that bordered both our houses (*my woods*, I'd thought of them then, with deep possessiveness). I heard her coming, crushing leaves underfoot, disturbing the tranquillity I'd come to take for granted. Irritation bubbled under my ribs as I thought of the plants she was trampling, the sanctuary of the woods destroyed.

Then I saw her, heading toward me through the trees, and forgot to be annoyed. She was about my age, I thought, sixteen or seventeen, with a spill of curly black hair that sparked blue in the sun. It fell to her waist, catching on branches, getting in her eyes so that she had to keep brushing it back. I found myself wondering what it would be like to run my hands through that fall of hair—if it would be silky to the touch, if it would slip heedless through my fingers like water, leaving nothing behind but sensation.

I shook my head, trying to chase the image away. Still, I could swear I felt the weight of her hair in my hands, sun-warm and smelling of pine needles. A strange feeling settled over me—restless, anticipatory. I leaned against the trunk of the birch tree nearest me and watched her. God, she made more noise than a herd of elephants, stomping on every fallen branch as if she was doing it on purpose, sending a murder of crows high into the air. How could such a delicate person make such an unbelievable racket?

Racket or no, she noticed when the crows took to the air. She lifted her head, gazing up through the trees to the clear patch of sky beyond. That was when I got my first clear glimpse of her face, and my heart stuttered in my chest. I couldn't have said, later, what made her so beautiful, just that I was drawn to her, in a way from which there was no turning back. It had nothing to do with her looks, although those were pretty enough—the curve of high cheekbones, the hint of full lips, dark-fringed eyes tilted upward to watch the birds' flight. No, this was something else. My aunt would have called it her aura, but I hated superstitious crap like that.

Whatever you chose to name it, the effect was the same: It struck me hard and I pressed the flat of one hand against my chest, willing my heart back to a normal rhythm. Inside me something resonated, vibrating against my bones so that the fingers of my other hand trembled, gripping the trunk of the birch.

The birds had gone now, flying in a V for safe harbor, but the girl still stood there. She looked lost, as if she'd misplaced something of great value and didn't think there was much chance of finding it. Seeing her look like that bothered me—but why? I'd never spoken a word to this strange girl, never seen her before in my life.

I called out to her, stepping into the sunlight. She didn't scream or run. Instead she simply looked at me, as if all along she'd expected to find me standing there. Her eyes were a deep, fathomless blue, like the sky after a storm.

Then she spoke, and I was the one who was lost.

Falling through the dark now, I can still hear her voice. I cling to it like a lifeline. Still I fall, tumbling alone through the pitch-black, moonless night.

My descent lasts forever. It's as if there's never been anything but the blackness, pressing in on me so that it's hard to breathe, expanding exponentially so that I scatter, flung into the far corners of the universe like so many beads of mercury. I open my eyes wide, straining to admit any particle of light, but it's useless; the darkness is impenetrable. I plummet in a permanent state of free fall, gravity abandoned.

In a desperate effort to keep myself together, I cast my mind back to the last memory I have, the moments before I fell—standing in the woods behind my parents' house, waiting for Isabel. The moment I saw a ghost, the moment I made my choice.

The woods went quiet. This was the first thing I noticed—the birds stopped singing, the squirrels ceased quarreling in the trees. Even the wind seemed to have quit blowing, so that the leaves and branches were still.

It came over me then—the instinct of the hunted, as if someone's gaze had fallen on me and rested there, patient, assessing. As if I was prey.

But I was alone in the silent woods.

A cold spot sprang up between my shoulder blades. Slowly, I turned.

And then I saw *him*, coming through the trees toward the clearing, looking just like he did in the antique portrait hanging in my parents' hallway. Dark hair and my gray eyes, beard and mustache neatly trimmed, wearing an honest-to-God frock coat.

Robert Adair.

At first I thought I was dreaming. It didn't matter what I'd seen in the woods all those years ago, what I'd come to believe really happened to Isabel's mother. This man couldn't be real. Because otherwise, I was standing fifteen feet away from my six-times-over grandfather.

We stared at each other. I was too shocked to speak, and for his part, how could he? He was a dead man.

Then I heard Isabel in the woods behind me, and my breath came harsh in my throat. How would I ever explain this to her? Although, come to think of it, Robert's appearance did lend credence to the confession I'd planned to make: *Well, see, your mother didn't just disappear—she followed a ghost into the woods and never came out again. And me, I've spent the past six years trying to find her.*

She'd think I was crazy. And then she'd hate me for not telling her that I was the last person to see Julia the day she disappeared.

I thought of our baby, little more than a collection of cells, and my heart twisted. Eyes fixed on the apparition of Robert Adair, I fingered my grandmother's wedding ring. I'd been carrying it around in my pocket all week, waiting for the right moment. Somehow, touching it gave me the courage to speak.

"What do you want?" I said to Robert, as if he were a real person and not one of my ancestors who'd died just after the Civil War.

He didn't reply. Instead, he lifted one hand in summons and then turned, heading back through the woods the way he'd come.

For a fraction of a second, I hesitated. And then I ran after him, pushing through the trees just in time to see him disappearing under the overhang of a big oak. Behind me, I heard Isabel calling my name: "Max, where are you going? Max, stop!"

Torn, I glanced over my shoulder into the clearing. I saw her standing there in a green sundress, the sun gleaming on her blue-black hair—my future. And then I looked ahead into the woods, where Robert Adair was barely visible.

This was my chance. Either I could follow him and risk finding out where Isabel's mother had really gone—or I could walk back into the clearing and lie my ass off. Pretend I'd never seen Julia Griffin the day she vanished. Get down on my knees, propose. Swallow the guilt.

"Stay there!" I yelled at her, and ran after Robert. Bursting through a stand of pine branches, I caught sight of him a few yards away. Then he disappeared around the curve of a giant oak, and, cursing, I redoubled my pace.

By now I could hear Isabel running—of course she hadn't listened to me. "Stop!" I yelled with all the air I had left in my lungs.

"Don't follow me, Isabel. Go back!" I'd be damned if I let her get caught up in this—her and my child.

She didn't answer, but the crashing behind me grew louder, faster. I rounded the oak tree where I'd last seen Robert . . . and stepped into emptiness.

It was as if I'd been pushed into an elevator shaft, or gone down a steep drop in the front car of a roller coaster. I was falling. The world blurred, moving faster and faster. I grabbed at the trees around me, trying to slow my descent, but they tore from my grip and sent me hurtling through cold darkness. The pressure on my lungs began, the pulling and the howling of a thousand voices.

And then as suddenly as it began, it is over. The earth rushes up to meet me and I hit the ground hard enough that my teeth slam shut on my tongue. Struggling to my hands and knees, I spit blood, then vomit until there's nothing left in my stomach. When I can catch my breath, I wipe the back of my hand across my mouth and sit up, forcing my eyes open against the corkscrewing ache in my head and the impossibly bright glare of the sun. Around me there is a strange, savage stillness—as if the world is waiting, or I am.

My first thought is that I'm still in the woods. Then my gaze clears and I see that I'm in a sea of thick, jointed brown stalks, topped with broad green leaves. Gripping one of the stalks for balance, I stagger to my feet. These plants are taller than I am, stretching as far as I can see in every direction. I extend a finger to touch the green leaves—and just as quickly pull it back again. They are sharp as hell, and now I am bleeding.

Putting the injured finger into my mouth, I bend to examine the plant more closely, as if I were at work in the greenhouse back home. I rummage in my pocket for my Swiss Army knife, feeling a pang of loss as my hand brushes the ring I'd planned to give Isabel. I shave off a piece of one of the fibrous brown stalks and inspect it, running my fingers over the rough, yellow-grained interior, then bringing it to my nose. It smells sweet. I put the shaving in my mouth and suck, drawing out the juice.

Sugarcane. I'm standing in a cane field, most likely close to the harvest, given the height of the stalks.

The thing is, I've never seen a cane field in South Carolina. Even when Robert Adair was alive, the plantations around Charleston were devoted to harvesting cotton. I try to remember what little I know about sugarcane cultivation in the States, but the only place I can come up with is rural Louisiana—and what the hell would I be doing there?

Regardless of how I ended up here, one thing is for sure—I can't just stand around waiting for something to happen. Taking a deep breath, I stride forward, one arm raised to protect my face from the sharp leaves of the cane.

And come face-to-face with a tall, broad-shouldered, onyx-skinned man, machete held high above his head.

Isabel

Somehow I fumble through the rest of the conversation with my daughter and hang up, robbed of what little peace I've been able to muster. Since Finn was a little girl, she's had an uncanny ability to tell what the people around her are thinking and feeling. It's disquieting, and most of the time I simply chalk it up to the fact that she's perceptive. "Sensitive," I tell her teachers and the parents of other children, when they regard her with the wary, dismayed gaze that I've come to recognize all too well. "Empathic," I add, a manic smile spreading across my face—nope, nothing wrong here!

The truth is, I don't know how Finn knows the things she does. Most of the time, she's just a normal little girl who likes purple nail polish and stuffed animals with big eyes, and Annie's boxed mac-and-cheese better than the real deal. But then sometimes she'll say something that so closely echoes what I'm thinking, it's as if she's read my mind. On other occasions, she'll bring me my phone and say, "It's Ryan," before the damn thing even rings. And I can't count the times she's found something I lost, or known that I've had a hard day at work before I've made it all the way through the door.

I suppose I could drag her to psychologists and evaluators

galore—but in the end she's healthy, and smart and sweet and kind to stray animals. So what if her intuition's a bit off the Richter scale? This is what I want to say to the parents who, one by one, have stopped letting their children play with her—the friends who have fallen away after Finn has said something strange one too many times. Plenty of kids are bullies who steal and hit and call other children names. Finn does none of these things. She's compassionate, almost to a fault, and it breaks my heart to see her spending more and more time alone.

Usually I'm Finn's staunchest defender. I'm so used to her little quirks that I hardly notice them anymore. But this time, her response to my unspoken thought—*Don't you know, Mama? It already has*—has sent me reeling.

I drive back to the dig, apologize for my absence, and finish out the day, but my heart's not in it. Moving like an automaton, I check my students' paperwork, oversee them as they gather their shovels and line levels and plumb bobs, argue over who had the audacity to dig with someone else's trowel—a cardinal sin in the world of field archaeology, where a worn trowel is a prize possession, a mark of experience and digs gone by.

We've been together for four weeks now, this team of mine, and the few people who haven't slept with each other have devolved into a grumpy sort of sibling rivalry. Normally I would see it as my job to defuse the bickering before it erupts into something more substantial, a disagreement that could compromise the dig. Today, though, I just ignore them, and aside from the occasional sidelong glance, they leave me be. Between my nervous breakdown and my sudden departure, it's clear enough that something is wrong—but I'm not saying, and they don't ask.

It's a good thing that this is almost the last day of our four-week dig, because I am able to issue only the most rudimentary of instructions as we cover the units for the night with tarps and plastic. I hear my voice coming from a long way off, telling Jake and Maura that the weather forecast is calling for wind, we need to take the sifting screens apart and use the legs to hold everything down. It seems a miracle to me that they comply, much less that the rest of my team does what they're supposed to—dumping water from the cooler, loading up the van, the buckets holding our finds wedged carefully upright so they won't spill.

Sitting on a forgotten camping chair, I make careful notes: *Broke down at 3 P.M. Conditions: Windy, but no rain. Temperature: 95 degrees Fahrenheit.* I nod at Maura as she walks past with the camera, check I have everyone's clipboard, do one last walk-through to ensure the site is secure. Then I drive us back to the house that doubles as our field lab, cranking the radio high to discourage conversation.

Everyone piles out of the van in high spirits, unloading with far more alacrity than usual. It's Friday night, and for once they don't have to be up at five-thirty A.M. They have big plans, most of which involve sharing a taxi to St. Lawrence Gap and getting wasted. I listen with half an ear, delivering the standard admonitions as I check all of the artifact bags against my notes. Finally the van is empty, and my team heads inside, arguing over who gets to take the first shower. I give the interior a final once-over, nearly hitting my head on the roof when I hear Jake's voice behind me.

"Um, Dr. Griffin . . ." he says, sounding more awkward than I've ever heard him.

I stand up and turn to look at him—scraggly brown hair pulled back in a ponytail, face sunburned beneath his Duke Blue Devils baseball cap, dirt-spattered T-shirt and shorts, uneasy expression. "Yes?" I say, doing my best to sound patient.

He shifts from one foot to the other, looking uncomfortable. "Before . . . this afternoon . . . well, you probably don't want to talk about it, I get that. But we all know that something happened, and I'm guessing it wasn't good. And I just wanted you to know that I . . . if you need someone to talk to . . . I mean, if there's anything I can do . . ." His voice trails off, and he looks down at his boots, covered in sandy soil.

Poor Jake, I think with the part of me that's still capable of having sympathy for others. As my second in command, it's fallen to him to deal with the hysterical, freaked-out supervisor. I can't imagine that the crush he has on me—which I've done my best to discourage—has made this moment any easier, unless he's harboring delusions that I'll suddenly swoon into his arms, wherein he will carry me off to the room he's sharing with two other students with questionable hygiene and comfort me to our mutual satisfaction. "Thank you," I say, with all of the sincerity I can muster. "I appreciate that, but what happened . . . it's private."

He lifts his head, but can't quite meet my eyes. Instead he stares at a point somewhere over my shoulder. More out of habit than actual curiosity, I turn my head and see the route taxi that has just swerved around the corner, reggae music blaring, the runner hanging half out of the sliding door, looking for passengers. "Okay," Jake says, eyes on the white van with its telltale red stripe as it screeches to a halt, disgorging two rowdy teenagers and then promptly taking off again, careening down the road at an alarming speed. "Just thought I'd ask. If you want to come with us tonight—you know the invitation's always open."

"Thanks," I say again, "but I think I'll just stay here and relax." I do my best to smile at him, but it must come off more like a grimace, because he winces again and heads into the house, neglecting to kick his shoes off at the door the way I've nagged him to do a thousand times.

For a moment I consider yelling after him, but then decide it's not worth it. He was trying to be nice, after all, the only one of the bunch brave enough to approach me. So instead I lock the van and head into the house, where I start in on some more of the day's never-ending paperwork in the common room, doing my best to give the appearance of normalcy as, one by one, my students emerge, ready for a night of partying. Clean-shaven and smelling of cologne, Jake asks once again if I want to come. Again I tell him no, and with a final, worried backward glance, he shepherds the lot of them out.

The moment the door closes behind them, I heave a huge sigh of relief. My team is my responsibility, no matter what else is going on in my life, but right now all I want to do is take a hot shower and go to bed. Food would be nice, but not essential. I'm pretty sure I have some CLIF Bars stashed in my bag if need be, not to mention some odds and ends in our shared refrigerator. Right now, my stomach is clenched in a ball so tight, the very idea of eating is repulsive.

Alone at last, I open the door to my bedroom and scan for danger—a long-standing habit born from the paranoia that whatever mysterious force kidnapped Max and my mother will seize me too. Nothing stirs. No one jumps out and claps their hand over my mouth. No one points a gun at my head.

Stepping inside, I close the door behind me and stand with my back against it, surveying the small space. It's just as I left it—generic pictures of island life on the walls, books and notes scattered across the small desk, the two sundresses I'd brought with me hanging lonely in the closet. Through the half-open curtains that cover the sliding door of the balcony, I can see palm trees swaying in the breeze.

I step outside and lean on the railing, looking down at the pool of the hotel next door—filled with folks in a far more jocular mood than I—and the Tiki bar. The breeze lifts my hair, carrying with it the smell of salt water and sunscreen, the sound of a woman's laughter. Beyond the bar, I can just make out the small stretch of beach, hear the susurrus of the waves.

It couldn't have been Max, I tell myself. *Of course it couldn't.* Except that it was.

I fumble for my phone, which I've slipped into the pocket of my shorts, and call Max yet again. Still the same damn message, in that irritating robotic voice. *I'm losing my mind*, I think. *This is how it goes. Not with a bang but a whimper.*

Disgusted, I step back inside, shutting the balcony door behind me and relatching it. Immediately, the quiet of the room envelops me, broken only by the hum of the air conditioner. With a dim sense of dislocation, I stride across to the bathroom—I've got my own, one of the fringe benefits of supervising—and push open the door. Surprise, surprise—the room is empty. For good measure, I brush the curtain aside and peek into the bathtub. No one in there, either— just the steady drip of a leaky faucet as water plinks into the tub. I lock the bathroom door behind me, strip off my sandy, dirty clothes, extract my cellphone from the pocket of my shorts, and place it on the back of the toilet tank, in easy reach in case it rings. And then I turn on the hot water and step under the soothing spray of the shower.

Mechanically, I reach for the little bar of soap, then for the travel-size shampoo, which smells faintly of almonds. As my hands slip through my hair, rinsing the sweat and grit away, I can't help but replay the phone call—Max's call, maybe. Or maybe not. Frustrated, I work conditioner into my hair with enough force to yank a few strands out by the roots. It takes a long time—my hair is curly and thick, and I have let it grow nearly to my waist out of sheer laziness.

Finally I am clean, but I'm reluctant to leave the sanctuary of the shower nonetheless. Rummaging through the toiletries I've brought with me—perched on the bathtub's ledge in a precarious little row—I exfoliate and shave, buff and scrub. At last there is nothing left to do but turn off the water and get out, and so I do.

For a moment I just stand on the white bath mat, listening. Nothing moves in the room beyond, and relief stirs within me, followed closely by disappointment. Dripping, I stand there and try to figure that one out. Do I *want* some stranger to be in my room while I'm naked and basically defenseless? Or am I just so undone that a physical altercation would give me a way to channel my emotions into something I understand? After all, I began my training at the dojo for just such an occasion—the threat that took my mother and Max, come to snatch Finn and me as well, to carry us off to places unknown.

Annoyed, I grab a towel from the rack over the toilet and start drying my hair. I've gotten about halfway done when it strikes me— it's not an intruder I'm listening for.

As much as I hate to admit it to myself, I didn't really think there was anyone here who meant me harm. No, I was searching every corner of this room for Max, thinking somehow he'd be here, that I'd open the door and see him lounging on the bed, hands knotted behind his head, smiling at me the way he used to. As unreasonable as it is, some small, hopeful part of me had believed that when I opened the balcony door, he'd be leaning against the railing, his arms wide open in welcome.

The realization widens my eyes, forces a high-pitched whimper from my throat, and the towel falls from my trembling hands to the floor. How could I be so stupid as to think Max would be here, in this ugly little room? That after everything, I'd find him waiting for me? Worse, how could I have hidden it from myself?

The keening sound comes again, and, horrified, I press my hand to my mouth to silence it. I haven't really cried in years, haven't thought I could afford to. If I started, I might not be able to stop, and then what?

Still, I can feel the tears pricking my eyes, feel a sob rising in the back of my throat. I clench my jaw, trying to force it back down. And then I snatch the towel off the floor, wrapping it around me as tightly as I can, as if that will hold me together. I grab the phone off the toilet tank and, gripping it in my hand like a lifeline, walk into the empty, silent bedroom. Perched on the edge of the bed, my breath coming harsh in my throat, I dial Ryan's cell.

He doesn't answer, and, fighting a rising feeling of panic, I try his work phone instead, at Mage, the digital media and comic design company he and a couple of his friends founded three years ago. It rings once, then twice, and I envision the phone sitting on his desk among the usual clutter of comic books and graphic novels. He could be in the room with it and not be able to locate the damn thing in time. Tapping my foot impatiently, I wait. Finally, on the fourth ring, he answers with a clipped, "Baxter."

Usually I'd give him a hard time about his crappy phone manners, but today I couldn't care less. Relief swamps me, and all I can manage is, "Ry?" in a small voice that doesn't sound much like mine.

"Isabel? What's the matter?" The clipped tone is gone, replaced with deep and immediate concern.

I try to answer, I really do. But to my eternal shame, I burst into tears instead. I've rarely cried in front of Ryan in all the years I've known him, and I don't want to do it now. But I can't seem to help myself.

"Isabel?" Ryan says again, as if he isn't sure it's really me. And then, when I don't reply, "Jesus, what is it? Is it Finn?"

I grope for a tissue from the box on the bedside table, blow my nose, and manage to clear my throat enough to say, "No. Well, maybe. I don't know." And then I cry some more—inelegant, messy tears that streak my face and mat my eyelashes together. In a last-ditch effort to regain control of myself, I dig my nails into my palms hard enough to leave little half-moons. It hurts, but instead of center-ing me, the pain just adds fuel to my hysteria, and I sob harder.

Ryan makes a frustrated noise. "You're not making any sense," he says, and I can hear the effort it takes for him to sound gentle, wor-ried as he is. "I can't help you if you won't tell me what's wrong."

"I don't know how to tell you," I say through my sobs. "I'm scared, Ry."

That seems to get through, because I hear him take a deep breath. Then he says, "Okay, sweetheart. Here's what I want you to do. Where are you?"

Even in my current state, the endearment takes me by surprise. Ryan's never called me anything like that before, and it unsettles me further, like the universe has slipped sideways, landing me some-where unrecognizable. I glance about in confusion. "In my room. On the bed. Why?"

"Is there any alcohol in the house? Hard liquor, I mean, not wine."

Puzzled by the non sequitur, I spare a glance for the room's tiny closet, where I'd stashed the bottle of Mount Gay Rum that the crew handed me last weekend as a joke, saying that if I wouldn't go out with them, maybe I'd prefer to party alone. "Yes," I say, pleased to have a definitive response to give him.

"All right. So, first I want you to get up. Stand up, okay?"

Obediently, I get to my feet. "I'm standing," I say, sniffling. "Now what?"

"Now walk into the bathroom and get a washcloth. Can you do that?" He sounds genuinely doubtful, and I am seized by the desire to reassure him.

"Of course," I say, try to laugh, and choke instead. "I'm not incapacitated."

He makes the noise again, but this time it holds more humor. "That's my girl. Wet the washcloth with cold water and wash your face."

"But I'll get the phone wet," I protest, and he gives a strained laugh.

"So put it on the counter. I won't go anywhere, I promise."

Numb, I do as he says. Then I pick up the phone again, filled with the sudden conviction that he'll have gotten sick of doing emotional triage and hung up. "Ry?" I say, hating the fear in my voice.

"I'm here," he says, and in his tone there is an unexpected tenderness. It undoes the fragile control I've been able to muster, and I start sobbing again.

"Jesus," Ryan says, sounding stunned. "Isabel, please. You're really frightening me. Is it Andrew, or—goddamn it, say something."

But I can't. Instead I cry harder, gasping for air, until Ryan says with some desperation, "Are you alone? Isabel?"

I nod, realize he can't see me, and manage to say "Yes." I can hear myself breathing, quick and choked with tears. Dizziness sweeps me, taking the room with it, and I am suddenly afraid that I might pass out.

Evidently the thought has also occurred to Ryan, because he mutters "Shit," almost to himself. "Iz, you know how I asked you about the hard liquor? Can you get to it?"

"Sure," I say, hiccupping. "Why?"

"Just humor me. You're in Barbados . . . there's rum, at least, right?"

I swallow hard. "Yes, there's rum. I've got some in here, even."

"Fine, then," he says, clear and calm, all evidence of frustration gone. It's a magic trick I've seen him pull off before—shutting his emotions down, so that the front he presents to the world is untroubled as the glassy surface of a pond, regardless of what's roiling beneath. Once I asked him how he did it—it seemed an enviable ability, if a bit duplicitous—and he'd just shrugged, looking deeply uncomfortable. Only later, after much consideration, did it occur to me that this was likely a survival strategy he'd developed after his parents abandoned him at age eight and social services dumped him in one shitty foster home after another. *Living like that, you learn fast or you don't make it,* he'd said in acknowledgment, when I'd summoned the courage to ask. *You decide that having feelings is too expensive, or you figure out how to disguise them when you have to, so no one can use them against you. Either way, you pay the price.*

"Okay," he says now, as careful as if he's talking a jumper off a ledge. "Get the bottle and take three big gulps. Go ahead, I'll wait."

"But I'll be drunk," I say, remembering the #1 Rum Punch, and he snorts.

"You'll be calm. Don't argue with me. Just go ahead."

I wrap the towel around myself and make my way to the closet. Yanking the door open, I swipe at my eyes with the back of my hand, viciously, over and over, until I can see. And then I grab the bottle off the shelf. With shaking fingers, I unscrew the top and follow his instructions. The liquor burns my throat and makes me cough, but once I get it down, it settles in my stomach, rushing outward to my limbs with a reassuring, solid heat. I take one last gulp and set the bottle down on the dresser, feeling empty of everything.

"Better now?" Ryan says, and I jump, startled.

Tentatively, I essay a deep breath, expecting to be met halfway by one of those horrible, tearing sobs, but it doesn't happen. I breathe in and out once, then again, and ease down onto the edge of the bed. Then I wipe my eyes and peer around. The world is outlined by a faint, warm glow, and I realize that for the first time since my phone rang this afternoon, I feel safe. I clear my throat, cough, and then say, "Much, thank you. I'm sorry. I don't know what—"

"Don't apologize, Isabel, for God's sake. Just talk to me."

"Well," I say, feeling self-conscious, "it's Max."

Ryan is silent. Then he says, "Max? Do you mean they found his—"

"No, no," I say hurriedly. "Nothing like that."

"Oh. So then—did they find him? Alive?" There's a fair measure of incredulity in Ryan's voice, shadowed by a hint of scorn. Ry has an intense contempt for fathers who abandon their children, and precious little compassion. He hasn't spoken to his own parents since social services took him. As far as he is concerned, they died that day.

"No, not that, either," I say, taking another gulp of rum for fortitude.

"Well, then what?" he says, with a distinct edge. "I don't get it."

"You and me both," I mumble, and manage a slight, hysterical laugh. The rum has done its job, distancing me nicely from the shock of Max's phone call and dissolving my inhibitions in alcohol. It's a refreshing change.

Ryan growls, a feral noise I've never heard him make. "Isabel, so help me God, if you don't tell me what's going on, I'm hanging up this phone, calling that irritating little acolyte of yours, and making him go comfort you in your time of need."

He means Jake, and despite myself, I giggle. "You wouldn't," I say. "Besides, I'm only wearing a towel."

"I don't give a good goddamn what you're wearing. If you don't want that little pedant to catch you in the altogether, you'd better start talking or put on some clothes."

I tilt the bottle of rum back and take a swig. "I've never heard you sound like this before, Ryan. You're really quite ferocious."

"Jesus, Isabel, so help me, if you don't start talking—" he says, and then suspiciously, as I stifle a belch, "Christ, are you still drinking? Stop it. Put the damn bottle down. You're drunk is what you are."

"I'm not," I say with as much dignity as I can manage. "I'm calm. You said so."

"I know what I said. But what I'm saying now is, screw the top on the freaking bottle and put it back where it came from." He exhales loudly. "I'm at work, you know. So I am going to put you on hold and go close my office door. Then I'm going to come back, and if you haven't become a hell of a lot more communicative than you are right this minute, I am calling Jake. I've got his number right here in my phone, in case you think I'm joking. You've got twenty seconds, starting now." I start to object, but the receiver has already clunked down onto his desk with a grim sort of finality.

I glance from my phone to the bottle, which is now resting companionably between my knees. Then, with what feels like an astronomical effort, I set the bottle on the bedside table. I adjust my towel, straighten my spine, and pull myself together. The problem is, now I can hear Max's voice again, saying my name. I squeeze my eyes tight shut and start counting aloud, "Nine . . . eight . . . seven . . . six . . . five . . ."

As I reach the end of my countdown and begin to panic, Ryan says, "I'm back. Now talk. Please," he adds as a hasty afterthought.

The glow of the rum has departed, leaving me with an icy sense of dread. "Max called me."

I hear Ryan's sharp intake of breath. "What? Just now?"

"Well, not just now. Just now I am talking to *you*," I say, and clap my hand over my mouth to halt the progression of another belch.

"Yes, Isabel, I realize that. What do you mean, Max called you? On your cellphone? What did he say?" Disbelief is clear in Ryan's voice—that, and a healthy dose of skepticism. I don't blame him for it, but it wrenches at me all the same.

"Yes, on my cellphone. He said my name. *Isabel.* And then he said *Keep her safe.* He said other things too, but I couldn't hear him.

There was static." I fiddle with a fraying thread at the edge of my towel. "But it was him, Ryan, I swear."

"How do you know?" he says, exactly the way he presses one of his interns when they declare a coding dilemma unsolvable in the absence of sufficient data. It irks me, and in my inebriated state, I don't have enough of a filter to keep my irritation to myself.

"Well, for one thing, it was his number on my caller ID," I snap.

"That doesn't mean anything," he says immediately. "Someone else could have his number now. You know that."

"It was his *voice*." Despite myself, tears fill my eyes again. "Don't you think I know what Max sounds like?"

"It's been almost eight years, Isabel. How can you be sure?" It's his patient voice, his teaching voice, and it sends me over the edge.

"Don't lecture me!" I yell at him, goaded into certainty. "I'm not one of your dumbass interns. And don't treat this like some kind of . . . of fucking logic proof. I know what I heard!"

There is silence in the wake of my outburst. Then Ryan takes another deep breath. I'm pretty sure he's trying not to lose his temper. "I am almost two thousand miles away from you, Isabel," he says, each syllable measured. "I feel helpless, can you understand that? What do you want me to do?"

It's a genuine question, and the anger drains from me in a rush, leaving me with an unmistakable sense of guilt. "I'm sorry," I say again. "I didn't mean to scream at you. You were just trying to help."

Ryan gives a grudging sound of acceptance. "It's okay. Just . . . humor me. Tell me everything that happened, from beginning to end. Don't leave anything out, even if you don't think it's important."

Wonder of wonders, he's taking me seriously—and if anyone can solve the puzzle of Max's phone call, it's Ryan. I sigh, feeling all of the air rush out of my body as I relax. Hearing this, Ryan coaxes me, "That's it. Sit back against the wall, okay? Close your eyes. Breathe. And then tell me everything. Take me there with you. Let me see it."

And so I do. He listens without interruption, although I can hear his keyboard clacking—he's taking notes, I realize, feeling strangely reassured. When I get to the part about coming back to the house, he speaks for the first time.

"You thought he'd be in your room. Max," he says, quiet now. "You thought he'd be there."

I want to argue with him, but it's the truth. "Yeah," I admit. "Stupid, huh?"

"Well, maybe not. If that really was him on the phone." His voice is soft, sympathetic even, and it crumbles my defenses into dust.

"It's crazy, Ry. Isn't it?" I stand up, letting the towel fall to the floor, and cross to my dresser, rummaging in one of the drawers for clothes. "It couldn't have been him. I mean, if it was, how would his number have been disconnected when I called back? And if it was disconnected, how could he have called me at all?"

"I don't know." His voice is thoughtful, musing. "A good hacker could've done it. Someone with enough skill to manipulate the system."

I slip on clean underwear and then step into a pair of blue linen pants, the most comfortable ones I own. "You?" I say, only half-joking. As a brilliant, disillusioned teenager, Ryan had gotten a kick out of secretly maneuvering his way past high-tech cybersecurity of all kinds. He'd told me about it in an offhand sort of way one day over coffee, the way someone else would confess a history of stealing lipstick or downloading illegal MP3 files. He hadn't offered details and I'd never asked—until now.

Ryan makes a dissentient, aggravated noise. "I could. But I wouldn't. Jesus, Isabel, you don't honestly think I would do that to you?"

"No," I say after a moment's hesitation, closing the clasp of my bra. "I just . . . I forget about that side of you sometimes. It's weird to be reminded."

"I don't do that stuff anymore. You know that." He sounds offended.

"Of course you don't," I say in my best conciliatory tone, tugging a T-shirt over my head.

"Anyway, it's just a possibility. But who would mess with you like that? Who would want to?"

"I have no idea," I admit. "Someone who's kidnapped Max, maybe? But what would anyone want him for? And why let him call, after all this time? None of it makes any sense. It was him, though, Ry, I swear. Yet how could it be? I don't understand."

I hear a thrumming, repetitive sound and am about to ask him about it when I realize what it is—Ryan, drumming his fingers on his desk over and over the way he does when he's trying to solve a problem. "Neither do I," he says after a moment. "But we'll figure it out."

A profound sense of comfort washes over me—at not being alone with the mystery of Max's phone call anymore, having someone else to help me deal with whatever comes. Feeling somehow lighter, I open the doors to the balcony and step outside again. There's a couple sitting on the deck chairs by the pool next door, sipping fancy drinks with umbrellas in them. Two children splash in the water, illuminated by the outdoor lights. Their playful laughter drifts up to me and I can't help but think of Finn. As I watch, the man gets up, setting his drink on the ground next to him, and does a cannonball right into the deep end. He streaks under the water and surfaces next to the two little kids, who shriek with delight and splash him, initiating an all-out war.

Max has never played with Finn like that. But Ryan has, every summer. In fact, he's the one who taught her to swim, long after I'd thrown up my hands in exasperation. Time after time, he stood in five feet of water, arms outstretched, and coaxed her to jump, promising he'd catch her. And finally she had. Because she'd trusted him.

"Thank you for being there for me, and not just tonight," I say on impulse. It's not how we usually talk to each other—any more than him calling me *sweetheart* earlier—but I can't seem to stop myself. "You've been a father to Finn. I know that. And I love you for it."

Ryan doesn't reply, and through the haze of the rum I wonder if I've said too much, overstepped the bounds of our friendship. After a long pause he says, "Do you?"

There's an uncharacteristic tone in his voice, something I can't quite identify. Maybe it's just that Ryan, who is always so confident, sounds suddenly as uncertain as I feel. I bet that if I were sober, I'd be able to figure it out. But I'm under the influence of a substantial amount of alcohol, and subtleties are beyond me, so I just say, with simple indignation, "Of course I do. How could I not?"

This makes him laugh, an outright, full-bodied chuckle. "Well, I love you too. But I think you're pretty damn wasted. Is there anything in that nasty refrigerator of yours? You need to get some dinner."

"Dinner? I'd settle for lunch." The rum lurches in my stomach, threatening to make a reappearance, and it occurs to me that Ryan is right—I had better eat something, and soon.

"Lunch?" he says, appalled. "Have you even eaten today?"

"I had a yogurt," I offer, searching my memory for anything else I'd grabbed out of the refrigerator this morning. "Oh, and a cup of coffee. I skipped lunch—we were working too hard. And then Max—" My voice breaks, but stubbornly I push through. "Anyway, after that, I forgot all about eating."

Ryan gives a disgusted snort. "A yogurt. And all that rum. No wonder you sound like this. No wonder you thought it was Max, with just yogurt in your system and all that sun. I'm surprised you didn't hallucinate a phone call from the President."

"I didn't hallucinate anything!" I say, starting to get angry again. The world sways, abruptly awash in streams of color, and I grab the rail for support, the flaking paint rough underneath my palms. "Why don't you believe me? My dad didn't, either. What's wrong with both of you? Am I that untrustworthy? Or erratic?"

"Of course you're not. But Isabel, come on. Listen to how this sounds. What would you do if your dad called you up with a story like this, about your mom? You'd want it to be true, of course you would. You'd do anything for it to be true, am I right?"

"Yes," I say, gripping the railing for dear life. The rum rises in my throat, unpredictable and dangerous, and I swallow it back down with effort.

"But," Ryan says, implacable as the tide lapping the small beach beyond the pool, pulling the waves out to shore. "Your dad's still here, and your mom's not. What would you want, even more than seeing her again? What would be your first instinct?"

I think of the way my father had looked in the wake of my mom's disappearance—worn and exhausted, his face lined with lack of sleep, his eyes sunk deep into his head with worry. With the immediacy that only vivid memories can bring, I see him walking away from me, retreating again and again into his office, thumbing over and over through the police reports. I see him pinning up flyers all over town, see him passing me in the kitchen, in the hallway, in the driveway without a word. Looking straight through me, as if I weren't there, until I'd become resigned to the fact that I'd lost him too. And had turned, broken and grieving, to Max.

I don't like these memories, had buried them deep down years ago. When Finn was born and my dad had proven to be a better grandfather to her than I could ever have imagined, I'd thought I'd put them to rest for good. But here they are, evoked by Ryan's relentless line of questioning, and I don't care for it one bit. I shake my head hard to dispel them, but this only succeeds in making me dizzy, and I have to sink into one of the white rocking chairs. In my mind's eye I can still see my father, back turned and stooped with the burden of his grief, walking away from me. Always walking away.

And just like that, I have my answer. "I'd want to protect him," I whisper. "So nothing would ever make him hurt like that again."

This time Ryan's silence has a different quality—pensive, as if it holds the weight of a thousand words. And finally he says, his voice as low as mine, "Elementary, sweetheart."

Max

Time slows down and I can see everything—the deep green of the cane, the harsh blue of the sky, and silhouetted against them, the figure of this man, his black skin gleaming with sweat, the muscles in his arms bulging as the metal blade whistles through the air. I see each drop of sweat that trickles down his face and the bare skin of his chest, each tear in his ragged white pants, smell the odor that bakes off of him, the thick scent of an unwashed body pushed past its limits, laboring too long in the hot sun.

Then time starts up again and I leap out of the path of the blade not a moment too soon. "What the hell do you think you're doing?" I yell. "You could have killed me!"

The man stares at me as if I am a ghost, and then his features morph into a terrified expression. He drops his gaze to the ground, and I can see that the hand holding the machete is trembling. "Sir," he manages, his eyes fixed on the roots of the cane, "I ain't mean you harm, truly. Master Alleyne sent me 'head to clear this part of the field. The last thing I 'spected was to find a man standin' here."

His speech bewilders me. Its rhythm and intonation is peculiar, somewhere between the lilt of the islanders I remember from a family vacation to the Caribbean and Gullah, the dialect of coastal

South Carolinians descended from West African slaves. Then there's the bizarre mention of "Master Alleyne," not to mention the man's fear—which doesn't make any sense, given that he's the one with a weapon. For a moment, I am so bewildered that all I can do is stare at him. He bows his head and the machete drops from his hand. I watch it hit the dirt and my mind churns, trying to come up with some kind of explanation for his appearance, the way he speaks.

My own hands trembling, I lean down to pick up the machete— and catch a glimpse of his legs, which are horribly scarred. I blink at them for a moment, then down at the machete, suddenly certain that those marks were made by this blade or another one like it, aiming for the sugarcane and missing its target, sinking instead deep into flesh.

Cane cutter, my mind supplies bloodlessly, dredging the term up from the seminar on West Indian history I'd taken last year. I'd written my senior thesis on the 1816 Barbados slave revolt and the Barbados–Carolina connection, trying to come to terms with my family's screwed-up legacy—among other things. The knowledge surfaces in my mind, impossible but clear and sure. *This man is a cane cutter. He's going through the field, preparing the canes for harvest. Which means he isn't alone.*

As if this thought has summoned them, I hear other voices, raised in song. A strong, cracked alto soars above the rest, joined by the chorus. I can't make out the words, not at this distance, but the pattern is familiar enough. It reminds me of the music in the black churches of Charleston, the rise and fall of the call and response.

My mind spinning, I pick up the blade and offer it back to its owner, who doesn't move. "Here," I say, doing my best to sound reassuring. "I know you weren't trying to hurt me. It's my own fault—no reasonable person would expect to find someone here. Really, don't worry about it."

His head snaps up and he flinches back from the machete, as if he hasn't heard anything I've said. Patiently, I try again. "Take it. It's yours."

Gingerly, he takes the machete from me. His eyes flick to my face, and I see the incredulity there, quickly masked by careful blankness. "I thank you, sir," he says, the "h" nearly silent, and turns to disappear back the way he came. I take a sharp breath of the humid, heat-soaked air—and choke when I see his bare back. It's covered in a tracing of ridged scars, overlaid by angry, fresh wounds.

"Wait!" I say, before I even know I've spoken. It's more of an entreaty than a command, but the man freezes all the same. "Who did this to you?"

He doesn't say a word. The singers are closer now, close enough that I can see the flash of their white clothes through the cane, the gleam of their blades in the sun. In a moment he will disappear into their midst, and I will lose my chance. "Answer me," I say, and then, when he doesn't make a sound, "please."

At this, his head jerks in surprise. So softly I can hardly hear him beneath the whoosh and snicker of the blades, the stomp of feet, and the chanting of voices, he says, with an air of dignity that belies his words, "Master Alleyne, sir."

The "t" in "master" is nearly imperceptible, the "r" little more than a suggestion. I'm sickened enough by the idea of one human being controlling another, but hearing the word pronounced this way, echoing every servile stereotype, sends nausea coiling in my stomach. "Why?" I say, as if there can ever be a justification for something like this. Close up, his back is a war zone—crisscrossing half-healed lash marks and thin, corded raised scars. Despite the heat, cold sweat breaks out all over my body.

The man shrugs, without turning. "I ain't been working hard enough. Been drinkin', he say. Been stealin'." His voice is empty, as if the words cost him nothing.

I open my mouth, but no sound comes out. It wouldn't matter if it had, though, because now the rest of the cane cutters are upon us, swinging their blades in synchrony with the doleful beat of their song. There must be thirty or forty of them, black men and women who move as one, clad in ripped, filthy white linen, cleaving through the cane. Behind them is a white man on horseback, a knife holstered at his waist and a whip strapped to his saddle, shouting insults and hoarse commands.

Slave driver, my mind says, in that same cold voice.

But how?

The man with the scarred back has melted into the group. I stand in the path of the oncoming gang of workers, stunned. In the moment before the rider sees me, I finally manage to decipher the verse of the song: "Master buy me, he won't kill me."

And the chorus, raised loud in response: "For I live with a bad man, oh la. For I live with a bad man."

Isabel

That night, I dream of Max, more vividly than I have in years. I'm walking toward him down a wide, paved road. The air is heavy and humid, redolent with the aroma of tropical flowers, and in the distance I can hear the pounding of waves. On one side of the road, a thick green stand of sugarcane rises up, taller than I am, rustling in the breeze. On the other there are fields, small wooden buildings, and, behind Max, a long, winding drive, flanked by towering palms and leading to a white, two-story house that can only be described as a mansion. It's a plantation house, I realize, not unlike the great house at Lowthers, where we've been digging, or the other, larger ones, like Bayleys or Drax Hall. The wooden buildings are housing, ramshackle and poorly kept in comparison.

Max is standing in the middle of the road, about fifty yards away, waiting for me. He's wearing the clothes I last saw him in, the ones he had on the day he disappeared: khaki cargo pants and a navy T-shirt, faded from too many washings. At this distance I shouldn't be able to see the slight smile that lifts his lips, but I see it all the same. He raises one hand and beckons to me in an unmistakable gesture: *Come on.*

I break into a run, closing the space between us—forty yards, thirty. Max's smile widens, and I quicken my pace. But as I get closer, his expression shifts from expectant to panicked. He turns away from me, toward the house. And then there is a massive boom, and smoke eats everything.

The force of the explosion knocks me off my feet. Gravel digs into my palms and scores my elbows. Desperate, I scramble back up, peering through the haze. I scream Max's name, but he doesn't answer. I'm sure I've lost him again.

Over and over again I wipe my streaming eyes, until finally I can make out the scene in front of me. Max is still there, but now he is standing in the midst of a world on fire. I hear screaming, and then the unmistakable report of gunshots. The road is littered with debris, and flames spill from the windows of the house, filling the air with smoke.

The screams split the air again, but somehow they are different. These are battle cries, driving and wild. And then they come, spilling out of the cane field in a relentless wave, black as the receding night, pitchforks and swords clutched in their hands. One of them brandishes a torch, and as I watch, he tosses it into the field. *Rebels*, I think.

The cane begins to smolder. Then it catches, tongues of red devouring the tall stalks. The pungent smell of burning leaves sears my lungs and ash rains down, coating everything. I try to run toward Max, to drag him to safety, but in the horrible way of dreams, I can't move. All I can do is watch as I lose him all over again.

"Max!" I shriek. "Max! Run!" But he stands, trapped between the smoldering plantation house and the burning cane. He makes no effort to save himself. And, standing there on the road, unable to move, neither can I.

But being paralyzed doesn't mean I can't feel. What I'd taken for the pound of surf was, in fact, the clattering of horses' hooves, closing fast. And my body senses them, pounding down the gravel, well before they come into my line of sight: thirty soldiers in red with old-fashioned muskets, charging toward me. Stampeding through me as

I stand on the road, as if I don't exist, headed for the field on fire. The black men do not have guns and I poise myself for a massacre.

Though the rebels may be sorely outnumbered and ill-equipped, they have one thing on their side—desperation. I watch as the torch-wielder raises a sword high above his head and brings it down hard, the muscles in his arms standing out beneath his skin. The blade pierces a soldier's red coat, sinking deep into his body. He falls to the ground, clutching his stomach, and the rebel kicks him viciously.

Then comes the deafening report of a musket, and a red stain blooms on the swordsman's chest. I barely have time to register the look of astonishment that flashes across his face before he collapses, shocked and bleeding, into the burning cane. The rebels behind him scream in outrage, and the musket booms again. But all this chaos fades to background noise when I hear a cry, high and plaintive, frantic—the cry of a child, coming from inside the plantation house. My child, trapped and terrified.

"Finn!" The scream tears my throat. I fight to free myself from my paralysis, harder than I've ever struggled against anything before, but the effort is pointless—I can't move. Max, however, has no such difficulty. Without hesitation, he runs for the house, throwing his shoulder against the front door, which splinters under his assault. I see him drop to his knees and crawl inside before the smoke obscures my vision and he is gone.

Finn screams again, and I watch as part of the roof gives way. Tears stream down my face, and I realize that I am praying, saying her name and Max's name over and over. The cloying smell of burnt sugar, the heat of the fire—they are everywhere, and it occurs to me that if there is a hell, it must be just like this.

And then I see it—a flash of movement in one of the upstairs windows, distinct from the smoke and flames. I strain my eyes, and there she is, blond hair piled on top of her head, her face streaked with soot, silhouetted in the window frame. I have no trouble recognizing her. It's been fourteen years, but I'd know her anywhere.

The woman at the window is my mother.

Max

When the man on the horse asks who I am, there's a split second in which I consider lying. But the man leans down, regarding me with such open curiosity, and all of the workers pause, machetes and hoes in hand, and I can't think of a damn thing.

Instead, I draw myself up to my full height and make a show of brushing off my clothes, which are wrinkled and covered with dirt. "Maxwell Adair," I say, inclining my head in my best aristocratic manner. "And you are?"

"Simon Alleyne," the man says, inclining his head equally stiffly. He speaks with a British accent, laced with a lilt I can't quite identify. "Overseer of this estate. I beg your pardon for asking, sir, but what brings you here? It's nowhere for a gentleman to be."

"I got lost," I say, sweeping my hand in a gesture meant to encompass the enormity of the cane field.

"Lost," the man repeats, his eyes raking over me. I'm wearing khaki pants, a blue T-shirt, and Vans—an outfit that seemed normal enough when I was waiting for Isabel in the woods, but not here, wherever here might be. The man swings down off his horse and strides toward me through the cleared cane, whip in hand. "Adair, eh?" he says, looking closely at my face. "You'll be kin to the master, then?"

When I say nothing, he rephrases: "Robert Adair, owner of this estate. Sweetwater. Are you a relation of his?"

Try as I might to maintain a neutral expression, my mouth drops open at this. Sweetwater was the name of my ancestors' Barbados plantation, held by the Adair family until a slave insurrection engulfed half the island in fire and destruction. The militia and the British garrison put the rebellion down in three or four days, but Robert Adair, much of his property destroyed and his wife dead in childbirth, lost his heart for Caribbean living—and his taste for slave ownership with it. The plantation was sold, to the best of my knowledge, and co-opted by the Wiltshire family, which owned much of the island back then. "Yes," I manage. "I'm a relative of his from America. South Carolina."

A smile breaks over the man's face. "American," he muses. "That explains your garb, I suppose. Well, sir, if your intention was to pay a visit to Mr. Adair, you've arrived at the right place. The great house is just over yonder." He gestures through the cane, back the way he'd come. "I regret to inform you, however, that Mr. Adair isn't here at present. In fact, he's gone to South Carolina himself. His wife is at home, though, and I am sure she'll be pleased to welcome you—and find you more suitable clothes. I would escort you myself, save that I have the responsibility of these Negroes. Perhaps you'll know how they are—leave them to their own devices but a moment and they subside into the most despicable form of laziness."

Simon Alleyne looks at me for confirmation, but I am too busy gaping at him—and the ragtag group of people standing next to him. Thoughts swirl through my head, coalescing into an impossible, bewildering version of reality. Did I really follow a ghost into the woods and wind up in the middle of Robert Adair's cane plantation? If so, the man with the scarred back, the singing woman, the others standing here with their stained white clothes, their straw hats and headcloths—these people are slaves. Slaves owned by my ancestor.

My stomach roils again, and I feel myself go pale under my summer tan.

"Here, you, Richard!" Alleyne snaps his fingers, and one of the men steps forward.

"Yessir?" he says, eyes downcast.

"Take Mr. Adair up to the house and make sure someone sees to him properly. He'll not be used to this heat. And then mind you come directly back here, or you'll pay a pretty price." He snaps the whip against his thigh in warning.

"Yessir," the man says again, and then to me, "This way, Master Adair, sir." He heads off through the path left by the cut cane, and I follow, for lack of a better option. I want to tell him not to call me "Master Adair," but I can't seem to find my voice.

We emerge into a wide yard, surrounded by a hum of activity. Five or six small dark-skinned children are scurrying back and forth, carrying piles of hay to feed the cattle, penned up at the far end of the yard near a barn. As the children draw closer, the cows low impatiently, sticking their huge heads through the slats in the fencing. An older woman, her hair tightly braided and bound by a bright red cloth, opens the gate for them and they run in, strew the hay around the pen and then, just as quickly, bolt out again. As I watch, they pick up buckets that are sitting outside the pen and trudge from the clearing, shepherded by the woman. I hear one of them call, "Sing us the song about the spider and the bear, Nanny Bec."

Her response is lost as they disappear from sight. Gazing after them, I can see the top of a huge stone windmill, and near it a metal-roofed structure with a smoking chimney. To my left stretches several acres of cleared land, covered in small, thatch-roofed wooden huts, with the occasional garden and fenced-in pen holding chickens, goats, and pigs. I take in a lungful of the manure-filled air, heavy with the cloying scent of what must be sugar and the aroma of flowers.

"What are those?" I ask at last, pointing at the huts.

If Richard is surprised by my question, he gives no sign. "The slave quarters, sir," he says, and then, with some timidity, "Life's so different in America, then?"

The slave quarters. I raise a hand and wipe the sweat from my forehead, staring in disbelief. "No," I say. "No, I guess not."

"But that there," Richard says with some pride, gesturing to my right, "that's the great house, where Master Adair and his wife live." I turn to see a massive white stone mansion surrounded by hedges of lime trees, looming over the rest of the property.

I've seen paintings of Sweetwater's great house before, but nothing can prepare me for it in person, the opulence of it in such sharp contrast to the slave village. It turns my stomach. Silently, I accompany Richard as he brings me to the door as promised. He waits until a maid opens the door to my knock and then departs hurriedly for the field.

The maid is a light-skinned teenager with angular cheekbones, her hair tied back with a blue scarf. There's something familiar about her, but I can't figure out what it is. She looks me over with some incredulity, but says, "Welcome to Sweetwater, sir," and opens the door wide so I can enter. Inside, the house is cool—well, cooler anyway—and dark, at least compared to the blinding glare of the sun. It smells of wood polish and the sharp bite of limes.

"You'll be thirsty, no doubt, sir?" the girl says. Her voice is high and clear, her accent less pronounced. "Come on into the drawing room and sit you down. Can I fix you something? Maybe a nice glass of rum punch, fresh-made just this morning. Ain't nothing more refreshing than punch on a hot day like this one."

She's looking up at me as if I'm an alien, and clumsily I fumble for my manners. "That would be great, thank you. I'm sorry, we haven't been introduced," I say. "I'm Max Adair."

This girl is not quite so guarded as Richard or the man with the scarred back. She smiles back and curtsies, lifting her skirts with a distinct sense of irony. "Hannah, sir," she replies, leading the way toward the drawing room, where she deposits me on an overstuffed settee and leaves in search of the rum punch.

I look around, trying to absorb my surroundings. The room is full of furniture, including uncomfortable-looking chairs that remind me of the ones in my mother's sitting room. In one corner, a bookshelf holds an ornate candelabrum, filled with tall white candles. The walls are covered in framed maps of the island, plus a painting of a busy port scene, complete with boats rowed by bearded, eye patch–wearing men, an honest-to-God monkey perched on one of their shoulders.

As odd as all of this is, it pales in comparison to what lies, face-down, half-concealed by a pillow, on the couch next to me: a news-paper.

Taking a deep breath, I flip the paper over. *Barbados Mercury*, the top line reads in bold black typeface, and beneath that, *And Bridgetown Gazette.*

I close my eyes, open them again. And then read one more line, just beneath the paper's masthead.

Saturday, March 30, 1816.

Isabel

I wake from the dream, heart hammering, covered in sweat. My eyes snap open, half-expecting to find myself standing on the road, throat seared from the heat of the flames and the ash sifting down like corrupted snow, my mother at the window and a rebel soldier dying at my feet. But no: I'm in my small rented bedroom, breathing only the stale, recycled air of the window unit, the drapes stirring in the slight breeze. I turn my head and see the bottle of rum standing sentinel on my bedside table, next to my phone. For a second, I consider calling Ryan, if only to hear another human voice, but it's still dark outside, and he's doubtless fast asleep — not necessarily alone, either. The last thing he needs is for me to bother him with what will surely seem like yet more evidence that I've flipped my lid.

Pushing myself up to a sitting position, I rub my eyes, then wince. They sting, and the flesh beneath them feels swollen. I can only imagine what I must look like, and send a brief prayer of gratitude winging upward for whomever invented concealer.

I swing my legs off the edge of the bed, then wander out to the small balcony, gazing out over the blackness of the sea. The sun is just beginning to rise, creeping over the horizon furtively, and I watch it come, thinking that no matter what Max's phone call might portend, no matter what demons stalked me in the night, here is something to cling to. Just like I did in the days after my mother disappeared, after I watched the second line on that pregnancy test appear, after Max vanished without a trace, I will keep going. It's what I know how to do, and today will be no exception.

It's the weekend, so at least I don't have to round everyone up and drag them out to the dig site. Instead, I put on shorts and a tank top, then grab my running shoes. I don't worry too much about waking up my housemates—I can tell from the detritus strewn around the common area that they made it home, and I have to trust Jake and Maura to play den mother in my absence, although the thought is more than a little terrifying.

And so I make my way out the front door and across to the beach, formulating a plan. Discomfiting as it might have been, the dream was just that—my subconscious, combining Max and my mother and Barbados into some sort of nightmarish scenario. It's not too difficult for me to analyze the storyline—my fear of losing Finn, of being trapped and unable to help her, combined with the old loss of my mother and my renewed anxiety about Max. The latter, though, I can do something about. I'll call Verizon as soon as they open, I tell myself, grabbing my left ankle to stretch my hamstring, then my right. They'll be able to confirm that I received a call from Max's number, and at least that will be a starting point. Maybe they'd even be able to trace the tower, tell me where the call came from.

It's not much, but it's a beginning—more than I dared hope for. As I pick up my pace, feet pounding the sand and the sun's orange glow suffusing the sky, for the first time in almost eight years, I allow myself to believe I might find him.

Max

The paper falls from my hands, tumbling onto the floor next to the couch, and my vision grays. I'd known something was terribly wrong, but this—it's not possible. Things like this don't happen to normal people. Not people who have a job and a girlfriend and a baby on the way.

What did you expect? the sardonic voice in my head supplies. *You followed a ghost into the woods and thought you'd end up . . . where? Disneyland?*

"Shut up," I mutter, and lean over, propping my elbows on my knees. I hang my head, letting the blood rush back into it, and blink until my vision clears.

When it does, Hannah is standing in front of me again, a tray in her hands. "Are you all right, sir?" she says. "You're white as a sheet, if you don't mind me saying so."

It takes considerable effort for me to sit up and smile at her, but I manage it. "I'm fine, Hannah, thank you. Just a little dizzy."

She gives me an appraising look. "I expect so, out there in the hot sun with nothin' to drink. Miss Lily ain't feeling so good, but she asks you to stay for supper, and stay the night too, 'less you have someplace else in mind."

My heart jolts at the mention of Lily's name, and I try not to let it show on my face. "Mrs. Lily Adair? Robert's first—I mean, his wife? She's here?"

Hannah's eyebrows lift in puzzlement, and I curse myself for my carelessness. "Yes sir," she says, holding out the glass of punch. "Where else would she be?"

"Where else indeed," I mumble, scrubbing a hand over my face to steady myself. When I look up, Hannah's eyebrows have nearly met her hairline.

"You know Master Robert?" she says, setting the tray down on one of the end tables and handing me a plate holding a small cake.

I take a huge gulp of the rum punch for fortitude. The alcohol hits my belly and spreads throughout my bloodstream, a warm and welcome comfort. "I haven't met him personally, no. He—we're distant relations. Cousins. I'd hoped to find him here." I drain the glass of punch and take a large bite of the cake, on the premise that having a mouthful of food and drink will prevent me from saying anything untoward.

Hannah reaches out and plucks the empty glass from my hand. "Cousins," she says, nodding sagely. "That makes sense. You got the look of him, for sure, 'specially round the eyes."

I'd thought this was the case, but it's a relief to hear Hannah say it—at least it substantiates my story. But as I regard Hannah, it occurs to me what seems so familiar about her. I nearly drop my plate.

I'm not the only one in this room who looks like Robert Adair.

I'd known that planters took advantage of the slaves in their employ, and unless I'm very much mistaken, Hannah is living proof of it. Her eyes are brown, not gray like mine, but their shape is the same. She has my long nose and the high cheekbones I inherited from my father. Still, she has to be at least seventeen—far too old to be Robert Adair's child, who was in his late twenties when Lily died and he lost everything.

I cast my mind back, trying to remember what I know of my family before 1816. Not much—they'd settled in Barbados sometime in

the seventeenth century, which means that there have been generations of Adairs on this land or a plantation like it. But for Robert to
own Sweetwater—that must mean that his father is dead. His father—
and maybe Hannah's too. This house should, by rights, belong to the
both of them.

Deftly, she refills my glass. I stare at her hands, the long, skillful
fingers that remind me of my own, and feel my face pale. "You sure
you all right, sir?" she says. "You need to lie down? We can make a
room up for you right quick."

I shake my head. "I'm okay. I just—today is the thirtieth of March,
right?"

She glances down at the paper, then bends and scoops it up from
the floor. I see her eyes flick to the date for confirmation, and feel a
rush of warmth—so she can read. "Yes sir," she says, refolding the
paper neatly and putting it on the end table. "Saturday."

"The weekend," I say before I can stop myself. "And they're still
working?" I gesture outside, in the direction of the fields.

Hannah gives me a sharp, curious look. "Field slaves, they have
off every other Saturday. And every Sunday. With the harvest just
'round the corner, it's a busy time."

I nod silently, not wanting to implicate myself further, and eat
the last of my cake. It's sweet enough, but the weight of it settles in
my stomach like a rock. "By any chance," I say before I can lose my
nerve, "do you know a woman named Julia Griffin? Blond hair,
brown eyes, not too tall?"

She tilts her head to the side, thinking. "Might be," she says after
a moment. "There's a Miss Julia who sets with the missus sometimes—
sounds like it might be her. She's got yellow hair. Can't say for sure—
I only call her Miss Julia."

"Thanks," I say, trying to disguise the hope surging through me.
If Julia is really here—then maybe I can figure out a way to get both
of us home. Wearily, I run my hand through my hair. "I really appreciate everything, Hannah—the drinks, the food, Mrs. Adair's hospitality. Please tell her I said so."

"You're welcome," she says, and refills my glass again. At this rate, I'll be drunk within the next five minutes.

In the hallway I can hear a woman's voice raised in command—and another, acquiescing. Hannah's head tilts, listening, and she turns to go. "Just one more thing," I say casually before she makes her escape. "What date is Easter this year?"

It's not an innocent question in the least. If I'm remembering correctly, the slave rebellion that shook the island launched on Easter Sunday of this year. I keep my expression blank, hoping that if Hannah has heard any rumors, she won't associate them with the arrival of Max Adair of South Carolina. Sipping my punch on the uncomfortable couch, wearing my out-of-place clothes, I wait for her answer.

"The fourteenth, I think," Hannah says after a moment. Her face is blank again. I can't tell if the date means anything to her. "You religious, Master Max?"

"No," I tell her, giving her my best smile—the one that could usually stop an argument with Isabel in its tracks, to her unending frustration. "Not terribly religious, just curious. I'd heard Easter is a great celebration here—I was looking forward to it."

She seems to accept this, and leaves me to my thoughts. *April fourteenth.* I sip my punch, calculating furiously. There are fifteen days left until the insurrection. Fifteen days before all hell breaks loose. Before the island goes up in flame, taking Sweetwater with it, sending Lily Adair into premature labor—and to her death. Fifteen days before the shit hits the fan.

I have got to get out of here before then.

Isabel

Despite my best intentions, the weekend doesn't go well.

For one thing, most of my team spends Saturday nursing a wicked hangover, creeping from room to room like extras from *The Walking Dead*. When I harass Jake about this, he just looks shamefaced and asks me if I have any extra Advil. Worse, from the way he and Maura are avoiding each other, I'm pretty sure something happened between them—and neither of them looks very happy about it. It's really too bad; as two of the senior members of the crew, they have to work closely. If this continues, our remaining days together are bound to be less than pleasant for all concerned.

On top of everything else, when I call Verizon, they inform me that they have no record of any incoming calls to my number yesterday. Not one. My call to my dad, yes, and the hysterical forty-five minutes I spent speaking to Ryan (at this, I clench my teeth, silently bemoaning the cost even with my international phone plan). No call from Max.

Goosebumps break out all over my body, as if I've stepped into the path of a freezing wind. I ask the Verizon rep to check again, then once more. Finally, I have to admit defeat—not one of my strengths—

and hang up, in no small part because she is beginning to become extremely irritated with our conversation. *No*, she assures me, *it can't be a computer snafu. It doesn't work that way. If someone called you, I'd see it here.*

Completely bewildered, I corner Jake again. He's lying on his bed with a cold washcloth over his eyes. Hearing me come in, he discards the cloth with a grimace and props himself up on his elbows, no doubt anticipating further scolding.

"I already said I was sorry for letting them get so wasted," he says, before I can get a word out. "It won't happen again."

"Of course it won't," I say, folding my arms across my chest. "Because this is our last weekend here. I don't know why I even bother."

Jake flops down on his back with a groan. "Dr. Griffin, did you just come in here to yell at me? Because I thought you did a pretty good job before, if you don't mind my saying so, and my head hurts like a mother."

I take a step closer to the bed, blocking the ray of sunlight that's managing to make its way through the drawn curtains. "If I was going to yell at you, Jake, you'd know it. I didn't come in here to give you a hard time."

"Then what do you want?" he says, opening one eye to squint at me. "No disrespect intended."

I pause before answering, trying to imbue my voice with its usual confidence. "At the dig yesterday—before I drove off—you saw me answer the phone, right?"

His eyes open wide, confused and bloodshot. "Of course I saw you answer the phone. It rang, and you fell over and gave me a dirty look when I laughed. You took one look at the caller ID, started crying, and took off like a bat out of hell. Ow," he concludes, rubbing his temples, the effort of assembling so many words proving too much for him.

Although I can't say I'm too thrilled with his description of my behavior, it's accurate enough—and, more than that, it confirms my faith in my own sanity, Verizon be damned. I'm so relieved, I could kiss Jake, but that would hardly be appropriate. Instead I say, feeling much more like myself again, "Good. That's what I wanted to know."

He rubs his head, eyes closed. "I guess you're not going to tell me why you asked, are you?"

"You guess right," I say, regarding him with a touch more pity than I had five minutes before. "Just one more thing. About Maura—"

At this he rolls over, pulling the pillow on top of his head. "Don't say it. I don't get how you always know these things. You're like a witch doctor, or something."

This makes me smile despite myself. I yank the pillow off, doing my best to look stern. "Hardly, Jake. Anyone can see that something's going on between the two of you. I don't need to know what happened—for God's sake, don't tell me!" I say, when he opens his mouth. "Just fix it, okay?"

His bloodshot eyes find mine, and the vulnerability I see in his expression reminds me just how young he is. "How am I supposed to do that?" he says.

With a sigh, I lean over, turning the pillow to its cool side, like I do for Finn when she has a fever. "Talk to her, for one thing. Apologize, if that's something you need to do. But for Christ's sake, stop pretending like it didn't happen. That goes for Maura too."

Jake turns his head so that his cheek presses against the pillow. "Why aren't you giving her a talking-to, then? Why am I the lucky one?"

"Because," I say, turning to head for the door, "you were the one who was responsible for making everyone behave. Hence, you get the lecture."

He groans again. "Fine, I'll talk to her. Now if you don't mind, Dr. Griffin, could I please get some sleep?"

"Certainly," I say, and leave him to it, closing the door behind me just a bit harder than necessary. From inside his darkened bedroom, I can hear Jake swear as I walk away.

My good mood lasts a little while longer—long enough for me to call home and have my father assure me that Finn's fine, and for Jake to emerge from his room and approach Maura, who's flung herself into an oversized easy chair in the common area and is reading *Gone Girl* with rapt attention. I'm pleased to see that whatever he says is enough to make her get up and follow him outside. He gives me a resigned look as they pass, like a man en route to his own execution, but he's going and that's enough for me.

It lasts through Sunday afternoon, in the field lab, as we sort through our finds from Friday, cleaning and packing things away for further analysis. Tomorrow is our last day here, and everything has to be as organized as possible before we hand it over to the team from the University of the West Indies at Cave Hill, just outside Bridgetown.

This is a joint dig, a collaboration between the College of Charleston and UWI, so we won't be closing up the site when we leave. They'll come in with their own team right after us and pick up where we left off. In some ways, this has made things easier—we were able to borrow a lot of their tools and buckets, instead of schlepping our own through the rigors of international air travel—but as lead archaeologist, I've had to relinquish a certain amount of control, which isn't easy for me.

Still, this is their country and their site; they've been kind to allow us access. I do my best to keep this in mind as I look over our latest finds with a proprietary eye, all salvaged from Lowthers: a metal buckle; buttons from what looks like a soldier's uniform; the remains of a cask that most likely held rum; a set of pipes, possibly played by a slave to relieve the tedium and misery of bondage.

Brushing the dry dirt away from the pipes with a toothbrush, I find myself wondering about the man or woman who owned them. I imagine them standing in the plot of open land surrounded by the slave quarters, playing a mournful tune as the sun went down. Holding the pipes in my gloved hand, I am consumed with longing, wishing I could rewind time to meet the musician, look them in the eye, and acknowledge the wrong done to them. I've felt this way before, holding an artifact, but rarely so strongly.

As I stand there, something peculiar happens. The image sharpens, bringing the pipes and their owner into focus. It's a man, shirtless, his back striped with lashes. Despite this, he stands tall at the center of a group of dancers, swaying to the music, his body illumined by the rays of the setting sun. Just before it slips below the horizon, he turns, the last of the light falling full on his face, and that is when I know him for who he is: the man from my dream, holding the sword high above his head, vengeance written on his features and sweat gleaming on his skin.

I am so startled that I nearly drop the pipes. It isn't like me to indulge in this type of fantasy, much less blend my waking life and dreams with such seamlessness. It unnerves me, and I suddenly want nothing more than to leave the lab and surround myself with normalcy, squabbling grad students, immature undergraduates, and all.

With less delicacy than is called for, I place the pipes back in their plastic bag, seal the top, and retreat to the common room. All around me, life proceeds as usual—the dinner crew debating the best way to make spaghetti and then lambasting Rob and Maura, who have chosen this inconvenient moment to freeze cups of water for the cooler. Still, I can't help but see the man with the sword, blood staining his chest, toppling backward into the fiery cane. I watch him fall, I see my mother at the window, I hear Finn scream. And then, as clearly as Jake's voice, rising above the kitchen's fray, I hear Max calling to me, desperation plain in his voice: *Isabel. Keep her safe.*

Max

Until dinner, I roam the grounds of Sweetwater. The estate is huge, populated by what must be over a hundred slaves. I hear them singing in the fields, the thwacks of their blades cutting the cane.

I'm standing in a grove of mango trees near an open yard when a group of children emerge from the fields, hauling cane on their bent backs and carrying buckets of water. One of them, a dark-skinned girl who is smaller than the others, trips over a stone and falls, water arcing out of her bucket to splash in the dust of the yard. Dazed, she rubs her knee and looks around for the fallen bucket. But before she can retrieve it, a man approaches from the stand of ferns that edges the other side of the yard. He is darker than the girl—his skin gleams ebony—and he is better dressed, which isn't saying much, given the rags she's wearing.

The girl shrinks back from him, opening her mouth as if to speak. Before she can say a word, his arm swings back and he strikes her, quick as a snake, sending her sprawling. I jerk back in surprise, my hands curling into fists. The twenty-first-century part of me wants to call the authorities, but the rest of me knows that there is no one to call, not here and certainly not now.

"Clumsy girl!" the man says, scowling at the other children. "The rest of you, ain't you got work to do? Quit your staring and go about your business. As for you, Mercy Nell," he says, nudging the girl with his foot, "you're no better than your mama. That how you want to end up? In the Cage?"

Mercy Nell shakes her head furiously. Her faded pink headscarf has come undone, and her braids tumble down. From where I stand, I can see that her knee is bleeding. "You see Mama when you go to town, Isaac?" she asks. "You know when she's coming home?"

At this, the man gives a derisive snort. "When the law say so, Mercy, and you should count yourself lucky that Missus Lily wants her back again, running off like she did to find your fool of a daddy. Much luck that did her—he got a wife up at Simmons, from what I hear. He ain't gonna hide the likes of your mama, not from the Negro hunters. She's flat crazy if that's what she thinks. And you watch you don't turn out just like her."

I expect Mercy to cower again, to tell Isaac whatever he wants to hear. But instead she braces her hands in the dirt and pushes to her feet, ignoring the blood that drips from her knee. "I'd be proud to turn out like my mama," she says in a voice that carries through the plantation yard. "She runs 'cause she wants to be free, like we're meant to be. 'Cause she believes we're as good as anyone else, even if our skin's dark as night. She got twice the courage of you, Isaac."

She straightens her spine and looks the man in the face. "I know why you care so much, why you're standing here calling me names when you got to be minding the sugar. I hear you at night, I know what you do to her. She wants to be free of them buckra, sure. But she want to be free of you too. You can take her body, much as you want, and ain't nothing she can do to stop you. But you can't get your greedy fingers 'round her heart."

She stands defiant, her small chin uptilted, staring Isaac down as if she were a snake charmer and he the cobra, helpless before her gaze. At the edge of the yard, the other children are frozen too. The

expression on their faces mirrors the one on my own—total incredulity, blended with pride and fear. I hold my breath.

Then Isaac breaks free of her spell and backhands her again. She
falls to her knees and he kicks her, over and over, until she rolls into
a ball, trying to protect her head.

Rage surges through me. Before I know what I'm doing, I charge
out of the grove and tackle Isaac, knocking him to the ground next to
Mercy Nell. "She's a child, you son of a bitch," I spit, standing over
him. "What kind of coward kicks a child?"

Isaac's mouth opens, then closes again. For a moment fury is
clear on his face. And then he gives me a second look and wipes his
expression clean. "Sorry, sir," he says, dropping his eyes. "I didn't see
you standing there."

I am breathing hard. "What the hell does that have to do with it?
I'm glad I *was* here—God knows what you might have done to her
otherwise."

He doesn't say a word, and it's all I can do to stop myself from
beating him to a pulp. Forcing myself to calm down, I extend a hand
to Mercy Nell, who has uncurled herself and is gazing up at me
warily, arms wrapped around her knees as if she is trying to make
herself invisible. "Are you all right?" I ask. "Can you stand?"

Mercy Nell eyes my hand as if she has never seen anything like it
before. "I beg your pardon, sir," she whispers, rubbing at a trickle of
blood on her cheek. "I ain't mean to cause trouble."

"You didn't cause anything," I say, and pull her to her feet. "I saw
the whole thing. Nothing that happened was your fault."

"Yes sir," she says automatically, but I see her eyes dart to Isaac.

"Don't worry about him. He won't bother you again. I'll see to it,"
I tell her, dusting off her clothes. She flinches when I touch her, and
with a sick sensation, I realize why that must be. Feeling disgusted
with my entire family, I drop my hands to my sides.

"Get up," I tell Isaac. He obeys at once, which sickens me even
further. He has to listen to me, doesn't he? He has no choice. But he

was abusing the little girl—hell, the whole thing is such a fucking mess. "You stay away from her, you hear me? If you put so much as a finger on this child and I find out about it, you won't like what happens. I'm staying at the great house. Mercy Nell, if this man touches you, you come tell me."

The child bites her lip. "What's your name, sir?" she says.

It occurs to me that, as a member of the family, I may have some actual power here, beyond what's conveyed by the color of my skin. And for once, I don't feel bad about using it. "My name is Max Adair," I say, looking Isaac in the eye. "Remember it."

Isaac's hands open and close, but never clench into fists. "Yes sir," he says. "If you don't need me no more, I got to get back to the sugar."

I nod and he turns, his back stiff as he strides away. As soon as he is gone, Mercy slumps, the tension running out of her body. She bends down to pick up her bucket, her free hand pressed to her ribs. "I thank you, sir," she says softly, her gaze fixed on the empty bucket swinging from her fingers. "I won't forget."

"You don't have to thank me. Anyone would have done the same."

She shakes her head. "Ain't no one stopped Isaac before."

"But Robert—" I say, and she shakes her head again.

"This is slave business. Master Robert pays it no nevermind." She peeks up at me through her lashes. "I'm grateful, and no mistake. But sir—you're a stranger here. You don't know me or my mama, neither. Why'd you stop Isaac?"

The puzzlement on her face strikes me like a blow to the chest. "Because it's wrong!" I say heatedly. "You're a child. Men don't hit or kick little girls. Where I come from, a man like that is no man at all."

Mercy smiles at me, one hand still flattened against her ribs. Two of her bottom teeth are missing, her dress is stained with dirt, and there is blood running down her face—but when she smiles like that, so that it lights up her eyes, she is beautiful. "I thank you," she says again, and drops me a small, unexpected curtsy. Then she hefts her bucket and disappears down the path, the hem of her torn dress dragging in the dust.

Adrenaline is still whipping through my body, seeking an outlet. I've never thought of myself as a violent person, but I would have happily bashed that abusive asshole's face in and damn the consequences. I run a hand down my face, and start walking again.

A few minutes later, I come upon what must be the sugar mill, right next to the boiling house. A series of slaves trudge up to the mill from the fields, bent almost double, cut cane piled heavy on their backs. Steam issues from the boiling house's chimney, and the air is full of the smell of scorched sugar, underlaid by a truly foul stench.

Curious, I open the door—and walk straight into a scene out of Dante's *Inferno*. The heat hits me first, a wall of steam so thick I can hardly see. As my eyes adjust, I can make out leaping flames, their glow reflected off the walls and illuminating the half-naked bodies of the workers, whose dark skin is oiled with sweat. A never-ending spill of bubbling, pale liquid flows directly to the boiling house from the mill, into a series of giant copper kettles, the source of steam billowing up in towering white clouds. A slave stands at each kettle, stirring the contents with a long wooden ladle. The smell is sour, so thick that it fills my nostrils and I choke, trying to swallow it down.

Running back and forth between each of the kettles is a man, his eyes fixed on their contents. "Now!" he yells, and two of the slaves transfer the boiling liquid from one of the huge kettles into a smaller one, stepping back to avoid the inevitable splatter. His air of absolute authority is such that it takes me a moment to realize he must be a slave himself. As I watch, he grabs a short, squat kettle-minder by the arm and jerks him back from the edge of one of the cauldrons. "Have a care, Ben," he says in a low voice. "You stay 'wake, or you wind up in there. Mind yourself, now."

The short man blinks and straightens up, eyes widening. He gives a quick nod and a mutter of thanks. Eyeing the vat of steaming cane mash, he begins to stir it with the long-handled ladle, blinking rapidly in an effort to stay conscious.

With a start, I realize what the other man meant—in another few seconds, Ben would have tipped forward into the kettle of boiling sugar and been burned alive. Horrified, I glance around the room—the blazing fires, the exhausted slaves, the awful smell—and begin backing out again. No one has taken any notice of me, and that's just as well—I have some choice words for the white man who is sitting cross-legged by one of the room's huge windows, observing the action, and they're best kept to myself.

I am halfway back to the great house when I hear the screams.

Isabel

Monday dawns hot and humid as ever, a light breeze blowing off the Atlantic. When the alarm goes off, I drag myself out of bed and holler at everyone to get up, making sure they gather our shovels, tarps, and trowels. I double-check the cooler, filled with plastic cups of ice and gallons of water from the bathtub, make sure there's enough food for lunch, and rifle through my backpack for my bug spray, sunscreen, and long-sleeved shirt. Satisfied, I jam my wide-brimmed hat on my head, shove my feet into my steel-shank hiking boots, and tell everyone that it's time to go.

As usual, no one but Maura has gotten up early enough to eat breakfast, so they're all cramming granola bars into their mouths in the van. Next to me, Rob sloshes coffee down his gray *Jurassic Park* T-shirt, baptizing the T. rex's head. With a sigh—this happens every morning—I hand him a napkin, pilfered from Chefette's, the island's main fast-food restaurant. He mutters something that sounds vaguely like "Thanks, Dr. Griffin" and dabs at the stain, succeeding only in making it worse.

I'm focused on driving—even after a month on the island, I'm not completely confident about navigating on the other side of the road. But as the green-and-brown fields of cane blur by me on the left and the small, decrepit houses on the right, chickens pecking in the yards and boys lounging on the porches, part of me is already at the dig, wondering if today the phone will ring again and Max will be on the other end of the line. It's silly, I know, but I can't help it.

The hope carries me through assigning partners for the day—always a challenge, since weaker students have to be spread throughout the group, sharing the love—through setting up our shade shelter and sharpening the shovels and trowels. It carries me through overseeing the assembly of the sifting screen and through the first two hours of painstaking work. I make it to our afternoon break—and then everything goes to hell.

We're digging in five-inch increments, what we archaeologists call levels. Every five inches down, the diggers need to trowel off cleanly, preparing the site to be sprayed with water to show the true color of the dirt, then drawn and photographed for the record. It's taken us four weeks to get to where we are today—from the detritus of twenty-first-century life to what was likely a late-nineteenth-century trash heap to the packed dirt floor of a slave hut, strewn with broken bits of pottery and the remains of an iron cooking pot. This was our goal—Barbados is approaching the 200th anniversary of the 1816 slave rebellion, and the College of Charleston and UWI have banded together to discover and preserve as many artifacts as possible, to commemorate the island's history.

This has been a complicated process. Most of the items that slaves used in their daily lives—eating utensils, drinking vessels, clothing, even the huts in which they lived—were comprised of organic materials and have long since rotted away, making my job that much harder. All I can do is guess at what ought to be here, and hope that I'll find a few artifacts that have survived the passage of time.

As the supervisor, I don't have that many chances to excavate—I'm too busy answering questions and making sure that everyone else takes care of what they need to do. Cleaning up the site for the day gives me the much-anticipated chance to get my hands dirty, and when Maura signals me, I don't hesitate.

It's funny how the smallest things stay with you. For the rest of my life, I think I will remember how the sandy soil feels as it gives way under my knees, how sweat drips into my eyes, even under the brim of my hat, and I wipe it away with a gloved hand, impatient to investigate their progress. The way Maura's face looks, reddened with sun and excitement, as she calls up to me that they've found something.

In that moment, I have no sense that my world is shifting on its axis, never to settle back into the same position again. Instead I feel the familiar spark of curiosity that led me to become an archaeologist in the first place—the desire to connect with people who came before me, to discover their secrets, the things that they'd left behind to mark their passage. Carefully, I climb down into the pit and crouch next to Maura, who has abandoned her trowel and is poking at something with a Popsicle stick to avoid damaging it. All around me rises the smell of wet earth, recently disturbed, and the acrid sweat of the diggers, mixed with coconut-scented sunscreen and the harsh bite of bug spray.

Maura is lying on her stomach. "Look," she says, and sits up, scooting backward so that I can see. "It's delicate. Maybe a piece of jewelry? What do you think?"

"Let me see," I say, unclipping my trowel from my belt and leaning closer. Buried as it is, I can still see what alerted Maura—the glint of something metallic, gleaming silver even through the layers of dirt. Feeling a thrill run through me, I glance at her record sheet to make sure she's documented everything—horizontal and vertical position, the nature of the soil, the context of the find and the location within our digging matrix. Then I gesture toward her trowel. "Do you mind?"

She shakes her head, handing it to me. As carefully as I can, I slide our two trowels beneath the mysterious object and lift up the dirt beneath it in one piece, Maura's find still safely cushioned inside. I place it on the ground atop a piece of tinfoil and begin chipping the dirt away with Maura's Popsicle stick, one painstaking bit at a time.

The other students gather around us, their faces lit with excitement. This is my favorite part of a dig, the part that makes all of the planning and paperwork worthwhile. It's the part that all of us archaeology geeks love—the suspense as we wait to see what a particular plot of land will yield, the magic of discovery when we find something special. Ryan calls it the Indiana Jones moment.

Bending over the clump of dirt is starting to hurt my back, so I take off my cotton shirt and lie down on it. Gingerly I prod at the find, rewarded by a cascade of loose dirt, and pick up a small paintbrush resting beside Maura's clipboard to clean away what remains. The more I brush, the brighter the glitter of metal becomes, until the last bit of earth falls away, revealing what it's been hiding all along—a silver chain, encrusted with dirt but remarkably intact. Hanging from it is a pendant I never thought I'd see again.

It can't be, I think, staring down at the aquamarine stone, its clear blue shimmer visible even through the grime I have yet to clean away. *It's not possible.*

Next to me I hear Maura suck in her breath, echoed by the rest of my students. "What is that?" she says. "It looks almost like a—"

"Like a dragonfly," I say, before I can stop myself. As filthy as the necklace is, most of it still cloaked in the sandy soil and one of the wings sheared away, I have no doubt. My chest tightens, and I swallow hard. *Not possible.* But then—

"It's beautiful," Maura says, sounding reverential. "Where do you think it came from, Dr. Griffin? It doesn't look like any of the other pieces we've found. I didn't know they did that type of silversmithing back in the early 1800s."

Taking in what my efforts have uncovered—a pendant half the size of my thumb, its remaining silver wing encrusted with dirt, the aquamarine stone peeking through the soil just where I imagine the dragonfly's heart would be—I feel my heart stutter to a halt. I breathe, inhaling sweat and sand and salt, and it starts up again, racing as if to make up for its earlier transgression. "No. They didn't," I say, blinking in an effort to reconcile the appearance of the necklace with what I know to be true.

This is the doppelganger of the necklace my mother was wearing the night she disappeared. The one my father and I had custom-made for her, a birthday gift, just three weeks before. We have no photos of her wearing it. I haven't seen it in fourteen years. But I still remember the way my father fastened it around her neck that night, the way it nestled in the hollow of her throat, a perfect fit, like it was meant to be there. I remember her standing on the edge of the crowd at Max's family's garden party, her face pensive, fingering the pendant as if the engraving on the back of one of the wings was stamped in Braille: *"The dream is the truth."* An excerpt from Zora Neale Hurston's *Their Eyes Were Watching God*, one of my mother's favorite books. *Love always, I. & A.*

Hands shaking, I sit back, eyeing the necklace as if it's a hazardous explosive. It just sits there, half-sunk in the dirt, mute and innocent.

It's not, I say to myself fiercely. *It can't be. It's not.* After all, what the hell would my mother's necklace be doing here, broken and abandoned in the detritus of a nineteenth-century Barbados plantation? As far as I know, she never even left the United States.

"All right," I say, pushing back my panic, willing myself to treat the necklace like any other find. "Who's got the camera? Someone sketch this and record what you need to. Then bring it up, wrapped and bagged, please, and we'll photograph it in the light."

Isabel

B ack at the house, I oversee the unloading of the van, then disappear into the field lab with the necklace. Setting it on the worktable, I remove it from the tinfoil and take a soft brush to the rest of the loose dirt. This is unusual enough that I'm sure the team will notice—usually it's their job to do grunt work like this, not mine—but there's no way I'd trust anyone else with this. I wash the necklace with care and set it down on the foil.

The necklace lies there, tarnished and broken. The delicate chain is more or less intact, snapped only where the metalsmith soldered it to the edge of the missing silver wing, the one with the stamped inscription—maybe.

Regardless of whether another wing was originally attached to the other side of the stone, *something* used to be there. This is clear enough from the unbalanced look of the necklace, the broken rivet, the snapped chain. Grabbing a magnifying glass, I lean over the table, examining the necklace more closely. The break is sharp, as if someone had grabbed the necklace and pulled, hard enough to sever metal from stone. And metal from metal, I realize, examining the end of the severed chain.

Imagining someone's hand around my mother's throat, jerking

hard enough to do this kind of damage, I shiver. My father and I had chosen each element of the necklace so carefully—aquamarine, for courage and communication, for trust and letting go, and the dragonfly, emblematic of a shift in perspective and self-realization. We'd designed it to represent the year that my mother had spent tracking down her birth family—a year fraught with emotional highs and lows, letters written and historical records sent, hopes raised only to be shattered again. Adopted as a child and raised in California, where I'd spent the first fifteen years of my life before we'd moved to Charleston for my dad's job at Grice Marine Lab, she'd only just discovered her roots before she disappeared.

We'd chosen the inscription engraved on the wing—*the dream is the truth*—to symbolize my mother's unrelenting identity quest. On the very first page of *Their Eyes Were Watching God*, the line is part of a quote about women's tricky relationship with memory that my mom often read to me. She'd only found out she was adopted when she was in her twenties, and the crevasse between the stories that families tell themselves and the difficult, messy truth troubled her no end.

The night she'd vanished, she'd been alight with excitement, showing me the family tree she'd created, drawn by hand in black ink, as far back as the early 1800s. She was on to something important, she believed, a link that would make all the difference. "You've always known who you are, Izzy," she said, tracing the letters of some long-dead ancestor's name with reverence. "I can't explain what it's been like, to feel adrift all these years. When my mother was alive— I promised her I wouldn't search. But now it's just me, and I feel like I can't go forward until I understand where I began. Does that make any sense to you, sweetheart?"

She turned to me, radiant in her white silk blouse, the necklace gleaming bright against her skin, her face expectant. And I nodded, forcing a smile, even though I didn't understand, not really. My mother's search for her roots had led to many an argument—she'd forgotten to pick me up from chorus practice, she'd let dinner burn, time and time again. She'd cried over leads lost and unreturned phone calls and letters, sat up late night after night poring over her papers.

In South Carolina, I thought, things would get better. They had to. After all, she'd finally found the link with the past that seemed to matter so much to her. I knew she'd follow it down the rabbit hole, like she had with all the others, but maybe—hopefully—this time she'd emerge satisfied. So I said, "Of course I understand, Mom. Does this look okay?" and turned in a circle, more to draw her attention away from the family tree than for her input on my sundress. After all, we were going to some kind of neighborhood celebration, nothing I cared about all that much.

My mom smiled, watching me twirl for her. "You look lovely," she said. "Do you know, I think the Adairs have a son about your age. Max, I think his name is."

I lift my gloved hand and touch the necklace, turning it over, looking for proof. There is none; the metalsmith left no mark on the blue-green stone or the remaining wing. All the proof I can hope to find is stamped on a missing bit of silver, a scant few inches long, most likely still lost somewhere in the pit—if I'm lucky. That, and the fact that an embossed insect wing like this has no business in the remains of a nineteenth-century plantation yard. Maura had been right—as talented as they might have been, metalsmiths just didn't do this kind of work back then. Whether it belonged to my mother or some stranger, this necklace is out of place—and out of time.

I unpack my camera, positioning the necklace under the light to make sure there are no shadows. My hands shaking, I photograph it from above, then turn it over to capture the back. And then I pick it up, heedless of the broken chain, and put it around my neck, feeling the featherlight weight of the metal against my skin, the cool press of the stone. *Mom,* I say, as if she can hear me. *What happened to you?*

The night she disappeared, we had all been at the Adairs' annual spring party. My mom had met Mrs. Adair—Jennifer, she'd said, with a pleased smile—at the grocery store, and she'd invited us. The fact that my mom had agreed took me by surprise—she'd never been an overly social person—but my father and I were happy that she wanted to do something other than obsess over genealogical charts, and we hadn't complained.

Of course, she'd had an ulterior motive. All that obsessive research had led her to believe that somehow, way back in the nineteenth century, her birth family had some connection with the Adairs. Max's family had owned land in the Charleston area for a century—and before that, in Barbados, where his great-great-great-whomever had run a sugar plantation. When my dad got the job at the Marine Lab, my mother thought fate had led us to find a house just behind their property. I had a sneaking suspicion that her desire to go to the party had something to do with this mysterious historical link, and prayed she wouldn't do anything too embarrassing. Either way, being invited to this gigantic bash was, she informed me, like a dream come true.

The party was huge, sure enough—outside under a tent, with an honest-to-God pig on a spit, coleslaw, fried nuggets that a server informed me were hush puppies, and an abundance of sweet tea. A jazz band was playing, and I stood at the edge of the makeshift dance floor, breathing in the scent of honeysuckle and watching the trumpet player bend and sway. Out of the corner of my eye, I could see women wearing large-brimmed hats and men in seersucker suits. The scene was such a far cry from southern California that I was immobilized, with plate and plastic cup of sweet tea in hand, taking in the spectacle as if it were a Tennessee Williams play.

From my spot by the dance floor, I watched as black servers circulated among the white crowd, feeling a tremendous sense of dislocation. The Adairs' son was nowhere to be seen. I could hardly blame him, given the profusion of Laura Ashley–wearing, giggly Southern belles everywhere. All they lacked were fans over which to bat their eyes. I might have tried to sneak off into the woods if I hadn't seen my mother standing at the edge of the party, her eyes fixed on me with a look that, at this distance, I was hard-pressed to decipher. I was worried that she would think I wasn't having a good time, so I raised my cup of tea and smiled. Then I turned back to the band and lost myself in the music.

The next time I looked, she was gone. I never saw her again.

I place the necklace carefully inside a small Tupperware container, foil and all. It seems anticlimactic to box it up like yesterday's leftovers, but this is what I have. I press the cover on top and stare down at it, wondering if I am losing my mind.

Of the seventy or so people at that party, none of them remembered seeing my mother after the first half hour or so. She was a new face, and Charleston society was insular, so people had noticed her. That, and she was beautiful, with thick, straight blond hair and almond-shaped brown eyes—neither of which I'd inherited. "One of these things is not like the other ones," she used to joke, when the three of us were together. "One of these things does not belong."

People noticed my mother, always had, and that party was no exception. A man in his thirties remembered her stopping a server to ask questions about the punch, her voice noticeably devoid of a Southern accent. Another recalled her standing by the azaleas, fingering a blossom, a look of deep concentration on her face.

But although a good handful of people could recall seeing her prior to six-thirty—around the same time that I'd glimpsed her standing at the edge of the gathering with that odd, wistful look on her face—no one reported seeing her afterward. Not the Adairs, not the servers, not the guests, and certainly not me. Not my father, who had come back from the bar, a glass of white wine in one hand and a tumbler of Scotch in the other, to find her missing. At first he'd assumed that she'd wandered off to tour the grounds. Then he'd gotten annoyed, thinking that she'd snuck into the house to pursue her obsessive hunt for her family's origins. Finally, when a search of the house and the grounds proved fruitless and she didn't answer her phone, he felt the first bolt of fear seize his heart.

The Adairs seemed genuinely distressed by my mother's disappearance, and they cooperated with the police investigation, which lasted for months. Still, I never really did trust them, and they didn't care for me much, either. At first they felt sorry for me, brought casseroles, and invited us over for Sunday dinner. And then—months later—when it became clear that Max liked me better than the far more suitable Southern girls with whom they tried to set him up time and time again, their pity for me alchemized into outright dislike that only the veneer of their good manners managed to conceal.

The investigation never turned up a single clue about what happened to my mother—not a credit card charge, a medical record, or a bank account. This necklace, sitting innocuously in a Tupperware container, is the first trace of her I've found since that spring night so long ago.

I would give a lot to be able to go back to the dig site tomorrow, to sift through the dirt myself and discover what it yields, but that's not an option. I have to go home, to see my students safely back to Charleston and to hold my daughter. *Keep her safe*, I hear again, and squeeze my eyes tight shut, trying to force the events of the last few days to make sense. *What if it wasn't Max?* I think, and then, just as quickly, *What if it was?*

With my eyes closed like this, my other senses are heightened—and a good thing too: It forces me to ground myself in the here and now. The scent of dinner wafts in from the kitchen—most likely some kind of stew, since I'd admonished everyone to use up the remaining food so that we'd create as little waste as possible. I can hear Jake asking Maura to pass the rice, hear her tease him that he's already had two helpings, and sigh with relief. Whatever happened the other night, they've worked it out. My stomach growls, reminding me that I need to eat. But first, there are a few things I have to do.

Sitting down at the field lab table, I pull out my laptop and write a quick email to Giselle Absolom, the UWI archaeology professor who will be overseeing the dig after our team leaves. I bring her up-to-date on our progress, let her know that I'll be coming by her office tomorrow morning before we leave to photocopy our field notebooks and record sheets. I'll bring the contents of the field lab and upload all of our photos.

And then, careful to maintain as much professional distance as possible, I tell her about the necklace. It will stay here with her—it has to, courtesy of the 2011 Preservation of Antiquities and Relics Act—and so the best I can do is let her know how important it is. I describe it, to the best of my ability, and then extract the camera's memory card and upload the latest images, attaching them to my email. Hiding behind the language of my profession, I tell her that the find is of particular relevance to my research, that I have reason to believe that there may be an inscription on the missing piece, and it is of the utmost significance that the piece be located.

By the time I emerge from the field lab, dinner is over. I shower, then grab a bowl of cereal and bring it to my room. I eat, paging through the day's notes, frustrated by my complete inability to concentrate. At last I give up and call Ryan.

For once he answers immediately. "Isabel?" he says, his voice pitched loud to compensate for background noise—the hum of people talking, the distant riff of a guitar.

"Hey, Ry," I say, feeling myself relax at the sound of his voice. "Am I interrupting something?"

He snorts, amused. "Oh, yeah. Oyster night at Vickery's. It's a party out here."

I imagine him sitting outside at the bar, drinking a Turbodog beer—his favorite—and watching Shem Creek for dolphins. But then I hear a woman's voice, raised high in the background, and have my doubts. "Seriously, Ry, are you on a date? Because if you are—"

"No, Isabel, I am not on a date," he says, sounding overly patient. "Nor am I looking for one. I came here with some of the folks from Mage, including Michelle—here, say hi to Isabel," he adds, holding the phone away and putting me on speaker so that I can hear everyone, his co-worker Michelle included, chorus dutifully *Hi, Isabel*. "Better?" he says, coming back on the line.

"Sure. I just didn't want to bother you, if you were in the middle of something."

"You're not. We finally wrapped up the design of that new app for Cumulus Comics—you know how it's been giving me fits?"

"I do," I say, with appreciation. I don't really understand the ins and outs of what Ryan does—most of it is way too technical—but I do know that some element of the coding in this particular app has been driving him crazy. He's been working late, going in early, and generally wanting to bash his head into the wall. "Congratulations."

"Thanks. Hold on, I'll walk down to the creek. Be right back, y'all," he says to Michelle and the others, and then, after a moment, "Okay, Iz. Go ahead and tell me."

"How do you know I have something to tell you?" I say, opening my laptop and looking at the images of the broken necklace. I'm not trying to be difficult—I'm stalling more than anything else—but Ryan snorts, anyhow.

"Don't you?" is all he says, and when I stay silent, "Come on, Isabel, I've been worried about you. If you don't say something, I'm just going to imagine whatever you have to tell me is worse than it actually is."

This sort of confession, uncharacteristic of Ryan, goads me to speak. I tell him everything, from the moment Maura called me over until I cleaned the necklace off in the lab. When I'm done, he is quiet for a long time. I step out on the balcony and listen to the waves crash against the shore, imagining that I'm sitting next to him, watching the fishing boats moored in the harbor, hearing the creek lap against the pilings.

Finally he says, his voice cautious, "You're not joking, right?"

"I know how it sounds, Ry. And I know what you're thinking. But no."

He gives a low whistle. "You know what I'm thinking? What am I thinking, then, Isabel?"

"Well," I say, bracing my hands on the back of one of the rocking chairs, "you think that the phone call has freaked me out so much

that I'm seeing connections where none exist. You think the necklace belonged to some loyal nineteenth-century British subject, and
it just happens to bear a passing resemblance to the one my mom
used to own. And you're afraid to tell me this directly, because you
think it's going to drive me straight back to sobbing into a bottle of
rum."

"That's about the size of it. Plus I'd give my next three beers to
have you sitting next to me, where I could look you in the eyes and
talk you out of this insanity."

"Three beers, Ry?" I say before I can help myself. "It's Monday
night. What kind of week are you planning on having?"

He makes that growling sound again. "The way you're talking,
Isabel, you're lucky I'm not drinking an entire case. Could we look at
this rationally, please?"

"I am being rational, Ry. If you could just see the necklace—"

"Well, I can't. And even if I could, I have no way of comparing it
to the one your mother used to wear. Which reminds me—you didn't
tell your dad about this, did you?"

"Of course not," I say, indignant. "I wouldn't say anything to him
unless I had some kind of proof. Why would I want to upset him that
way?"

Ryan gives a sigh of relief. "Thank God for small favors. While
we're on the subject of unlikely events, did you ever call Verizon and
try to trace that phone call?"

This arrow hits the mark, and I pause, mid-retort, chastened.
"Yes," I admit.

"And?" he presses.

"They had no record of the call," I say, and then rush on before
he can reply. "But *someone* called me, Ryan. I'm not crazy. I asked
Jake, just to be sure I hadn't lost my mind entirely. And he confirmed
it—someone called me that afternoon, for sure."

"Jake would probably agree that the sky was made of cheese, if
you asked him to. But fine, point taken. So the phone company
screwed up. It doesn't prove anything."

"It doesn't disprove anything, either," I say, and he makes an aggravated noise.

"Look," he says at last, "would you please just take care of yourself, Isabel? Do that for me, okay?"

"I am taking care of myself," I say, annoyed. "Myself and eight students. And I don't think I'm doing such a bad job. Nobody's gotten arrested for public drunkenness, everyone's still speaking to one another, and I'm pretty sure there's still one person here who hasn't slept with someone else."

At this, Ryan chuckles. "Please don't think I'm overstepping my bounds when I say that I hope you're referring to yourself."

"Besides me," I say, smiling despite my irritation. "Seriously, Ry, I'm okay."

"Sure you are." His voice is wry. "You'd say that if you were standing in hell and the devil poured some kerosene on top of you."

"Says the pot to the kettle," I retort, and now he laughs in earnest.

"Touché. Six o'clock tomorrow, right?"

"You don't have to pick me up," I say for the thousandth time. "I can take a cab—"

"For Christ's sake, Isabel, I'll be there, if for no other reason than to see you and make sure you're all right. You scared me the other night, crying that way. I've never heard you sound like that before."

"I said I was sorry." My face burns, hot with embarrassment.

His voice drops low, into the gentle register he usually reserves for Finn. "And I told you, don't apologize. Just—come home."

There doesn't seem to be too much to say after that, so I tell him to have a good time and we hang up. I go back inside, haul my suitcase onto the bed, and start packing, relishing the mindless challenge of making all of my clothes and gifts and notebooks fit into a single suitcase, wondering what the future holds.

Max

I didn't turn around when the woman started screaming. Maybe that makes me a coward, but I've seen enough for one day. I can't shake the feeling that something terrible has happened, though, and as I make my way into the dining room, summoned by Hannah, I notice that she's been crying.

"What's the matter?" I ask. She wipes her eyes but doesn't speak, so I try again. "I heard screaming before—did something bad happen?"

Hannah hiccups, tries to speak, and finally says, "An accident at the mill, sir. My auntie Moll, she got too close to the rollers. It happen sometimes. The foreman, he stands by with an axe, just in case. But not in time for Auntie Moll."

"What?" I say, stunned. "You mean she—"

"She's killed," Hannah says, and wipes her eyes again. "My cousin Peggy, she saw her mama die. That ain't no sight for a child."

My stomach churns. *The foreman stands by with an axe, just in case* . . . so the only options must be chopping off a limb, or death. If I'd stayed in the yard for two more minutes, I likely would have seen the whole thing. "They couldn't do anything?" I say, even though I know better.

Hannah shakes her head, sniffling miserably. "Once the rollers get you, ain't no stopping the mill. Ain't no shutting it down. By the time they stop it, Moll's long gone."

Looking at her wet, crumpled face, I feel a painful sense of guilt. If I'd been there, if I'd turned around when I heard the screams, maybe I could have figured something out. Maybe I would have known something, seen something that could have saved Moll.

I swallow hard and make up my mind. No matter what I witness here, no matter what it costs me, I will not turn my back again.

"I'm sorry," I say, putting a hand on Hannah's shoulder.

She jerks away from my touch as if it's burned her, then gives me an apologetic smile. "Thank you," she says, and ushers me to my seat. I sit—although I have never felt less like eating in my life—and glance around.

The dining room at Sweetwater is imposing, lit only by candelabras. I'm sitting at a huge mahogany table, surrounded by high-back chairs. It's set for one, but with as much fanfare as if there were ten honored guests.

A regal woman with skin the color of burnt sienna appears at my elbow, so suddenly that I start. "Master Max?" she says, a smile lifting her full lips at my surprise.

"Yes," I say, scrambling hastily to my feet. It's pure reflex—I was raised to stand in the presence of what my mother insisted on referring to as "a lady"—but from the way her lips twitch in ironic amusement, I might as well have paraded a trained seal across the table.

"I am Penelope," she says, gesturing for me to sit down. "Housekeeper of this estate. I apologize for not seeing to you sooner. As you may know, we have had some difficulties this afternoon." Her speech is clipped, bearing a British accent with a heavy Barbadian lilt, but clearly more cultured than Hannah's.

"It's nice to meet you. There's no need to apologize—I do know what happened this afternoon. Hannah told me."

"Ah," she says, casting her eyes toward the floor. "The missus sends her regrets—she is indisposed, but hopes to be able to speak with you in the morning. Until then, she bids me tell you that any relation of her husband is more than welcome in this house."

"Thank you," I tell her. "I appreciate it." And sit back down, just as another girl comes into the room, clad in a worn green dress, her hair tied back neatly. She's holding a tray bearing some sort of roasted bird, which she promptly deposits onto my plate, followed by a sweet potato topped with butter and brown sugar. I try to thank her, but she's already stepped away from the table and is retreating from the room.

There's a clinking of glass on glass, and Penelope presents me with a tumbler of wine. "Drink," she says, with unexpected sympathy. "You've likely had a long day, Master Max, what with all of your traveling and then hearing about the mill. This is good Madeira, just came in off the docks yesterday. You have a few glasses, you'll feel better."

I accept the tumbler. I've had more to drink today than in the last two months combined, but I feel like I need it. Grimly, I fork sweet potatoes and chicken into my mouth. Maybe when I wake up tomorrow, all of this—Hannah's aunt, Mercy Nell's bloody face, the hell of the boiling house—will have been some kind of vivid nightmare. In the meantime, all I can do is try to not give myself away.

After dinner, the girl in the green dress—"Sarey," she says shyly when I ask her name—leads me upstairs to my bedroom. The room is large, with a four-poster bed shrouded in mosquito netting, a tall wooden dresser and wardrobe. A large basin filled with steaming water sits on the ground, and beside it are a stack of towels and a bar of soap. Clothes are folded neatly on top of the dresser.

"Thank you," I say, and she nods, brushing past me to light the oil lamps. The room comes to life with an odd, eerie glow, wavering as if we're underwater.

"Sarey," I say impulsively, "what does 'buckra' mean?"

She turns to me, arching a dark eyebrow in surprise. The light plays over her face, throwing her broad cheekbones and pointed chin into relief. "Where you hear that word?"

I explain about Mercy and Isaac, and she listens, her face pained. At last she says, "Buckra—that's what some call folk with skin like yours. White folk." Nervously, she picks at a small thread dangling from the sleeve of her dress. "Isaac is no friend of mine, but he's right about one thing. That girl trouble. If she's not careful, she'll join her mama in the Cage, no matter she's just twelve years old—if he don't do for her first."

The matter-of-fact way she says this makes me shiver. I don't want to ask, but I can't help myself. "What's the Cage, Sarey?"

Her lips purse at this and her eyes flash to mine. "The Cage in Bridgetown. Where they lock up runaways, and keep 'em for everyone to see. The windows got grates so you can look inside. I did once, when Miss Lily sent me to Sunday market. It's dark, bodies everywhere—crouching, moaning. People in irons, can't spread their hands more than this far apart." She holds her palms a foot away from each other. "And the smell . . ." She shudders. "I never got it off my skin, never mind I scrubbed 'til Penelope yelled at me for wasting the soap. Sometimes I smell it still."

"And that's where Mercy's mother is?" I ask, horrified. "Because she ran away?"

Sarey's eyes refocus on me, and she shakes her head. Then she rubs her hands together briskly, as if trying to rid herself of the conversation. "Best not to think 'bout such things before you sleep. Gives you the nightmare something awful." She crosses to the shutters, drawing them against the darkness. "Nightshirt's in the top drawer," she says, gesturing at the dresser, "and banyan hanging up in there. You best take your bath before the water cools—unless you need anything else?"

I shake my head, and she ducks her own, murmuring, "Good night, then." She turns away in a swish of green skirt, pulling the door to behind her.

Alone at last, I strip off my filthy clothes, set the ring and my Swiss Army knife on the bedside table, and climb into the tub with a sigh of relief. Even though it's too small to hold me comfortably, this

is the best I've felt since my world turned upside down. I sink beneath the surface, holding my breath. Thoughts race through my
mind. If Julia is really here, if I find her, how the hell will we get
home?

I resurface, taking in a lungful of air, and then go back under
again. There has to be a reason Robert brought me to Sweetwater.
Am I supposed to stop the rebellion, which is doomed to fail, and
save his wife and child? Even if that's possible, how can I justify
standing by as an entire country of oppressed people continues to be
abused—even knowing, as I do, that hundreds of slaves will lose their
lives in the insurrection or be put to death afterward, as punishment?

Morality aside, there are the theoretical questions to consider:
Do I have any business getting involved? I'd be changing the path of
history. Who knows what ripples such an action might cause, what
implications for the future?

There's a part of me that feels I'm meant to be here, to stand with
the slaves against this awful system that my ancestors helped to create. But I also want to go home to Isabel. I feel her absence like an
ache, a fist clenched around my heart.

I take another breath, sliding down in the tub again—and then
resurface, gasping, as a truly paradoxical thought occurs to me. If I
succeed in stopping the rebellion, I might not exist. If I save Lily and
her baby, Robert won't start over in South Carolina and create a new
family. I will never be born. I won't meet Isabel for the first time the
week after her mother disappears. I won't love her. I won't lose her. I
won't father our baby.

I climb out of the tub—the water's started to cool, anyhow—and
dry myself roughly with a towel. Of course I exist, I think. If I don't
exist in the future—then how can I wind up here? Maybe Lily and
the baby will die no matter what I do. Maybe Robert will never come
back to Barbados, at least not to live and raise a family.

I yank the nightshirt Sarey left me over my head, feeling like a
Charles Dickens character, and sit down on the side of the bed, deep
in thought. What about Julia? Why did Lily lead her into the woods

that day? There must be some kind of connection between them—Isabel has told me often enough that her mother was searching for her family's roots when she disappeared.

I've replayed the afternoon I saw Julia in the woods so often without any luck. Still, if I think it through again, maybe after all that's happened today I'll see it in a new light, find something that I missed. Something that will make sense of all this.

Through the window I can hear the lilting notes of a song—fiddles and drums, and what sounds like a banjo. The music fills my ears. I lose myself to the driving beat and let myself remember.

Isabel

Our plane is delayed on the ground in Barbados, then again in Atlanta. By the time we make it to Charleston, it's ten P.M. and I am exhausted. I'd texted Ryan to let him know yet again that he didn't have to pick me up—I'd be perfectly happy to take a cab—but he wouldn't hear of it. So when I stagger off the plane with the rest of the crew and make my weary way down to baggage claim, there he is, leaning against the wall, scrolling through his phone, his dirty-blond hair in typical disarray, wearing a forest-green T-shirt and jeans with a rip in the knee. Even in my altered state, I notice a couple girls eyeing him. The taller one whispers something, and her friend giggles.

Ryan looks up at the noise, but his gaze passes right over them and finds me. His face lights with a smile, and he pushes off the wall. "Isabel," he says, and comes to meet me, wrapping his arms around me in a hug. For a second I let myself relax against him, breathing in the clean-laundry scent of his shirt and the Ivory soap that he's used as long as I've known him. He's been drinking coffee; I can smell it, deep and rich, when he rests his chin on the top of my head—a habit he knows I hate.

"Quit it. I'm not a chin rest," I say, pushing away from him. He grins down at me, unrepentant.

"Welcome home," he says. "I'm thrilled to see you too."

"Thank you for coming to pick me up," I say, and he shrugs.

"Not a problem. Here, give me that. You look beat." He grabs the strap of my backpack, slung over my shoulder.

I twist out of his grasp. "I'm fine," I insist, a statement whose effectiveness is substantially compromised by the yawn that interrupts the second word, mid-syllable.

Ryan narrows his eyes at me just as the baggage carousel for our flight begins to hum, dumping the first of many suitcases onto the conveyor belt. "Sure you are," he says, heading toward the carousel. "Wide awake. I guess that means you don't want the double mochaccino with whipped cream waiting for you in the car?"

My mouth begins to water at the thought, and I ball his T-shirt in my fist, holding him still. "Seriously, Ry? Are you teasing me? Because if you are, that's just cruel."

He shakes his head, mouth quirking upward. "I know better than to mess with you where caffeine's concerned, Griffin. I picked it up on the way here. Scout's honor."

I throw my arms around him again. "Have I ever mentioned that I love you?" I say with great fervor.

"You have," Ryan says dryly. "Twice now. Once when you were wasted, and now, when you're exhausted. Flattery like that will go to a man's head. Unless your intention is to make poor Jake jealous as hell, in which case you're succeeding."

Puzzled, I gaze up at him. "What do you mean?"

"Well, he's heading this way, and you're wrapped around me like kudzu. Let's just say he looks less than pleased."

"Hmmm," I say, and twine my arms around Ryan's neck. "That's the best news I've heard all day. Maybe we should start making out."

Ryan exhales, chuckling. "Or . . . maybe not," he says, disentangling himself from me. "Isn't that your bag?"

I look where he's pointing and see my battered blue suitcase bumping down the belt, nearly making its way past us. "Shit!" I say, and dive for it, almost colliding with Jake, who's on the same trajectory.

"I've got it," I say to him. "But thanks."

"No worries," he says, cutting his eyes sideways. I follow his gaze and see him giving Ryan a distinctly mistrustful look. Never one to let an opportunity pass him by, Ry grins and lifts one hand in a desultory wave.

"Hey there," he says, cheerful as can be. "Need a ride?"

Twenty awkward minutes later, we've dropped Jake off at his crappy grad school apartment and are en route to my father's house. Ryan drives with one hand on the wheel, the other resting lightly on the gearshift. As for me, I'm clutching what remains of my fancy coffee, determined to stay awake long enough to make it home.

"You didn't have to do that," I admonish Ryan, stifling a yawn with the back of my hand. "Tease him that way."

Ryan snorts. "I guess you're right. But he makes it so easy, mooning after you with those puppy-dog eyes. I'd feel for the guy, if he wasn't annoying as hell."

"Sure you would," I say, imbuing it with the full weight of my considerable skepticism, and ruin the delivery by yawning again.

"You can go to sleep," Ryan says. "I won't be offended."

I'm not much for sleeping in moving vehicles. Maybe it's a trust issue. I prefer to be the one behind the wheel, but I can't very well relegate Ryan to the passenger seat of his Forerunner. "I think I'll be okay for the next twenty minutes," I say, ignoring Ryan when he rolls his eyes.

Instead I gulp coffee and watch the cars flash by on I-26, wondering idly about the lives of the people in each of them. Tired as I am, I get lost in my imaginings, and Ryan doesn't interrupt. Silence falls between us, and I can't help but replay the bizarre events of the past few days. I stare out the window into the night, trying to string all of the incidents together in a way that makes the pieces fall into place. Try as I might, though, clarity eludes me, and without meaning to, I sigh.

Beside me, Ryan shifts in his seat. "You want to talk about it?"

"Not especially. You'll just tell me again that I'm crazy." I set my coffee in the cup holder and brace my elbows on my knees, in preparation for the onslaught.

"That's not fair, Isabel." His voice is even. "I never once said you were crazy."

"Imagining things, then. Deluding myself. What's the difference?"

"There's a big difference," Ryan says, quieter than before. "But if you don't want to talk about it, fine. I won't force you."

"I just want to go home," I say. "I want to see Finn."

"Fair enough." His fingers tighten on the wheel. "If you don't feel like talking, can I tell you something instead?"

My curiosity piqued, I sit up straight and look over at him. His gaze is fixed on the road, his expression inscrutable. "Sure," I say. "What is it?"

"I got offered a job at Marvel."

It takes me a second to process what he's said. Then it sinks in and I shriek so loudly that Ryan jumps. "Christ, Isabel. Don't *do* that. You'll run us off the road."

"The hell with the road." I grab my coffee again and take a sip, for fortitude this time. "What's the job? When did this happen? Why didn't you tell me this before?"

"Slow down, Speed Racer. It's a product manager position with Marvel Digital, in New York. They offered it to me yesterday. And I was planning to tell you, but you've been a wee bit preoccupied."

I look at him, the lights from passing cars playing across his face, and try to imagine a world in which I don't see him every day. In which he doesn't join us for Sunday brunch or come over on Christmas Eve to help me put Finn's new bike together. Loss wrenches through me at the thought, and I force it away, feeling terribly selfish.

"Wow," I say with as much enthusiasm as I can manage. "That's incredible, Ry. When do you start?"

"That's it? That's all you have to say?" There's an unmistakable note of anger in his voice, and I peer at him through the darkness, bewildered.

"What do you mean?" I say. "Why are you mad?"

He drums the fingers of his free hand on his thigh. "You really think I'd leave — just like that? And you'd let me go, without any kind of discussion?"

"I don't own you," I say, more confused than ever. "It's an incredible opportunity. Of course I'd miss you, Ry. And so would Finn. You're my best friend. I don't want you to leave. But it's not fair to keep you here with us when you have this kind of chance. Besides, you'd just be a few hours away. It's not like you'd be moving to Peru."

Ryan sucks in another breath, louder this time. "Would you stop being so goddamn reasonable?"

I glance at him again, trying to figure out where all of this is coming from. He's sitting ramrod straight, his fingers so tight on the wheel that the knuckles are white. "Help me out here," I say, as delicately as possible. "What minefield have I stumbled into, exactly? I don't want you to go anywhere, Ryan. Obviously. Other than Finn and my father, there's no one who means more to me. But I'm not so selfish that I'm going to rend my garments and wail and cry about it to try to guilt you into staying. What kind of friend would I be?"

For a moment Ryan doesn't reply. Then his lips twitch, as if he's trying not to smile. They twitch again, and finally he does smile, a complicated, rueful grin. "A little rending and wailing wouldn't come amiss," he says.

"Seriously?" I say, peering at him in disbelief. "You thought I didn't *care*?"

He shrugs, eyes still on the road, and doesn't say a word.

"Jesus," I say, sliding down as far as my seatbelt will allow. "And I thought women were supposed to be the moody ones."

This earns me a grudging laugh. "Sorry," he mutters.

"Of course I care, Ry. I was trying to be *supportive*. God." I run a hand through my hair, wincing as my fingers snag in a tangle of unbrushed curls. "Okay, Dr. Mercurial. If you don't want me to be reasonable, what would you like me to do instead?"

He clears his throat. "I want you to come with me."

The words fall one by one into the dim light of the car, and for a second, I think I've heard him wrong. But then I take in the stillness of his body, the set of his jaw, and know that I haven't. Stunned into silence, I just stare at him.

"Say something, Isabel." His voice is expressionless, no hint of the anger that colored it just a moment ago, but I know him well enough to realize how little this signifies. He's waiting for my reaction before showing me his own, hedging his bets.

"You want us to come with you? To New York?" It emerges as a squeak.

"You said it yourself, Iz. It's not the end of the world, just a few hours away."

"But what about my job? Finn's school? The dojo? My dad? My house?"

"There are other jobs up there. Better ones," he points out, signaling for the exit. "As for Finn, we could find her a great school. Houses can be rented. Or sold. There are dojos in New York. And your dad could come visit. A lot."

I shake my head, as if that will force all of this to make sense. "Are you asking me to live with you?"

"No, no," he says hurriedly. "Not unless you wanted to. Nothing like that."

"Because I don't really think Finn would benefit from a display of your procession of girlfriends," I say, envisioning a fresh incarnation of the parade of women who've made their way through Ryan's life since I've known him. "Not to mention, the two of us would be a little hard to explain. A bit of a buzz kill on a Saturday night."

"Don't do that. Don't make a joke out of it." He takes the exit and slows down, pulling off the highway and up to the light.

Cautiously, I regard him. He's upset, that much is clear—maybe more upset than I've ever seen him. After his initial outburst, he's keeping it under wraps, but I can tell. I peer at him in the glow of the streetlights, trying to figure out what he's thinking.

Ryan must feel the weight of my gaze, because he shoots me an irritated glance. "Quit staring at me, Griffin, would you? It's making me nervous." His fingers drum faster, a blur on the wheel.

I have no idea what's going on in his head, but whatever it is, I don't feel equipped to address it in a moving vehicle. "Stop the car, Ryan," I say.

"It is stopped."

"You know what I mean. Pull over." I put a hand on his arm, feeling his muscles tense beneath my touch. "Please."

He eyes me suspiciously but pulls into a McDonald's parking lot. The two of us sit there for a moment, listening to the engine idle. Ryan rolls down his window, and the smell of French fries fills the space between us. I inhale with satisfaction—McDonald's fries are one of my guilty pleasures—and then breathe out, steeling myself for this conversation. At last I say, "What's this all about, Ry?"

"What do you mean?" he says, eyes trained on the golden arches.

Maybe if the last few days hadn't happened, I'd have more patience. As it is, though, to say that I'm on edge is putting it lightly, and Ryan's Mystery Man act is the last straw. "Oh, quit being so fucking enigmatic!" I say, slamming my hand against the dash for emphasis. "First you tell me you've been offered this amazing job, then get mad at me when I'm happy for you. Now you're accusing me of not caring enough, asking me to give up my life and come live with you, as—what? I don't get it, and in case you haven't noticed, the past seventy-two hours haven't exactly been easy for me. Explain yourself, or I'm going to start screaming."

Silence falls between us again, heavy enough to touch, and for a long moment I don't think he's going to answer. Finally he mumbles, looking anywhere but at me, "I don't want to leave Finn behind."

A wave of compassion breaks over me then, mixed with relief:

However misguided, his answer makes sense. I was beginning to feel like I'd disembarked from the plane and wandered straight into the Twilight Zone. "That's what this is about?" I put a hand on his shoulder, try to turn him to face me, but he resists, and after a minute I give up. "Ry, I know you love her," I say, doing my best to sound soothing. "She knows that too. None of that will change, just because you take this job."

"I don't want to leave her," he repeats stubbornly. "You said it yourself. I've been like a father to her. First Max leaves, then me. What's she going to think? That it's her fault? That it's just what men do?"

"She won't think that," I say, even as a small, cynical voice inside my head whispers, *Won't she?* I'd thought a version of that same thing myself, after my mom disappeared and my dad did his best to follow. If it hadn't been for Max, I would have never trusted anyone again.

"How do you know?" He turns to look at me, his expression as raw as I've ever seen it. "I want the job, Isabel, I'm not gonna lie. But I can't do it. I can't leave her."

Uncomfortable, I shift in my seat. "Ry, I don't know what to say. I know you love her. And I appreciate beyond words all you've done for her. But to say you won't leave unless we come too, to make me responsible for your decision—it's not fair."

"I can't help it," he says, and then presses his lips together into a thin line.

"What do you mean? Can't help what?"

Ryan looks stricken. "Forget it, okay? Forget I said anything."

"But—"

He looks over his shoulder and then steps on the gas, backing the car out of the parking spot with the speed and precision of an escape maneuver. I bet that if we were in my car instead of his, he'd have gotten out and taken a cab home. "Drop it, Isabel," he says, in a tone that brooks no contradiction. "Don't pick at this. You're right, I put you in an awkward position. Let's talk about something else. That damn necklace. The phone call. The dig. Anything. You choose."

Part of me wants to keep pushing. But the rest of me—the rational part—knows I owe it to him to respect his request. When I told him I didn't want to talk about what was on my mind, he let it go. I can't do any less. "Okay," I say, searching for a neutral topic. "Finn has to make a diorama based on a summer reading book, for when school starts up again in August. She wants to do it on A Wrinkle in Time by Madeleine L'Engle. I read it to her and now she's obsessed with Charles Wallace. You know how I hate crafty projects—any ideas?"

Ryan shoots me a wry grin. "Now you're speaking my language. Remind me. What's the book about again?"

"You remember. There's the main character, Meg, and then her little brother, Charles Wallace. Their father is missing, and—oh, God." My voice trails off. "I didn't even think about it from that angle. Do you think that's why she . . ."

Eyes fixed on the road, he reaches over and grips my hand, hard. "Nah, Iz. It's probably because Charles Wallace is so damn smart. Wasn't he some kind of über-genius? And really perceptive, like Finn. No wonder she's into him."

I squeeze his fingers in gratitude, and he lets me go. We spend the next fifteen minutes chatting about the Murry family and tesseracts and alternate universes, and by the time we pull up in front of my dad's two-story Colonial, it's as if the tension between us never existed. As he gives me a hug goodbye and promises to help Finn with the cursed diorama soon, it's easy to pretend he didn't ask us to give up our lives here and follow him to New York. But I know better, and the puzzle of it nags at me all the way up the steps and into the front hallway, into the little blue bedroom where my daughter sleeps, toy penguin clutched to her chest and quilt thrown off; safe and well cared-for. I look down at her small form, visible in the glow of her Snoopy night-light, and hear Ryan's voice, low and rough as if revealing the most shameful of confessions: *I can't do it. I can't leave her.*

I must have made some small noise, because Finn stirs, blinking owlishly at me from her nest of stuffed animals. "Mama?"

"It's the middle of the night," I say, sitting on the side of the bed and smoothing her rumpled hair—black, like mine, spilling over her shoulders in a mass of tangled curls. "Go back to sleep, sweetheart."

Finn sits up, wrapping her arms around her knees. Her toes peek out from beneath the hem of her white cotton nightgown, revealing the remnants of the purple polish we'd applied together before I left. With her huge gray eyes and the long nightgown, she looks like a girl from a fairy tale.

"You're home," she says, and yawns. "But you're late."

I tuck the quilt around her, suppressing my own yawn. "My flight got delayed. I called Grandpa. Didn't he tell you?"

"He told me," Finn says, and scoots forward to lean against me. I wrap my arms around her, relishing how solid she feels, a warm bundle of sleepy child. "I wanted to wait up for you, but I couldn't. You took too long."

"Sorry." I tuck a strand of her wayward hair behind her ear. "I would've been home earlier if I could. Believe me, I would rather have had dinner with you and Grandpa than be stranded in an airport with a bunch of grumpy archaeologists."

Finn giggles against my shoulder, then settles back on her pillow. One by one, I resettle her stuffed animals around her. "Go back to sleep, baby," I say.

"Will you stay until I do?"

"Of course." I kick my shoes off and lie down next to her, pulling the quilt over both of us. For a moment we are silent, listening to the hum of her fish tank's filter and the whir of the ceiling fan. And then Finn stirs, snuggling against me.

"Mama?" she says, tangling one hand in my hair.

"Hmmm?" I am warm and comfortable, slipping sideways into sleep despite my best efforts, and it's a struggle to answer her.

"I wanted to stay awake to tell you. You don't have to keep me safe," she says. "Don't worry about what Daddy said. I'm fine."

A moment ago, it was all I could do to remain conscious. Now I feel as if my body's been electrified. My eyes spring open, and my heart starts pounding. "What?" I say, trying to keep my voice even. "What did you say, Finn?"

But there is no answer. She is asleep, and I am left lying beside her, wondering if I've misheard her, knowing I haven't, wondering if I am losing my mind.

Max

The afternoon Isabel's mother disappeared, my parents were having their annual garden party. I hated the damn thing, with its Southern belles in period costume—there didn't seem to be any this year, fortunately—and black servers everywhere, just as if the War Between the States, as my grandmother always called it, had never happened. My parents insisted on showing me off like a prize pig at the fair—*Do you remember Anna, Max? The two of you used to play together. Oh, you were so adorable! Max, Anna plays piano too. She's in tenth grade, just a year younger than you. I'm sure the two of you have a lot in common. We'll just leave you to chat, shall we?*

My parents had a real obsession with Anna Prudhomme, who came from even older Charleston money than we did. Their dearest wish was to unite our families, for me to work my way up to partner in my father's law firm and dutifully produce no more than three beautifully behaved children. My dearest wish was to do almost anything else.

It was a problem.

That day, I'd said all my hellos, shaken hands, even danced with Anna, one of the least interesting—and most snobbish—human beings on the planet. Then I'd nicked some food and headed for the tree house my father and I had built the summer I turned nine. It was one of the few good memories I had of him.

He was easy to please, my father, as long as you did exactly what he wanted and agreed with him about everything. Deviate in the slightest—as I always seemed to do—and there were problems. He never laid a finger on me, didn't even yell. But he made it clear when he was unhappy, mostly via icy silences broken only by speeches about how disappointed he was, how he expected better.

I'd reached the tree house and climbed the ladder, then leaned back against the rough wall and sighed with relief. In the distance, I could make out the sounds of the party, voices raised in conversation and the fizz of jazz music, but they were no more than background noise. I loved the tree house for this reason, always had. It was the perfect escape.

Family legend held that this clearing was some sort of sacred space, but I'd never put any stock in that. It was where Robert Adair had always claimed the entrance to the Thin Place lay, a spot where the living could communicate with the dead. He'd chosen the land for this purpose, had spent the rest of his life in a vain attempt to make amends to his lost wife. It was one of our dirty family secrets, a little nugget that had never made it into the historical literature or the garden tours.

Thin Place or no, the clearing was undeniably peaceful, especially in contrast to my parents' over-the-top shindig. I dug around on the floor for the book I'd left up here last time—*The Great Gatsby*—devoured my sandwich, the vinegary taste of the barbeque making me wish I'd grabbed a bottle of water, and read, letting my mind drift where it would.

Where it would, as it turned out, was into sleep. I jerked awake some time later on the sun-warmed floor of the tree house, with the unmistakable sense that I was not alone.

I sat upright and glanced around. The sun had begun to go down, but I could still see clearly enough. The room was empty; no one was here but me.

The feeling was still there, though, a clear sense of another presence. Unnerved, I crawled to the open door and looked down into the clearing.

Despite whatever instinct had woken me, I hadn't really expected to see anyone. People make noise, and I didn't hear a damn thing except for the buzz of cicadas and the whine of a mosquito, too close to my face. I swatted it away and blinked in confusion. A woman was standing in the clearing, and I could have sworn she looked familiar.

"Hey!" I called down to her. "Are you lost?" After all, we were in the heart of my family's property, a good quarter mile away from the party.

The woman didn't respond, and I hung my legs over the edge of the ladder to get a closer look. "Hello?" I called again, louder this time, but still she didn't turn to look at me. There was something off about her clothes—she had on an old-fashioned yellow dress, like the ones I'd seen women wear on the Magnolia Plantation tours all the times my parents made me go. I couldn't figure out what a woman would be doing dressed like that in the middle of the woods.

Puzzled, I called out again, but she didn't seem to hear me this time, either. In fact she was staring straight ahead, peering into the trees as if she was expecting someone. A chill ran straight down my spine, and I dismissed it as superstition—too much time spent around a campfire, listening to the Adair family legends about ghosts and revenge. Maybe my parents had hired some folks in period dress, after all, and one of them had wandered into the woods and lost her way.

But I couldn't shake the sense that I'd seen her before. I reached for the top rung of the ladder to climb down—and froze. Now I did hear something—the sound of crunching leaves. The woman heard it too; she cocked her head to the side, and an expectant smile spread across her face just as a second woman stepped into the clearing.

There was nothing bizarre about this newcomer; she was short but curvy, with a fall of long blond hair, and she had on a perfectly normal blue skirt and white shirt, something my mother would have worn. As I watched, she made her way to the woman in the old-fashioned dress. "Hello," she said, and her voice sounded shy.

The woman in yellow held out her hand. The blond woman took it, and together they walked into the woods on the other side of the clearing.

As they vanished into the trees, I realized where I'd seen the first woman before. The chill that had been creeping up my spine swept over my entire body, and I leapt up, banging my head on the ceiling. Ignoring the pain, I leaned over the edge of the tree house and yelled, "Hey! Where are you going? Stop!"

The woman in costume never turned, but the blond one did. She looked over her shoulder at me in the fading light, and then—just before she disappeared into the woods—she lifted one hand in fare-well.

I sank to the floor, my body covered in a cold sweat. Like it or not, I'd recognized the woman in the strange dress. A portrait of her hung in the upstairs hallway. As far as I knew, it had been there for over a century, since Robert Adair had commissioned it from a miniature of the woman he'd loved and lost—his first wife, Lily.

Lily Adair had died during the 1816 slave rebellion, taking most of Robert Adair's soul with her. Family legends or no, she wasn't hanging about in the woods, kidnapping party guests. The idea was nuts.

But I'd *seen* her.

I climbed down the ladder as fast as I could and sprinted after the two women. I knew these woods. If the women were here, I'd find them. With each step, I fully expected to hear their voices or the sounds they'd make moving through the trees. But I heard nothing, and no matter how hard I looked, I couldn't see anything out of place—no flash of a white shirt or a full, sweeping yellow skirt.

Night had fallen by the time I made it through the woods and to the road bordering my family's property. No headlights pierced the darkness, and there was no one on the road as far as I could see. I listened for all I was worth, but the noises I heard were familiar—mosquitos, cicadas, the far-off croak of frogs in the creek.

It was as impossible as it was true: The two women were gone.

Isabel

Despite my exhaustion, I sleep uneasily, half-expecting another terrible dream. But none come, and in the morning I find myself alone in my daughter's small bed with its purple-and-white quilt. The quilt was a birthday gift from Max's mother and father, and I'm grateful for it, as well as for the fact that they've taken an active interest in Finn, picking her up from school when my father, Ryan, or I can't manage it, spoiling her with new clothes. I've never quite forgiven them for how they treated me when Max and I were together—like I wasn't good enough for their son by a country mile. They wanted him to marry a nice, old-money, Cotillion-indoctrinated Southern girl. But I also know how much they've lost. Finn is all they have left of Max, and so I do my best to be gracious, even though their impenetrable civility and insistence on never discussing anything that really matters drive me insane.

It's a mark of my distance from them that I never even thought to tell them about Max's bizarre phone call—and I won't now, I conclude, sliding out of bed and stretching. Like my dad with the necklace, all it would do is upset them.

Then again, I think, if I were my father, wouldn't I want to know?

If someone found anything that looked like it could have possibly belonged to Max and didn't tell me, I'd be furious. I decide then and there to show him the photos of the necklace, and let him come to his own conclusions.

I dig in my suitcase for the last of my clean clothes, pull them on, and go into the bathroom to wash my face. Padding down the hallway, with its floor-to-ceiling windows and curving staircase, I breathe deep, happy to be home. Then I make my way downstairs into the bright yellow kitchen, where Finn and my father are having breakfast.

"Mommy!" Finn hails me. She's scooping eggs into her mouth, mostly without the benefit of chewing, in between gulps of milk. "You woke up in time for camp. Grandpa said maybe you wouldn't, and I should let you sleep because you were super-tired. But I was hoping and hoping you would wake up, and here you are."

"Oh . . . camp," I say, vaguely disoriented. "Yesterday was the first day, right? How's it going? Do you like it okay?"

Finn gives me a wide-eyed look, only slightly disingenuous. "It's good," she says, and I narrow my own eyes at her, trying to ferret out the truth. Last year I sent her to the YMCA for most of the summer, which was a disaster of epic proportions. She shied away from the group sports activities—which, at the Y, were most of them— preferring instead to sit in the corner with her sketchbook or to wander around, looking for butterflies the way my dad had taught her. The other campers ignored her, which was bad enough, but the counselors were even worse.

At first they'd seemed to like her. I'd drop her off in the morning and she'd go willingly enough, hopping out of the car with a wave and a smile. Gradually, though, things changed. Finn never complained, but the pinched look on her face and the way she'd pick at her breakfast were red flags enough for me. It took me a while to figure it out, but ultimately I pieced together what happened. Apparently, Finn had somehow realized that two of the counselors had embezzled from the field trip fund the year before, and were planning to do it again. She'd walked up to them and said, face earnest, "Stealing is wrong. Don't do it. Not twice."

The counselor who told me this story swore up and down that the two culprits had never talked about their plan at work, hadn't said a word where Finn could hear them. Regarding my daughter as a tiny, malevolent oracle, they'd confessed, paid the money back, and then been fired, regardless.

I'd retorted that this was ridiculous—that if they'd stolen money, didn't it stand to reason that they'd lie about it too? How could Finn possibly have known, otherwise? Really, the Y should be thanking her. But my words fell on deaf ears. The counselor turned away, a familiar, uneasy look on her face, mumbling that if this had been the only incident, that would be one thing, but, well, she was sure I'd understand . . .

I hadn't understood a thing, other than that my daughter, who was only trying to be helpful, had somehow once again wound up a pariah. Heartsick, I'd pulled her out of the camp early and ranted to Ryan about the unfairness of the whole situation. It had taken half a bottle of wine and a good forty-five minutes to resign myself to the fact that, as much as I loved my daughter, the world was never going to be a place where she easily fit in. This time around, I'm sending her to two weeklong camps, one focused on art, the other on gardening. It seems like an ideal environment for Finn, but we've been burned too many times for this to mean much.

"Good, huh," I say now, eyeing my dad for corroboration. He smiles at me and shrugs, cracking an egg into the frying pan.

"Over easy?" he says to me. "Also, welcome back."

"Thanks. And yes, please. I see you've quit shaving."

"Do you like it?" He strokes his salt-and-pepper beard, grown out for the first time in years. "It was Finn's suggestion. She thought it would make me look—what did you say, Finn? Oh yes, distinguished."

I grin at this and ruffle my daughter's hair, pulled back into a ponytail. "Did Grandpa pack your lunch?"

She nods enthusiastically. "He made me a ham-and-cheese sandwich. And I have grapes and goldfish and applesauce. Oh, and eight gummy bears, which," she says with a sidelong look at my dad, "I just remembered I wasn't supposed to tell you about. But you're not mad, right? You won't take them away?"

My dad is wearing a sheepish expression, looking more like a seven-year-old than the seven-year-old herself. "They're organic," he offers in his defense. "From Whole Foods. Probably cost more than your whole post-graduate education combined. How bad can they be?"

Fetching myself some coffee and a plate, I roll my eyes at both of them. "It's fine."

Finn pushes her chair back from the table, turning toward me so that I can see her *I Dig Archaeology* T-shirt. "I'm wearing a shirt that can get dirty, see? Don't you think it's a good choice? Because when you go on a dig, you come back all muddy, right?"

I laugh out loud at this. "It's a great choice, sweetpea. Why did you have to wear a shirt that could get dirty, though?"

"Because we're doing splatter painting today," Finn says, getting to her feet. "Miss Josie says it's just like Jackson Pollock." She pronounces the last two words with care, then skips over to the sink and places her plate and cup carefully inside. "And you know what else? Maybe today I'll make a friend!"

She smiles at me brightly, and I do my best to disguise the fact that this little comment has torn a fissure straight through my heart. "I'm sure you will," I tell her, planting a kiss on top of her head as she skips by the table. "Come on, I'll drive you."

All the way to camp at Sundrops Montessori, Finn chatters about what she's been up to while I was gone—how Ryan took her kayaking and then for ice cream and a movie, how she and my dad broke their frog-catching record, how Grandma and Grandpa Adair brought her fancy combs for her hair and then treated her to brunch at High Cotton. She asks lots of questions about Barbados and I answer, telling her I've gotten her a special present that will be waiting at home for her, that I took lots of pictures and I'll make a slide show for us to look at together.

I don't say anything about Max—not about his phone call or her comment the night before—nor, of course, do I mention the necklace. The last thing she needs is to worry about stuff like this. All I want is for her to have a nice, normal day. So I pull up in front of the school and hug her goodbye, inhaling her little-girl scent of breakfast and toothpaste and crayons. I watch her go inside, new blue backpack, bouncy ponytail, archaeology T-shirt, and all, a smile pasted to my face, just in case she looks back. Only when she is out of sight do I cross the fingers of both hands on the steering wheel and hope— out loud, so the universe is sure to hear—that this time will be different.

When I make it back to my dad's, he's outside, watering the garden behind the house. In his retirement, my dad has developed quite the green thumb. He grows most of his own vegetables, which, in the summer, translates to tomatoes, squash, eggplant, and bumper crops of parsley. It gets hot early here and if you wait until the afternoon to water, you're bound to burn the leaves—not to mention that the water will evaporate in a matter of minutes. Ideally, you're supposed to water in the evening, so that moisture has the best chance of soaking into the soil while the temperature is cooler—a fact that Max drilled into my head so many times I could recite it as well as my own phone number—but somehow I don't think my dad will appreciate being chastised about how he tends his own garden, and so I keep my opinion to myself.

My father lives in Mount Pleasant, just over the bridge from Charleston proper, in a historic community called Old Village. His property backs the Adairs', separated by a thick patch of woods, in the midst of which is Max's tree house. All these years later, his tree house is still standing. I know this because sometimes I'll go and sit there, staring down into the clearing where I saw him last, trying once again to solve the puzzle of his disappearance. Between my mother and Max, it hardly takes a Freudian analyst to determine why I've dedicated my career to the pursuit of finding lost things.

The Adairs have the largest property in Old Village, by far. I can't even imagine how much they could get for the land if they cleared it and sold it off in parcels, but as far as I can tell, they have never even considered this. Not that they need to—Max's dad, Thomas, is a very successful lawyer, and their house, which has been in the family for years, is worth a ton of money in its own right. I've never quite been able to figure out why they've turned away multiple developers' offers for the woods behind their house, unless it's a matter of pride.

When I'd asked Max about it, he'd shrugged, looking uncomfortable, the way he always did when I brought up anything related to his family's wealth. "Why the hell do they do anything?" he said, poking about at the edge of the pond for flat rocks to skip across the water. "Besides, if they sold the land"—he sidearmed a rock along the surface of the pond with enough force that it skipped halfway across before subsiding beneath the flat green leaf of a water lily—"it wouldn't feel like home anymore."

The house in Mount Pleasant has been home to Max's family for a long, long time, passed down through the generations. Unlike my parents, who moved here when I was in high school, the Adairs have been here since the early 1800s.

Max was always too embarrassed to talk about it, but I know that Robert Adair, his great-great-great, however many times back, grandfather, owned slaves on his plantation in Barbados. When the rebellion broke out, he was in Charleston, scouting land. According to family lore, his nine-months-pregnant wife was killed in the chaos of the revolt. Robert never forgave himself for leaving her, nor for taking part in a system that birthed the rebellion that caused her death. He never went back to Barbados. Settling in Mount Pleasant, he became a dedicated abolitionist—much to the horror of his new wife and family. He also insisted on hanging a portrait of his late wife in the upstairs hallway—something I can't imagine that his second wife appreciated, either. The portrait still hangs there today, a testament to a man's guilt and regret.

Max's family is proud of the role Robert played in the abolitionist movement. Every year, on the Mount Pleasant Garden Tour, they spend a fair amount of time telling their guests about Robert's efforts to secure humane treatment and freedom for Southern slaves. In fact, Max's father, Thomas, still works at the law firm Robert founded when he put down roots in Charleston. Max's parents wanted him to be a lawyer too, but he had his heart set on owning his own green-house. He loved being outside, knew the names of every plant, could make anything grow. On our way to school, to get coffee, to the mov-ies, he'd swerve over to the side of the road to rescue scraggly, half-dead potted plants, muttering under his breath about wastefulness and insensitivity.

Watching my dad do battle with the hose as he stretches it far enough to reach his tomatoes, I am hard-pressed to put Max out of my mind. "Hey," I say, coming up next to him. "Thanks for looking after Finn."

He sprays the last of the tomatoes, soaking the dirt. "Of course. The dig go okay?"

"It did," I say carefully. "Relatively uneventful—nothing unexpected—until the last couple of days."

Coiling the rest of the hose, my father shoots me a sharp look. "Are you talking about that phone call again? Because I don't think it's healthy for you to dwell on it—"

"I'm not dwelling, Dad. The phone call happened. I can't pre-tend it didn't. What do you want me to do? If you thought Mom had called you, what would you do? Would you listen to me if I told you not to dwell on it?"

My dad does his slow blink, the one he employs when he wants more time to think. "I'd want to," he says eventually. "But I think we both know I didn't do the best job of behaving reasonably where your mother was concerned. We never talked about it, Iz, but I failed you. The thing is, I'll be goddamned if I'll do it again."

"Come on, Dad," I say, uncomfortable. "You were devastated. Anyone would be. It's—it's admirable, the way you never gave up on finding her."

"Is it?" he says, fixing me with an uncompromising stare, the way he used to when I'd sneak in late, thinking I'd gotten away with it, and find him sitting in the overstuffed chair in the living room, waiting for me. "Is it *admirable* to make your daughter into collateral damage?"

"Dad!" I say, shocked. "I'm not—you didn't—"

"It's the truth," he says grimly. "Maybe if I'd been a better father, you wouldn't have fled right into the arms of that boy."

I feel my eyebrows lower in puzzlement, trying to work out what he's talking about. "That boy? You mean Max? He was my best friend. He never hurt me."

"No?" my father says, turning to march back into the house. "He knocked you up before you'd even graduated from college. He abandoned you. If that's not your definition of hurt, then I'd like to hear what is."

My father has never spoken to me like this before—not when Max and I were together, not when I told him I was pregnant, and not in the long months afterward, when I spent hour after hour at the police station, hunting online for leads and filing missing persons' reports. He was nothing but supportive, so that at some point I came out of my fog and realized that I'd gotten my dad back, the one that I'd lost the night my mom disappeared. I had no idea that this was how he really felt, which makes me wonder what else I don't know— and, in turn, makes me lash out.

"That's not true," I say, grabbing him by the shoulder and stopping him halfway through the screened-in porch. "He didn't abandon me, any more than Mom abandoned you. Max was *happy* I was pregnant. He had no intention of going anywhere. Something happened to him, Dad. I know it did. And now I might have the chance to find out what it was. Do you really want to take that away from me?"

My father's features soften. "Of course not," he says, sinking onto the wicker couch. "But Isabel, I just don't want you to fall down the rabbit hole, and hurt yourself and Finn in the process. I know what that feels like, honey. I want better for you."

I drop my hand from his shoulder, knowing it's now or never. "Dad," I say, hating the way my voice trembles, "I have something to show you. Something bizarre."

Reaching into my pocket, I pull out my cellphone and find the photos of the necklace. Without a word, I pass the phone to him.

My dad stares at my iPhone, stunned. He flips through the images, turning the phone left and right for a better view. Finally he says, his voice cracking, "Is this a joke, Isabel? Because if so, I assure you that it's in terrible taste."

"No," I say. "It's something we recovered on the last day of the dig. I didn't want to make any assumptions—or to draw connections where there aren't any, like Ryan thinks I'm doing—but Dad, it looks just like her necklace. Doesn't it?"

On his face, I can see the disbelief and recognition that mirrors my own, the day I pulled the necklace out of the sandy soil. For a moment, I can see that he believes.

Then he shakes his head, handing the phone back to me. "Isabel," he says, getting to his feet, "it looks like your mother's necklace, sure. But it can't be. Julia never left the country, and if someone kidnapped her—why would they go to the trouble of concealing her necklace in some old plantation site, thousands of miles from here?" He rubs his eyes, looking more tired than I've ever seen him. "Much as I hate to say it, I agree with Ryan. You're seeing what you want to see, stirring up old memories that are best left alone. Julia's been gone for almost fifteen years, and she's not coming back, any more than Max is. I know how hard it is, but you need to move on. You need to let them go."

Max

The sun wakes me in the morning, streaming through the gaps in the blinds. Yawning so wide that my jaw cracks, I stretch, extending my fisted hands over my head. To my surprise, my fists meet solid wood instead of drywall. For a moment I'm puzzled — and then reality comes rushing back in.

I'm still in the four-poster bed with its tall headboard, surrounded by clouds of mosquito netting. Heart pounding, I lurch to my feet, entangle myself in the netting, and tumble to the floor with a crash. I stagger to my feet, unravel myself, and stand still, trying to put body and soul together.

I cross to the wardrobe and throw it open. There's a hideous purple-and-blue robe in there, but my crumpled clothes are gone. Someone must have taken them away in the night. Feeling a pointless sense of loss — I wasn't particularly attached to them or anything, but they were one of the few links I had to my normal life — I shut the door and cross to the dresser, where a flowered basin and matching pitcher sit. My mother has something that looks like this at home, an antique she calls an ewer. Cautiously, I peer inside and discover that it's filled with water. I pour some into the basin and wash my face, patting it dry with a towel, and feel a bit more human.

The room is warm already. By the time I pull on the shirt and trousers—the former a loose white linen number that makes me look like a pirate, and the latter an insanely tight garment with too many buttons—I am sweating. I walk over to one of the big windows and swing the shutters wide. Bracing my hands on the frame, I lean out.

From up here, I can see much more of Sweetwater—the expanse of the cane fields, quiet today in honor of the Sabbath; the barns and outbuildings; the slave village with its expanse of thatched-roof huts and the occasional limestone shack; the boiling house; and the mill. I can see the gardens too, full of beautifully manicured tropical plants.

In the light of day, it seems ludicrous to think that I am capable of singlehandedly stopping a rebellion, even if that's the right thing to do—but maybe once I find Julia, she'll have some answers. Either way, I'm not going to make any progress standing here.

Peering into the looking glass over the dresser, I sigh. I look as shocked as I feel, and my hair is standing up every which way, as distressed as I am. With some effort, I am able to tame it. Then I pull on the stockings that Sarey has left for me, grimace at my reflection—behold Max Adair, nineteenth-century gentleman!—and slip on a pair of shoes someone has left for me.

As soon as I open the bedroom door, I can smell the enticing scent of hot coffee and hear the buzz of activity. Motivated by the notion of caffeine, I make my way to the first floor and step into the dining room.

A woman is sitting at the table, chestnut head bowed, sipping from a teacup. Next to her stands Hannah. "Morning, Master Max," she says when she sees me. "Did you sleep well?"

"Yes, thank you," I say. I'm about to ask if I can have some coffee when the woman lifts her head. Her clear brown eyes meet mine, and I feel a chime of recognition that shakes me to my bones. Without a doubt, I am looking at Lily Adair.

I might have gone on gaping if she hadn't risen to her feet with some effort, one hand at the small of her back. Hannah instantly springs forward to support her. Her features are as finely drawn as they are in the portrait that hangs in my parents' upstairs hallway, as they were the day that I saw her leading Julia into the woods—but as she gets to her feet, I can clearly see a bulge beneath the fall of her purple, lace-trimmed dress.

My mother would love this dress, I think distantly. *She'd have it commissioned for a belle to wear at one of her garden parties in a hot minute.* But none of the belles I've ever seen at my parents' parties come within a mile of approaching Lily Adair, who is, quite simply, stunning. Her hair is tied back from her face with a ribbon, spilling down in a cascade of curls, and her skin is a delicate, flushed shade of peach. For a moment all I can think of is that I can understand how Robert spent the rest of his life pining after her.

"Miss Lily," Hannah says, startling me out of my daze, "may I present Master Maxwell Adair, of South Carolina."

Lily looks at me expectantly. For want of something else to do, I bow. Thank God for Cotillion; I never imagined that the boring hours I spent dancing waltzes and learning which fork to use for dessert would actually be useful. "The pleasure is mine. Thank you for your hospitality."

I must not have screwed up too badly, because Lily curtsies as much as her pregnancy will allow. "Welcome to Sweetwater, sir," she says in a low, clear voice, and settles back into her chair. "I'm Lily Adair, mistress of this house. Please, help yourself to some food, and tell me how you came to be here. I have only heard the slightest of rumors, and I confess that I am most powerfully curious as to the details of your arrival."

Oh, boy. What the hell am I going to say? I buy myself some time by sitting down and regarding the table, which is creaking with food—chicken, whitefish, a bowl of peppers, small ginger cakes, a plate of buttered plantains, and a platter of yams. "I'd be happy to tell you. But first—Hannah, could I maybe trouble you for some coffee?"

"Where are my manners?" Lily says, sounding so horrified that I have to swallow a laugh. "Here I am pestering you, when you've only just woken up—and not eaten or drunk a thing. What must you think of me? Hannah, a dish of coffee for Mr. Adair, and cream and sugar as well."

But Hannah is already handing me a cup of steaming coffee. I bury my nose in my cup, breathing deeply, and then take a sip. *Ah, heaven.* Fortified, I take another sip, listening to Lily, who is still talking. "We are so isolated here. And as you can see, I am near to commencing my confinement. Not living in town, we depend on visitors for entertainment and news. A guest from America—that is a rare treat. Forgive me if you sent a letter informing us of your intention to pay a visit to Sweetwater—the mail is so irregular, with ships often blown off course by storms and such."

I seize on this idea. "I did send a letter," I say, helping myself to some chicken, lest my face reveal more than I intend. "I'm sorry it didn't arrive. As to how I came to be here—I'm from Charleston, born in America. My father is from England." That fits with what I know of the Adairs prior to their arrival in Barbados—English, every one of them, except for a Scottish branch somewhere. "My father has it in mind for me to be a lawyer—an attorney," I continue. When in doubt, stick with the truth. "But I wasn't sure that was what I wanted to do. So he suggested I come to Barbados, to see if island life would suit me better. He knew that Mr. Adair had settled here—they're distant cousins, I believe—and thought perhaps he would be kind enough to show me around."

I have no idea how well my story meshes with the daily business of how folks conduct their lives in the nineteenth century, but it's the best I could think of. I take another sip of coffee and raise my eyes to look at Lily Adair's face. To my surprise, she is smiling. "Indeed," she says, nibbling at the edge of one of the ginger cakes. "And why do you not wish to obey your father's wishes?"

Uh-oh. "Honestly," I say, "I don't have the right attitude to be an attorney. All of those hours spent behind a desk, or in court, arguing—

all of that paperwork—it doesn't really appeal to me. I would rather be outside, in fresh air."

At this, Lily laughs. "Well, we have enough of that here, if you don't mind the mosquitos and the infernal heat. Tell me, what is it you prefer to do in the fresh air?"

"I'm a botanist," I say, spooning some plantains onto my plate. "Or at least I intend to be." There, that sounds better than saying I'm a gardener.

"Really," she says, sipping her tea. "Perhaps you can help us with some of the plants on the estate, then. Mr. Alleyne—the overseer, I believe you've met him—has been telling me about some kind of plague that's afflicted the grapefruits this year." She eyes me over the rim of her cup, and I have the distinct sense that there's more to this conversation than what she's saying aloud.

"Yes, I've met Mr. Alleyne," I say cautiously.

"Mr. Alleyne informed Penelope that he came upon you in the midst of the cane field," Lily says. "That one of the field slaves nearly decapitated you with his machete."

I shake my head. The last thing I want is for Lily to punish the slave for some imagined offense. "I got lost, looking for the great house. I wouldn't say I was nearly decapitated, though—that's an exaggeration. We just . . . surprised each other."

"Wandering into the cane field during the harvest—it is lucky you were not killed," Lily says, her face flushing. "But did you not have a horse? How did you come to Sweetwater?"

"I caught a ride. From Bridgetown," I say. The capital was once a major port—I remember that from my thesis research. "They dropped me off on the grounds, but left me to find my own way."

"Oh, dear," Lily says, raising her napkin to her lips to hide her laughter. "I suppose we will need to exercise extreme caution in allowing you to ride about the countryside alone, Mr. Adair, lest you canter straight off the cliffs and into the sea." Her brown eyes meet mine, sparkling with amusement. "Tell me, how goes it in Charleston? My husband is there himself at present, inspecting properties. It is really quite unfortunate that you have missed him."

As an Eagle Scout, I was always the kid who could find his way out of the woods, even if my map was ruined and my compass lost. Nineteenth-century Barbados or no, my pride is piqued at the idea that I'd need an escort to traverse a 166-square-mile island. I unclench my jaw, force a polite smile onto my face, and try to remember what South Carolina would have been like in the early 1800s. "Charleston is . . . busy," I say finally. "A thriving port city, with many opportunities. I hope your husband finds what he's looking for." I swallow hard, because I know good and well what Robert will find—not in Charleston proper, but across the river, in Mount Pleasant. I also know what he will lose—this woman sitting across the table from me, smiling brightly, and the baby she carries.

"I hope so as well." An odd expression crosses her face—worry, maybe, or discomfort—and she settles back in her chair, one hand on her belly. At this, Hannah steps forward, and, with a nod from her mistress, whisks away Lily's plate. She returns in a moment with a fan, which Lily plucks from her fingers with a murmur of thanks. The air in the room is hot and still, and all three of us are sweating.

"I'll do it for you, missus," Hannah protests, but Lily shakes her head.

"You'll not," she says firmly. "With child or no, I can still fan myself, Hannah."

"Mrs. Adair," I say as Hannah utters a low sound of disapproval, "I don't mean to presume—but do you know a woman named Julia Griffin? She's the mother of a good friend, and I think she might be living here on the island."

My heart is in my throat as I ask this question, and I almost can't look at her. But when I do, she is nodding. "Mrs. Griffin?" she says. "Yes, I surely do. Come from Charleston, this twelve-month past. A most fascinating lady."

"Really?" My pulse is pounding. "Does she have blond hair and brown eyes . . . about your height?"

Lily eyes me curiously. "Why, yes. She is the mother of your particular friend, you said?"

I feel a surge of adrenaline. "Yes," I manage. "Do you know where I might be able to find her?"

"I do. Less than an hour's ride from here, on John Simmons's estate. She's been tutoring Mr. Simmons's girls—and an excellent teacher she is too." She fans herself harder. "Today is Sunday, of course, but tomorrow I could send word with one of the rangers to see if an arrangement could be made for you two to meet—if you so desire."

"I could go myself," I say before it occurs to me that this might sound unseemly. "It's just . . . it's been such a long time since I've seen her, and Isabel—her daughter—has been worried. I know it would ease her mind to know that I'd seen Mrs. Griffin and found her in good health."

Something Lily said nags at me, but I ignore it, high on having found Julia. Presumably Lily will lend me a horse to get to Simmons— here's hoping I can still remember how to ride one. Who would've thought those damned equestrian lessons my parents made me take every summer, in further pursuit of transforming me into the perfect Southern gentleman, would come in handy?

Lily makes an odd noise, and when I look up at her, I see that she is laughing. "Isabel?" she says, giving me a knowing glance over the top of her fan. "Are the two of you engaged, then?"

This suddenly seems like the best reason possible for my eagerness, and I leap at it. I pull my grandmother's ring from my pocket. "I want us to be," I say, which is no less than the truth. "If I found her mother—well, I'd hoped to ask her permission."

"May I?" she says, and I hold out the ring. She turns it this way and that to catch the light. "It's quite pretty," she says at last, smiling. "And as for asking Mrs. Griffin's permission—she did say she was widowed. Her husband died of the flux on the journey here, poor man. It's kind of you to think of asking her for her daughter's hand; many men would not bother to solicit a woman's opinion in the matter, beyond that of the lady to whom they hope to become affianced—and sometimes not even then, more's the pity."

"Widowed?" I repeat in bewilderment, thinking of Andrew. Then the other shoe drops. Of course life would be much easier here for a respectable woman who'd lost her husband than it would be for a single woman with no explanation for her state of affairs. "Oh, yes—Isabel did tell me about her father," I say quickly. "That was before we'd met, though. So sad."

She leans forward conspiratorially, dropping the ring back into my hand. "Suddenly your desire to pursue your love of botany in our fair climate has taken on a different hue, my dear Mr. Adair." Her bright laughter fills the room. "In this case, I completely understand your desire to pay a visit to Mrs. Griffin. But I rather think I will send someone with you, anyhow, else you wind up in St. Lucy by mistake—or in a cane field again. Forgive me for saying so, but it sounds as if you might be in desperate need of a guide."

I thank her for her generosity, standing as she gets to her feet, and Hannah emerges from her silent post in the shadows to take Lily back to her bedroom to rest. It's only after I've made my way out to the veranda, wondering what Julia is doing at this very moment, that I realize what's been troubling me about my conversation with Lily.

It must be over ninety degrees outside, but a cold sweat breaks out all over my body nonetheless.

Come from Charleston this twelve-month past. But Isabel's mother has been missing for six years.

Isabel

ow that the dig is over—or at least my part in it—my professional obligations dial down considerably. Still, I have to go to campus today, to meet with the department chair, file my notebooks, and Skype with Dr. Absolom to make sure her team has everything it needs. Our appointment's not until four P.M., and by then they'll have finished their first day at the site. I feel a frisson of excitement, wondering if the other wing of the necklace will be among the items that they unearth.

With Finn at camp and some free time on my hands, I decide to screw unpacking and drive over to the dojo for a workout. Try as I might to stay in shape during our time in Barbados, I've missed being part of a group, challenging myself in sparring sessions, and learning new combinations. After my disturbing conversation with my father, I'm craving some form of physical release, and right now this is the best one available to me. Before I can go, though, I have to drive home and get my gear bag.

Finn and I live in Charleston's upper peninsula, in a neighborhood called Wagener Terrace. I bought the house five years ago, when Finn was two. It needed a lot of work, so I got a great deal. Between me, Ryan, and my dad, we've managed to overhaul it almost completely, and now I can't imagine living anywhere else. It's over a hundred years old, with everything you'd expect—crown molding, high ceilings, multiple sets of French doors, and a cozy porch swing. But my favorite part is the backyard, invisible from the street, a tiny oasis complete with hammock and koi pond.

I know Ryan's been looking after it for me—he lives about a ten-minute walk away, in a Victorian split into a duplex—but I still breathe a sigh of relief when I pull up in front of my little white house and see the grass neatly cut, the wind chimes swaying in the breeze. I haul my suitcase out of the car and then dig in my purse for my keys—always a masterful endeavor, since I am convinced that my bag has a black hole at its center that devours all things vital at the precise moment that I require them.

At long last I find them and swing the door inward, inhaling deeply. Everything is as I left it—the family room with its two worn couches and easy chair, its round coffee table that Ry and I found at a yard sale last year and strapped to the top of his Forerunner. I turn in a circle, taking in the small white bookshelf with its fully stocked shelves, the large windows, blinds covering only the bottom half so that light can still come in. Someone—Ry, I suppose—has plugged in my lavender diffuser, and the aroma fills the air, familiar and welcoming.

After so much time away—and especially after the events of the last few days—being back home is more comforting than I could have imagined. I walk through the rest of the first floor, making sure that none of my plants have bitten the dust. Then I make my way upstairs to my bedroom, looking for my gear bag. I change in record time and drive out to the gym, on a mission.

An hour later, I am soaked in sweat and have a spot on my back that's probably going to bruise, thanks to a particularly effective shoulder throw by Jenna, one of the other black belts. She apologizes profusely, but I don't mind. Instead I retaliate with a *tomoe nage* throw, pulling her onto her toes, then getting my feet under her belly and launching her halfway across the mat. She lands with a thud and struggles up onto her elbows. Her belt has come undone, and her gi is half off one shoulder.

"You all right?" I say, offering her a hand up just as the buzzer sounds, signaling the conclusion of the match—and with it, the end of class. She rolls her eyes, pushing her sweat-soaked blond hair away from her face, and plucks her ponytail holder, sprung loose by the impact of her fall, off the mat.

"What do you *think*?" she says, but then she grins at me and lets me pull her to her feet. "Didn't know you had it in you, Griffin. What the hell did you have for breakfast? Steroids?"

"It hasn't been the best week," I admit as we walk off the mat, skirting a group of guys who have stayed behind to talk about an upcoming competition. One of them, a purple belt named Rafe I've slept with a time or two—after extracting a promise that he'd keep the encounters strictly to himself, on pain of death—gives me a high five.

"Nice throw," he says, and beside me, Jenna snorts, stripping off her gi. A deep red mark is already blooming on her arm where she hit the floor. Seeing it, I wince. A few hours from now, that's going to be a nasty bruise, and I'd bet money there's one just like it on her hip and thigh.

She catches me eyeing her arm and snorts again. "Yeah," she says, "nice throw. Were you planning on stopping before you put me through the wall or was that just a happy accident?"

"Sorry," I tell her, embarrassed. "I didn't mean to send you flying like that—well, not so far. I've actually never had much luck with that move before. Maybe frustration is a prerequisite."

She elbows me good-naturedly. "Don't apologize, Iz. Just make sure you bring it next time, girl. Because you aren't gonna get the drop on me like that twice."

"Uh-oh," I say, laughing as we make our way into the locker room. She tosses me a towel from the folded stack, then grabs one for herself. "I'll keep that in mind."

"You do that," she says, and disappears into the shower, signaling her transformation from martial artist into school librarian and dedicated mother of two.

I don't know if it's the effect of normal social interaction—what passes for girl talk with me—or the sublime relief of physical activity, but suddenly I feel much more like myself. Riding the wave of my good mood, I shower in another stall, make myself presentable, and then call Ryan to see if he wants to meet for lunch.

As it turns out, he's busy until four o'clock, by which point I've filed my paperwork, met with everyone and their brother, and finished up my Skype conference with Dr. Absolom. Much to my disappointment, the team hasn't turned up the missing fragment, although she assures me that they'll keep looking.

I get off the phone and walk out into the hallway in time to see Jake round the corner, Blue Devils baseball cap jammed onto his head. He's joking with someone—Maura, I see when she turns—but when he sees me, his attention refocuses, like a compass needle swinging north. His gaze travels over me from head to toe.

Beside him, Maura makes an aggravated sound. "Hello, Dr. Griffin," she says, enunciating every syllable.

At this, Jake's head snaps up, and he blushes a deep, dark red. "Hi," he mutters. "I'm sorry—I didn't mean to—"

I stare at him in disbelief, at a loss for words. Luckily, Maura has no such difficulty. "For God's sake," she mutters, disgusted. "Shut your mouth, Jake, before you step in it any further. I apologize, Dr. Griffin. We were just going." She grabs Jake by the elbow, dragging him off down the hallway before I can utter a syllable.

Bewildered, I look down to see what could possibly have provoked such a reaction—perhaps I neglected to get dressed after my workout at the gym and have been conducting all of my subsequent business in the nude? But no, I am wearing clothes. True, they're nicer than the cutoffs and battered tank tops I favored on the dig. After weeks of crawling around in the dirt, I opted for a denim skirt that ends a few inches above my knees, heels, and a baby blue sleeveless shirt with three tiny buttons at the top. The top button of my shirt is undone and the skirt is tighter than, say, a sack, but I don't see how this warranted Jake giving me the once-over like he would a freshman girl at a frat party.

I'm still fuming fifteen minutes later when Ryan shows up at my door, a coffee from Kudu in each hand. He's barely made it in the door before I kick it shut and dump the incident on him, complete with visual effects. He stands by my bookshelf, pleating a piece of paper between sips of caffeine. An airplane takes shape under his fingers.

"And then Maura dragged him off down the hall," I conclude, hands on my hips. "Isn't that the most obnoxious thing you've ever heard of?"

"Yes, that's thrilling," Ryan says, and yawns.

"You're not listening to me!" I snatch the paper airplane from his fingers and aim it at his head. It veers sharply, and he leans forward, catching it before it reaches the floor. Eyeing it critically, he adds a paper clip to the nose.

"I'm listening," he says, essaying another short flight. This one is far more successful; the plane glides smoothly, landing on the desk next to a manila folder. "I'm just sleep-deprived. After I dropped you off, I stayed up late working on this new comic we're digitizing. Then I was too wired to sleep, so I watched a bunch of *Walking Dead* reruns. And now I'm burnt crispy." Settling himself in my chair, he props his feet on my desk, rummages in the drawer for my stash of dark-chocolate-covered almonds and pops two into his mouth, blinking at me in sleepy exaggeration.

"Stop stealing my food, you cretin." I push his feet off my desk, and he puts them right back up, grinning at me. Flinging myself into the chair opposite him—the one I usually use for student conferences—I let out an exasperated sigh.

Hearing it, he looks up at me from under his lashes, hazel eyes wide and plaintive as a puppy's. "Are you mad at me?"

"No," I say, sighing again. He grins in mock relief and extends the almonds to me, a peace offering. I take one and crunch it contemplatively. "I'm just sick of . . . that." I gesture at the hallway, encompassing my encounter with Jake. "What does he want with me? I've got to have at least five years on him."

"Oooh, five years," Ryan says, rolling his eyes. "You Mrs. Robinson you."

"Shut up."

"Seriously, Izzy, you don't know?"

I shrug. "Don't tell me it's the whole 'single mom' thing. I've got a kid, so I must be easy. Oh, plus lonely and desperate."

Ryan draws a deep, put-upon breath. "Take it from me. Easy is the last thing you are."

"Thanks a lot."

"It's not an insult, just the truth." He shifts his feet, coming perilously close to knocking over a blue ceramic dragon that Finn made me for Mother's Day. I scoop it up, airlifting the dragon to safety.

"Please take your feet off my desk. Also, if you've got a point, this would be an excellent time to make it."

Ryan doesn't budge. "It's not the single mom thing. It's the Lara Croft thing," he says, and ducks as I toss the manila folder at his head. "Seriously. Archaeologist, martial artist, sassy chick. You've got the whole package."

"You must be kidding," I say, staring at him.

"Nope."

"Oh, yeah, sure." I let the full measure of my skepticism fill my tone. "Me and Angelina Jolie. How could I miss the comparison?"

Ryan tilts his head to one side, regarding me, and something in his expression takes me by surprise. I shift, uneasy under his scrutiny for the first time since we've known each other. He's seen me in a bikini more times than I can count, but I've never felt he was looking at me as anything other than his friend. Now, though, something is different and I am hard-pressed to say exactly what. He hasn't moved, hasn't done anything but look. Still, I can feel a change in the energy between us, feel the weight of his gaze on me in a way I never have before. His eyes are fixed on my face, considering.

Then he smiles, a mischievous grin that makes me think I've imagined the last few seconds. Either that, I think, or he did it just to mess with me. "Of course," he says, leaning back so the chair is balanced on two legs, "he could just be all about that bass."

I feel the color heat my cheeks. "You did not just say that."

The grin spreads across his face. "Yeah, well, if the skirt fits . . ."

"Jesus Christ," I say, as my face flames even hotter. "Get out of my office. I have to go pick up my daughter. And," I hiss, my voice as quiet as I can manage, in case there's anyone in the hallway to overhear, "kindly refrain from talking about my ass."

Ryan bursts out laughing. "Your wish is my command," he says, and lets the chair crash to the floor with a bang. I fume as he saunters past me, whistling all the way to the door. It's not until he's gone mostly down the hall that I make out what it is—the chorus to Meghan Trainor's "All About That Bass."

"I can still hear you," I yell after him. His only response is a low-pitched chuckle. Then he disappears through the swinging doors and, mercifully, all is silent.

Max

Lily is true to her word. One of the plantation's rangers, Tommy, and I set out for Simmons the following morning. The only snag in the plan is that we have to stop at Bayleys Plantation first to deliver a letter from Simon Alleyne.

Shifting in the saddle to find a comfortable position, I try to remember everything I know about these two plantations, Bayleys and Simmons. Each housed key players in the insurrection. Bussa, one of the main leaders of the rebellion, worked on Bayleys—I wonder if I'd recognize him from the pictures I've seen of his statue in Bridgetown, arms raised high as he bursts the chains of slavery. As for Simmons, Nanny Grigg, one of the primary female organizers of the revolt, called that plantation home, as did Jackey, the estate's head driver, who held secret meetings at his house in the slave village.

Lost in my thoughts, I almost fail to notice that Tommy has stopped, and have to rein up hard to avoid riding past him. "We're here," he says, gesturing at a graveled road to the right. "Bayleys."

Following him, I look around the sprawling plantation. Tommy clearly knows his way, because he takes us directly to the barn to leave our horses. Then he leads me up to the great house, a huge limestone building with a gray roof and a wide front porch.

Despite my eagerness to be off, we've arrived in time for lunch, a complicated affair with a number of guests seated around the wide table. They rise to their feet as I'm led into the dining room and introduce themselves—John Rycroft Best, the attorney who handles Bayleys while the owner is abroad, Christopher Barrow of Edgecumbe Plantation, and Robert Haynes, a member of the House of Assembly, general of militia, and planter.

Tommy presents the letter to John Best and then vanishes, absorbed into the complex machinations of the estate. Reluctantly, I take a seat.

"So," Best says, brushing his fall of dark hair back from his face and pushing back in his chair, a tumbler of punch in his hand. "You're recently arrived from South Carolina, Mr. Adair—I should be most interested to hear what you think of Barbados."

Accepting a glass of lime water from the young girl who stands silently by our table, I struggle to think of something positive to say. "It's very beautiful," I venture. "And I'm impressed with your level of industry. But it seems incredibly dangerous. Just yesterday, a woman at Sweetwater was killed by the rollers in the sugar mill."

John Best's mouth twists. "A woman," he repeats. "You mean a slave."

At my nod, he tugs at his frock coat, straightening it with brisk, efficient motions. "Well, yes, that is a hazard, I'll admit. And it's unfortunate to lose a good worker, especially during the harvest. But were they not so lazy, so careless, like children, allowing themselves to be distracted whilst feeding cane into the mill, the risk would be vastly diminished. Nonetheless, it is regrettable."

"Actually, they seemed to be working quite hard," I say, trying not to sound curt. "Surely there must be safety measures you can implement."

His lips tighten. "We have the plough now, you know," he says. "So in truth, their workload is greatly reduced. They have a generous schedule—into the field at six in the morning, a break at nine for breakfast, then back at work until one, whereupon they have a two-hour break for lunch, which we supply. Then back in the fields at three. When their work is done for the day at six, they are at liberty to go about their business, tending their small plots and their stock. So you see, their lives are quite simple."

"Come now, John," Barrow says. "Mr. Adair is not amiss in noting the dangerous nature of the mill."

Haynes nods at this. "God knows amelioration has its dangers, but in the current climate, it is we who would be careless to dismiss such views. I believe something untoward is afoot. Numbers of the slave population can read, as you know, and they have certainly seen the debates over the Registry Bill in the *Mercury and Gazette*—not to mention the publications that arrive here regularly from England, describing the progress of the abolitionist movement." He looks around the room, then leans forward to whisper, "I fear the worst— that they will interpret the Registry Bill as having but one objective: to hasten their freedom. Seeing us as their primary impediment, they will rise up and butcher us in our beds."

"Nonsense!" Best retorts. "There's not been an insurrection here in over a hundred years. You give too much credit to our slaves. They possess neither the spirit nor intellect to organize—not to mention the liberty and time to do so."

Barrow makes a low sound and tosses back the rest of his wine. "Liberty and time they may not possess, John. But motivation they have aplenty."

I've been trying to place John Rycroft Best—his name is familiar, and now I remember why. He is famous for his role in putting down the insurrection as commander of a local militia, his belief in its improbability notwithstanding.

"Excuse me," I interject. "The Registry Bill—why is it such cause for concern?"

All three men swivel to face me, and then Robert Haynes replies, "I'm surprised the news hasn't reached you in South Carolina, Mr. Adair. This farce of a bill—put forth by that abolitionist arse Wilberforce in Parliament—requires West Indian planters to register all of our slaves by name to prevent illegal trading in the wake of the Abolition Act."

At this, Best nods, an expression of disdain marking his thick features. "An absurd, unnecessary bill. We have no need of illegal slaves. In fact, we have implemented a most effective breeding policy: We encourage the Negroes to reproduce and then, once they have caught pregnant, to do little work. Indeed, if you look at our books, you will see that we set aside generous funds each year specifically for the nourishment of women during their lying-in, expenses associated with breeding, and midwifery fees besides."

"I see," I say carefully, trying to keep the disgust from showing on my face. "So what's the difficulty, then?"

"Difficulty," Barrow says in wry amusement, fanning his hand to swat away a fly, "is one way of putting it. The difficulty, as you say, Mr. Adair, is that well-meaning as they may be, Parliament and the Throne do not have a true understanding of conditions here in the West Indies. We believe that, even as we are subject to their laws, they are remiss in requiring us to submit to this legislation. Our own House of Assembly should have the ability to make such decisions. And yet, despite their rejection of the bill last November, we remain subject to it."

He looks over at Robert Haynes. "What say you? Is that an accurate assessment? I myself am loath to say, given that I was voted out of the House and eighteen head of my cattle bayoneted in my fields, besides."

The bitterness in his tone is unmistakable, and Haynes lays both hands on the table, splaying his fingers wide. "You know that was none of my doing. And should we find the miscreants who perpetrated the act, I would gladly see them tried for such indecency. It was a conflict of classes, Mr. Adair," he says, turning to me. "Mr. Barrow earned his position in the House through hard work rather than inheritance, and advocated amelioration for our slaves—

improvement of their treatment. Worse still, he suggested that we grant additional rights to the free coloreds on the island. This was not a popular suggestion, as you can imagine."

"I don't understand. If they were free already, then why—"

Best gives me a sharp eye. "They may be free, Mr. Adair, but they are not white men. We would do well to remember that—as would they. They petitioned for the right to testify against white men in court—as if we would ever allow such a thing. Absurd," he mutters, snaring a slice of grapefruit from a nearby platter and biting down with such intensity that juice sprays everywhere, arcing across the table to stain my jacket.

Best is beginning to look incensed—as if he might go off again at any moment—so I direct my question to the table at large. "If it's so ridiculous, then why would it matter what they ask for? How would they have the power to remove Mr. Barrow?"

Barrow laughs, a full-bodied chuckle. "Not the free coloreds," he says when he winds down. "The poor whites. If the coloreds have the same rights as they do—well, who's to say where the difference lies between them? They were threatened, you see, by my position. And so they ousted me—along with my poor friend William Grazette."

Robert Haynes stands up and stretches, his fists reaching toward the ceiling. He's a tall man for these times, around 5'10", with a long nose and hair that has begun to gray and recede. "Couldn't have anything to do with the fact that you drove those men mercilessly during their militia training, could it, Barrow? Your reputation precedes you, sir."

"Bah," Christopher says, getting to his feet. "Those lazy wretches couldn't load a musket were they to be given a set of instructions at the start and the promise of a whore's services at the end. They should count themselves lucky to have had the benefit of my instruction."

All three men laugh uproariously at this, and then John Best turns to me, placing his napkin on the table. "I thank you for joining us for lunch, Mr. Adair, and for inciting such lively discussion. I regret that I must depart for another one of my properties at present—

but it would be my great pleasure for you to enjoy a tour of this estate."

"That's most kind of you," I say with tremendous relief, "but I'm afraid I have an appointment at Simmons this afternoon, and I should really be on my way. Thank you for lunch, though—it was very . . . edifying."

"You are most welcome," he says, and then there ensues a dizzying flurry of bows. Christopher Barrow and Robert Haynes depart, both extending invitations for me to visit their estates as time permits, and then—after summoning a slave to take me to the stable and locate Tommy—John Rycroft Best leaves as well. I follow the slave— whose name, he informs me, is Charles—down the front steps, the fish and plantains I've eaten shifting uneasily in my stomach.

Isabel

To thank my dad for looking after Finn while I was gone, I have him over for dinner on Thursday night—an all-American meal of roast chicken and apple pie. I love to cook—there's something satisfying to me about the entire process—but I don't have that much free time during the year. My lighter summer schedule is a blessing in more ways than one, including the fact that Finn and I are able to stand next to each other in the kitchen, me with my cutting board and her on her step stool, peeling apples and talking.

"So," I say, endeavoring to sound as casual as possible. "How's camp going?"

Finn sets her apple down and reties her red apron, with as much gravity as if we were planning an appearance on *Emeril*. "It's fine, Mama. You don't have to worry."

"But do you like it?" I press, chopping the top off a carrot.

She hops down off the step stool, tossing her apple peels into the compost bin that we keep for my dad's benefit, then clambers back up. "I like it fine. Miss Josie's nice. And today Lucy shared her cookies with me. But then . . ." Her voice trails off, and she picks up her apple again, clearly thinking she's said too much.

"Then what?" I say, feeling the familiar anxiety clench my stomach.

"Nothing. Did you say five apples or six, Mama? For the pie? Because look, I've done all these." She tilts the bowl toward me, so I can see.

"I said seven, actually. But honey, what happened after Lucy shared her cookies with you? Was she mean?"

Finn's lower lip trembles, and she shakes her head. "Not exactly."

Pretense abandoned, I set the knife and carrots down on the cutting board. "What does that mean, sweetpea? Either she was mean or she wasn't, right? Did she hurt your feelings? Or call you names, maybe?"

Eyes downcast, Finn shakes her head. "I don't want to say," she mumbles. "You'll just get upset."

Steeling myself for whatever unpleasant thing is coming, I turn to face my daughter. There's flour on her forehead and another streak of it across her red apron, which has tiny white polka dots on the front. The hand that isn't holding the apple clutches at her braid, using the end of it to hide her trembling lips. With a pang, I notice that her nails are chewed to the quick, the purple polish more chipped than ever. "I won't, baby," I tell her. "I promise. Mommy just wants to help you. I can't help if you won't tell me what's wrong."

Tears well in Finn's eyes, and she does her best to blink them away. "It's just—" she starts, and then bites down on the end of her braid, hard.

As gently as I can, I reach for her, disentangling the braid from her mouth and then scooping her into my arms. I carry her over to one of the kitchen chairs and settle down next to our old wooden table, Finn in my lap. Her shoulders heave, and I can feel the wetness of her tears, warm on my neck. Finally she says, so quietly I have trouble making out the words, "It's just, sometimes I can't tell when people have really said a thing. I think they've said it out loud but really they're just thinking it in their heads. And I answer them, and they look at me all weird and then they don't want to be my friend anymore."

My stomach clenches, and I feel myself break out in a sweat. There are a thousand questions I want to ask—for instance, whether Finn can hear what I'm thinking right now, as crazy as that sounds. I'm not sure I really want to know the answer.

"Is that what happened with Lucy?" I ask instead, rubbing slow circles on her back.

Finn nods, her breath congested with tears. "I didn't mean to. I thought she'd said out loud how she was excited to go to the beach this weekend. So I told her that I liked the beach, and how you and me and Ryan and Grandpa were probably going fishing Saturday and maybe she could come too." She hiccups, wiping her face on my shoulder. "But then her eyes got really big and she picked up her Oreos and her lunch and slid all the way down the picnic bench. And I knew she hadn't really said it all the way out loud. She'd only thought it and then she told everyone and no one will talk to me anymore."

The tears come in earnest now, but I don't say a word. I'm too stunned. Instead I just sit there, holding her in the straight-backed wooden chair, letting her sobs shake us both. For all the bizarre things people have told me she's said or done, the times she's known who was on the phone before it rang or at the door before they knocked, Finn has never said anything like this. On top of Max's call and the necklace, it's almost too much. Aside from my dad and Ryan, Finn is all I have. I need her to be okay.

I sit there, rocking her, rubbing her back, until her sobs taper off. And then I say the only thing I can think of. "There's nothing wrong with you, honey. You're just a little more sensitive than other people, that's all, and sometimes that's scary to them. But I think it's really a good thing. You don't hurt other people's feelings, or leave them out, or say mean stuff. Even Lucy—you were just trying to invite her out on the boat with us. It's not your fault she reacted that way."

Slowly, Finn raises her face from my shoulder. Her eyes are wet, the long dark lashes she inherited from Max pasted together in spikes, and her nose is as red as her apron. "Do you really think so?" she says, sniffling.

"I know so. Here, blow your nose." I take a napkin from the pottery holder on the table and hand it to her, smiling as she complies, with a noise like a duck being trampled. "And if you ask Ryan and Grandpa, I'm sure they'll tell you the same thing. Now, come on, let's wash your face and finish making that pie. Otherwise Grandpa's going to have to eat apple peels out of the compost pile for dessert."

Obediently, Finn climbs off my lap and washes her face at the sink, patting her tear-stained cheeks dry with the dish towel. Watching her, my heart hurts anew. She's so small, so vulnerable. Is it possible that she can really tell what people are thinking, or was what I told her no more or less than the truth—that she's a sensitive, intuitive child, far more attuned to emotions than the average seven-year-old?

One thing is for sure—the world isn't kind to people who are different. Again I think of Max saying, *Keep her safe*, and feel tears rise to my own eyes. Regardless of who was really on the other end of that phone line, his message isn't lost on me.

Finn is watching me, her small face scrunched up with worry, and I make myself get to my feet. "Okay," I say. "Time to make the crust, and then you can help me get the chicken ready for immolation."

I've chosen the word on purpose, hoping Finn won't have a clue what it means. Sure enough, she doesn't, and by the time I've explained the nature of a fire sacrifice, including a G-rated version of Aztec cultural history, she's giggling, asking if I know why the chicken skeleton didn't cross the road (answer: He didn't have enough guts).

Still, our conversation stays with me all through dinner, while my dad carves the chicken and pronounces it perfect ("Perfectly mimmolated!" Finn announces, earning a snort of laughter from yours truly and a puzzled look from Grandpa). It's with me while we devour apple pie and vanilla bean ice cream, while Finn showers and I tell my dad not to worry about the dishes, I'll take care of them later.

It's still with me thirty minutes later, after I tuck Finn into bed, make sure her windows are closed and latched, and—when I'm sure she's fallen asleep—sneak back to plug in the baby monitor I've unearthed from the back of my closet. I conceal it underneath her bedside table, where she won't notice it unless she's overwhelmed by a sudden desire to vacuum—not likely, I think with a grin—and retreat to the kitchen. Turning on the second monitor, I push up my sleeves and tackle the dishes.

The window above the sink looks out on my backyard, which is bordered by a six-foot fence. Trees overhang the yard on both sides— one a giant oak, the other a nut-laden pecan. At the back of the yard is the koi pond, with a small iron bench next to it. I'm not much of a gardener, despite everything Max tried to teach me, but a previous tenant loved wildflowers, and I haven't killed them off yet. They surround the patio, barely visible in the glow of the light from the screened-in porch, bending slightly in the breeze.

I open the window, inhaling the scent of the honeysuckle Ryan trained to grow over the arbor he'd built for me as a moving-in present five years ago. He'd argued for a grapevine, saying we'd make scuppernong wine, but I'd told him I had enough to do without stamping grapes in my spare time. Reluctantly, he'd planted honeysuckle instead.

The wind has picked up outside, and in the distance, thunder booms once, then again. Rain begins to sprinkle the patio. Then, with the abruptness typical of Southern summer storms, the sky opens up and rain comes down in earnest. Now it is pouring, the wind blowing freshets of water into my face and whipping the trees into frenzy. Hastily, I slam the window shut just as thunder roars again, closer this time.

As is so often the case, the thunderstorm makes me think of Max. He loved storms, would climb up to his tree house to watch them wreak havoc on the woods, despite the danger. It was part of the thrill, he'd admitted the one time he'd convinced me to join him up there. We'd sat in the doorway, my back against his chest and his lips against my hair, watching the trees sway and lightning flash against the sky.

I stand at the sink, my hands immersed in soapy water, watching the rain come down outside, and think how Ryan and my father must be right—the phone call was a fluke, an accident of the airwaves. It had just sounded like Max. I'd seen the number and my brain had automatically substituted his voice for the random caller's on the other end.

But, the little voice in the back of my mind protested, *what about when I called back, and the number had been disconnected? What about the necklace, besides?*

Thinking about this makes my head hurt, and I attack the chicken pan with renewed vigor. A few minutes pass before I raise the roaster out of the water, eye it critically, and settle it onto the drying rack next to the sink. I plunge my hands back into the water, intending to tackle the silverware next. And then I freeze.

On the rain-slick stones of the patio, clearly visible in the moonlight, is Max.

My heart pounding in that alarming triple-time rhythm, I lean closer to the window, wipe the glass with the dish towel. I blink, rub my eyes, but he is still there. He's dressed oddly, in a long-sleeved, ruffled white shirt and tight pants, but it is unmistakably him. The rain comes down, pelting him and plastering his dark hair to his face, but he doesn't seem to notice. Instead he stares at me through the glass, eyes wide and imploring. His mouth moves, but I can't make out the words.

I want to run to him, but my limbs won't cooperate. Instead I stand frozen, one hand still in the dirty dishwater. "Max," I whisper, and then louder, "Max!"

At the edge of the yard, lightning strikes. I see it streak from the sky, cleaving the oak tree in half with savage simplicity. As terrifying as this is, it galvanizes me into action. I drop the dish towel and run across the screened-in porch to the back door. Yanking it open so hard it slams into the wall, I leap down the back steps and into the storm.

Rain pours down so hard it blinds me, and as soon as I manage to shove my wet hair out of my face and take a few steps into the yard, blinking my eyes to clear them, the motion sensor light comes on, blinding me all over again. Above the scorched ozone of the lightning strike, I can smell wood burning. Sure enough, the oak is in flames, despite the downpour.

"Max," I say again, reaching out my hands for him. "Oh, God, Max, where have you been? Why don't you say something?"

Maybe he replies, maybe he doesn't. I can't tell. Thunder rolls again, close to the house and so loud, I can barely hear my own breathing, let alone another human voice. Desperate, I open my eyes wide, peering through the sheets of rain for a glimpse of him. And then I gasp, a sharp, painful inhalation. Shock floods through my veins and pools in my belly, cold as ice and twice as treacherous.

My patio is empty. Max is gone.

Max

Charles turns out to have been born at Bayleys, and lived here his entire life. He is a carpenter, skilled in his trade—and once he realizes I am interested, he points out examples of his work throughout the plantation, a railing here, a window frame and gutter there. I admire them, and he says shyly that he loves what he does.

"I learn from King Wiltshire," he says. "He's the best, everyone says so. Master John, he says King Wiltshire can craft a table as beautiful as any that come from England. He and Master Edward, they let King hire himself out, maybe one day earn enough money so he can be free. He goes all over the island, anywhere folks ask. If I work hard, one day maybe I can do the same."

King Wiltshire—I recognize that name, it's not exactly the kind you forget. He's one of the slaves who was—will be?—involved in the rebellion, I'm sure of it.

"Master Edward?" I ask automatically, even though my mind is churning.

"Master Edward Thomas. He's the manager of Bayleys, an' Wiltshire too—"

Whatever Charles was about to say is lost, drowned in the sound of a man's screams, and another noise, one I can't quite place, in their wake. "What is that?" I say, my voice sharper than I intend.

"Oh," he says, clearly uncomfortable, "Cuffee, most likely, getting in trouble again. He's always on the wrong side a things, seem like. I say, one day Master Edward kill him if he don't stop. But he'd rather die a free man, speakin' his own mind, than live a slave." There's sadness in his voice, laced with a certain amount of pride.

"Getting in trouble," I echo. "What do you mean? Getting whipped?"

I have my answer as we round the corner of the stable and come face-to-face with a crowd of slaves in the plantation yard, all staring at a naked, brown-skinned man, suspended from a tree by his bound wrists. Behind him is a big-bellied, red-faced man, bullwhip in hand, raising his arm to strike.

Before I even know what I'm doing, I leap forward. "Cut him down!" I snap, and grab the man's wrist, staying the whip.

He turns to look at me. His bushy eyebrows creep upward, his eyes wide in his reddened, fleshy face. Then his gaze drops to my hand where it grips his wrist. The smell of raw alcohol wafts off him, mingling with the dirt and sweat to form a truly appalling stench. "I don't believe this is your business, sirrah," he snarls. "This man has been caught stealing. He deserves every lash of this whip. Stand back, and let me do my job."

He jerks back from me, trying to loosen my grasp on his wrist, but I won't let go. "I don't care what he's taken, or what he won't do," I say, and twist, hard. "Cut him down, you drunk son of a bitch, and do it now."

At this, a low murmur rises from the gathered slaves. Too late, I surmise that this must be Edward Thomas. Most likely, stopping the manager of Bayleys Plantation mid-whipping is a stupid thing to do, but I don't care. I feel a wave of fury building inside me, seasoned by pity for Cuffee, and my grip on his wrist tightens even further.

"Call me names, will you? You'll not tell me what to do, or interfere with estate business, either." Thomas raises his other hand and punches Cuffee in the kidneys, grinding his knuckles into one of the bleeding wounds left by the bullwhip. The slave lets out a low, agonized moan, and his body sways. I glare at Thomas, digging my fingernails into his wrist.

"What's *wrong* with you?" I say. "Have you lost your mind?"

"He'll behave for his betters," the man sneers, "or he'll pay for his mistakes. I'm manager here, not you. And you'll not stop me."

Again he tries to wrest his hand free, but I hang on to it like death. I wrench the whip from his grasp, tossing it into the trees. "Watch me," I say. And then I hit him in the stomach, using my grip on his wrist to pull him into the punch.

He grunts, doubling over, and I kick him, hard, so that he topples into the dirt. Blood roars in my ears. "You strung him up from a tree?" I say between gritted teeth. "You're whipping him like an animal—and you think that makes you a man?"

Thomas doesn't reply. Instead he lunges at me. I have just enough time to dodge his attack, to see a knife in his hand; the blade only slices through my jacket.

Before yesterday, I hadn't hit anyone in years—not since high school when some jackass broke into my locker. This is different, though. This is life or death. I'm no good to Isabel or Julia if I bleed out in a plantation yard at the feet of a beaten slave. This image, more than anything else, propels me into action, and I bring the side of my hand down on his with all the force I have. He loses his grip and the knife spins free.

I'm so shocked that this move actually worked that I freeze for just a moment. And a moment is all it takes for Thomas to tackle me, his face inches above mine, purple and congested with rage. "I'll show you," he mutters, pinning my arms with his knees, fists windmilling, sending spit flying onto my face with every word. "Think you can tell me how to manage my own slaves? What d'you have to say for yourself, Negro-loving American bastard?" His lips pull back in a nasty grin, revealing a row of graying teeth.

My head aches and I can feel blood trickling from my lip. I work my mouth for a moment, watching the world spin. There are two of him, then one, then three, then two again, and I need a few seconds to take aim. But when all of the versions of him converge into a single, venom-spewing asshole, I spit directly up into his face, as hard as I can. It lands on his cheek and slides down in a smear of red. "I already said it," I say, forcing the words out. "But in case you're too stupid to understand, I'll repeat myself. Cut—the—man—down."

At this, his eyes narrow and he raises his fist with renewed intent. The slaves gathered in the yard are yelling, and above the noise, I hear a woman scream. My ears are ringing, but I could swear she's screaming my name.

I twist, trying to get my arms free, but it's too late. His fist comes down, colliding with my temple, and then the world goes dark.

Just before it does, though, I catch a glimpse of the woman who's been screaming, a pale face in a sea of dark ones. She's wearing a bonnet and holding some kind of parasol. She does not look the same. But I have seen her face in my mind's eye every day for the last six years, and I recognize her immediately.

The woman screaming my name is Julia Griffin.

Isabel

I might have stood on the patio indefinitely, soaking wet and gaping at the spot where Max had so lately been, if it weren't for Finn. She appears in the doorway in her white nightgown, clutching Raggedy Ann. "Mommy?" she says in a small voice. "I heard a bad noise." And then louder, when I don't respond, "Mama! The tree is on fire."

I make myself focus on my daughter, who is starting to shiver. "Go back inside," I say automatically. "You're getting wet."

"So are you," Finn says. "And the tree is burning. Look." She points. "What if it catches the whole house on fire?"

Her voice is trembling now, and it snaps me out of my trance. "Go back inside, Finn. Right this minute."

"But Mama—"

"Come on," I say, my hands on her shoulders, steering her across the screened-in porch and into the kitchen. Through the window I can see the tree blazing, see lights coming on in the houses around mine. As I grab for my cellphone to dial 911, I can't help but think of my dream, of Finn screaming from inside that burning house and Max running inside to rescue her. My fingers tremble on the touch screen of my phone. It takes me several tries to punch in those three little numbers.

After I've told the 911 operator about the fire, after I've wrapped Finn in a thick towel and then made her change her nightgown, I sink down on the couch. Finn is at the kitchen table, drinking micro-waved hot chocolate and gazing wide-eyed at the wreckage that used to be our oak tree. The fire seems to be well under control—more of a sizzle than a conflagration, thanks to the downpour—but it's still pretty spectacular, all things considered.

I watch her for a minute or so as she stirs the hot chocolate, scooping up the marshmallows one at a time with her spoon just the way I used to. And then I call Ryan, who has been working late at Mage recently and is fast asleep—although how he can sleep through a storm like this is beyond me. It takes him three rings to answer, and when he does, he sounds thoroughly disoriented. "What?" he says, bewildered. "You saw who? Did you say something was on fire?"

When he finally understands what I'm talking about, he lets out a long, low whistle. "I'm coming. I'll be there in five minutes."

I bristle at this—not a reasonable response, I know, but I resent the implication that I need a white knight to ride in and save the day. "Don't be ridiculous, Ryan. It's pouring. And the fire department's on their way."

"You called me, Isabel," he says, sounding thoroughly awake now and more than a little unnerved. "You don't want me to come?"

"I didn't say that." I wrap my arms around myself, trying to stop the shivering. "It was so bizarre, Ry, seeing him that way. And then the poor tree. I loved that tree."

"I know you did," Ryan says, and now his tone is gentle. There are odd noises in the background on his end, shuffling and then a door slamming.

"Ry?" I say into the silence.

"Yeah?"

"If you wanted to come, I guess it would be okay. For Finn, you know."

He snorts. "I'm already in the car, Isabel. Do me a favor and try not to get into any more trouble in the next few minutes, all right? It's hard on the heart."

I start to protest—after all, it's not like I set the tree on fire myself, or airlifted Max magically into my backyard—but it's immaterial. He's already hung up.

Feeling inexplicably better, I walk into the kitchen and gaze out at the fire, which is down to an aggressive sort of sputter. Finn comes up beside me—she's finished her hot chocolate, and sets the cup carefully in the sink. Together, we stare at the remains of the tree, and I sigh. It sounds stupid, but I did love it. When Finn was two, my dad and I hung a tire swing from one of its branches for her. It was the first tree she ever climbed, and the first one she fell out of, much to our mutual dismay.

"I'm sorry, Mommy," Finn says, slipping her hand into mine. "Maybe it will grow back?"

"I don't think so," I tell her, letting my eyes drift from the tree to the place where I'd seen Max. "But we're safe, that's the important thing. The fire's almost gone, and the fire department will be here soon, just to make sure. And Ryan's coming over."

Her eyes widen. "Now? But he'll get wet."

Despite everything, this makes me laugh. "He won't melt, sweetie."

"Not like the Wicked Witch of the West," Finn observes. Before I left for Barbados, we'd been reading *The Wizard of Oz* at night. My dad must have kept at it while I was gone. I should probably call him too, I think, reaching for my phone.

"Don't," Finn says absently. She's wandered back over to the table and gathered up Raggedy Ann, propping the doll in her lap. "He's sleeping. You'll just wake him up and scare him. Besides, the fire's almost out. You said so."

I open my mouth, then shut it again. "Finn?" I say at last. "Why did you wake up?"

She fiddles with Raggedy Ann's hair. "I dreamed that Daddy

came here. That's what woke me up, at first. And then the lightning scared me."

I've been holding it together fairly well, but this is the last straw. The phone drops from my hand, clattering onto the countertop and nearly sliding into the sink. "You dreamed that Daddy was here? Where?"

"I don't know," Finn says, glancing up in alarm. "Here. In our house. But when I woke up, he was gone."

"Did you see him, Finn?" Without meaning to, I've crossed the room and am kneeling in front of her, my hands on her upper arms. "Did he say anything to you?"

Her eyes slide away from mine. "You're hurting me, Mommy."

Sure enough, I'm gripping her too tightly for comfort. I make myself let go. "Sorry, baby. I just—have you ever dreamed that Daddy came here before?"

Wide-eyed, she shakes her head. I'm about to question her further when I hear the sirens. Finn and I open the door just in time to see the fire engine pull up. Right behind it is Ryan, who leaps out of his car and makes a run for our house, heedless of the downpour.

"You're all right?" he says to me, stepping into the foyer and lifting Finn into his arms. His hair is plastered to his face, and his clothes are soaked.

"I'm fine. It's around back," I say to the firemen, who begin trekking around the house and through the side gate. "You've got her, Ry?"

"Of course I do," he says, pulling the front door shut behind him. Finn twines her arms around his neck, heedless of his wet clothing, and he tosses her in the air, making her giggle.

I leave the two of them and walk through the house to the screened-in porch, where I can see the firefighters surrounding the tree. One of them sees me standing in the doorway and gives me a wave.

I close my eyes and rub them until I see sparks. When I open them again, I half expect to see Max standing on the patio, but there

is no one there. And so I make my way back inside, eventually finding Ryan with Finn in her room. He's unearthed a towel from the
linen closet and is foisting it upon her, insisting that she dry her hair.
She, in turn, is trying to give it back to him. "You're way wetter than
I am," I can hear her saying as I approach. "And you're dripping on
my floor."

I arrive just in time to see the sheepish expression on Ryan's face.
"Sorry, Iz," he says when he sees me. "I didn't mean to get her all
wet."

In light of the rest of the evening's events, this hardly seems to
matter. "It's no big deal. Here, Finnish. Into the bathroom with you."
I grab yet another nightgown out of Finn's dresser, shepherd her into
the hallway to get another towel, and go through the whole drying-
and-changing ritual again. Finally I have her all put back together, at
which point she wants to see the firefighters. We rendezvous with a
somewhat wrung-out Ryan on the screened-in porch, and all three of
us watch as Charleston's finest put my tree out of its misery.

"Damn," Ryan says softly. "I mean, that sucks," he corrects himself, glancing down at my daughter.

"I don't think 'that sucks' is actually much of an improvement," I
tell him, my arm around Finn's shoulders.

His lips twitch. "I guess you're right. Sorry—I don't think I'm all
the way awake."

"It was really sweet of you to come. Thank you."

Ryan snorts in derision. "Isabel, your house was practically on
fire. What was I supposed to do—roll over and go back to sleep?"

"I bet a lot of guys would have."

"Well, I'm not a lot of guys. I'm me. And there's no way I could've
done that." He sounds more than a little offended.

I don't know how I would have replied, but Finn decides the
issue by giving a jaw-cracking yawn, complete with sound effects that
make both of us laugh. "Come on," I tell her. "Fun's over. Back to
bed with you."

Ryan scoops her up in his arms like she's Scarlett O'Hara and takes her down the hall while I say goodbye to the firefighters. It takes a little while, and by the time I make it to the living room, he's already there, eating a tangerine and channel surfing. He turns the television off when he sees me and tosses the remote onto the coffee table just as I collapse on the couch next to him, thoroughly exhausted.

"Here," he says, pulling the chenille blanket off the back of the couch. I wrap it around myself and glance sideways at him, still in his rain-splattered shorts and T-shirt. His hair has dried in dirty-blond spikes, like a skater version of his normal self.

"Some night," he says, running a hand through it so that it stands up in even wilder disarray. "Some week, actually."

"No kidding."

"Did you call your dad?" he asks. "About the tree, I mean."

I debate telling him about Finn's comment and then decide against it. "No, just you. I'll tell him tomorrow. The fire's out, no one got hurt. He'd just worry."

"Why did you call me, then?" His tone's merely curious, but knowing him as I do, I can't help but wonder if there's something more behind it. Puzzled, I stare at him.

"I don't know," I say eventually. "I didn't consider not calling you. I felt like you'd want to know. Plus I thought you'd be mad if you found out about it after the fact."

"Fair enough. But you wanted me here, Griffin. Admit it." He gives me a crooked grin.

"God, you're a difficult son of a bitch." I extricate one of my arms from the blanket and punch him on the shoulder.

"Ow," he says, still smiling. "I'll take that as a yes."

"I didn't say that," I protest.

"You didn't have to." He rubs his shoulder, grimacing, and tilts his head to one side like the RCA dog, an unreadable expression on his face. "You don't really think it was Max out there, do you?"

Irritated, I disentangle myself from the blanket and fold my arms across my chest. "You don't believe me?"

Ryan shrugs, looking uncomfortable. "I believe there was a guy in your backyard, Isabel, and that you should probably call the police. I'll stay here tonight, if you want."

I ignore this invitation. Heat fills my face. "You don't think I know what Max looks like? You think I'd confuse him with some stranger?"

Ryan gives me a wary glance. "Well," he says, "for one thing, it *has* been almost eight years. And for another, it was dark—and it was pouring so hard you could barely see. You told me that yourself."

"It was Max," I insist. "And it didn't start raining that badly until I got outside."

"Isabel," Ryan says, and he reaches out to take my hand. "I know you want it to have been Max, so badly that maybe you saw him there. But if it was him, why would he run away from you?" He rubs his other hand through his hair, tousling it further. "Why just stand out there, to begin with?"

I am trying to formulate a rebuttal to this—not the easiest thing to do, given its logical premise—when something else occurs to me. I can feel myself blanch. "It was dark," I say, almost to myself. "But it shouldn't have been."

Now Ryan looks truly alarmed, as if this is proof that I've gone around the bend. "What do you mean?" he says, squeezing my hand in what I imagine is an attempt to bring me back to reality.

"When I looked out into the yard," I say, the words coming haltingly, "I could see him, but only because of the moon. It's big tonight, you know? But it wasn't until I went outside that the motion detector light came on."

Ryan's grip on my hand tightens, and I lift my eyes to his. "That isn't possible, is it?" I say, a chill creeping down my spine. "If there was a man in my backyard—Max or anyone else—that light should have come on right away."

"Unless it was broken, yeah. Or unless whoever it was stood absolutely still for a long time." His tone is even, careful not to imply anything, but the implications are clear enough nonetheless.

"What the hell, Ry?" Despite myself, my teeth start to chatter.

He puts his arm around my shoulders and draws me in against him. Even through the blanket, I can feel the warmth of his skin, and it comforts me. This close to him, I can smell the Ivory soap he always uses, and a faint whiff of spearmint gum.

"It'll be okay," he says, resting his chin on top of my head. "I promise."

"There was someone there, I swear. I'm not crazy, Ryan."

"Of course you're not," he says, in such an obvious effort to sound conciliatory that I roll my eyes.

"That's exactly what you'd say to a crazy person," I tell him. "Right before you called the men in white coats."

Ryan gives an uneasy chuckle. "I'm not calling anyone, Isabel, don't worry. But I do think you need to get some rest. Maybe in the morning we'll be able to think of a reasonable explanation for all of this." He strokes my hair absently, the way you'd pet a kitten.

"You don't believe me," I say sadly. "You don't believe me and now you think I've lost my mind."

"I never said that."

"But you're thinking it," I say, twisting so I can see his face. There are dark circles under his eyes, and I feel renewed guilt about yanking him out of bed.

He yawns. "What I think is that you're under a lot of stress. Take a hot bath and go to bed, all right? We'll talk about it in the morning."

I slide out from under his arm and raise an eyebrow at him. "What makes you think you can tell me what to do?" I mean it as a joke, but it comes out confrontational instead. Ryan sighs, so loudly I worry that he'll wake up Finn.

"I'm not telling you what to do. I'm trying to take care of you, and I've got to tell you, Griffin, you're not making it very easy."

Unused to caretaking as I am, this idea never occurred to me. Once it does, I'm ashamed of my attitude. "Oh," I say, doing my best to sound penitent. "I didn't realize."

"Well, now you know." His voice is brusque. "So do me a favor and get your butt upstairs, will you? I'll sleep in the guest room."

It's my first instinct to argue, to tell him I can take care of myself and my daughter, that he should go home and get a good night's sleep. But then I look at him sitting there, his hair rumpled and his shirt still damp from the rain, braced for battle, and I don't have the heart. Because I can tell that, as far as Ryan's concerned, where he belongs is right here, watching over us. Normally this kind of posturing would just piss me off, but tonight it doesn't. Tonight I'm scared, and as much as I hate to admit it, I'd feel better if he was here. I bite my lip, trying to hold myself together.

Ryan must misinterpret my silence, because he grabs me by the shoulders. "That came out wrong. Please let me stay," he says. "It's not for you, all right? I know you don't need me here, Isabel. It's for me. You and Finn are the closest thing to family that I have, and I couldn't stand it if anything happened to either of you. If you think that's protective alpha bullshit, fine. I won't argue. But don't make me go."

I've never heard Ryan sound like this. He doesn't talk about his parents, about what it was like to grow up bouncing from one foster home to another. In fact, aside from the first time he told me about his childhood and a passing reference here and there, he never mentions it. I've had my own share of loss, and I know what it's like to feel adrift in the world, but I didn't realize Finn and I were Ryan's anchors, that the wounds left by his childhood were still this raw. How could I? In his own way, he's as guarded as I am.

I try hard to keep my face expressionless, but I must not have succeeded, because Ryan's eyes narrow. "Don't look at me like that," he says fiercely. "Don't you pity me." His hands tighten on my shoulders with an intensity that borders on savagery, but I don't flinch. I know this kind of anger, have pulled it around myself often enough so no one would see what it concealed—hurt, running deep and inexorable like a river to the sea.

I look at Ryan and see the boy he used to be, skinny and blond and hazel-eyed, unwanted and afraid. I think of myself, sitting alone in the house as my father sorted through old photographs of my mom. I think of the weeks after Max disappeared, how I sat in the police station with my hands clasped over my belly, desperate to keep Finn inside me, to not lose her too.

"Ry." I lift one hand to touch his face, slowly, so I won't spook him. His eyes flash wide, but he doesn't move. "I understand," I say, and let my hand fall.

Ryan swallows hard. I want to tell him that I do need him. That, aside from Finn and my father, he's all I have left in the world. But the words stick in my throat and in the end I just lean closer and rest my face against his chest, hiding the tears that slip down my cheeks. "You can stay," I whisper, and hope that he can't tell I am crying.

His arms close around me, holding me tight. Gently, he rocks me from side to side, and I know I haven't fooled him for a moment. He has to clear his throat twice before he speaks, and when he does, his voice is thick. But all he says is, "Thank you."

Max

I wake up in a dark room, my head throbbing and my mouth as dry as the Gobi. For a moment I have no idea where I am—just that I'd kill for some aspirin. The room is close and hot, but I feel a welcome current of air eddying over my face. I turn my head in the direction of the breeze—and jerk, startled, as a wet cloth touches my forehead.

The movement jars my head, and I let out a moan. Then a cool hand is on my head, steadying me. "It's all right," a voice says, low, soothing—and unmistakably American. "You're okay. Just lie still."

Blinking my eyes to clear them, I work my tongue, trying to unstick it from the roof of my mouth to speak . . . even though I hardly know what to say. Because right there, next to me, is Julia—her blond hair swept back under a bonnet, her almond-shaped brown eyes fixed on mine. "It's okay," she says again, patting my hand.

Her words are comforting enough, but the expression on her face is not. She's staring at me, hard—as if she's trying to communicate something without words. Through my all-consuming headache, it occurs to me that maybe we are not alone.

I shift my eyes right and see a house slave sitting on a chair by the bed. Next to her is a table with a basin and an ewer, as well as a small earthenware cup. She's eyeing me every bit as intensely as Julia, but the look on her face isn't cautionary—it's puzzled, like she's trying to figure out who or what I am.

"Water," I croak. "Please."

Immediately, she pours some into the cup and then lifts my head so that I can drink. "Slow," she says in a firm voice, and I do my best to obey, even though the feel of the water flowing over my cracked lips and down my throat is the best thing I can remember tasting in a long time.

With a nod of approval, she pulls the cup away and sets it down on the table next to the bed. "That enough for now. How you feel?" she says.

"I—my head hurts." I lift one hand and press it to my temple, feeling for damage. "Am I bleeding?"

"You were," Julia says, with a faint air of accusation. "All over your shirt. Jubah was able to stop it. She's a healer."

I look at the woman sitting to the left of my bed, her hair pulled back by a neat white kerchief, clothed in a nut-brown dress. Her eyes are a startling shade of amber, clear and bright in the light that streams through the open window. "Thank you," I say, and she nods.

"My pleasure," she says, the island lilt stronger than any I've heard before. "I hear what you did for Cuffee. Ain't no one stand up to Master Edward in a long time 'cept Cuffee himself, and you see how that turn out. No one do a thing but you. So why you do it?"

Her direct gaze unnerves me, as does her voice—husky and mellifluous, but with an unmistakable edge. I swallow hard. "I don't know," I say at last, forcing the words through my abraded throat. "I just—I couldn't stand by and watch something like that, not if I could stop it. What happened to Cuffee?" The question dies in my throat as I remember the bloody, laid-open back of the man who hung from the tree, the way his body had swayed with each lash of the whip.

Jubah looks down, tracing her finger along the pattern of the quilt. "Oh, Master Edward cut him down," she says bitterly. "And rub his back with salt an' pepper an' lime juice, like he a cut of pork, marinating for dinner."

"What?" My voice cracks on the word, so that it emerges in an outraged croak.

"You pay that no mind," Jubah says, watching my face. "He plan to do that, anyhow, say it make Cuffee remember his place. But what you do, it give us hope. And sometime hope be all you have."

I can think of no response. You'd think it would be a good thing, to stand up for someone who's being abused, to instill hope where there was none before. But what if my choice pushes the rebellion from possibility to probability, from talk to action? What if by confronting Edward Thomas, I've condemned hundreds of people to death, including Lily Adair and her unborn child?

This line of thought only makes my headache worse, and I fall back onto the pillow with a groan, closing my eyes. Jubah makes a low noise in her throat, and then I hear the clinking sound of porcelain. "Drink this," she says in that same authoritative voice. "For your head."

"What is it?" I say, opening my eyes again to see her holding another cup in her hand. Steam rises from it, filling the air with the aromatic scent of herbs. I sniff suspiciously as she gives me the cup, and Julia makes an impatient sound.

"Just drink it. It won't hurt you," she says, pleating the material of her skirt between her fingers. It's a nervous gesture, and it occurs to me that she must be as eager to speak to me as I am to her—but there's no way for us to have a frank conversation with Jubah present.

I take the cup from Jubah and peer into it doubtfully, eyeing the swirling contents. "Fine. But what is it?" I say, taking a small sip and letting the hot liquid linger in my mouth before I swallow. "Cinnamon, lime, peppermint, bay leaf, basil, and . . . something else?" My eyes flick to Jubah's face for confirmation.

She nods. "Willow bark. For the headache. You know somethin' 'bout plants, then?"

"A little," I say, gulping more of the tea. "I studied them—at home. In South Carolina," I add for Julia's benefit, watching her face.

If I wasn't watching her so closely, I'd likely have missed the flash of pain that moves across her face, filling her eyes—but I am, and I don't. "At home," she echoes softly. "And how is home, Mr. Adair?"

It's strange to hear her call me this—Mr. Adair is my father—but I know that here, having her call me by my first name would be inappropriate. "Well enough," I reply, turning my head to see her more clearly. "Your daughter sends her regards."

"Isabel's all right, then?" She leans forward, gripping my hand too tightly in her excitement. Her nails dig into my palm.

"Yes, she's more than all right. She's—" I close my mouth precipitously on the word "pregnant," realizing that this is likely the last thing a mother wants to hear about her unmarried daughter. "Doing really well," I finish lamely. "Andrew too." The last is an exaggeration, given that Andrew has spent the last six years falling down a black hole in search of his wife, but that hardly seems like the right thing to say.

Julia's eyes narrow, and she turns to Jubah, who is watching us with interest. "Could you please excuse us?" she says. "Mr. Adair and I have some matters to discuss."

Jubah rises without a word. At the doorway, she turns and looks back at me. "What you do today—" She halts, her gaze resting on my face with disconcerting intensity. "You need anything—medicine, healing, something else—you come see Jubah."

I open my mouth to thank her, but she shakes her head in adjuration and is gone. As soon as she disappears, Julia grabs my arm again.

"What are you doing here?" she says, her face alight. "It is you, isn't it, Max?"

I barely have time to nod before she leans in, whispering. "Are you here alone?"

Again, I nod, and her face falls. "That's good, I suppose," she says. "I shouldn't want them to be here, with me—but I just miss them so much." Her eyes fill with tears, and she dabs at them with her free hand, gripping my arm tightly. "I want to know everything. But we can't talk here. There's more privacy in the gardens, though. Maybe we could go for a walk."

"A walk?" I say incredulously. "What makes you think I can go for a walk? I can barely hold up my head."

"Maybe if you sat up and started moving around, you'd feel better." Her voice is urgent. "We have to talk, Max—please."

"Of course we have to talk. I came here to find you, after all," I tell her, struggling up to my elbows. "Did you think I hung around on nineteenth-century slave plantations in the two weeks leading up to a rebellion for fun?"

At this, her face goes white. "A rebellion?" she says blankly.

"Oh, hell. You didn't know." Gulping down the rest of my tea, I lever myself up to a seated position.

"A rebellion?" she repeats. "Here? But what—when—"

"We really can't talk about *that* right now. Hang on, let me see if I can get up." I reach for the bedside table, pushing myself to my feet. "Jesus, I think I have a concussion or something," I mutter, waving away her offer of help as the world swims around me, my vision gone to streamers. "Just give me a second. Christ, that man packs a hell of a punch."

She giggles, an unexpected, silvery sound that reminds me so much of Isabel, it sends a bolt of pain straight through my chest. "You should've seen his face when you karate-chopped his hand. Not to mention when you spat on him."

"I saw his face *then*," I mutter, grabbing the edge of the table to steady myself. "I was right underneath him, if you recall. God, my head."

"Here. Maybe this will help," Julia says, offering me another cup of nasty tea. "She brought the whole pitcher."

I take the cup and down its contents, bracing my legs against the bed to stay upright. Julia is eyeing me, a worried expression on her face. "I'm not going to fall over," I assure her. "I'll be okay, as long as we go slowly. I don't know how I'm going to sit on a horse, though."

I grimace at the thought, then put the idea firmly out of mind. "Well, I guess I'll worry about that when the time comes."

She nods, satisfied, and grips my arm, her voice a fierce, determined whisper. "Good. Rebellion or not, I didn't survive a year in this godforsaken, dehumanizing place to give up now, Max. We'll find a private place to talk. And then—you'll tell me what you know."

I think of Isabel, pregnant and alone. Andrew, grieving and desperate. This island, torn apart and aflame. Resigned, I square my shoulders. "Be careful what you wish for," I tell Julia, and gesture for her to lead the way.

Isabel

I get Ryan settled in the guest room, digging out an extra blanket from the linen closet despite his protestations and surreptitiously peeking at the sheets to make sure that they're clean. He blinks at me owlishly from the armchair that he's commandeered and sighs. "Isabel, you do realize that at this point, I could probably sleep on the floor and it wouldn't matter," he says, sounding resigned. "The moment you quit fussing and shut that door behind you, I'm going to fall facedown on the closest surface, bed or no bed. But by all means, keep fluffing the pillows. It gives me a warm and fuzzy feeling inside."

I roll my eyes. "I guess that means you don't want me to bother hunting for the spare toothbrush that Finn's dentist gave her, huh?"

He makes a sarcastic sort of snort, the effectiveness of which is significantly compromised by the fact that it ends in a yawn. Pushing himself to his feet, he walks over to the bed and sits down on the edge. "Get out of here, would you? Wake me up if anything freaky happens. Otherwise . . . good night."

"Some guardian you are. A meteor could fall on the house and you'd probably turn over and keep snoring."

He lies back on the pillows, fingers knitted behind his head. "It's the thought that counts, right?" he says, and closes his eyes.

With his hair tousled and his long, parti-colored lashes sweeping the top of his cheekbones, he looks about eight years old. Swept by sudden tenderness, I pull the spare blanket over him, tucking him in as if he were Finn, and am rewarded with a small smile. "Can't help yourself, can you, Griffin?" he says lightly.

"I guess not," I say, bending over to switch off the bedside lamp. The room is plunged into darkness, the dresser and bookshelf looming, humped shapes in the dim glow of the streetlight, and Ryan himself barely visible.

"Ry?" I say, without intending to. Really, all I want to do is let him be—he's so clearly worn out. But I'm sick of being trapped in my own head, going in circles like some sort of demented, treadmill-obsessed hamster.

For a second he doesn't reply, and I think that he might already be asleep. But then I hear a catch in his breathing, and the springs creak as he rolls over to face me. "Yeah?" he says, voice drowsy.

"Never mind," I say hastily. "You're tired, you need to get some rest. Forget it."

There's a pause, and then he sighs, sounding more awake. "That's not fair, Isabel. Go ahead. What were you going to say?"

"Well," I say, before I think better of it, "you said Finn and I are the closest thing to family that you have. Which I get. I won't ask you about your parents, don't worry. But I just wondered—if you had no one, Ry—and you were always in trouble, like you told me—how did you get as far as you have? Going to school, starting Mage?"

Silence falls between us, and then I hear the unmistakable noise of Ryan struggling up onto his elbows. "Seriously, Isabel?" he says, and there's a peculiar note in his voice—maybe annoyance, maybe something else entirely. "After eight years, you're asking me this now because . . . why?"

"I don't know," I say, biting my lip. "Maybe because—well,

you've never talked about your family before. Not the way you did tonight."

The headboard thuds against the wall as Ryan sits up all the way. "I did not talk about my family," he says pointedly. "Or I did, but only insofar as it relates to you and Finn. And I don't particularly care to talk about them now."

"Okay, okay," I say, holding up my hands in surrender—not that he can see me. "I'm sorry. I shouldn't have asked."

I start to back away from the bed, intending to retreat from the room and shut the door behind me. But before I can move more than a step, Ry's hand closes around my wrist, pulling me toward him. Dark as it is, I didn't see this coming, and let out a squeak of alarm, which makes him laugh. "I'm the one who should be apologizing," he says, tugging harder, so that I sit down next to him on the bed. His hand is still circling my wrist, and I can feel his leg pressing against me, warm beneath the blanket. I start to fidget, to try to get up, but he holds me fast. "Things like this," he says, "they're easier to talk about in the dark. So. You remember the day we met, at Metto?"

"Of course I do," I say, thinking back to that long-ago afternoon when I'd sat in a Mount Pleasant coffee shop, so sick of the confines of my apartment that I couldn't stand to look at them anymore— a three-month-old Finn in her car seat next to me, rocking her with one foot as I tried over and over again to make sense out of the math that I needed to pass the GRE. Finn had been fussing, and I'd picked her up, cradling her in one arm, turning pages with the other, so frustrated that I'd begun to think that there was no point in taking the test at all. Until a shadow had fallen over me, and I'd looked up to see a guy standing there, dressed in a black suit and dark green tie, his blond hair falling into his eyes and a sympathetic expression on his face. *I'm sure this is going to sound like the worst kind of pick-up line,* he'd said, *but it isn't, I promise.*

For God's sake, I'd thought, staring at him, who the hell would have the least bit of interest in picking me up? There were dark cir-

cles under my eyes from nights spent studying and staying up with
Finn, I had a diaper bag at my feet and a halfway-to-squalling infant
in my arms, and my shirt was stained in ways I didn't care to contem-
plate.

His eyes had traveled over my table—the half-drunk cup of coffee, the well-thumbed book, the crumpled pages of notes, the baby
giving the hitching cries that meant she was working herself into a
real fit—and then he'd smiled, a sardonic, self-deprecating grin. *The
thing is,* he'd said, as shamefacedly as if he were confessing to a pre-
dilection for engaging in sexual congress with small animals, *I'm
really, really good at math.*

Um . . . congratulations, I'd said, clutching Finn tighter, wondering if he was some kind of well-dressed, academically-minded lunatic. *And?*

And I can help you, he'd said, as gingerly as if I were an armed
bomb, one ill-chosen word away from detonation. *That is, if you'll
let me.*

Puzzled, I'd looked up at him, wondering if I'd fallen asleep with
my head on my book and was, in fact, hallucinating. *But,* I'd said finally, *why would you want to?*

The smile had faded then, so that he just stood there regarding
me—untidy braid, messy clothes, colicky infant, and all. His tie had
come undone, I saw, loosened at the neck, and there were dark circles underneath his own eyes, as if he hadn't been sleeping too well,
either. But his gaze met mine straight on, and in it I saw a painful sort
of honesty. *Because,* he'd said, *I promised someone that I'd pay it forward, when the opportunity presented itself. And here you are.*

The open way he was looking at me, the sudden vulnerability in
his voice—all of it made me uneasy. The last thing I needed was
someone else to worry about, when I could barely take care of myself
and my daughter. *I don't even know you,* I'd said, lifting my chin.
What makes you think I'd want your help—much less accept it?

His lips had twitched, as if he was trying not to smile. *Well,* he'd
said, *I'm Ryan. So now you know my name, at least. As for accepting*

my help— He'd glanced sideways at the table, strewn with my failed attempts at problem-solving, then at the increasingly restive baby in my arms. *Not for yourself, you wouldn't,* he'd said. *But maybe—for her?*

Common sense told me to say no, to gather my hysterical daughter and my books and hightail it for my beat-up Honda Civic. But something made me hesitate. He reminded me, I'd thought for one strange instant, of myself: bravado, layered so thickly over an abyss that most people would never guess the truth.

What's the catch? I'd said, and he'd smiled at me in acknowledgment, sharp-edged as broken glass.

No questions, he'd said. *I'll keep my promise, if you keep yours.*

I'd considered him for a long moment—his guarded expression, at once foreign and familiar. And then I'd imagined a world in which I didn't get into graduate school and had to abandon my dream of becoming an archaeologist, much less supporting my daughter. If Ryan could help me pass the GRE, I decided, I didn't care if he had a fetish for doing the nasty with a hundred and one Dalmatians. *You have a deal,* I'd said, and, juggling the baby, stuck out a sticky hand. *I'm Isabel, by the way.*

I'd kept my promise—and so had he, drilling me on math day after day, hour after painful hour, until I'd aced the test. And then I'd invited him over for dinner, in thanks, and he'd held Finn and read to her, and almost eight years later—here we are.

"Of course I remember," I say again, peering at him through the gloom. "What does that have to do with anything?"

Lightning splits the sky outside the window, and in its harsh illumination I see him square his shoulders against the headboard. "I was wearing a suit the day I met you," he says levelly, "because I was coming from a funeral."

He's loosened his grip on my wrist, but I don't dare move. *No questions,* he'd said that day, and so I had never asked. Nor had he volunteered the information—until now.

"You're right," he says with equanimity. "If someone hadn't taken

a chance on me, I'd probably be rotting in jail or a trailer park somewhere." He drums his fingers on the blanket between us, a slow, dis-
jointed rhythm. "It's kind of a long story, actually. But I figure we've
got time . . . provided that neither of us falls asleep before I finish."

He smiles at me then, a forced, unpleasant sort of grin, and I
know that whatever else this story of his may be, it will not be pretty.
I open my mouth to tell him he doesn't have to go on, but before I
can say a word, he waves a hand, dismissing this. "It's okay, Isabel.
Don't feel guilty. You want to know? You can know." The grin fades,
and he looks me in the eye, all pretense gone. "If I didn't want to tell
you," he says simply, "I wouldn't. You ought to understand that by
now."

"I do. But still—I feel bad, Ryan. I didn't mean to dig all this up."

"And I said, don't feel bad." He gives me a genuine smile now,
meant to take the sting from his words. "It ends well, I guess. Or
badly, depending on your point of view."

I raise my eyebrows, inviting him to continue, and he does. "My
junior year of high school, I hacked into the school's computer system, deleted a bunch of people's records. It was a game to me, something to do for fun, just to prove I could. Except this time I got lazy,
and I got caught. The principal wanted to expel me, and the
superintendent—well, let's just say he was a big fan of corporal punishment, and this being South Carolina, it was good and legal then.
Still is." His fingers move faster now, a dark blur, hard enough to
shake the bed.

"That fat fucker took a paddle to me himself, the kind with the
holes punched out so that it whistles when someone swings at you.
He wanted me to yell, I think, or fight, or cry—who knows what he
had in mind, sick bastard. But when I just stood there bent over his
fancy damn desk and took it, I think it pissed him off worse. He'd
read my file. He should've known better than to think a little thing
like that would make shit difference." He laughs then, low and so
bitter, it catches in his throat.

"Ryan—" I say, horrified, but he ignores me, plowing onward.

"So, that was that. Everyone was ready to write me off, my latest foster mother included. She'd never liked me much, not that I gave her reason to. A match made in hell, that one." He shrugs, dismissing this as inconsequential. "But this teacher, Mr. Owens—I'd had him for math two years running, and we got along—he spoke up on my behalf. He said if I could do something like that, with no training—well, who knew what I'd be capable of, if I used my powers for good instead of evil?"

A tree bangs against the house, and Ryan's eyes flick toward the bay windows, then away. "I was already bored to death when he said that, waiting to see if they were going to boot me out on my ass or pass me on to juvenile hall. By then I didn't care, so long as it meant that I wouldn't have to sit through one more lecture about how worthless and misguided I was." He snorts, disgusted. "When Mr. Owens said that—like I was some kind of conflicted superhero—I laughed, but no one else did. The superintendent—God, he hated me!—he said there was nothing funny about the situation, that kids like me belonged locked up somewhere that they couldn't do any more damage." The last part of this sentence comes out stilted and nasal, an eerie mockery, and I shudder.

"I thought Mr. Owens was going to punch him," Ryan says in his normal voice, sounding gratified. "His face got all red and he muttered something under his breath, so only I could hear. *Officious, entitled son of a bitch*, he said. And I'd never liked anyone more." In the pale beam of lamplight streaming in through the curtains, I see him smile.

"Anyway, he persuaded the principal and the superintendent to let me have independent study with him, three periods a day. He tutored me himself, got me enrolled in a coding class, took me to the library, bought me my first computer, made me apply for scholarships. When I got in trouble after that, he spoke up for me, always." I hear him swallow, hard, all humor gone.

"After graduation, he took me out to dinner, and then he gave me a check for ten thousand dollars. At first I thought it was a joke. When

I realized he was serious, I told him I couldn't take it, but he wouldn't listen. He'd saved it up, he said, and there was no one he'd rather give it to. I had to go to school, because one day I'd be somebody special. I was worth something, he said. No one had ever told me anything like that before."

He's silent then, for so long that I think he isn't going to say anything else. But finally he goes on, each word falling like a weight into the night. "So I went to school, like he wanted. I graduated with honors, to make him proud. And then two years later—he got sick. Cancer. I went to see him every day. He didn't have much family, either. I think maybe that's why he—" He closes his mouth with a snap on whatever he was about to say, then tries again. "Anyhow, I thanked him for what he'd done for me. I told him I didn't understand why he'd bothered, but that it had changed everything. And he told me he didn't need thanks, that one day I'd be able to do for someone else what he'd done for me. He made me promise. And when I went back the next day, he was dead."

"Jesus, Ryan," I say, and reach for his hand in the dark. For a moment his fingers close around mine, his grip tight, holding on. And then he lets go.

"Not much of a bedtime story, is it," he says, his voice empty. "Sorry about that. But when I saw you, after his funeral . . . well, I don't believe in signs, Isabel, you know that. But the way you looked—so tired, so determined, all by yourself with the baby—if there ever was a time to pay forward what he'd given me, that was it."

"Because I looked so pathetic, you mean." With a pang, I remember how I'd felt that day, as if everything had spun hopelessly out of control.

He gives an incredulous chuckle. "Is that what you think? You were a lot of things that day. Overwhelmed, yes. Sleep-deprived, sure. But pathetic? Not hardly. I looked at you and I saw someone who would do whatever it took to make a better life for herself and her daughter. Someone who wouldn't give up, even if it meant sacrificing her pride and accepting help from a stranger. And I thought—"

He clears his throat, and when he speaks again his voice is uneven, rough as water running over a jagged bed of stones. "I thought that you'd be worth it," he says at last. "That day in the coffee shop, with you—for the first time I understood, maybe, what he'd seen in me all those years ago. Why he took the chance."

Without meaning to, I've shifted closer to Ryan, so that I'm almost touching him. He stirs, rolling to face me. "You're a survivor, Isabel," he says. "You're the strongest person I've ever known. You and me—we'll get through this."

Now the tears do come, coursing silently down my cheeks, and I'm grateful for the dark. But something must give me away—a hitch in my breathing, maybe, or just the fact that he knows me so well—because his hand rises, silent in the dark, and brushes the wetness from my face. "Hold on," he says quietly. "That's all you need to do. Hold on, just like you always have. And I'll be right here. I won't leave you."

I try to speak, to thank him, but my throat is too tight. Instead I close my eyes, steadying myself, listening to the whir of the overhead fan and the pounding of the rain. I reach for Ryan and feel his fingers close around mine, wet with my tears. His hand is as familiar to me as my own—the silvery texture of the scar that spans the base of his thumb, the sharp edge of a splinter, buried beneath his skin. *Hold on*, he said, and so I do.

For an instant, I feel him hesitate. And then he brushes one finger across my knuckles, a delicate, inquiring touch. I run my nails along his palm in answer and hear his sudden intake of breath, involuntary and as sharp as if I've hit him. His hand moves in mine, skimming the hollows between my fingers—a stranger's touch, warm on my skin—making me shiver. Featherlight, his fingertips graze my palm, and I return the favor, tracing my nails across the inside of his wrist in wordless reply. A shudder runs through him, but he doesn't pull away.

Outside, the storm is still raging, the crack of the lightning and the answering growl of the thunder a counterpoint to the rapid beat of my heart. I open my eyes, watching the shadows of tree limbs on the wall as they bend and twist, lashed by the wind.

Slowly, as if he expects me to slap him away, Ryan lifts his other hand to cup my face. Moved by sudden tenderness, I turn toward him, pressing my lips into the curve of his palm. He smells of soap and ink, citrus and rainwater, and part of me wants nothing more than to lie down next to him—safe in the warmth of his body—until morning finds us. I have the strangest sense of dislocation, as if none of this is real.

"Ry—" I say, and then can't think how to go on.

He runs his free hand through my hair, winding one of the errant curls around his finger. "What is it?" he says, voice hushed.

So many words come to me then. I want to ask him if he feels the same way I do—as if we've slid sideways, into a surreal version of reality. If he feels the tension arcing between us, or if I've imagined it, along with the vision of Max standing on my patio, pelted with rain. But in the end exhaustion breaks over me, and I just don't have the heart. "Good night, Ry," I say at last. "Thank you for trusting me. For telling me the truth. And—for staying."

Both of his hands—the one that's holding mine, the one twined in my hair—grow still. He takes a deep breath—and then he lets me go. "You're welcome," he says, his voice expressionless, and slides away from me, across the bed. "Good night, Isabel. Sleep well."

Max

"Six years?" Julia grasps my arm to keep her balance. We're standing near the stables, where I can easily say that I went to check on my horse if need be. There's no one within earshot, but we're pitching our voices low, just the same. "But I've only been here a year. When I saw you, I knew you'd changed—but I was hoping it was some kind of trick, you know, something that happened when you—came."

I shake my head. "No. In fact, I'm surprised you did recognize me, Julia. You'd only seen me that one time, in the woods, right?"

"Oh, no. I'd seen you before, in the grocery store with your mother. I knew who you were, that day at the garden party. But you were seventeen then, right? You've grown." She fiddles with a pendant hanging around her neck—an aquamarine stone, flanked by narrow wings, pressed in silver—a dragonfly. When she looks up, I see that her lips are trembling. "Max, is there something you aren't telling me?"

"After six years, there's probably a whole lot I'm not telling you," I say, defensive. She just stares at me, arms crossed over her chest, and I figure I might as well get it over with. "Isabel's pregnant," I say, and wait for the axe to fall.

But when I summon the courage to look at her face, she is smiling at me—glowing, in fact, as if someone has lit a candle beneath her fair skin. "Really?" she says, and sits down suddenly on a bench outside the stables.

For a moment neither of us says anything. Tears are running down her face, but she makes no effort to wipe them away. Finally she manages in a choked voice, "I'm assuming you're the father?"

I jerk my head up, wearing what must be a ferocious expression, because she snorts through her tears and starts to laugh. "I'll take that as a yes. Really, Max, you should see your face."

I sink down onto the bench next to her. "She only told me the day before yesterday. Or what I think is the day before yesterday," I mutter, thinking about the way that time has passed—or not passed, rather—for Julia. "She's not very far along. It was March when we—" Embarrassed, I clear my throat. "Anyway, when I left . . . it was May, back there. So it can't be more than six or eight weeks. But she told me—and then I knew I had to tell her the truth, about seeing you in the woods that day. I couldn't imagine going through the pregnancy with her, marrying her, and keeping that kind of secret. So I asked her to meet me in the clearing—you know, where my tree house is. Where I saw you with Lily that day. I was going to tell her the truth. But I never got the chance."

Julia blots her eyes with a handkerchief that she's produced from the bodice of her dress. "What happened? You were waiting for Isabel in the clearing, but Robert got there first, is that it? And then . . . you followed him?"

"What else could I do?" I tug at the arms of the frock coat, sweat running down my sides. How people go around dressed like this, I have no idea.

"And so here you are. And you . . . what? Thought you'd ride in on your white horse and rescue me, like John Wayne or something?" Her lips twitch.

"Not exactly," I mutter. "But I had to try. What kind of person would I be if I didn't?"

At this, the amusement fades from Julia's face. "You're a good person, Max. Obviously. I didn't mean to make light of what you've done." Her eyes meet mine, and she swallows hard. "The rebellion," she says, low-voiced. "When?"

"It's supposed to start on Easter Sunday. There'll be a dance on Good Friday at River Plantation, and the slaves will finish planning there."

"Easter Sunday? That soon?" Her face goes white and she presses her lips together. In the distance, I can hear slaves singing in the fields, see smoke belching up from the chimney of the boiling house. The air is thick with the smell of roasting meat.

I scuff my boots in the dirt of the stable yard. "How did you end up here, Julia? What were you doing in the middle of my parents' woods like that?"

Her eyes rest on my face for a moment, then dart away. She doesn't say anything for a long moment, and neither do I. The silence stretches between us, uncomfortable, but I wait her out. Finally she says, "Here at Bayleys, today? John Best asked me to tea to discuss another teaching arrangement. It was just luck, finding you. But here in Barbados—well. I was adopted—maybe Isabel's told you?"

"Sure." I shrug. "And after your adoptive mom died, you became obsessed with finding out where you'd come from. Isabel said that was all you did—write letters, go on websites, call people. That right before you disappeared, you thought you'd discovered something important."

"Obsessed," she says thoughtfully. "It's not the kindest of words, but I see how she could say that. And she's right—before that afternoon at the garden party, I'd finally traced my roots back as far as the 1800s. I'd discovered that I was descended from the Brightmore family, here on the island—good friends of the Adairs, actually. I've had the chance to get to know them, and they're lovely people—although they've lost two children recently, and Alicia Brightmore's been pretty miserable. But yes—I'd discovered a connection between our two families, yours and mine. I was so excited, thinking that I might be able to find information about the Brightmores through the Adair papers. But I hadn't begun to do any of that research. I never got to."

A far-off look clouds her eyes. "At your parents' party—the woman at the edge of the woods, wearing that beautiful yellow dress—I couldn't imagine what she wanted with me. But when I got closer . . . she spoke to me, Max. She said, *I know your face.*"

An icy centipede skitters down my spine, and I have to force myself to keep my expression blank as Julia goes on. "*You have so many questions,* she said. *But I can show you what you want to know.* I never should have followed her."

Tears fill her eyes, and she swipes at them furiously with the back of her hand. "But it was like she'd hypnotized me, or something. The whole way into the woods, she spoke to me, but I can't tell you a thing she said. I just followed her, like an idiot. I remember you shouting after us, and I waved. But it never occurred me to turn back. I'm a fool," she concludes bitterly, blowing her nose. "And now here we are, the both of us."

I pat her clumsily on the shoulder. "It's okay. We'll figure something out."

Julia turns on me, her eyes glossy with tears and the tip of her nose red-rimmed. "How?" she says. "I've already been here for twelve horrible months . . . and I can't escape no matter what I do. And now my daughter is pregnant and I can't even get to her! What if we're stuck here for the rest of our lives?"

"Look," I say, striving for calm, "I refuse to believe that the two of us are here for no reason whatsoever. Maybe you got stuck here for so long because you were waiting for me. Maybe there's something we're supposed to do. But one thing I do know—we're not going to resolve anything by freaking out. We can't afford it. We don't have time. We need a plan."

Isabel

After the multiple shocks of this evening, nothing would please me more than to comply with Ryan's suggestion that I get some sleep. Listening to the pounding of the rain on the roof, burrowed under the covers in my four-poster bed, I do my best to clear my mind. Now that I'm safe in my own room, everything that happened with Ryan—the story about finding and losing his mentor, the feel of his fingers, moving slow and sure with mine—feels like little more than a dream. Remembering my absurd impulse to clamber into bed with him, I smile, wondering what he would have done if I *had*. He'd probably have been so shocked, he'd have dumped me unceremoniously onto the floor.

I envision myself sprawled at length on the floorboards of the guest room, Ryan peering down at me with an appalled expression on his face, and laugh aloud. Tension drains from my body, and I'm finally able to relax, closing my eyes and imagining myself wandering through each room of my house the way I often do on the verge of sleep. I don't know why I find this so soothing—maybe it's the sense that everything is undisturbed, just the way I left it—but for whatever reason, it usually works wonders. I start on the first floor, just like always, and make my way through the living room with its couches and overstuffed bookshelves, through the dining room with the bouquet of wildflowers my dad brought over for Finn, and to the kitchen, where I stand at the sink, hands braced on the rim, and stare out the window, into the waning storm.

This must have been my destination all along. Because there is Max on my patio, the rain coming down on him and his lips moving, saying something I can't understand, no matter how hard I try. I will myself to focus on him, to see his face, in the hopes that somehow I'll be able to make out the words. But as sleep overtakes me, his features dim. Time runs backward, through that last day in the woods and beyond, rewinding until it strands me in the hallway in front of Max's bedroom, the night that everything changed.

This is a memory, this dream, and I should be able to put a stop to it. But with the eerie inevitability that accompanies predestination, I throw the closed door of his room wide. Heat hits me, fierce as a slap: There is a fire burning in the grate tonight, just like there was then, and there is seventeen-year-old Max, as I knew he would be— staring at me in horror, the flicker of the flames reflected in his gray eyes.

We haven't seen each other for weeks, except in the hallways at school—not since I told him we were spending too much time together, that we needed to make other friends. It hurt him, badly— I saw it in the way his eyes flashed wide before they narrowed in anger, the way he bit his lip, hard enough to draw blood—but then he turned away, stalking off through the woods. *Fine,* he said. *If that's the way you feel, I will.* And apparently he has, because here he is, sitting on his bed, holding another girl's hand. He and I have never even kissed, but I feel rage spark through my body all the same, electric and dangerous.

I open my mouth to say something, but before I can, Max leaps to his feet, mouth gaping like a goldfish's, and jerks his hand away. I've never seen him look so shocked—not even the time he found me running shirtless through the woods, wanting to feel the rain on my skin. Under other circumstances, it would have been funny.

"Isabel—" he says. "What are you doing here?"

The girl is standing now too, spots of red burning high on her cheeks. "Who are you?" she says, putting a proprietary hand on Max's arm.

I want to smack her hand away. Instead, I ignore her, turning all of my attention to Max. "I came to see you. But I guess I'm interrupting something."

Max looks from me to the girl, who is peering down her nose at me, a sneer curving up one side of her pretty mouth. I expect him to introduce me to her, to tell whoever this stranger is that I have every right to be here. But instead he shifts his weight uneasily and says, "This is kind of a bad time, Isabel. You should go."

"I should *what*?" I say, feeling the color fill my own face.

"Go home," he says, his voice remote.

A nasty look of triumph crosses the girl's face, but it barely registers; I'm too stunned to do anything but stare at Max. He's standing there on the worn Oriental rug in dark blue jeans and the Sonic Youth T-shirt I gave him for Christmas, the flames from the fireplace leaping high to cast shadows on his face. He looks like the same boy as always, except that when I look into his wide gray eyes, they hold none of their usual warmth or humor. Instead they're as empty as his voice, and tears prick my own eyes at the sight. Humiliated, I spin on my heel and run down the stairs, taking them two at a time.

Upstairs I can hear a commotion. "No," Max says, and then, insistent, "Stay here." The floorboards creak, and footsteps sound in the hallway above, coming my way.

At this, I vault the low bannister and dash for the front door. The last thing I want is Max's pity. It had obviously been a mistake, coming here, and it's too late for me to take it back—but I'll be damned if he'll see me cry over him. I burst through the door and sprint across the damp grass of the meadow, heading for the woods. The threat of whatever nocturnal creatures might be prowling in there is infinitely preferable to facing Max. I hear the front door slam, and then his voice again: "Isabel, wait! Come back. I'm sorry. Isabel, damn it, stop!" His voice carries easily in the quiet night air, but I'm not about to obey him, like an animal called to heel.

Still, I can't help but look back. Almost at the tree line, I spare a moment to glance over my shoulder. In the light of the moon, I can see him crossing the meadow at a dead run. I've never seen him move so fast, and, heart pounding hard, I step up my pace, crashing the last few steps into the thick stand of trees that border the woods.

Immediately, darkness descends, like someone's dropped a curtain. There's no clear path here, just a tangle of trees and bushes and vines that catch at my legs and impede my progress. Determined, I plow through anyway, one hand up to protect my face. Max wanted me to go home—well, fine, I'm going. Let him try to stop me.

The woods by night are strange, alien—shadows dart toward me from the corners of my eyes, only to vanish when I turn my head to look at them dead-on. The deeper I move through the trees, searching for a landmark that will lead me home, the more poorly the moon illuminates my way—until finally I can see nothing but vague shapes in the dark.

Then something grabs me, and I scream.

A hand covers my mouth, silencing me, and reflexively, I bite. I hear a grunt of pain, and then Max's voice comes out of the inky blackness. "Ow," he says, his chest heaving against my back. "It's me, Isabel, for Christ's sake. It's just me."

For a moment I am so relieved, I want to throw my arms around him. Then the feeling retreats, subsumed by annoyance at being muzzled like a recalcitrant dog. "Let go!" I say, the words muffled by his fingers, which are still clamped firmly over my mouth. He shakes his head.

"Be quiet and I will," he says.

I do my best to twist out of his grasp. What does he care if I scream? We're in the middle of the woods. And who does he think he is, snatching me like that?

"Stop it," he says, not loosening his hold. "Quit fighting me, and I'll let you go."

I redouble my efforts, kicking him in the shins. He retaliates by knocking me to the ground and pinning me. "Be still," he says, his face inches from mine.

I try to throw him off, but he's too heavy. Leaves crackle under my body, and a branch pokes me in the back. Max's weight is solid on top of me, immovable. One of his hands traps my wrists above my head; the other is still over my mouth. I glare up at him, even though he can't see my face. Aggravated beyond comprehension, I sink my teeth into his hand again, hard enough to break the skin.

He draws in a sharp breath, startled, and I buck, trying in vain to dislodge him. Grimly, he pinions me. "*Stop*, Isabel. Why are you doing this? I don't want to hurt you."

With tremendous effort, I wrench my head free and take a big gulp of air, the smell of pine needles and leaf mulch mingling with the silvery taste of Max's blood. "Too late," I say.

His body tenses on top of mine, ready for a fight. "It's not what you think."

Despite the fact that I'm lying on my back in a pile of leaves, I do my best to sound self-righteous. "That is the lamest thing I've ever heard, Max Adair. Besides, how do you know what I think?"

"I don't care about her." His voice is flat, matter-of-fact.

"Oh, that's nice."

"I didn't mean it that way." He exhales through his nose in frustration. "She's not—I don't know how to explain, Isabel. Damn it, I never meant for you to see her—"

"Obviously," I say. "Let me up."

If my icy tone bothers Max, he doesn't let it show. "No," he says. "Not until you listen to me."

"I've been listening. You haven't said anything worth hearing. Get the fuck off."

"I won't," he says stubbornly, and adjusts his weight, centering his hips on mine. He smells like smoke and sweat—and beneath that, like Max: a faint scent of fir trees and cinnamon that always makes me think of Christmas.

I sigh, all of the fight leaking out of me. "This is really stupid. There are leaves in my hair, and probably bugs too. Are we going to lie here until the sun comes up?"

"If we have to," he says, sounding amused, damn him. "I could think of worse ways to spend an evening."

"This isn't funny, Max."

"I'm not laughing," he says. "Are you?"

I shake my head. Now that I'm not quite so enraged, I see our situation for what it is—we're alone in the woods. Max is lying on top of me. Anything could happen, I realize, here in the dark where nothing seems quite real and the outside world might as well not exist. I struggle to focus on the incident that brought the two of us here in the first place—Max, sitting on his bed with a pretty, red-haired stranger. "Who was that girl?" I say, squirming beneath him in a renewed effort to get free.

"Why do you care? And don't do that, please. I can't think when you do."

"Really," I say, and very deliberately I move beneath him again, rolling my hips. "Who was she, Max?"

His breath comes in a gasp, and his hand grips my wrists so hard, I'll have bruises the next day. "You left me," he says, not bothering to hide the bitterness in his voice. "Remember? You were the one who said we were spending too much time together. So why do you care who's in my room at night?"

I feel a pang of guilt shoot through me—I'd been so furious with Max, so determined to make my point, that I hadn't stopped to think about how my absence might have affected him. Lying there, I realize that I am jealous—and worse. An atavistic, unfamiliar desire trembles in my limbs: to mark Max, claim him as my own. It's as if the wildness of the woods has gotten inside me somehow, riding in my blood, clouding my thoughts. The weight of the dark, the crush of the leaves, the call of frogs, and the far-off fall of branches—Max and I are just another part of it, an indistinguishable thread woven into the fabric of the night. Right and wrong are irrelevant; reason has fallen away.

Emboldened, I wrap my legs around Max's hips, drawing him closer. He resists for a moment, then gives in, shuddering against me. "What are you doing?" he says, dropping his head so that his lips almost brush mine. I can feel the stubble on his cheekbones, the tickle of his hair when it falls forward, into my eyes.

"I don't know," I say. "Who was that girl?"

"Her name is Anna. My family wants me to marry her." With his free hand—the bloody one—he traces the outline of my face in the dark. His fingers pause on my lips. "Go ahead," he whispers. "Do it again. I dare you."

"They want you to *what*?" I say, so surprised that I ignore this challenge completely. Undeterred, his fingers begin exploring the bare skin of my shoulder, where he's pushed my sweater aside.

"You heard me." His lips are warm on my collarbone. "God, you feel good."

A shiver runs through me, and I struggle to focus. "What do you mean? Like an arranged marriage? What are you talking about?"

"Don't worry," Max says, his voice lazy. He's let go of my wrists and is kneeling between my legs, looking down at me. My eyes have adjusted to the dark now, and I can see his face, focused on me with a single-minded intensity that belies his tone. "I'm not going to marry her. It doesn't matter what they want."

"I don't understand," I say, my voice uncertain. I sit up, and he takes my hands, holding them in both of his.

"What do *you* want, Isabel? That's all I need to know." He squeezes my hands. "Why did you come to my house tonight?"

My mouth goes dry. I clear my throat, considering all of the things that I'd planned to say, my carefully rehearsed speech. They seem ridiculous now, childish. "I came to give you this," I say, and, leaning forward, I press my lips to his.

I mean for the kiss to be brief—a statement of sorts, a simple acknowledgment of my intentions—but in the moment before my lips touch his, I see Max's eyes widen. He sits still for a moment, unmoving. And then his mouth opens under mine. One hand rests between my shoulder blades, light as a thought; the other tightens in my hair, demanding.

"Isabel," he says again, his voice hoarse, "what do you want?"

In response, I run my hand under his shirt, raking my nails along his bare skin. He trembles at my touch, and the sting of pine needles, the night noises of the forest, the cool air with its scent of wild things, all of it courses through me like a drug. "You," I whisper, and know it is no more or less than the truth. "I want you, Max."

Despite the dark, I can see him smile. "I want you too," he says. "I always have." And then his mouth closes on mine again, and he bears me down onto the leaves, his hands shaking but sure, my body open to his.

I come to consciousness with the feel of Max's touch still on my skin. In the darkness of my bedroom, I shudder. I can still smell him—smoke and sweat and fir trees—as clearly as if he were next to me. "Isabel," he whispers, once, then again.

Blinking, I sit upright against the pillows. And there he is, standing with one hand wrapped around the foot of my four-poster, saying my name. There he is, less than three feet away, and the look on his face—it is so sad. "Wake up, baby," he says.

I'm still dreaming. That has to be it, right? The alternative is too bizarre to consider. Viciously, I rub my eyes. When I open them again, sure enough, I am alone.

And then I hear Finn scream.

Isabel

I am on my feet before I even intend to move. In the hallway I almost collide with Ryan. Our eyes meet, and then he yields, stepping back so I can go first. I push past, still under the spell of my dream and half-terrified by what I might find—Max, escaping through the window with Finn like a goblin in an evil fairy tale? A stranger, who—not satisfied with lurking on my patio and invading my bedroom—has crept down the hall to steal her away?

Her door swings open, and I brace myself for the worst. But there is Finn, sitting up in bed, alone and unharmed. Her face is pale, and her dark hair is pasted to her face with sweat—but she is here, and that seems like the biggest blessing imaginable.

"What is it?" I say, sitting down next to her as my pounding heart slows. "Did you have a nightmare?"

As soon as I wrap my arms around her, she bursts into tears. "Daddy," is all she says, clinging to me like I am the last life raft in a hurricane-tossed ocean. "Daddy!"

For a disorienting moment I think she is talking to Ryan, who is standing in the doorway, scanning the room for threats, clad only in his boxers. Like me, he must have leapt out of bed and come running when she screamed. But she doesn't spare him a glance, and I know then that she means Max.

"What about Daddy?" I say, doing my best to sound soothing. It isn't all that easy. I tell myself that of course Max wasn't in my room, that I only dreamed about him because of what happened—or didn't happen—with Ryan. However logical this might be, though, it doesn't do much to ease the disconcerting sense that something is amiss—nor does the feel of my child, trembling and sobbing in my arms.

"He was here," Finn says, raising her tearstained face. "Right here, with me. But then bad men chased him away. You have to help him, Mommy. You have to!"

Dread ripples through me, chilling my skin. I glance over Finn's head at Ryan for help and see that his eyes are wide, the pupils dilated with alarm. "What the fuck?" he mouths, and I shake my head, at a loss. Finn doesn't usually have nightmares, not like this. I can't remember the last time she woke up screaming—and aside from earlier tonight, she's never talked about seeing Max in her room. The whole scenario gives me the creeps, and based on Ryan's expression, I'm not the only one.

I rock Finn like I did when she was smaller, rubbing her shoulders through the thin material of the nightgown. "There aren't any bad men here. Ryan and I would never let anyone like that near you. Would we, Ry?"

"Of course not," Ryan says, and I am relieved to hear that his voice sounds reassuring, no hint of the apprehension that was clear on his features just a moment before. "You're safe, sweetheart. Your mom and I are here."

For good measure, he crosses to the window next to Finn's dresser, pushing the curtain aside to gaze out into the rain. It's still pouring, coming down in sheets and blowing sideways with the force of the storm. I can see the big oak at the front of the house bending in the wind, leaf-laden branches scraping the siding.

Finn looks from me to Ryan in desperation. "Not *here*," she says, her gray eyes huge in her white face. "There's no one here but us."

Ryan turns from the window. Kneeling on the floor next to the bed, he peers into her face. "I don't understand. What do you mean, then, baby?"

"The bad men weren't here." Her voice is earnest with conviction. "They were *there*. There, where Daddy is."

Ryan's hand goes to his stomach, rubbing absently along the length of his scar. He's had it as long as I've known him—*Got it in a knife fight freshman year of high school,* he'd told me when I asked—but I've never seen him touch it this way, like some kind of worry stone. "Where, Finn? In your dream?"

She nods, trembling. "There was a fire. Everyone was yelling. There were horses, and guns. Everything was burning. And Daddy—" Biting her lower lip, she burrows deeper into my arms. "They wanted to hurt him," she says in a small voice. "They know who he is now and they won't ever let him go."

"It was just a dream, Finn," I say, taking her hand in mine and wincing at the ice-cold, clammy grip of her fingers. "Maybe you had fire on your mind because of the tree. But nothing's burning here. There are no horses or guns." *And no Daddy, either,* I think.

"Not here," she says again. "There was a house, on fire. And grass, taller than me. It smelled funny—like burnt cookies. Daddy was hiding in the grass. And then he was running, but they came after him. He has to be fast. But I don't think he'll be fast enough."

Struck speechless, I look over her head at Ry, wishing that I'd told him about the dream I had in Barbados. I can't think of a single thing to say, at least nothing that will help. Truly, I'm about five seconds from a meltdown myself.

Ryan must see this on my face, because he gets off his knees and sits down on the bed, careful not to touch me. He opens his arms to Finn, and she crawls from my lap to his, still sniffling. Reaching for her quilt, he wraps it around her. "It's okay," he says, smoothing her hair back from her face. "It's over now."

Finn looks between the two of us again. Her eyes come to rest on my face, and in them I imagine that I see the reflection of a thousand tiny flames. "No," she says with simple finality. "It's not."

Without being asked, Ryan disappears to search the house, returning in time to see me tuck Finn back under the covers, her face washed and her hair freshly braided. He pulls the curtains closed and makes a fuss over checking under the bed and in the closet, the go-to hiding spots for the green, squishy monster Finn used to claim came out after the grown-ups went to sleep. I haven't heard a word about this particular villain in years—not since Ryan cleansed the entire second floor with some sort of do-it-yourself monster spray he read about online—and I don't think she's frightened of it tonight. Still, she giggles as Ry gets down on his stomach and wriggles the top half of his body underneath the bed frame, emerging much the worse for wear. He brushes dust bunnies from his hair and gives her a courtly bow, and she laughs out loud. "You look silly," she says.

"Thanks a lot," Ry replies in mock offense, but as he turns away to peruse her bookshelf, an unmistakable look of gratification marks his features. "*The Penderwicks*?" he suggests, rifling through the shelves. "Shel Silverstein? Septimus Heap?"

She nods at this, and he pulls *Magyk* free. I sit next to her, listening, while Ryan reads one chapter after another about Boy 412 and sassy, independent Princess Jenna. At first Finn offers helpful commentary on the twists and turns of the plot, like a tiny, less critical version of the aliens in *Mystery Science Theater*. After a while, though, she grows quiet, her eyes flickering shut and Raggedy Ann tucked up safe under her chin. Ry reads a few lines more, then glances over at me, one eyebrow raised in inquiry. When I nod, he shuts the book and sets it on her bedside table. Together we creep silently out of the room, closing the door behind us.

"Wow," he says when we've gone a few steps down the hallway. "That was rough, huh?"

"No kidding," I say, looking anywhere but at him. Now that the crisis is over, I am painfully aware that he's wearing next to nothing—which wouldn't usually bother me, but tonight is different. I remember the warmth of his hand in mine, the scent of his skin when I pressed my lips against his palm, and shiver all over again. What is the matter with me?

Ry clears his throat. "Um. We're probably not going back to sleep, right? I'll make coffee."

He sounds as normal as ever, but I still can't bring myself to look at him directly. "Good idea," I say, examining a floorboard crack in dire need of repair. "But maybe you should put on some pants first."

Out of the corner of my eye, I see him glance down at himself, amused. "Oh, that's why you're acting so weird. I came running the second I heard her scream. It could be worse, you know."

At this, my cheeks flame red, and I turn away from him to hide it. "Go get dressed, for God's sake. I'll make the coffee."

Without another word, he complies, arriving downstairs a few minutes later in the shorts and T-shirt he'd worn the night before. We sit around the kitchen table as the sky lightens, an ocean of unspoken words between us. Then Ryan clears his throat again, breaking the silence. "This is a new thing, right? Nightmares like this?"

"It is. But like I told you, she thought Max was here earlier tonight—before lightning hit the tree, when I saw him standing on the patio. And I'll tell you something even weirder—right before she screamed, I was dreaming about him." I will my features to inscrutability, afraid that Ry will somehow be able to divine the nature of the dream from my expression. "He woke me up, actually, saying my name. And I could have sworn I saw him, standing at the foot of the bed."

Ryan's eyes widen. "In the house? Christ, Isabel. You should have said something."

"Like what?" I snap, goaded into irritability. *"Don't worry, Finn. There's no need to worry about your father, because I just saw him in my bedroom?"*

He grips the edge of the table, hard enough that his knuckles whiten. "If there was a man in your room—"

"You searched the house, Ry. And when I came downstairs, I checked all the windows and doors. They were still locked. So he wasn't really here. He couldn't have been." I stare into the depths of my cup, as if it contains tea leaves that will reveal the future rather than rapidly cooling Sumatran blend. "Except," I add quietly, "that he was."

Ryan pushes his chair back and starts pacing, the way he always does when he gets upset. "I don't like this, Isabel. I don't like it at all." He runs a hand through his hair, rumpling it further. "Even if someone was messing with you—pretending to be him on the phone, showing up at your house—it doesn't make any sense."

"No. It doesn't. But Ryan—when I was in Barbados, I had this crazy dream. I thought it was just a stupid nightmare. But now—" I dig my nails into my palms, hard enough to draw blood.

He comes to a halt, bracing his hands on the back of his chair. "Tell me," he says, eyes fixed on mine.

So I do.

Ryan doesn't say a word until I'm done. And then he shakes his head, hard, like a horse trying to rid itself of flies. "What the fuck," he says, and starts pacing again. "It's a coincidence, that's all. It has to be."

"And if it isn't?"

He turns on me and for a moment I see the shadow of the boy he used to be. "It is," he says, his jaw set in a stubborn, defiant line. "What else could it be?"

Taken aback, I say the first thing that comes to mind. "Well, you know what Sherlock Holmes would say. 'When you have eliminated the impossible, whatever remains, however improbable, must be the truth.'" I cradle my mug, letting the remaining warmth seep into my fingers.

This earns me a grudging smile. "Fine, then. Let's eliminate the idea that a criminal mastermind with paranormal powers is channeling your ex-boyfriend and invading your dreams—not to mention Finn's—and take it from there."

"Okay," I say, striving to sound reasonable. "That leaves us with the idea that—however improbably—Max is still alive."

He exhales through his nose, narrowing his eyes at me, and opens his mouth to speak. Anticipating an argument, I stare him down—but he doesn't blink, and in the end, I am the one who looks away. "Isabel, I'm not trying to be cruel," he says. "But I think there's a vast amount of territory between the criminal mastermind theory and the idea that Max is alive. I want that—for you. But I also don't want you to get hurt, any worse than you already have been. And dwelling on something that's not likely to be true—" He breaks off mid-sentence and stalks over to the coffeemaker, refilling his cup. From the way his shoulders tense, I can tell he's doing his best to bite his tongue.

"You don't know it's not true," I say to his back.

He thumps the carafe down onto the counter and spins to face me. "No, but I do know that it's not *likely* to be true. Not after eight years. And the more you get yourself worked up about this, the worse it will be for you—and for Finn."

I've been doing my best to hold myself together, but this pushes me over the edge. "I am not worked up," I say with icy calm.

"No? You called me from another country, completely hysterical. Hell, I've hardly ever seen you cry, Isabel. And that night—you couldn't even talk to me." His voice is heated. "You scared me to fucking death. And ever since then—that goddamn necklace, these crazy dreams . . ." He dumps sugar into his cup and stirs it so viciously that coffee slops over the edge, spilling onto the counter. "I don't know what's going on," he says finally. "All I know is that nothing feels right. And I don't know how to fix it."

"You don't have to!" Despite myself, my voice is rising. "Why do men always feel like it's their job to solve every problem? No one asked you to fix this for me, Ryan. And if you recall, I'm not the one who wanted you to stay here tonight. If you don't want to deal with this—if you don't believe me—then get in your car and go home."

At this, Ryan's face pales. Then color flames in his cheekbones, sudden as a brushfire. He glares at me, eyes bright with anger. "You're really going to throw that in my face—that I wanted to stay in case something went wrong?"

"I—"

"I know you didn't ask me to fix this," he says, each word measured, as if he's fighting the urge to yell. "But I want to, because I care about you and Finn. If that's unacceptable to you, then I think we have a larger problem."

I take a deep breath. Then I look him over. He's leaning against the counter, hands shoved in his pockets, tension clear in every line of his body and his jaw set in anger. But he's still here, and that counts for a lot. He came when I called, he crawled under the bed looking for monsters, he read to Finn until she fell asleep. And none of this, I remind myself, is his fault.

"Also—" he continues in incensed tones, just as I say, "I'm sorry."

Ryan's teeth come together with an audible click, cutting off whatever he was about to say next. "Excuse me. Did you just apologize?"

"I did. You're only trying to help, Ry. And if I were you, I'd probably be saying the exact same things. I can't blame you for that."

Ryan picks up his coffee and comes back to the table. Eyeing me warily, he sinks into his chair. "I don't think I've ever heard you apologize during an argument before."

"Well, don't get used to it. Because it probably won't happen again."

He's grinning at me now, the smile at odds with his disheveled hair and the dark circles under his eyes. "I won't," he drawls, tilting the chair onto its back legs. "But now that we've established that I'm not a total ass, can we talk about this without you biting my head off?"

I nod, rolling my eyes, and he says, "So, then. What are you going to do?"

"Well," I say, "I'm going to see if Dr. Absolom has turned up the rest of that necklace. And I think I might go see Max's parents. Finn's sleeping over there tonight anyway. I might as well feel them out and see if . . . well, if anything strange is going on."

Ryan's eyebrows knit, and the chair bangs down onto the floor. "For the love of God, Isabel, don't tell them you saw Max. If you won't listen to me about anything else, please listen about this."

"I'm not planning on telling them," I say stiffly. "But I can't just do nothing."

The storm has stopped, and the trees outside the kitchen window are still. Light streams through the gap in the curtains, slanting across the old wooden table and striking Ryan's face. I watch as the sun works its alchemy, transforming his hazel eyes into clear, bottle-glass green. "Fair enough," he says, tracing the rim of his cup with one finger.

"And," I add, "I think I might take Finn to see a therapist."

Ryan sits up straight. "You hate shrinks."

"I don't hate them. I just think that they're overrated." I shrug. "But I don't know how to help her, Ry. The way you want to fix things for us—I want that too, for Finn. And maybe someone else can see things more clearly. Maybe they can do what we can't."

He makes a skeptical noise, shifting restlessly in the chair. "I don't know, Isabel."

"It can't hurt," I say, sipping the last of my coffee. I mean it as a joke, but his eyes flash to mine, flat and unreadable in the sunlight. When he speaks, it is without a hint of humor.

"That's what *you* think," he says.

Max

By the time I get back to Sweetwater, it's all I can do to force down some dinner and make polite conversation with Lily, who has somehow gotten wind of my encounter with Edward Thomas and wants to hear all about it.

"Good for you," she pronounces, to my surprise. "He is a terrible man, vicious in the way he treats the slaves, without the slightest fear of retribution. And you went for him right there in the plantation yard. Oh, what I would have given to see it! I'm surprised he didn't call you out on the spot."

My eyes widen. "Call me out? Like—a duel? I don't think there was any need for that. After all, he'd already knocked me unconscious."

She motions for me to turn my head so that she can see the bruising on my temple, clicking her tongue in sympathy. "And when you woke up, Julia was there to tend to you. Oh, it is as if you planned it!"

"What?" I say, confused.

"Well, you did intend to ask for her daughter's hand, yes? And yet it will be some time since she has seen you, with no real evidence as to your character. Why should she give her consent? But to see you come down upon Edward Thomas like an avenging angel—could you hope for a finer demonstration of valor? Why, you were a veritable Sir Galahad!"

"Not really. I just . . . I couldn't stand to watch it, that's all."

She gives me a direct look out of those dark brown eyes. "Do you not understand how extraordinary that is? Or maybe not . . . since you are so recently come from America . . ." Her voice trails off, and she stares down at her lap as if she's said too much.

A suspicion wakes in my mind then. Lily had refused to let Hannah fan her. She'd described Edward Thomas as vicious. Her husband had grieved the loss of her, and then dedicated his life to freedom for America's enslaved.

Lily Adair is an abolitionist.

This is more than I could have hoped for. Maybe, I think with growing excitement, if we go to her with information about the rebellion, she will help us.

Lily's pale throat moves as she swallows. And then she speaks, confirming my suspicion. "There are many who come from overseas—especially from England—who despise how the slaves are used here. Who protest, and write missives home about the deplorable habits of the West Indian planters. When they are first come, they cringe at the screams in the fields and in the yards, and find it incomprehensible that so many of us do not turn a hair, as accustomed as we are to such sounds. They declare it an injustice and an abuse of humanity, and opine that they could never do the same. But then time passes . . . and they don't cringe anymore."

Color heats her cheeks. "It is a sad fact of the human condition that individuals become accustomed to anything after a time. Worse still, given the opportunity to assume a position of power, they will take the whip into their own hands—and soon forget the awkward feel of it, in the rush of power that accompanies such actions."

Her gaze drifts to one of the scenes of plantation life that decorate the walls of the salon. "But I . . ." she says softly, "I have never grown accustomed to the screams, nor the actions that provoke them. I believe that all human life is sacred, and that the color of my skin lends me no special dispensation to use other people so. It is an old argument between the two of us, Robert and I, because as you see, he depends on the slaves to make our living. He discourages me from thinking about such things, from reading the work of such progressive thinkers as Mary Wollstonecraft, who opines that all humanity deserves equal treatment." Closing her eyes, she recites: "*Is one half of the human species, like the poor African slaves, to be subject to prejudices that brutalize them, when principles would be a surer guard, only to sweeten the cup of man?*"

Her eyes open, and she fixes me with an unblinking stare. "I have resolved not to be the 'domestic brute' to which Mrs. Wollstonecraft refers—to refrain from rendering this household my fiefdom, and I the hapless, indolent tyrant. But here I find myself, nonetheless." She knots her hands atop the mound of her stomach, gripping fiercely.

"Were it not for the babe, I would take ship for America and set up house in Charleston or Savannah, rather than continue with the arrangement in which I find myself. For to be party to such horrors is to be complicit in their ultimate commission. And bit by bit, one day after the next, these are the sins that blacken a person's soul."

I make my way to my room that night with Lily's words echoing in my head, which throbs in dull counterpoint to my racing thoughts. My discussion with Julia plays over and over, her shock when I'd told her about the rebellion, her insistence that the past wasn't ours to change.

"Haven't you ever heard of the grandfather paradox?" she'd said impatiently. "You can't go back in time and meet your great-great-great-grandfather, because you'd change the course of history. You might end up not being born."

"My great-great-great-grandfather isn't here," I'd pointed out.

"No," she'd agreed. "He's not. But I can see it in your face—you want to save her, Max. You want to save Lily. And if you do—if you somehow stop the rebellion, and she lives—then Robert will come back, and you'll cease to be."

I'd growled at her that I'd thought of all of this, and turned away to watch the sun sink down over the endless fields of cane, bathing the horizon in a wash of red and orange, setting the world aflame. But she'd put a hand on my arm and uttered the words that sent an icicle straight through my heart: "And if you're not born, Max, what then? Then you'll never meet Isabel, and your child . . . will never exist."

Murderer, I think. *I'd be a murderer.* Except if I know that I might have the power to save Lily and her baby—to save the lives of the slaves—how can I simply stand back and let them die? I am a murderer, no matter what I choose.

Thoughts swarm my head like a hive of bees, and sleep doesn't so much come over me as take me, pulling me inexorably down into its depths. I dream first of a field of cane that stretches to the horizon, of the whisper of the stalks as they sway in the wind. Someone is running away from me, trampling the cane as they go—but all I can see is their back, disappearing as the leaves close around them.

Over the hiss and shuffle of the cane, I hear a child's high, piercing laugh. I run after it, ignoring the leaves slicing at my skin and the hot sun battering down on me, but I can't catch up, and now I'm lost in the middle of the field. Around me, the cane dips and waves. The clear blue eye of the sky peers down at me, indifferent.

I turn in a circle, trying to quash the panic welling up in my chest. Far away, I can smell something burning, sharp and acrid.

And then I see her, standing no more than twenty feet away, framed by the tall stalks of the cane: a small, pale girl in a white nightgown, her hair tumbling nearly to her waist in a mass of black curls. She fixes me with a clear gray gaze, and then her face lights with a huge smile. "Daddy!" she says. "I knew I would find you."

Stunned, I stand there, staring at her. My mouth opens, but I can't say a word.

Her dark brows lower, and her mouth sets in a determined, familiar line. "Don't you recognize me?" she says, taking a step closer. "It's me. Finn."

And suddenly, I know just who she is. She has Isabel's dark curly hair, my mutable gray eyes. I know this is my daughter—but she's not a baby. Not even a toddler.

"How old are you?" I blurt.

She casts her eyes down, as if she understands that the answer will hurt. "I'm almost eight," she says finally. "I'll be eight in October."

"Eight?" I echo in disbelief. "But then—"

"You've been gone a long time. I've been looking and looking for you." A note of pride creeps into her voice. "And now I've found you. Mommy will be so happy."

"Found me? But we're not really here. It's just a dream." I close the distance between us and take her hands in mine. She smells of chocolate and sleepy child, of apples and fresh shampoo. "You're not even real yet," I whisper. "You're a collection of cells. A person in the making."

She shakes her head. "I'm real. You'll see. I'll find a way—I'll bring you home."

Terror seizes me then. "You can't, Finn. It's too dangerous."

Stubbornly, she pulls her hands away. "I can too. I'll save you and Grandma Julia both and you can't stop me."

"Julia?" I say. "How do you know about—"

But before I can finish, the dream shifts, changes. The field is gone, and with it, Finn. I am kneeling in the dirt, sun beating down on my back, facing Isabel. She's looking at the ground, her long dark hair tied back in a messy ponytail.

I call to her over and over, but she doesn't answer. At last I reach out and grab her arm, my fingers pressing into her skin. "Isabel," I say, my voice thick with everything I'm feeling—all the loneliness and confusion of the last few days, my fear that I'll never get home, that I'll make the wrong choice. "Can you hear me?"

This time her head jerks up. "Max?" she says. "Max, is that you?"

"Isabel." I move closer, but it's as if an invisible barrier has sprung up between us. My hand falls away from her arm, and I can't reach her, no matter how hard I try.

"Oh my God, Max. Where—"

She's still speaking, I can see that, but I can't hear a word. The smell of burning is back, closer now. Static hums between us, and above it, the crackle and sputter of leaping flames. They rise for a second, obscuring her face, and I panic. "Isabel! Are you okay?"

She doesn't reply—or if she does, I can't hear her above the roar of the blaze. Then the flames die down, and beyond them I can see the silhouette of a small figure—Finn. She looks at the fire, at me, and then she moves forward. Her nightgown flares in the breeze that's sprung up between us, the flames rise higher, and still she comes, curls flowing free down her back, face set and determined. And I know what she means to do—to cross through the fire, just as she'd promised, and bring me home.

"Finn, no!" I scream, but she doesn't stop. Panic sweeps me. If she sets foot in those flames, she'll burn up; she'll die. In desperation, I turn to Isabel. "Stop her. Keep her safe," I yell, gesturing at Finn. I have some stupid hope that Isabel will be able to grab her, to keep her from walking through the fire. But Isabel doesn't move.

The dream changes again. I stand in the middle of a road, strewn with rum bottles and broken furniture. The smell of alcohol rises, strong in the air. Behind me looms Sweetwater's great house, and before me is a cane field. On its edge stands Isabel.

I beckon to her: *Come on.* Something is wrong here, but I cannot bring myself to care. Isabel will come to me, we will be together, and everything will be all right.

Then I hear it: the thunder of horses' hooves, men's agitated voices. And another sound—the smash of breaking glass, close by. I turn my head and see Cuffee, a rag wrapped around one hand and a flaming torch in the other. He gives me an apologetic shrug and then flings the torch, end over end, into the house through the broken window.

The curtains catch, and Sweetwater goes up in flame. Before I can react, a company of slaves charges out of the cane, setting it on fire behind them. They barrel forward, flowing around me as if I were a rock in the path of a stream, wielding their makeshift weaponry—pitchforks, hoes, shovels, the occasional sword. Through the smoke, I can see Isabel standing in the road, yelling for me to run.

I'll run, all right, I decide—straight for her. But before I can, red-coated soldiers are upon us, wielding muskets and pistols. They fall on the slaves, who shriek and fight back with incredible ferocity.

I don't know how I hear it above the melee, but somehow I do—Finn's scream, piercing and filled with fear, coming from the house. I do the only thing I can think of—I run for the front door and ram my shoulder against it. It gives way, and I drop to my knees and crawl through the smoke, coughing.

"Finn!" I yell, and she screams again.

"Daddy!"

"I'm here, Finn!" Choking on ash, lungs burning, I crawl up the staircase, then down the hall, following the sound of her voice to a bedroom. Lily is huddled in the corner, clutching her belly. At the window stands Julia, watching the chaos in the courtyard. And leaning against her, gray eyes little more than holes in her soot-smeared face, is my daughter.

"Daddy," she says, and reaches for me.

I open my arms, but it is too late—the roof caves in, and all three of them are lost to me in a rush of smoke and flames. I scream and scream, but it makes no difference.

I can't save Finn or Isabel. I can't save Julia or Lily. I can't save me.

I wake panting, soaked in sweat, Finn's cries echoing in my ears. And I know what I have to do.

Isabel

It's seven A.M. when Ryan finally leaves, making me promise to call him if anything else happens. I agree, more to appease him than anything else. As soon as the front door shuts, a fresh mug of coffee in hand, I check my work email for a message from Dr. Absolom. She's written to me, all right, and my heart pounds as I open the message. This is the crew's last day of digging for the week, and I cross my fingers, hoping for news about the necklace—but no, her email just contains a list of queries about our previous finds. I respond, then sort through the rest of my mail—a departmental meeting memo, a request for a letter of recommendation from a student, a list of archaeological job opportunities across the country.

Browsing idly through the latter, my eyebrows furrow, thinking about Ryan's offer from Marvel. It's an incredible opportunity, one that I'd hate to think he'd turn down for Finn's sake. Even though the decision is his, how could he not come to resent us, in time?

The phone rings as I'm pondering this, providing a welcome distraction. It's my dad, and, gritting my teeth, I give him an edited version of last night's events. When I finish talking, my dad sighs. "Don't get mad at me, Isabel, please, but would you maybe consider seeing someone? A therapist, I mean, to work through all of this."

Despite my annoyance, this makes me laugh. "Funny you should say that. To answer your question—no, I don't think I need one, although I appreciate the suggestion. But I'm worried about Finn. And actually, I told Ry this morning that I was thinking about taking her to a psychologist, just to talk. She's having a hard time at camp. I think she's lonely. And that nightmare—it's not like her."

"Well," my father says cautiously, "if you're serious about this, I have a referral for you. You know my friend Jack, the one I play golf with? His granddaughter's got some stuff going on, and he speaks very highly of her therapist—says he's seen real progress in the little girl. So I asked him for the name."

I want to ask when he was planning on mentioning this, but decide it's not worth it. Instead I reach for a notepad and pen. "Okay," I say. "Tell me who it is."

Finn doesn't wake up until ten o'clock, too late for camp, so we decide to play hooky at Folly Beach, where Max's parents have a house. He and I used to spend weekend nights there, stealing his dad's beer and sneaking onto the beach for midnight swims. It makes me happy to imagine Max seeing his daughter here, splashing in the waves, sprawled on a beach towel, wearing heart-shaped sunglasses, looking for all the world like a tiny movie star.

Thrilled by the prospect of this adventure, Finn helps me make PB&Js for lunch with such enthusiasm that the sandwiches ooze raspberry jam in a manner evocative of small, slaughtered creatures. By the time she's finished, there's a blob of jam on her chin and several more on the counter, smeared into sticky patches. My lips twitching with the effort not to smile—she's so proud of her handiwork—I hand her a damp towel and send her off with instructions to look in the mirror. Then I tuck the squishy sandwiches into Ziploc bags, cut up some strawberries, and declare our picnic complete.

We have a great time—Finn spots a pod of dolphins swimming just offshore, I find a huge starfish that's washed up on the beach, and, after our requisite trip to the Morris Island lighthouse, we wind up at Dolce Banana, where I let her load up her frozen yogurt with as many toppings as she wants. She piles on Nutella and cookie dough, then adds M&M's, cheesecake, and Oreos. In the end, it takes two hands to carry her concoction to the table, and she gets a massive sugar rush, babbling nonstop most of the way home before passing out cold. I have to wake her when we pull up in front of our house, then shoo her into the shower and pack a bag for her overnight with the Adairs.

Finn stays with them every other weekend, and usually our exchange is little more than a handoff, with a few pleasantries exchanged for good measure. Jennifer and Thomas are unfailingly polite to me, and I to them, but it's been many years since we've discussed anything of substance. Tonight is no exception. At six P.M. precisely—the Adairs equate lateness with poor manners, surely an indication of how my child and I have gone to the devil—I pull up in the curving driveway of the old white house, bracketed by its stands of azaleas and camellias. Jennifer is already waiting on the wide porch, holding her habitual evening glass of Chardonnay, and I can't help but wonder if I'm late, after all, and her presence outside is meant to convey subtle irritation at my rudeness. When I check the time on my phone, though, sure enough, it's exactly six P.M. *Get a grip, Griffin*, I tell myself, and paste a smile on my face as I get out of the car.

The Adairs' chocolate Lab, Blair, almost knocks Finn over with the force of his greeting. Grabbing her overnight bag, I carry it up onto the porch and set it down on the weathered gray boards. "Hi, Jennifer," I say, as Finn extricates herself from Blair long enough to hug her grandmother.

She waves at me in greeting, but her attention is on Finn. "Hello, sweetheart," she says, kissing the top of my daughter's head. "Pop's out back, grilling shrimp skewers, if you want to go see him. He's got a special treat for you."

I eye her, regal as ever in her pale pink shell and tan slacks. Her hair, dyed a tasteful chestnut, is twisted up in some impossibly complicated hairdo, and her makeup is perfect—subtle enough that you have to look closely to be sure that it's there. As always, I feel ill put-together next to her, as if I've committed some cardinal faux pas. *I should have worn a skirt,* I think, glancing at my capris. *And given myself a pedicure.*

As quickly as the thought comes, I dismiss it. How is it that, without saying a word, Jennifer Adair has made me feel inferior? Worse yet, how have I let her? I'm not a sixteen-year-old San Diego transplant anymore, with no knowledge of the intricacies of Southern culture and a propensity for blunt honesty regardless of the circumstances. Watching Finn roll around on the porch with Blair, giggling as the big dog does his best to sit in her lap, I draw myself up straight.

"You look great, Jennifer. That's a good color on you," I say, nodding at her shirt. Inane as the comment might be, it's the best I can manage.

"Thank you," she says, accepting the compliment as her due. "By the way, I've been meaning to tell you—I met the most wonderful hairdresser the other day. Mine was sick, and, well, I was a bit concerned—but Stephan worked wonders with me. I'm sure you'd love him. All of those beautiful curls . . . he could make you look just darling."

Annoyance bubbles in me, and I can't help but take the bait. "That's so kind of you," I say, eyeing her impeccable dye job, "but I'm letting it grow out. Trying out the natural look, you know?"

She shoots me a sharp glance out of her pale blue eyes. Leaning back against one of the white columns flanking the porch, I give her an innocent smile—*who, me?* And then I sigh, disgusted with both of us. How can we have an honest conversation about Max if we can't even manage basic civility? "I appreciate the offer," I say, trying again. "Really, I do. Maybe you can write his name down for me."

"Of course," she says, regarding me frostily, and turns her eyes to the tumbling mass of Lab and child at her feet. "Finn, dear, don't let Blair do that. You're all over fur."

I bend down, extracting Finn from underneath eighty pounds of overeager dog, and brush her off. "There. Good as new. Here's your bag, lovey."

"Bye, Mama," she says, throwing her arms around me. "See you tomorrow."

Shower or no shower, she still smells faintly of the ocean and sunscreen, with a hint of Nutella. I hold her close, and then make myself let go.

Between worrying about Finn and half-expecting Max to appear every time I doze off, I don't rest well. By the time ten A.M. rolls around—our designated pick-up time—I am more than ready.

On my way over the bridge, I steel myself to speak with Jennifer, although I have no idea how I'm going to broach the subject. I grip the wheel harder and cringe, imagining the unpleasant conversation that's bound to ensue. Maybe Ry is right, I think, pulling into the driveway. Maybe I shouldn't say anything. But how can I not?

Back straight, I march up to the front door and ring the bell. Jennifer answers, looking just as put together as yesterday—this time in a navy blue scoop-neck blouse and pearl earrings. "Finn's out back," she says, holding the door open. "I'll get her."

Standing in the front hallway, with its burnished wood floors and high ceilings, its crystal chandelier and oil painting of the dunes at Folly Beach, I gather my courage. "No," I say. "Don't. I wanted to ask you something—about Max."

"So," Jennifer says, "ask away."

Finn's playing in the backyard, and we're sitting in the living room—what Jennifer calls the front parlor—with glasses of sweet tea, which is, naturally, homemade. I've always found this room intimidating; the majority of the furniture is antique, owned by generations of Adairs, and what isn't an heirloom is absurdly expensive and uncomfortable, from the eighteenth-century French carved Louis XV sofa to the stiff-backed, pink-and-white damask armchairs. A baby grand piano dominates one corner—Max took lessons for years, and they used to trot him out at parties to entertain the guests. When his parents weren't home, we used to come in here and he'd play for me—ironic, pissed-off, faux rock-god interpretations of songs by the Violent Femmes and the Dead Kennedys that would've driven his mother right over the edge if she'd heard.

"Well," I say, trying not to think about how horribly this conversation could end, "this is awkward. And I'm afraid I'm going to sound crazy, but—" I pause and then blurt out my question. "I have to ask—you haven't heard from Max at all, have you?"

The color drains from her face, and she sets the tea down on a coaster, ice rattling in her glass. "Why would you ask that?"

I reach up, running my fingers over the rough surface of my turquoise pendant. Max had given it to me on my seventeenth birthday—*for strength and protection*, he'd said, fastening the clasp around my neck. His hands had been shaking, making him uncharacteristically clumsy, and in the end I'd batted him away and put the necklace on myself. *Do you like it?* he'd said, doing his best to sound offhand, as if it didn't really matter—but when I'd nodded, his face had lit like the sun. *Good. Because it looks beautiful on you. You'll wear it, Isabel? Say you will.*

I try to fix that image in my mind so that I won't see Jennifer, blanched to the lips, eyeing me accusingly. But then she speaks, and I can't pretend anymore. "Well?" she says sharply. "What would make you say such a thing?"

"I—"

"Is it some kind of joke?"

"No! Oh, God." I'm not the least bit thirsty, but, in urgent need of a diversion, I reach out for my iced tea and take a sip. It's too sweet, the way Jennifer's tea always is.

"You *what*?" Her voice is steely. "Out with it, Isabel. You must have had a reason for saying such a thing. Tell me what it is. Have *you* heard from him?" She's trying to hide it, but I can hear the note of pleading that's crept into her voice. Ryan's right. What could I have been thinking, giving her false hope like this?

"Um," I say. "Well, I—sort of. Maybe. I don't know how to explain."

"What are you talking about?" She leans forward, urgency clear in every line of her body.

And I tell her everything.

By the time I finish, Jennifer's face is bone-white. Her lips part, but she says nothing. Watching her, I think again that Ryan was right—that I've been insensitive and cruel, and a fool, besides. "I shouldn't have said anything," I say hurriedly, in an effort to forestall out-and-out warfare. "It was a mistake. Obviously. I'll just go get Finn, and then the two of us will be out of your hair."

Her mouth closes, then opens again. She reaches a hand toward me, catching at my sleeve. And then she throws her arms around me and bursts into tears.

I sit there, as stunned as if she had bitten me. In all the years that I've known Jennifer Adair, I don't ever recall her touching me voluntarily. Now here she is with her arms around my neck, sobbing into my shoulder. At a loss for what to do, I lift one hand cautiously and pat her back. She feels surprisingly fragile, her bones pressing against the material of the scoop-neck shirt.

"I didn't mean to . . ." I say, wishing I could rewind the last few minutes. I can't imagine that Jennifer will ever forgive me for having seen her like this—which means that I can kiss whatever goodwill existed between us goodbye. *Oh well*, I think, patting her back as if she were Finn, *it's not as if she ever liked me anyway.*

At last she pulls away from me, eyes still streaming. Reaching into my purse, I fumble around until I find a tissue. It's crumpled and stained with lipstick at the edges, but for once she doesn't utter a word of criticism. Instead she wipes her face and then blows her nose. "Thank you," she says, without a hint of her usual haughtiness.

"You're welcome," I say, setting my purse back down on the floor. "Jennifer, if I said something—"

"If you said something!" she says, and gives a brittle sort of laugh. "I thought I was going crazy. That I was losing my mind."

"What are you talking about?"

"Last night—" Her eyes dart away from me, focusing on the polished wood floor. There's a knot in the pine by her feet, and she stares at it fixedly, as if she can smooth it out by force of will. "I put Finn to bed in Max's old room, the way I always do. We read her a story. *Emily of New Moon*—it used to be one of my favorites. And then we stayed up a while longer—Thomas was on the computer, and I was watching *Downton Abbey*."

Of course you were, I think unkindly, *because your greatest ambition is to be a member of the Crawley family.* But then I look at her—really take her in, with her rumpled hair and smudged makeup, the end of her nose gone pink from crying, the way Finn's always does—and make a tremendous effort to curb my cynicism. "Okay," I say in what I hope is an encouraging manner. "And then? Did something happen to Finn?"

Her gaze flits over my face. "Not to Finn," she says uneasily. "No. But I—I went to check on her, like I always do. To make sure she was okay. And when I came down the upstairs hall, toward her room—I could swear I heard voices. Hers, but a man's too." She's got the tissue in both of her hands now, rending it to bits. Drifts of white paper dust her lap, but she doesn't seem to notice. "I thought that maybe you'd let her bring her iPad. But when I got closer, I realized—I recognized the other voice." She's speaking more and more quietly, so that I need to lean forward to hear. "It was Max," she says, almost to herself. "I know it was."

I've always thought that having your heart leap into your throat was a figure of speech—and an anatomically inaccurate one at that. When Jennifer says this, though, I can barely swallow around my pulse, beating fast and irregular in the hollow beneath my turquoise pendant. "What was he saying?" I ask, the words tumbling over each other in my haste to get them out. "Did you see him?"

She shakes her head. "I couldn't make out the words. At first, I just felt—frozen. I couldn't move a muscle, just stood there under that awful portrait of Robert Adair, listening. And then I heard him again, and I ran down the hall as quickly as I could. But when I opened the door—" Her voice catches, and she dabs at her face with the remains of the tissue. "He wasn't there," she says, and her eyes meet mine as if daring me to contradict her. "Finn was alone."

I sit back in my chair, gripping the arms hard enough so that the tips of my fingers go numb. "Was she awake?"

"Oh, yes. Sitting right up in bed looking at me." Carefully, she draws a fingertip underneath her eyes, wiping away her smeared mascara. "She said *Hi, Grandma,* as sweet as you please. And when I asked her who she'd been talking to, she said . . . she said . . ." Tears well up in her eyes again, slipping down her cheeks, and she blots them away fiercely. "She said, *I was talking to my daddy.*"

"Oh," I say faintly, and then, louder, "She did?"

Jennifer folds her hands in her lap. "I . . . I was so shocked. I asked her how that could be. And she said, *He was right here.* She patted the bed next to her, and then she smiled at me, like that was the most natural thing in the world to say." She gulps, holding back the tears. "But Isabel, no one was there. Not on the bed, and not anywhere else, either. The room was empty—I even checked in the closet and under the bed. And the windows . . . they were locked from the inside, too high for her to reach. I always make sure of that, even when it's a lovely night. With her, I'm not taking any chances."

"I appreciate that," I say. "More than you can imagine."

An odd look passes over her face then. "Do you know, I think that may be the nicest thing you've said to me. It's certainly the most sincere."

Before I can think of an appropriate way to respond to this, she presses on. "Standing there, I got the most peculiar feeling. Chills, all down my spine. And—I'm embarrassed to say this, but it's the truth—I ran downstairs and left her there. I went and found Thomas in his study, and I told him all about it, but he . . . he . . . ."

"Let me guess," I say dryly. "He didn't believe you."

"Not for one moment. He said I was hysterical. That she must have been dreaming. And when he went up to check on her himself, she was fast asleep, tucked up under the covers. He wouldn't say one more word to me about it after that, just sat back down at his computer and poured himself a drink." The last few words are laden with scorn—the most emotion I've ever seen her show where Thomas is concerned. "I don't care what he says, Isabel. I know what I heard."

"I believe you," I say, and watch the look of defiance on her face fade into something else—surprise, and then relief. "I believe you, Jennifer. I do."

"Well, then," she says, with her usual decorum, crossing her legs at the ankle and lifting her chin, "then I believe you too." And for the first time since I've met Jennifer Adair, we share a moment of perfect understanding.

"Wow," I say, relinquishing my grip on the chair. "For the past week, Ryan and my dad—they've pretty much said I was insane. Sorry to be rude, but—well, you're the last person I would have expected to be on my side."

At this, she gives a haughty sniff. "Let's put our cards on the table, shall we?"

Warily, I shrug. "Sure."

"I know you don't like me. You never have." She pats her hair, restoring her chignon to its former impeccable state. "You think I'm petty and overly concerned with appearances. That Thomas and I had unreasonable expectations where Max was concerned, and we should have let him make his own choices rather than trying to foist our own upon him. The only reason you let Finn have as much to do with us as you do is because you think it's what Max would have wanted. Does that sound about right?"

I've always found Max's mother to be fairly predictable. In the past ten minutes, though, she's surprised me more than she has in the past fourteen years. "It does," I say, meeting her eyes. "But in the interest of honesty—you've never liked me, either. You tried to set Max up with another girl, for God's sake. You've never said one kind thing to me. Every time you see me, you find some way to insult me. Yesterday it was my hair, and before that it was leaving my daughter behind to go to Barbados—never mind that I was working, not gallivanting off on a tropical vacation. Sometimes I think you secretly believe that I did Max in myself and have just been lying about it all these years."

This last emerges thick with derision, and Jennifer winces in response. I press my fingers against my lips, trying to keep myself from alienating her completely. *She's Finn's grandmother,* I tell myself. *Max's mom. Try to hold your tongue.* But the dam has broken, and I forge ahead. "I guess I just want to know—what did I ever do to make you hate me so much? All I ever did was love him, Jennifer. I loved him and I lost him too. I know you hate that Finn's illegitimate—but at least you have a granddaughter. At least you have something left of him."

Her lips tremble, and I know I ought to stop—but it's too late. I've waited a long time to say these things to her, and now that I've begun, there's no turning back. "I can't help that I'm not from some fancy old Charleston family, or that I have to work long hours sometimes, or that my mother wasn't part of the Junior League before she walked off the earth. And actually I don't think I've done such an awful job, raising your granddaughter on my own. But it doesn't matter what I do, does it? You hated me from the moment you saw me. And I was just a kid."

She slides to the edge of the sofa, twisting her wedding band so that the diamond sparks in the sunlight. It's an oddly familiar gesture, and after a moment I realize when I've seen her do it before—in the weeks after Max disappeared, giving a statement to the police, sitting in my dad's living room asking me to tell her, once again, what happened that afternoon in the woods. "Is that what you think?" she asks. "That I hate you?"

It's the most straightforward thing she's ever said to me, and I reply in kind. "What else am I supposed to think?"

A sad smile lifts her lips, and she shakes her head. "Oh, Isabel. I never hated you." She twists her ring again, looking down at her hands. And then she looks up, eyes meeting mine. Her gaze is direct, all pretensions gone, and for a moment I see Max looking back at me. "I was frightened," she says simply. "And I was jealous."

"Jealous? Of me? What are you talking about?" My voice cracks.

"Not of you, necessarily. Of the choices you and Max made. Of your relationship with each other." The sunlight sparks off her ring again, but this time she doesn't touch it. Instead she stares down at the stone—*the largest rock this side of Colorado*, Max used to call it. "You have to understand, Isabel—my parents had expectations for me, the way we did for Max. I went to college, sure, but that was mainly for what we used to call my MRS degree. After I graduated, I knew I'd marry a rich man. I'd serve on charity committees, and volunteer, and make our house look beautiful—just like my mother did. He'd work, and I'd raise our children—or child, as it turns out." Her mouth twists.

"When I met Thomas, it seemed like the natural order of things. He was a lawyer; his family had been here since the early 1800s; he would inherit this house. I could see our life stretching out in front of us, just like I'd always imagined." Her gaze is distant, dreamy. "Only," she says at last, refocusing on my face, "it turns out I didn't have that much imagination, after all."

She pauses to take a sip of her tea. Outside, I can hear the rumble of a mower, and above it, Finn's carefree laugh. Jennifer cocks her head, listening—and then she turns back to me. "You see, I never thought about what I wanted. Just what I was supposed to do. My parents had lost most of their money by the time I was a teenager. My father made some bad investments, and—well, it's ancient history now. But I knew good and well that my family name was all I had to trade on. That, and my innate charm," she says with an ironic smile. "I went into my marriage with Thomas victorious—a lot of girls wanted him, but I'd won. I didn't understand until later that in no small part, I'd married him out of obligation."

"But you love him," I say, my mouth dry. "Don't you?"

She lifts one shoulder in a graceful shrug. "I do, but not the way Max felt about you—enough to go against his family, to say that he wanted you more than everything that Thomas and I had built for him. Everything I'd sacrificed so that he could have." She glances around the room, her gaze lighting on the antique credenza and grandfather clock, the Oriental rug and damask-covered chair where I sit. "First it was you—and then it was that gardening business. Thomas wanted to make him a partner in the firm, but what did he want to do? He wanted to dig in the dirt."

"He liked to make things grow. To make the world a more beautiful place."

She waves a hand, dismissing this. "We kept thinking that he'd change his mind, that he'd want to intern at the law firm in the summer. But all he ever did was work at that greenhouse and come home covered in mud. I couldn't understand it, and Thomas was furious."

Her eyes flick toward the backyard, and she twirls her wedding ring again. "Back then, I stood by Thomas, the way I'd always done. But after we lost Max, I had so much time to think. And I realized I'd been a fool. What did Thomas know about compromises, or seeing the world from someone else's point of view? And what did I know about making choices that mattered, deep down in your heart?" Disgust weights her voice. "But you—you knew from the time I met you what you wanted to do with your life. You made Max wait when you went to school, to get your degree."

"I never made him do anything!" I say, nettled. "He could have come with me, if he wanted. He chose to stay here."

"But that's just it, don't you see?" She traces the outline of her glass with one manicured finger, blurring the drops of condensation.

"You're strong, Isabel, in a way I've never been. After your mother—after whatever happened to her—you weren't the one who fell apart. I felt sorry for you, at first. I wanted Max to show you around, to help you make friends. I thought I could guide you, help you, since Julia was gone, and your father had . . . well, bless his heart."

She lifts one eyebrow in a gesture that is Max to the life, and I realize that she'd seen the inner workings of my adolescent household far more clearly than she'd ever let on. "But you didn't want any part of it, or of me, either. You took care of yourself, and then you set your sights on my son. I saw the way you looked at him, and I figured it wouldn't matter, as long as he wasn't looking back. But then one day I understood—he'd been looking back all along, and I was the one who'd been blind."

Aggravated, I get to my feet. "You make me sound like some kind of predator. And what do you mean, I didn't want any part of you? You just kept bringing us casseroles. And telling me that my clothes were all wrong. The one time I took you up on an invitation to the country club—I've never been so humiliated in my life. All those forks—how was I supposed to know which one to use? You did it on purpose, just so Max could see how unsuitable I was."

"The country club—I may have," she admits, dipping her head in concession. "But the rest of it—it was genuine, Isabel. I wasn't trying to be critical, at least not in the beginning. But you just looked at me like I was something on the bottom of your shoe."

At this, I start to laugh—and once I start, I can't seem to stop. Jennifer eyes me austerely, sipping her tea, until I get myself back under control and sink into my chair. Finally I say, "Are you saying—what, that I hurt your feelings? That we got off on the wrong foot because you thought *I* rejected *you*?"

She tilts her head ever so slightly in affirmation. "After Finn was born," she says, "you stayed in school, you got that job teaching at the college, just the way you'd planned."

"What else could I have done?" It's a genuine question, but she doesn't reply—and as I sit there, looking at her, I know why. "Oh," I say, realization dawning. "You thought that I'd come to you for money. That I'd ask you to support the two of us."

She doesn't say a word, but from the expression on her face—recognition, laced with what I could swear is shame—I know that I am right. "Really, Jennifer?" I say, enunciating each syllable. "After the way you treated me, I wouldn't have asked you and Thomas to put out the flames if I was on fire—much less beg at your doorstep."

Her head snaps back, as if I've hit her. "Oh," she says in a small voice. "Oh, dear."

We sit in silence for a moment. "You did say that we should put our cards on the table," I say finally. "I'm sorry if that was too honest."

Jennifer doesn't say a word. Instead, she looks down her nose at me the way that Max used to do when he was trying to affect an air of superiority—his default defense mechanism. Then she straightens up, setting down her glass, and folds her hands in her lap. Her eyes fix on my face. "I don't suppose honesty has ever been your problem," she says. "But it's certainly been mine. I never disliked you, Isabel. And now—now I need to tell you a story."

Max

"I don't like it," Julia says when I tell her my plan. We're sitting on the veranda of Simmons's great house, ostensibly engaged in a game of backgammon, but neither of us is concentrating on the board.

I sigh. "Well, me neither. Do you have a better idea? I'm open to suggestions."

"No," she admits. "But Max—it's so dangerous. You could be killed. And how, exactly, do you plan to put a stop to an entire rebellion? These people don't know you."

"I know they don't. That's where you come in," I tell her, rolling the dice and sliding my checkers accordingly. "You've been here for a year already, and people do know *you*. They trust you. Maybe you can get them to listen."

Julia raises her chin. "I'll help you, if you've made up your mind." With great precision, she airlifts my checker into purgatory, placing it on the bar that divides the board. "What do you need me to do?"

"There's a woman here," I say, lowering my voice. "Nanny Grigg. She works in the house. If I remember correctly, she was—will be—instrumental in organizing the rebellion. I need to talk with her."

Julia nods. "Come to dinner tonight. Afterward, look for Jackey—

the head driver. He knows I'm sympathetic—if I ask, he'll take you to her. Your move."

I roll a six, bringing my checker back into play. To anyone who happened to glance out of the French doors, we're just two people playing backgammon—not time travelers hatching what is likely a doomed plot. But both of us know better.

That night, we sit down to a huge meal of Thanksgiving-esque proportions, presided over by John Simmons and his round-faced, snub-featured wife, the unfortunately-named Mehitabell. The table is covered with several stuffed roast chickens, yams mashed with sugar and butter, roasted plantains, fried okra, and even a small suckling pig, which eyes me reproachfully from its silver platter.

Disentangling myself after dinner with some difficulty, I make my way through the grounds to Simmons's slave village, lit from afar by the glow of small bonfires. As Julia promised, a man is waiting for me at the edge of the village. He's thin but tightly muscled, a knife strapped to his belt. There's a scar high up on his right cheek, and though I can't see it well enough to tell for sure, it looks deliberate—as if someone cut him on purpose, carving a pattern into his dark skin.

"How can I be of help to you, sir?" he says in a deep, formal voice.

"I'm Max Adair. You're Jackey, right?" I say, just to be certain. It would be a hell of a mess if I'd gotten the wrong guy, despite Julia's explicit instructions.

He nods, eyeing me suspiciously, and turns on his heel without another word, gesturing for me to follow. So I do.

The houses here are similar to the ones at Sweetwater—mostly constructed of rough boards, with thatched roofs that come down low over the front door. Rude windows are cut in the exteriors, without shutters or curtains to prevent the flies and mosquitos from getting in. Here and there throughout the village there are nicer houses, made of tumbled stone, and this is where Jackey takes me.

"Wait here," he says, and leaves me standing outside his door.

I stand still, looking around. Everywhere there are people—women clustered at fire pits, children running and shouting, men sitting on their haunches, playing some kind of game involving a board and greenish seeds. The slaves seem different here—their voices louder, their backs straighter.

In the fading light, I can see a family sitting near one of the fires, having dinner. The eldest, a voluptuous, fifty-ish woman, squats in front of an iron pot, the fabric of her white dress stretched across her broad thighs. Smoke rises from the pot, thick and aromatic, bearing with it the mingled scents of yams, fish, and roasted corn. Pursing her lips, she dips an earthenware ladle and tastes the contents, then reaches between her feet and scoops up a twist of fabric. Carefully, she opens the cloth and tilts it over the pot, stirs and tastes again, and then nods with satisfaction.

The small boy next to her tugs at her dress. "Is it done, Nanny?"

Smiling, she raises one of her hands and rests it on his head. "You be patient, Charles. Everything worth doing takes time, and this stew's no different. Eat, and then I'll tell you a story." Her voice travels across the space between us, clear and resonant, and I see families grouped around the other fires look up in anticipation.

"Tonight a storytellin' night, Nanny G.?" one man calls in response. I can't see his face—just his short, powerful build, visible in the span of his shoulders and the air of authority with which he carries himself, even crouched in the dirt.

Nanny G., I think, my heart speeding up. *Nanny Grigg?*

The woman turns in the direction of his voice, grinning. "I don't know, John. Tonight a fiddle-playing night?"

He rocks back on his heels and takes a swig from a gourd with a hole punched in the top—a makeshift flask. "Anythin' for you," he says, and, pouring a bit of liquid into his cupped hand, flings it onto the fire. The flames flare brightly in response, the little girl sitting next to him jumps in surprise, and John throws his head back and laughs.

As I watch, Nanny Grigg ladles stew into hollowed-out calabashes and passes it to the children and adults squatting around the fire. She must feel my gaze resting on her, because she turns her head and her eyes meet mine, sparks from the fire reflected in their depths. Her face is expressionless, but I can tell from the way she stiffens that my presence here disturbs her. She opens her mouth to speak—and then Jackey materializes from the shadows behind her, one hand coming down firmly on her shoulder. He bends to whisper in her ear and she straightens, tilting her head in John's direction. Immediately, he rises as well, and the three of them come toward me, moving with purpose.

Jackey jerks his head, motioning to the doorway of the hut. "Come," he says, and pushes the door wide.

Inside, the hut is dark and close. He moves quickly about, lighting candles, illuminating a space no larger than a few hundred square feet. The floor is packed earth, and although there is furniture, it is sparse—a table and four chairs, a battered wooden dresser and a simple bed, just a rough mattress and blanket. There's a chipped mirror on the dresser, and brightly colored paintings on the walls. As head driver, Jackey's home is likely nicer than most—still, it verges on destitution.

Nanny Grigg pulls the door shut behind the four of us. "Who are you?" she says without preamble.

"Max Adair." Idiotically, I stick out my hand for her to shake. She peers at it as disdainfully as if I have offered her a dead fish. And then her eyes flick to my face.

"Max Adair," she says. "You the man who spoke for Cuffee, then?"

"I am," I say, and turn my head so that the candlelight falls full on my bruised temple. "And you are?"

"I am Nanny Grigg," she says, folding her arms across her chest. "This is John, a ranger here." She gestures to the other man. "Now that our introductions are over—what you want with us?"

The three of them regard me, their eyes inscrutable in the light of the leaping flames. Heart pounding, I speak. "I know about the rebellion—all about it. I know that the two of you are leaders"—

I motion to Nanny Grigg and Jackey—"and about Bussa and Joseph Franklyn, how you plan for him to govern if the rebellion succeeds. I know you've been mobilizing slaves everywhere, making them believe that the Registry Bill is really a declaration of emancipation, blocked in the House of Assembly by the planters. I know you want the slaves to rise up and fight. In theory, it's noble and it's brave. But it will fail. And almost all of you will die. You can't let that happen. You have to stop it."

My speech is greeted with silence, broken only by the whine of a mosquito. I look from one of them to the other and find them frozen, Jackey with his hand on the back of a chair, John leaning against the wall, and Nanny Grigg, arms folded across her chest. Finally she comes to life, slapping the mosquito away. "How do you know this?"

"I can't say. But I'm not on their side. I'm on yours."

"Hmmm," she says. "You on our side, Max Adair? But you tell us not to fight? Forgive me, sir, if this seems like peculiar advice."

"It's because I'm on your side that I don't want you to fight! Because I know what will happen to you. If I thought there was the slightest chance of success—but there isn't. And they'll just win all over again."

Nanny Grigg eyes me. When she speaks, her voice is hard. "You say you know what will happen. But I tell you that no one but God knows that. What say you, Max Adair? You the next comin' of Great Master himself, arrived on this earth to deliver us from misery?" Her tone drips with sarcasm. "Or an obeah man, wrapped in a white man's skin? You must be something, must you not, to divine what the future holds."

"Nanny G.," Jackey says in warning, but she turns on him.

"Don't you tell me not to speak my mind, Jackey. Don't you dare. If I can't speak it here—then ain't no place for me." She fixes me with a glare. "What you have to say for yourself, then?"

I open my mouth with no idea how I plan to respond, but John beats me to it. "Well," he says, "there's something strange about this man, that much be true. Ophran over at Sweetwater, he's working the fields, cuttin' cane, and sudden as you please, there's Master Max, standing right in the middle of noplace, wearing the oddest clothes he ever did see. It gave him the all-overs, he told me." He cuts his eyes in my direction, and I see the stark traces of fear on his face. "'Cause when a man tramping through the cane, you can't help but hear him coming your way. But ain't no sound, Ophran say. Just Master Max, standin' there starin'."

Nanny Grigg makes an impatient noise at this. "What you think happened, John? He dropped straight out the sky? Maybe he ain't a man, after all, or the Lord Jesus, neither. Maybe he's a bird, you ever think of that?" She snorts with amusement. "That the answer, Master Max?" The last two words are laden with irony. "You a pelican, or a gull? Or just a man?"

"I'm a man," I say. "But Ophran wasn't wrong."

The air in Jackey's hut has been still, almost fetid. But now a breeze sweeps through the room, making the candle flames dance wildly. Jackey takes a step back, one hand going to the knife that's still in his belt. "What you mean?" he says, voice hoarse.

Nanny G. slams her hand down on the table. "Don't be a fool, Jackey! You too, John. Superstitious nonsense, is what I say." But her eyes dart between the three of us, and for the first time I see a hint of doubt on her face. "Leave us," she says to them.

"With him? So he can do you a bit of no good? I won't. 'Sides, this my house." Jackey's jaw sets in a stubborn line, and he glares at me as if daring me to defy him.

She laughs the light, easy laugh of a much younger woman. "You think he gonna have his way with me, with the lot of you right outside, and me three times his age? Or what? Spirit me up into the sky and fly me away?" She shakes her head. "You go on. By the time you finish eatin', this man and I be done, and he on his way. Ain't that right, sir?"

"I won't hurt her," I say to the two men. "You can trust me."

At this, Jackey gives a short laugh. "I may be a lot a things," he says. "But one thing I ain't is stupid." Then the two of them move past me, out into the yard, and the door slams shut behind them.

Nanny Grigg points to one of the chairs. "Sit," she suggests, but I pull the chair out for her instead and stand, waiting. She eyes me, incredulous, and laughs again.

"Well, that's a first," she says, sliding into the seat. "I thank you."

I sit down opposite her, resting my elbows on the scratched surface of the table. "I wasn't lying. The rebellion will fail. I know what you've been told. What you believe—that the king's soldiers will come to your rescue, that they'll join you against the militia—it isn't true." I close my eyes, calling up the names of the fallen rebels. "Bussa will die in battle. Franklyn, Jackey—they'll be tried and executed. Johnny Cooper will be hanged. Do you want me to go on?"

Between us, the candle flame leaps and gutters. I can hear the steady call of a drum outside, joining a fiddler and a singer, and then the stomp of feet. Across from me, her eyes widen. "What are you?" she whispers.

"A friend."

"Ain't no white man a friend of mine."

"A seer, then. Call me whatever you want. But one thing I am is right." I lean forward, feeling the heat of the candle flame on my face. "Half the island will be destroyed. Slaves hunted, hung, sent away. Families divided. And for nothing."

Her eyes fix on mine, bright and intent as a hawk's. "No. Not for nothing. It takes something out of a person, day after day, bending to someone else's will. It's the big things, sure—the whippings, the way the white men use our women, like it's their right—but it be the little things too. The small indignities. We're like this candle, burnin' smaller and smaller, 'til the light be gone." Her voice comes low now, vehement. "But some of us, see—we're stubborn. The hotter we burn, the brighter our flame. And even if we lose—it will be worth it, to know we fought."

I feel my shoulders sag. "I can't convince you, can I?"

Hands spread wide on the table, she shakes her head. "If you truly see the future—what say you of my own fate? Will I live to see the destruction of all I hold dear?"

"If the answer to your question was 'no,' would it change anything?"

She settles back in her seat, her face in shadow, considering. "No," she says at last. "We must be free. And they'll not give it us, them buckra, that much be sure. The only way to get our freedom is to fight for it, the way they did on St. Domingo." She bares her teeth at me, saliva-wet and gleaming in the candlelight. There are dark gaps where several of them should be. "We'll fight with fire. And them bastards that use us so shamefully, we'll make them little before us. We'll watch 'em burn."

I regard her in silence, and she leans forward. The candlelight throws strange shadows on her face—an old woman one moment, a warrior the next. "You see the future, Max Adair?" she says, eyes steady on mine. "Well, then, give me something I can use."

Isabel

"You know about Robert Adair," Jennifer says. "Max's ancestor."

Bewildered, I regard her. "The one who came here back in the 1800s? Sure. What does he have to do with anything?"

"Well," she says, her eyes roving over the miniatures in the curio cabinet and the marble statue of Venus on its pedestal in the corner, finally coming to rest on my face, "not a thing, maybe. Or maybe . . . everything. It's hard to tell."

"Is this a riddle?" I say, doing my best not to sound impatient. "Or a Zen koan?"

This earns me a wry smile. "No. It's just that I can't really figure out how to begin." She sighs. "You know that he owned a large sugar plantation in Barbados. It was successful, but he saw the writing on the wall after the Haitian slave rebellion led by Toussaint L'Ouverture. The slaves on Barbados wanted their freedom, and after what happened in Haiti, an insurrection was every plantation owner's worst nightmare."

"I know all this, Jennifer. In fact, I think all of Charleston knows it. The insurrection is what drove him to move to America and free his slaves, right?"

She takes a sip of her iced tea, eyeing me over the top of the glass. "Was it, Isabel? That's not the way most of the plantation owners reacted."

"I know that too," I say. "So Robert was an anomaly. What does any of this have to do with seeing Max in my garden, or hearing him talking to Finn last night?"

Jennifer sighs again. "What I'm saying, Isabel, is that Robert's change of heart started much closer to home. According to his diaries at the Historical Society, he was thousands of miles away in Charleston when the insurrection erupted. Much of his plantation was destroyed, including the cane crop. But Robert suffered a much greater loss. His wife, Lily, died in childbirth, and took the baby with her. He was never the same man after that. He married again, but it was a marriage of obligation, to give him heirs."

"All of which is tragic," I say. "But still . . ."

"Have you ever noticed how large our patch of woods is, Isabel? The houses in Old Village—they're beautiful, sure, but most of them are fairly close together, on smaller plots of land. Did you ever wonder why ours is different?"

I shrug, puzzled. "I figured it was a holdover from when there were plantations here. Or that you kept the patch of woods for privacy."

"Reasonable enough." She drains her glass, then looks me directly in the eye. "But wrong. The truth is, Robert Adair chose this plot of land for that patch of woods."

"What?" I say stupidly. "Why would he do that?"

"Well," she says, fingering her necklace, "Robert was English, and a Presbyterian at that. But his grandmother was Scottish, and he grew up listening to her stories of the old ways. After Lily's death, Robert clung to one of these legends in particular—the thin places, where the boundary dividing the living and the dead was little more than a veil. Where, at the right time of year and in the right circumstances, you could talk to the ones you'd lost. Could ask their advice or beg their forgiveness. The places where you could walk in two worlds at once, she said."

In the warmth of the sunny living room, I shiver. "Don't tell me he thought he'd found a place like that here—in the woods?"

Reluctantly, Jennifer nods. "He did. His diaries allude to local superstitions, strange lights seen in the woods at night, things he'd heard the locals whispering about. Whatever the reason, he believed that these woods held such a place. He bought the land after Lily died, and spent the rest of his life trying to contact her—to apologize for leaving her behind. He blamed himself for his slaves' role in the insurrection. And he certainly blamed himself for Lily's death, and the death of their child. He thought it was a punishment from God for owning slaves. *The invidious institution*, he called it." She tugs at her skirt, clearly uncomfortable with the turn that our conversation has taken.

"Well," I ask, "did he ever hear from Lily? Dispatches from the great beyond?"

Her eyes flash to mine, and the look in them gives me pause. "Don't make a joke of it, Isabel. He dedicated his life to this. Other than abolition, it was his one great passion. Not his marriage, not his children. His second wife hated him for it. Imagine living in that shadow—knowing that no matter how hard you tried, you could never be the person that your husband wanted, simply because you weren't *her*."

The bitterness in her voice is genuine, and for the first time I wonder if Max's father has been faithful to his wife. I'd rather drink antifreeze than go down *that* road, though, so I simply say, "I didn't mean to make light of it. But . . . did he ever think that he'd suc-ceeded?"

She shakes her head. "No. It devastated him. And in his will, he stated that in order for the property to pass to his son, the woods had to be left unmolested. It's been a traditional clause, year after year, descendant after descendant. Of course, with Max gone, there is no direct heir to inherit the property. It will go to Finn. If she doesn't want it"—she lifts one graceful shoulder, then lets it fall—"there's no telling what will happen."

Somehow I'd never brought myself to consider what might happen when Jennifer and Thomas die. I try to imagine someone else living in Max's house, tearing down the tree house and selling off the land in parcels, and fight back tears. And then I imagine the alternative—me and Finn, rattling around together in Max's childhood home—and feel closer to crying than ever. Other than the woods and my house, this place holds most of my memories of him. I don't know what would be worse—letting the house slip from my hands, or haunting its hallways like Miss Havisham, unable to let him go.

I'm sure Jennifer sees how her comment has affected me—she doesn't miss much—but all she says is, "The Thin Place . . . it's . . ."

I stare at her for a moment, trying to puzzle out what she's trying to say. And then suddenly I am on my feet, sadness transmuted into shock. "The clearing by Max's tree house. Where I saw him disappear? Are you saying— What are you saying?"

She bows her head, looking anywhere but at me, and I know that I'm right. "Your mother—all those years ago—the last time anyone saw her, she was standing at the edge of the woods. It's foolishness— I know it is; however, I can't help but wonder . . ."

"Stop it, Jennifer. Just stop. You can't honestly think Max and my mother wandered through the woods and got sucked into the land of the dead. Or into an interdimensional portal? For real?"

Her eyes meet mine, the expression in them defensive. "I heard him, Isabel. I heard him talking to Finn. And you said he called you—that you saw him in your garden, in your room. That he spoke to you. How can we both be crazy?"

"I'm not saying that we're crazy. Just that there has to be a more reasonable explanation. A logical one. I mean, if there's some kind of . . . of thin place in your woods, why hasn't it been sucking people in and spitting them out for centuries? And if Max was trapped in there, why would he suddenly reach out to us now? He's been gone almost eight years. It doesn't make any sense."

"Well," Jennifer says, her words coming slow and deliberate, "maybe he was waiting for the right person to come along."

"What do you mean?" I say, but I have a sneaking suspicion that I know. Fear prickles along my spine, settles in my stomach, cold and coiling.

She leans forward, eyes fixed on mine. "What if the Thin Place is like a lock? And Finn is the key?"

"That's ridiculous. Finn wasn't in Barbados. Or in the garden. Or in my bedroom."

"No. But she's special, Isabel, you know she is. What if—what if we just took her down there, to the clearing? I know it sounds insane, but—what if she could talk to him?"

I'm about to snap at her, but the note of pleading in her voice brings me up short. Max is her child, I remind myself, just as Finn is mine. If Finn were lost to me, wouldn't I do anything to find her? So instead I say, my voice as gentle as I can make it, "I don't think that's a good idea, Jennifer. What would we tell Finn? *Come on down here and try to talk to your father . . . let's see if he answers you from the void?* It would scare the heck out of her. I can't use her that way. She's just a little kid."

"But what if it worked, Isabel? What if we could have him back again?" She's twisting her ring again, her hands trembling, and I feel a tremendous sense of pity for her—but not enough to compromise my child.

"I'm sorry," I say. "No matter how much I miss your son, I can't do that to Finn. She has to be my first priority. Max—if that really was him on the phone—asked me to do one thing. To keep Finn safe. And if he's out there somewhere, I have to believe that he'll find us . . . that he'll come home. I don't understand what's happening here any better than you do, but as far as I'm concerned, if by a crazy chance there is some kind of weird gateway in the woods—if there's the slightest chance, what if it took Finn too? I can't lose anyone else, Jennifer. I can't lose Finn." I rub my upper arms, trying to dispel the icy sense of dread that's taken me over from the inside out.

Jennifer's shoulders sag. "I hadn't thought of that," she says, all of the fight gone out of her. "You're right, of course. It's probably just a silly superstition, anyhow. But I can't stop thinking, Isabel—what if it isn't? What if he's out there . . . somewhere . . . trying to get to us, but he just can't? I couldn't sleep all night after I heard his voice. I kept getting up and going down the hall to check on Finn, thinking somehow I'd see him standing there. But I never did."

I nod in what I hope is a calm, reassuring manner, but my heart is racing. "Jennifer," I say carefully, "I want him back as much as you do. And if there was anything I could do to make it happen that didn't put Finn at risk, I would do it in a heartbeat. But as it is . . . I think I need to take her home."

"Of course," she says, and gets to her feet. I follow her out to the backyard, afraid all over again. Jennifer would never deliberately do anything to hurt Finn. Still, I know what it's like to feel desperate, to be willing to do anything. I'm sure there's nothing to this Thin Place business—how could there be? But if there were . . . what's to stop her from telling all of this to Finn, or from taking Finn into the woods the next time she stays over with the Adairs, just to see what will happen? Do I really trust her that much?

It's ironic, really. For the first time since I met her, I don't feel as if Jennifer Adair is my enemy. But now more than ever, I want her to stay the hell away from my daughter.

Max

Maybe it is a mistake to tell Nanny Grigg what I do—where the major battles of the rebellion will be fought, where the slaves will suffer the worst defeats. But I get it in my head that if I can give her that much, then maybe the rebels will have a chance—plus I can draw the worst of the conflict away from Sweetwater. Julia will be safe, and with any luck at all, fewer slaves will die in the fighting. If the information I give her saves even one life, it will be worth it.

Nanny G. listens to everything I say with grim intensity, asking pointed questions that I answer as best I can. By the time the candle burns down to nothing and I stand to go, my throat is hoarse from talking. I pass through the silent slave village without a word, collect my horse from the stables, and ride for home.

Back at Sweetwater, I dream the burning dream again. Isabel is stranded in the road. Lily, Finn, and Julia are trapped in a house on fire. I am helpless. But then the dream shifts. The hell of the plantation yard is gone. Instead I am standing on the flagstones of an unfamiliar courtyard, rain pelting down, drenching me. Through the downpour I can see the bright lights of a house—electric lights, not the uncertain, wavering glow of oil lamps or candles. I rub my eyes, trying to clear them, and realize that I am looking through a kitchen window, watching a woman wash dishes as she stares wistfully out into the rain. Blink again, and realize the woman is Isabel.

I call out to her, but her expression doesn't change and I realize she can't hear me. But then she leans forward, peering out the window. Her eyes widen, her mouth opens in shock, and she is running, running toward me. Thunder roars overhead, but I can still hear her calling my name, hear doors slam as she races through them. My heart beats faster—finally I will get to see her, hold her, and all of this madness will end.

Overhead there is a bright flash of lightning. It blinds me for a moment, and in the darkness I smell burning again. My vision clears, and I turn to see a blazing column of flame. Turn again, and Isabel is gone.

The dream shifts. Changes.

I am lying on the ground in the woods behind my parents' house, smelling the sharp scent of pine trees, the sweet perfume of honeysuckle. Isabel lies beneath me, laughing, and I duck my head to kiss her, brushing her lips with mine. Her hair spills to the ground, mingling with the shadows in the fading light. She tastes like I remember—sunlight and strawberry lip gloss—and she smells like coming home. Desire grips my belly, as hope rises in my heart. And the pine needles come down around us, a green blanket falling, a cover and a shield against the night.

Beneath me she shivers. I slip my hands under her, lifting her, so that we move together, and she shifts against me in demand. I remember our first time, the way she wrapped her legs around me and drew me down, how I knew then I couldn't stop, not unless she pushed me away. I want this so badly—to lose myself in her, erase the distance between us.

Teasing, she bites my neck, and I groan. "Please," I say, closing one hand on her breast, feeling the nipple harden under my palm. I take it between my thumb and forefinger, pinch gently, then harder, until she cries out. Trembling, I trace my lips down her body, over her belly, then lower. I spread her legs, and she arches beneath my mouth.

Her hand twines in my hair, and for a moment she yields to the heat that's growing between us—yields to *me*. I can feel it in the weight of her hand where it rests on my head, in the way she lets my fingers go where they will, pressing into her through the fabric of her jeans. "I need you," I say, my breath coming warm against her skin. Already I can feel it—the slow burn that spreads through me whenever I'm with her like this, searing all of my caution away. "Careful," I whisper, without knowing why.

"I'm tired of being careful," she whispers back, and tugs me upward, centering me above her. Even through our clothes I can feel her heat, and my breath catches in my throat. She hears it and arches against me once, then again. It's a question, and I feel my body answer, feel myself moving traitorously against her in response, regardless of the intentions of my higher faculties.

Inside my head a small voice is screaming that this is wrong, that there is something that I ought to know, a question that I ought to ask, but for the life of me I can't figure out what it is. I try my best to ignore it, but to no avail—it's there between us, nagging at me. Finally I surrender, pinning her with my hips, holding her still. "What's the matter, Isabel? Tell me."

I can't see her shake her head, but I feel it all the same. "Nothing."

"I don't believe you." My hands are roving over her, trying to read her body like Braille, as if the truth is engraved on her skin.

She takes a deep breath. I can feel the air fill her lungs, feel her breasts lift to press against my chest. "Do you want me, Max? Or not?"

"Yes, I want you," I say. "Too goddamn much, if you want to know the truth." I drop my head and kiss her, slow and easy, finding her tongue with mine. She's been eating something sweet—chocolate, maybe?—but beyond that I can taste something more elemental, more purely herself. I can't define it, but I would know her taste anywhere. "Of course I want you," I say, an admission that's easier to make here in the dark, where she can't see my face. "I want to make love to you, to take my time and show you just how much I missed you every second I was away."

That's it—I've been somewhere else, a place where she couldn't follow. But where? The answer dances just out of reach, tantalizing me.

She lifts her hand to press against my face, but doesn't make a sound, and I wonder if I've said too much. Darkness or no darkness, I can feel her eyes on me, feel her looking right through me, the way she's always been able to do. In a vain effort to protect myself, I close my eyes and breathe the scent of pine needles and honeysuckle, the familiar lavender-and-vanilla of Isabel's shampoo. Time slips sideways and I forget the feeling that something is terribly wrong between us, forget about everything but her.

Here in the dark it is hard to tell where her body ends and mine begins. My fear bleeds into hers, her regret into mine—but for what?—blurring the boundaries between us so that I am dizzy. And through it all runs that dangerous current of lust, threatening to sweep both of us away.

"I want that," I say, my voice coming low and husky, so that even I have a hard time recognizing it as my own. "But I also want to pin you down and fuck you until you can't say anything but my name. I want to prove that you're mine, even if it means I have to leave a mark." My breath comes in rough, staccato beats, and I raise my eyes to hers. "And so probably I shouldn't touch you anymore right now, Isabel. Probably I should be a gentleman and drive you home."

There is a beat of silence while Isabel digests this. I wait for her to throw me off of her, to tell me I'm a male chauvinist pig or some kind of twisted sadist. But instead, she grips my hair and pulls me down to her. "Oh, Max. What did they *do* to you back in the nineteenth century?" she whispers, the ghost of a laugh in her voice. She wraps her legs around my hips, pressing into me in a way that nearly unravels my fraying self-control.

I rear back, shaking, and free myself. "Stop," I say. "When you do that . . . I can't, Isabel." I kneel between her legs, wishing I could see her face more clearly. Because what she said—about the nineteenth century—that is the missing piece.

I am not here, I realize, not in the woods with her. And neither is she.

We are both elsewhere. Else*when*.

Fear fills me anew, and I gaze down at her, seeking solace. But she lies silent and still, eyes closed as if asleep. I reach down and stroke her face, call her name, but she doesn't respond—and suddenly I am afraid that she is dead, that she's died here in the pine needles and the shadows, leaving me alone.

"Wake up, baby," I whisper. "Wake up."

Her eyes open then, blue gone to black in the dim light, and fix on me. Her mouth forms my name.

And then I am awake, lying alone in the four-poster bed at Sweetwater, my face sheened with sweat. I swear I can still smell Isabel on my skin. I can feel the warmth of her, feel her roll her hips in that way I've never been able to resist, urging me on.

I close my eyes, imagine I can feel her sliding over me, wet and tight, feel the soft weight of her breasts filling my palms. I imagine her body rising and falling over mine, imagine the way she gasps when I take her nipple in my mouth and bite, hard enough to tease, not enough to hurt. By the time I imagine taking her hips in my hands and moving her how I want, imagine the way she always says my name when she's close to the edge—part benediction, part demand—I am panting. I cling tight to the feeling so I won't lose it, rising helpless into the memory of her flesh mated with mine, and at last lie still, breath coming hard.

In the morning, when I finally go downstairs, I discover that Lily is still in bed, and likely to remain so for some time. Hannah won't say much about it when I ask her, other than, "Missus ain't feeling well," and, when I press, "She's tryin' to do too much. That child's coming early, if she don't take her ease." A wave of nausea washes over me. Is it possible that history's gotten it wrong—that this baby will die no matter what I do?

I am still pondering this when Julia arrives for lunch, an engagement that Lily was determined to keep, no matter how she felt. Selfishly, I'm relieved—we'd planned to tell her about the rebellion today, to try to persuade her to leave Sweetwater.

Hannah ushers Julia in and then tucks a knitted blanket around Lily, who has insisted on greeting her visitor in the salon, ensconced on the couch. "You all right, Miss Lily?" she asks. "Not too warm?"

"I'm fine," Lily says, patting Hannah's hand. "Women have been having babies for thousands of years. If something is going to go wrong, it's no more likely to do so on this settee than in my own bed, and I want to see Julia—I've been starving for gossip, cooped up like this. Don't you worry."

Hannah gives her a look that suggests this little speech has not fooled her in the slightest, but bustles off to fetch tea for the three of us nonetheless. When she disappears through the swinging doors, Lily gives a deep sigh.

"She's kind to me, Hannah is. But she worries too much. When my time comes, John Best has promised to send his most skilled midwife from Bayleys—Jubah is her name. She's worked miracles, saving little ones who were half-strangled from the cord and turning breech babes in the womb, so they dropped and came headfirst. But you'll excuse me, Mr. Adair," she says, flushing red. "This is women's talk."

I sit back in my chair and smile at her, trying to put her at ease. "It doesn't bother me at all. I've met Jubah—she brewed me a medicinal tea when I was at Bayleys. She seems extremely capable."

"Oh, she is," Julia interjects, setting her teacup down on the end table next to her. "She calls herself a healer—but John Best and Edward Thomas both think she's more than that. They're afraid of her, if you want to know the truth."

At this, Lily nods. "It's Jubah I want," she says. "John Best and his ilk are frightened of her because they know how much influence she has over the slaves at Bayleys—they respect her, you see, and will often do as she commands. And I will tell you something else—if she can indeed communicate with the spirits of her ancestors, if she can stir their bones and call them up to do as she will—then those men are right to fear her. For they have done her and her people an incalculable wrong, and she would not be remiss in taking her vengeance."

There is steel in her voice, and I am glad of it. She'll need all of her strength to deal with what we have to tell her, and the time has come.

I turn to Julia, who leans forward, grasping Lily's hands in both of hers. "Lily," she says, "I am proud to call you my friend. Would you call me the same?"

Lily shifts her weight beneath the blanket, puzzled. "You know that I would. Why do you ask me that, Julia? Is something wrong?"

"Do you trust me?" Julia asks, her gaze fixed on Lily's face.

"I do. But what—do you ask something of me, a service rendered, a secret kept?" Her eyes scan Julia's face, flick to mine, and then back to Julia's. "Whatever it is, you may have it, if it is in my power to give. You have been a good friend to me these many months, keeping me company when I might otherwise have been alone, offering me succor and support. Were it not for you and Alicia Brightmore, I fear that I might have lost heart entirely, isolated as I have been. If there is something that you need, or want—only ask, and I will accept gladly."

Julia nods. "I need you to trust me. Trust us," she says, gesturing at me.

"Trust you," Lily says, considering. "As I said before, I do trust you, Julia. As for Mr. Adair—I have only just made his acquaintance. But a friend of yours is, as they say, a friend of mine."

"There's going to be a rebellion, Lily. Soon." Julia's voice comes clear and low, pitched just loud enough that Lily can hear it. "The slaves are going to rise up and fight for their freedom."

At first I think Lily hasn't heard. But then her face goes red, then white, then red again. "How do you know this?" she asks, leaning forward as far as her belly will allow.

"I can't tell you that. But it's the truth. Lily, you won't be safe here. Not you or the child." She frees one of her hands and places it on the rise of Lily's belly, sheltering the infant within. "For the sake of the trust you have in me—you need to leave here."

"Leave?" Her eyebrows rise. "And go where?"

"It doesn't matter," I say, sliding my chair closer to hers. "Parts of the island will be safe. Go there—or take a ship for somewhere else."

Lily sits up straight, one hand tight on the arm of the couch. "I still don't understand. How do you know all this?"

"We can't say how we know," I say. "I'm sorry, but we can't."

"Is it because you don't want to get anyone in trouble?" Her voice is eager now, face flushed bright with excitement. "Because I wouldn't do that—you know I wouldn't. You're aware how I feel about the way slaves are treated here. I know it could be the end of Sweetwater—Robert couldn't run it without his workers . . . but perhaps he could pay them. Or we could go back to London, or move to the Carolinas or Georgia to raise our child. I would rather live in poverty than see another man flogged for refusing to do his master's bidding, or witness more human beings penned up like chattel in the Bridgetown cage."

Neither Julia nor I say anything. I don't know about her, but hearing Lily's dreams for the future—a world in which Robert Adair pays his former slaves a decent wage, where Lily and her husband raise their child together in the shady squares of Savannah or the busy streets of Charleston—breaks something inside me. Perhaps Julia feels the same, because as Lily looks from one of us to the other, her face falls. "You think I am terribly naïve," she says. "Perhaps it is you who do not trust *me*."

"If we didn't trust you, we wouldn't be telling you this." Julia knots her fingers together, twisting. "Speaking up is a huge risk, but when your safety hangs in the balance—we can't stay quiet."

"My safety," Lily says slowly. "The revolt—it will be here, then? At Sweetwater?" She wraps her arms around herself, clutching the blanket.

"Not primarily. But Sweetwater will be affected, Mrs. Adair— and you can't be here when it is." Now I am the one who's leaning forward urgently. "You've got to go."

For a second Lily eyes me in silence. And then she shakes her head. "This is my home," she says, her voice soft but firm. "I'll not leave it."

"But you just said—"

With a wave of her hand, she cuts me off. "I'll leave to start a new life, yes. With my husband and our child. But I'll not run away like a coward, nor will I interfere with an oppressed people's right to fight for their freedom. We'll take what precautions we must. And when it is over, I will rejoice with them, that they need no longer bow to my whim."

"You don't understand!" I say, leaping to my feet. "The rebellion will fail. Hundreds of slaves will die. Maybe even thousands. The island will be in ruins. Sweetwater will go up in flames. And you—you and your baby—"

The words stick in my throat, and a good thing too, because God only knows what I might have said next. I turn away, and then Julia is beside me, her hand on my shoulder, pressing hard. She doesn't speak, but I can hear her just as clearly as if she had: *Shut up, Max.*

I shake off her hand, stalk to the sideboard beneath the window and pour a healthy shot of rum. The alcohol burns a clear path from my throat to my stomach, where it roils uneasily. I stare out the window, seeing the cane on fire, riots and murder in the road.

"What do you mean?" Lily says behind me, sounding frightened. "How can you know such a thing?"

But I have already said too much.

"That doesn't matter," Julia says after a moment. "Max—Mr. Adair—he speaks the truth."

"The truth as he imagines it will be!" she says, furious now. "That is such arrogance—to believe that because the slaves do not have formal training, because they are not members of the militia or the garrison, their efforts will not succeed. Do you seek to scare me, sir? To frighten me into leaving my land, for your own ends? Because I assure you, I am made of stronger stuff than that."

At this, I turn from the window. "Frighten you? God, that's the last thing I want to do. But unless we can stop the rebellion, you won't be safe here."

She heaves herself to her feet, ignoring Julia's attempts to help her. "So you would seek to drive me off my estate and deprive innocent people of the right to stand up for their freedom? How abominable of you, sir. Where is your sense of honor?"

"Honor!" I say, and just like that, I snap. I can see Julia's face, white to the lips, see her mouth moving, imploring me to stop, but I can't seem to help myself. "Is it honorable to allow men and women to walk straight into their own slaughter? To allow a woman and a child to die, knowing that I might have stopped it? Because if that is your idea of honor, you're damn right. I have none."

"To allow a woman and child to die," she echoes. "So now you'll threaten me, after I've opened my home to you. This is my thanks, is it?" She rears back and slaps me, hard, across the face. "You, sir, are a heartless bounder, a liar, and a coward. As for you, Mrs. Griffin, how have you allowed this fellow—for he is no gentleman—to fill your ears with such fustian nonsense? I would have credited you with better judgment indeed."

I have no idea what a bounder is—nor the exact definition of fustian—but obviously it's no compliment. Looking miserable, Julia steps between us. "It isn't nonsense," she says, "and he's not a liar, or a coward. Please, Lily—just listen to us."

Lily's eyes search mine, and for a moment her expression softens. "You will think me insane," she says, "but the other night I had the strangest dream. I dreamed I stood in the woods, but they were no woods I had ever seen—not the cold, damp forests of England, nor yet the overgrown tangles of this island. I stood alone, but I was not afraid. I knew that I waited for someone there, and if I were but patient, she would appear."

An icy finger traces the length of my spine. Next to me, Julia makes a choked, convulsive sound, and when I turn to look at her, she has gone bone-white. "Who were you waiting for, Lily?" she says.

Lily smiles. "You, Julia. I was waiting for you. And sure enough, you came, though the clothes you wore—they were like nothing I had ever seen. They were made of a strange material, and the blue of your skirts—it was so vivid, as if someone had captured a piece of the sky." She shrugs, dismissing this. "Such is the nature of dreams, no? But you came, and you took my hand."

She turns her gaze to me again. "We walked away into the woods, the two of us. But before we went—I saw you, Mr. Adair. You were watching over us, like a guardian angel. I knew in my heart that you meant us no harm."

"I don't," I say. "I promise."

Lily nods, that beatific smile still on her lips, as if she sees the woods from her dream—*my* woods—and not this stuffy drawing room. "I felt that you and Julia both—that you'd been meant to come to me. And even when I woke, I could not dismiss the feeling, though I knew it to be foolish and the stuff of fantasy."

Her eyes focus on us now, lit with fervor. "Don't you see? This is the proof that my dream was real, that the three of us were brought together for a reason that lies beyond the realm of mere coincidence. Together, we can accomplish what I have only imagined. We can cleanse ourselves of the role we have played in these horrors. We can help to free the slaves—and sever the ropes of guilt and blood that bind our souls."

She knots her hands over her belly, drawing breath, and when she speaks again, her voice is gentle, meant to persuade. "Mr. Adair, I know you do not condone the ways of our island. I have heard how you intervened on Mercy Nell's behalf, how you confronted Mr. Thomas and risked yourself to protect a slave who was a stranger to you. I have seen the kindness with which you treat Hannah and Sarey. Will you not welcome me into your confidence, sir, that we might stand together? I have trusted you with my secrets. Will you not trust me with your own?"

Everything in me wants to say yes. But how can I? "I can't," I say, feeling like the worst kind of bastard. "I wish I could. I'm sorry."

Her jaw tightens. "I see. And what about you, Julia? We have never spoken of such things directly, but I have long suspected you share my sympathies. Now is not the time to run. With child I may be, but still I am the mistress of this plantation, with all of its re-sources at my disposal. Now is our moment. Only tell me what you know."

Julia looks miserable. "I do share your sympathies, Lily. Of course I do."

"Then you understand why I cannot leave, do you not? Now of all times, I must stay here and offer what aid is in my power." Her voice breaks. "Do you not see—no matter what the nature of my beliefs, I am as guilty of perpetuating the institution of slavery as is my husband. Childbirth is a dangerous business, and survival far from certain—both for me and for the babe. Had I the choice, I would not go to my grave with my soul tarnished by these sins. I beg you—do not deny me."

Tears well up in Julia's eyes. "I can't," she says, her voice waver-ing. "We can't. But your dream—maybe it did mean something. Maybe it meant that we've come to help you when you need us most. Please, Lily. Please let us help you."

Anger flashes clear in Lily's eyes, chased by desperation. "If you truly wished to help me," she says, "you would consider what it is that I want, rather than what you think is in my best interest. Do I not have the right to choose such things?"

Neither Julia nor I reply, and Lily goes on, voice rising. "Who are you to decide what is mine to risk? How dare you say that my life and the life of my child outweigh the lives of the multitude of human beings, held in slavery, who call this plantation home? No, I will not run. And if I must die, I will do so with my conscience clear and my soul washed clean of atrocity."

She straightens, looking first at me and then at Julia. Her eyes linger on Julia's face, imploring. "I beg you—will you not help me?"

Julia is crying freely now. She tries to speak, but all that emerges is a choked sob, and instead she shakes her head—once, twice, then again.

Lily's expression hardens, and she widens her glare to include both of us. "I see that my trust in you has been sorely misplaced," she says, cold as snow. "Get out of my house. I never want to see either of you again."

Turning her back on us, she walks ponderously through the swinging doors of the salon, one hand underneath the great swell of her belly, and disappears from sight.

Isabel

"Okay," Ryan says. "You can look now."

We're standing in the studio at the back of his house, his hands over my eyes. It's Sunday, and we've spent most of the day together—breakfast with Finn at the Early Bird Diner, then a bike ride at Hampton Park, followed by lunch under one of the park's huge old oak trees, featuring slightly squashed ham sandwiches and a bag of peaches we picked up at a roadside stand. Ry had juggled three of the peaches for Finn's benefit, catching one in his mouth for the grand finale, splitting the skin so that juice trickled down his chin, dripping onto his shirt. She'd giggled uncontrollably, foisting a napkin on him and then grabbing a peach for herself. Ry had handed the last one to me—"Only a little bruised," he'd assured me with a grin—and I'd taken it, rolling my eyes at his theatrics, even though my heart leapt to see Finn so happy.

After lunch, I'd coaxed Ryan into getting up—no easy feat, given that he was sprawled on his back, one arm crooked over his eyes to block the sun, Finn's head pillowed on his stomach—gathered our bikes and the remains of our lunch, and driven over the bridge to Mount Pleasant. My father had promised to take Finn on a boat ride—she wanted to go up Shem Creek to sketch the dolphins, if they could find any—and she'd been filled with excitement, chattering the whole way there, telling Ry she'd give him one of the pictures for his office. We'd dropped her off, Finn practically hopping with anticipation, and Ry had let out a long, low whistle.

"God save the dolphins," he'd said as we drove away. "And your father, for that matter. What was in those peaches, I wonder? Because the way she's acting, it was straight-up crack cocaine. I hope she doesn't launch herself right out of the boat."

"She won't," I'd assured him. "Or if she does, at least you taught her to swim."

He'd snorted at this, swabbing peach juice from his hands with one of the baby wipes I always keep in the car. "Small consolation when she grabs some unsuspecting dolphin's fin and gives your father a heart attack. But I guess you're right—she won't drown in the process, so that's a plus."

Smiling at the idea of a peach-powered Finn cavorting with a pod of dolphins, I'd turned to Ry and asked him what he wanted to do next—go get a beer, or see a movie. He'd looked at me from under his lashes then, suddenly diffident, and his answer had surprised me. "Actually, would you mind stopping by my house?" he'd said, digging in his pocket for a pack of gum and offering me a piece. "I've got something to show you."

Which brings us to where we are now—standing in his studio, my eyes covered by his hands, still faintly redolent of the sweet scent of peaches. He drops them, and spins me around with a flourish.

For a second, all I can do is gape. On his worktable is a perfectly crafted miniature version of our house, porch swing, white wood siding, chimney, and all. It's sitting on a lazy Susan, and he reaches out, rotating the turntable so that I can see the interior. Somehow he's made the house hinge in the middle, so that it opens to reveal our cozy family room, our living room with its fireplace and capacious bookshelves. There's even a staircase leading upstairs, where I can see Finn's room, complete with canopy bed and quilt, my room with its rag rug and huge windows, and the guest room, with its window seat and twin beds. I don't start tearing up, though, until he spins the lazy Susan again, showing off the backyard, with its picnic table, hammock, and—restored to its former, if tiny, glory—my old oak tree.

Next to me, Ryan fidgets. "Do you like it, Isabel? Say something, would you?"

I run a finger reverently over the steps of the staircase. "Like it? My God, Ry, it's incredible. Did you make all this?"

Shyly, he nods. "Not all the furniture, but the house itself, yeah. I just thought—Finn's been having a hard time. She keeps talking about how she wants a dollhouse—and I know you told her she had to wait for her birthday—but that's not until October, and so I thought maybe—well, I thought it would make her happy. I was going to buy one, but everything I looked at was such total crap, I figured I could make something better. And I think it's turned out okay, right?"

"It's more than okay," I marvel, spinning the lazy Susan again so I can inspect the porch swing, suspended from infinitesimal chain links. "I had no idea you could do stuff like this."

He shrugs, embarrassed. "Yeah, well, neither did I. But there're a lot of YouTube videos out there, and I figured it couldn't be that hard. And if I sucked at it, well, nothing ventured and all that."

"So this is what you've been doing," I say, giving him a gimlet eye. "Watching reruns of *The Walking Dead*, my ass."

Ryan grins at me in wry acknowledgment. "It wasn't a total lie. I streamed them on my iPad while I was building the chimney. Very relaxing."

"She's going to love it. Give it to her whenever you want. God, she'll go insane."

"It's not done yet," he says. "In a week, maybe. I just wanted you to see it first."

"Yeah, because you knew once I saw it, there was no way I'd say no."

"That too," he says, amusement clear in his voice.

Watching him, I suppress a sigh. He isn't going to like what I have to tell him next—but there's no way around it. "Hey, Ry."

"Hmmm?" He messes with something on the worktable, making a small adjustment to the roofline.

I swallow hard, digging deep for courage. "I talked to Max's mom. And I told her—everything."

"You did what?" Ryan says, his hands suddenly still.

"She's Finn's grandmother, for God's sake. And I thought she ought to know what's been going on." I lean back against the table, bracing myself for an argument.

Sure enough, Ryan looks mutinous. "I thought we'd talked about this. Nothing's going on, Isabel. I can't believe you'd fill her head with all this crazy stuff. She lost her son. Let the woman have some peace."

"She was glad I told her," I say defensively. "She didn't think I was crazy."

He picks up a tube of glue, tossing it from one hand to the other. "Oh, yeah?"

This is the tough part. "Not at all." I take a deep breath, trying to figure out how to go on. Ryan just stands there, waiting. Finally, I tell him everything Jennifer told me. It doesn't sound much saner the second time around, and I have a hard time meeting his eyes. He doesn't interrupt, just looks more horrified by the moment.

"Oh Jesus," he says when I've finished. "No wonder she didn't think you were crazy. She's downright certifiable. What the hell did you say?"

"It's not important, Ry. The point is, she thought this whole Thin Place thing might be real. And that maybe—maybe that's why Max disappeared."

"What?" His voice cracks. "She thinks he got sucked into an alternate dimension? Christ. I hope you told her she was a first-rate lunatic, and got the hell out of there."

Uncomfortably, I shrug.

Ryan shakes his head. "If I were you, I wouldn't let her near Finn," he says, starting to pace. "Who knows what ideas she's already put in her head?"

It's not as if I haven't considered this and come to the same conclusion. Still, hearing Ryan say it makes me bristle—as if I'm an incompetent, neglectful mother. "She said she hadn't told Finn any of this. That she wanted to talk to me first." Even to me, this sounds like a flimsy excuse. When has Jennifer ever wanted to talk to me? Still, she'd sounded sincere, and I have a hard time believing that, for all of her less-than-desirable qualities, she would actually want to do Finn harm. Not on purpose anyway.

I open my mouth to tell Ryan this, but one look and I know my words would be wasted on him. His hands are clenched at his sides, and his pupils are dilated, showing a thin rim of hazel. Back and forth across the room he paces, making me dizzy. Just when I'm about to ask him to stop, he comes to a halt in front of me, close enough that I'm forced to look up at him. "So what did you do, Isabel? What did you tell her?"

"I left," I say, resisting the urge to back away. "And I told Finn I didn't want her going over there for a while. Would you relax, please? You're starting to freak me out."

Ryan takes a deep breath, and just like that, I see him perform the magic trick I've never been able to master. This close, it's a little unsettling to watch. He closes his eyes, and when he opens them again, his face is as blank as I've ever seen it. "I'm sorry," he says, taking a step away from me and shoving his hands into his pockets.

"I'm seriously considering making an appointment for Finn with a therapist, like I told you I might. My dad gave me a referral."

"You really think that's necessary?"

"Something's going on with her, Ryan. And in light of everything else, I don't think I can just dismiss it."

Ryan sighs. "For the thousandth time, there is no *everything else*, Isabel. There's reality, which isn't always how we want it to be, and then there's fantasy land."

My face tightens at this, and he must see it, because when he speaks again, his tone is gentle. "If I could change it for you, I would," he says. "I hate to see you hurting."

At this, my eyes well with tears, and I turn, heading for the door. Before I can reach it, though, Ryan puts a restraining hand on my arm. "Where are you going?"

I twist free of his grip. "I don't know. Away. I can't talk about this anymore."

"So don't talk about it." He steps in front of me, and now his face isn't blank at all. There's determination in his expression, and something else I can't quite read. "Stop looking backward, Isabel. Think about the future, yours and Finn's. And mine."

"What do you mean?" I say. But I have a sudden, sinking feeling that I know.

"You're ignoring what's right in front of you to go after a dead guy. You know that, don't you?" He blocks the doorway.

"Move, Ryan," I say, trying in vain to get past him.

"I won't. Not until you hear me out." He comes closer, trapping me between his body and the worktable. Instinctively, I step backward, but there's nowhere for me to go. Behind me I hear the unmistakable sound of small figures toppling, and then tinkling glass as something—perhaps a small lamppost—hits the floor. "Now look what you did," I say. It's a stalling tactic, and perhaps Ryan realizes this, because he lifts my face to his.

"I didn't do it. You did," he says. "And either way, I don't care." Then his lips are on mine, and he is kissing me—tentatively at first, then, when I don't pull away, with greater confidence. He tastes like peaches and a faint hint of wintergreen. I gasp and he makes a sound deep in his throat, pinning me against the table, his breath coming fast. His eagerness is contagious, and despite my better judgment, I kiss him back, let him run his hands over me.

Somehow we are lying on the table. The pieces of the dollhouse scatter, but Ryan, who's normally so conscientious about his work, doesn't seem to notice. He's pushed up my skirt, has one trembling hand on my thigh. I breathe in his familiar smell—ink and Ivory soap—as he unhooks my bra and lets it drop to the floor.

"God, Izzy," he murmurs into my hair, and the joy that's clear in his voice moves me more than the feel of his hands on my skin. I've rarely heard him sound so happy, and it fills my veins with ice. What am I doing, using him this way?

I shove at his chest. "Ryan, stop." My voice comes out more quietly than I'd intended, little more than a whisper.

He hears it, though, and freezes. "What?" he says at once. "Am I hurting you?" He pushes away from me slightly, balanced on his elbows. Beneath my palms, which are still pressed against his T-shirt, I can feel his heart pounding.

"No," I say, and then can't find the words to go on. He's looking down at me, hazel eyes narrowed in concern. This close, I can see the flecks of green in their depths.

"Is it too much?" he says. "Too fast?"

"No," I say again.

"Then what?" he says, and waits. When I don't answer, he gives a heavy sigh and sits up. His feet hit the floor with a thud.

"Let's not play twenty questions," he says. "You're thinking about him."

I swipe a hand across my mouth guiltily. "This isn't right," I say. "You know it isn't." I sit up, straighten my skirt, and, suddenly shy, look around for my tank top. Ryan crouches and picks it up, his mouth a thin line.

"The hell I do," he says, handing it to me.

I pull the shirt over my head. "We've been friends forever, Ry," I say, my voice muffled by the thin cotton. "This—whatever this is— it's not us."

When my head emerges from the shirt, I can see him glaring at me. "Maybe it's not you," he says, a slight emphasis on the last word.

"What are you saying?"

"Come on. Are you that blind, Isabel?" He takes a step back, hands in his pockets.

"About what?" I say, a sinking feeling in my stomach.

His voice is low, bitter. "I got offered a job at goddamn Marvel. Why do you think I stuck around here? For the international cuisine?"

"Oh, Ry," I say, and my eyes fill.

He's still angry, I can see it, but at the sight of my tears, he reaches for me again. I step back, away from him, without thinking, and he drops his arms, hurt clear on his face. "Why, Isabel?" he says, and the pleading in his voice takes me off guard. "We're perfect together. We like the same things. We think the same way. We even watch the same nerdy sci-fi flicks. Finn loves me. You know I'd do anything for either of you. I don't get it. What do you need me to be that I'm not? Tell me, and I'll try my best, I swear it."

I don't want to hurt him, but there doesn't seem to be any way around it. He's standing there in his juice-splattered shirt and blue board shorts, regarding me with such hopefulness—like I can give him a prescription for loving him. "Can you be Max?" I ask, and watch his face close, his expression shifting seamlessly from expectation to anger.

"For Christ's sake," he says, hands balling into fists. "He's dead. You know that, Isabel, deep down, don't you? Please tell me you do. You're chasing a ghost. Obsessing over your daughter, doing this"— he gestures between us—"for nothing. All this crap about phone calls and sightings, you've got to give it up. If not for me, for Finn."

"Finn is the reason I'm doing this!"

"Bullshit." His tone is icy. "You're doing it for you."

The way he's looking at me—like I'm a stranger, and a despicable one at that—breaks my heart. "That's not true," I say. "Ryan, come on. You know me."

"Yeah," he says, his voice level. "I do. Here's what I know: You make up your mind about something, you do it, and damn anything that stands in your way."

"That's not true," I say again. "It's not fair."

Ryan gives me a sad smile. "Really?" He puts his hands on my shoulders, turning me so I can see the destruction we've wrought—the dollhouse he's built for Finn, window boxes, oak tree, and all, in pieces on the floor. "Go home, Isabel," he says, and turns his back on me.

Max

The next week passes in a blur. Evicted from Sweetwater, I make my way to Bridgetown, which I figure is my best hope of finding a place to stay—not to mention fitting in, inasmuch as such a thing is possible. It breaks something inside me to do it, but I sell my grandmother's gold engagement ring and use the money to rent a room at Chadbourne's Inn. It's far from fancy—just a place to sleep—but right now that's all I need. In my mind, a countdown to Easter Sunday is ticking away. Just ten more days. Ten days are all we have to convince the slaves that their rebellion will fail, to save Lily.

After some thought, I take a chunk of the leftovers and purchase a smoothbore musket and a pistol, plus a cartridge box, musket balls, paper cartridges, and powder. One thing's for sure—getting back to Isabel will be damn near impossible if I die in this rebellion because I don't know how to shoot a nineteenth-century gun. I grew up target shooting and deer hunting, so I'm a good shot, but I've never fired guns like these.

Sitting in my room at night, I lay the whole shooting match out on my bed and experiment until I piece together how it works. Of course, loading a gun is not the same as firing one, so my next step is to find a place where I can practice. This means making my way into the country, somewhere uninhabited—and for that, I'll need transportation.

Thank God my grandfather didn't skimp on my grandmother's wedding ring, because I still have enough money left over to buy a horse and stable him. The man who sells him to me informs me that his name is Havoc, and after a few minutes with him, I can see why. He's a huge black monster, stubborn as hell, and headstrong. Also, he bites. But he's what I can afford, along with a used saddle and bridle, so I make the deal.

I spend a couple of hours each day in the most secluded places I can find—not easy on this deforested island—loading and firing until I'm confident. I practice making my own cartridges—dropping the ball into the cylinder of paper, dumping in the powder, and tying the whole thing off. By the time I make it back to Bridgetown, I've committed the process to muscle memory.

Feeling comfortable in Bridgetown itself, however, is an entirely different challenge. The city is as populated as Sweetwater was isolated. It's a thriving port, filled with street musicians, hucksters, and sailors who spill off the boats in the Careenage in search of alcohol and prostitutes.

It takes me a while to get used to the gorgeous mulatto women who stand in the doorways of taverns, hands on cocked hips and hair spilling down, calling to passersby. The first time I sit down to dinner and the dark-eyed waitress who brings my food rests her hand on my thigh, the warmth of her hand searing through my trousers, I nearly spill my wine. She laughs, a full-throated chuckle, and moves closer, so that her breasts brush my arm. "Mmmm?" she says, eyes fixed on mine in clear invitation.

Despite myself, my body responds. I take a sip of wine and shift in my chair, looking anywhere but at her. Yet she steps closer still, and I can't help but breathe in her scent—floral perfume, and beneath it, an earthy aroma. The frustration of the last week builds inside me, seeking release.

"No," I choke, pushing my chair back. She laughs again.

"All right," she says, her eyes raking me from head to toe. Her gaze lingers just a little too long on the fly of my trousers, and I swear I can feel the weight of it. "Suit yourself." And she turns on her heel, bearing the tray back toward the kitchen.

Shaking, I empty my glass. I've been with Isabel since I was seventeen, and before her there were one or two girls that I'd dated with anything approaching seriousness. With Isabel away at school, I've had plenty of experience with abstinence—but she was just a couple of hours down the road, not two hundred years out of my reach.

I stare after the woman retreating to the kitchen, at the swell and sway of her hips beneath the thin material of her dress, and wish more than anything that I could call Isabel now—not just out of lust, though God knows that's a part of it, but for comfort. Sitting in a tavern surrounded by sailors and gamblers, men looking for a few hours of pleasure and a glass or two of ale, I have never felt so alone.

The path before me forks. In one direction lies Isabel and my daughter. And in the other—what? A corrupt inheritance I might hold the power to change, a cause worth fighting for. Is it really Lily and her baby I mean to save, or myself?

Jubah's words echo in my ears—*You need something, you come see Jubah.* Here's hoping she meant it. If she's truly as powerful as people suspect—with the ability not just to heal but to see the future—maybe she will be able to light my way.

Isabel

All the way to my dad's house to pick Finn up, I replay what happened with Ryan, trying to figure out what I could have done differently. I keep hearing his accusations, seeing him turn away from me, and it hurts more than I want to admit. Then I remember the taste of his mouth, hear him saying *God, Izzy*, and feel purely confused. In that moment, I wanted him—didn't I? I let him touch me, I kissed him back. And then I pushed him away. What kind of person does that make me?

No sooner do I ask myself this than I hit a dead end. Ryan and I have been friends for years—or at least that's what I thought. All this time, has he been lying to me, concealing a romantic agenda? If that's the case, what about his procession of girlfriends, some of whom stuck around for quite a while? Was he just using them?

I think about this for a minute and get so aggravated, I nearly run a red light, earning me horn blasts from the other drivers. Stuck at the intersection of King and Poplar, I drum my fingers on the wheel in frustration, consumed by the need to go somewhere—anywhere—rather than be alone with my thoughts.

His invitation to go to New York with him—what was that all about, then? Did it have anything to do with Finn? Or was it really some backward way of alluding to his feelings for me? What would he have done if he'd actually managed to convince me to move— gotten me up there and then confessed everything?

"Goddamn it, Ry," I mutter, pulling ahead as the light changes. He was the one place I had that was safe, my sounding board, my rock. I can't help it—I feel betrayed. No matter whether Ryan and I agree about what's going on with Max and Finn, we're in it together. That's what he promised me that day over the phone in Barbados, and I believed him. I let myself trust him, let myself lean on him. And now this.

"Goddamn it!" I say again, louder this time, and hit the wheel with my fist. It hurts, but somehow that reassures me. The wheel is a solid object, unlikely to morph into something inexplicable or disap- pear. It's simple cause and effect—slamming my hand into it causes pain, however fleeting.

Maybe that's what I need—to go to the dojo and work off some of this insanity the simplest way I know how. I check the car's clock— it's open mat time, with almost an hour before the next class starts. My dad isn't expecting me back until three, which means I have time enough, and my gear bag's in the trunk, workout clothes and all.

Decided, I make the left onto Poinsett, forcing myself to take deep breaths. Somehow, all of this will be okay, and until then, I will do whatever is necessary to hang on.

For the first time in years, I wonder what it would be like to still have a mother. Someone I could go to who would understand, who'd make me a pot of chamomile tea and lemon cookies and listen to me rant, the way my mom used to do. I let myself miss my mother, and it hurts more than I expect it would.

By the time I pull up in front of the gym, all I can think of is shut- ting the lid on Pandora's box, and fast. I grab my gear bag out of the trunk and go straight to the locker room to change, barely acknowl- edging Jenna and Rafe, who wave at me. I suit up, remembering to duct tape my gloves—which are in dire need of replacement, along with most of the rest of my gear. Back in the gym, I go straight for the heavy bag in the corner, starting out slow and then attacking the bag with everything I have.

It works, and it doesn't. I wanted the racing thoughts to stop, and they do. My mind narrows to a single, focused point and everything fades away so there's only me, pounding the bag. After a while I un-Velcro my pads and let them drop to the floor, slamming my bare fists and my feet into the bag again and again. Dimly I am aware that people are staring. From far away I hear Jenna say, "Damn, girl." I don't stop, though. I can't. Stopping would mean letting the world back in.

Like I said, it works, and then again, it doesn't. Because even as I work the heavy bag until I can barely raise my arms and my vision blurs, as I kick the freestanding bag over and over so that my legs ache and I'm soaked in sweat, I can't erase the hurt look in Ryan's eyes when I backed away from him, or the cold sound of his voice saying, *Bullshit. You're doing it for you.*

Max

Finding Jubah isn't hard. The next night, I ride out to Bayleys Plantation at sunset and simply ask a small boy in the slave village for directions. He points, one hand over his mouth to conceal his gap-toothed grin. I skirt a cookfire, smoored for the night, edge around a goat pen, and find myself in front of the hut the boy indicated, its thatched roof dipping low and ominous in the dimming light.

The door to Jubah's hut is open, but I knock just the same. She's sitting at a wooden table, the light of a single candle burning before her. The table is empty otherwise, except for an earthenware cup of tea that's sending tendrils of fragrant steam into the air. At my knock, her head turns toward the sound, a slow, near-predatory movement. "Master Max," she says.

Disconcerted, I say the first thing that comes to mind. "Hello, Jubah. You don't look surprised to see me."

"I been waitin' for you," she says, shrugging. "The bones tell me you come."

A shiver runs down my spine, and part of me wants nothing more than to run. Instead I duck my head and step into the close dusk of Jubah's hut.

Her braids are wound into a complicated twist atop her head, and when she turns to look at me, I can see the flames reflected in the obsidian depths of her eyes. Half her face is in the light, half in shadow, so that for a moment I feel as if I am looking at two different people—one here, with me, the other lost to darkness.

"Sit," she says, and gestures at the chair across from her.

I sit down, spreading my hands wide on the worn surface of the table. "I don't know exactly why I'm here," I say. "That is—I know, but I don't know what it is that I hope you can tell me."

"Oh, you know all right." Her voice is serene, as placid as the surface of an untroubled pool of water—but her own hands are moving, turning a small object over and over in their grasp. "You know, and I do too. The spirits, they always know."

As if my fingers belong to someone else, I see them tighten on the edge of the table, gripping hard. "Is it possible, then?" It emerges as a whisper, hoarse and strained.

"Perhaps," she says in that same indifferent voice. "Or perhaps not. That is not for me to say. We ask the spirits, they tell us true. But first—you drink."

"Drink?" I ask. "Drink what?"

Tilting her head, she nods at the cup on the table. "For you. You drink, you see things. Then—we talk."

My heart picks up speed, hammering my sternum like a captive bird. I suck in air, trying to slow it down—and get a solid lungful of the steam drifting upward from the mug of tea. The world expands, contracts to a single point of light, and then widens like a fish-eye lens. At the center of it I can see Jubah, her dark eyes fixed on mine, miniature candle flames blazing in each of her pupils. I know this is just an illusion, but it seems as if she has somehow absorbed the light—as if she has become the candle, holding fire and heat and mutability deep within.

"The spirits always know." Her voice is smoother now, coaxing— honey spread over a thin, perilous layer of ice. "They know where you come from. They know where you go. But to tell Jubah—that require sacrifice. Now drink," she says, and sets the small object on the table. It is bleached white by the sun, with hollow sockets where the eyes should be, and sharp, yellowed incisors. I'm pretty sure it's a cat's skull.

I close my eyes, wondering whether I am really going to do this. God only knows what is in that cup, or what it will do to me. But then my hand wraps itself around the handle—finding it unerringly, an arrow to its target. I lift the cup to my mouth and drain it, tasting bitterness and dust, the fresh bite of green plants and the musk of spices ground to powder. The liquid sears the membranes of my mouth and slides down my throat, hot and potent and utterly unfamiliar.

When the cup is empty, I open my eyes. Through the blue heart of the flame I see Jubah regarding me, as if from very far away. I know the table is no more than two feet wide, but I could swear she sits at the other end of a long, narrow room, the wavering light of the candle the only bridge between us. "Can you hear me, Maxwell Adair?"

I feel myself nod, the movement jerky, not completely under my control. "I hear."

"Good," she says. "What do you see?"

"You," I say, the word thick in my mouth. "I see you."

"Mmmm. That all? Nothin' else? Look hard."

This time her words have the unmistakable ring of command, and I do my best to obey. I narrow my eyes, and Jubah's image flickers, going in and out like the picture on an old-fashioned TV. For a moment I can see *through* her to what lies beyond. Then she is gone, and I see only what remains.

I am standing in my old bedroom, at my parents' house. I haven't slept there since I graduated from college, but I can see it clearly, all the same—the pale blue wallpaper, the hardwood floor with its rag rug, the huge fireplace. But as I pad silently across the floorboards, avoiding the one by the closet that always creaks, I see that someone is asleep in my bed, underneath the quilt my grandmother made the Christmas before she died.

From where I stand, all that is visible above the covers is a fall of curly black hair, and at first, I think it's Isabel. But the form beneath the quilt is too small, and as I step closer and the figure lifts its head, I see that it is Finn.

"Daddy!" she says, sounding delighted. Sitting up, she wraps her arms around her knees and reaches to turn on the lamp beside the bed. "What are you doing here?"

"You're in my room," I point out, sitting down beside her.

"No, I'm not. This is *my* room," she says, pouting prettily.

"Well, it used to be mine. What are you doing here?"

"Visiting Nana and Grandpa." She toys with one of her curls, uncoiling it, letting it bounce back again. "I'm sleeping over. We had shrimp skewers for dinner. Grandpa grilled. And then Nana and I baked cookies. My favorite kind, with M&M's in."

My mother used to bake those cookies for me, when I was little. Dazedly, I lift one hand and rest it on Finn's head, smoothing her hair. She allows this, smiling shyly at me. "Your eyes are like mine," she offers after a moment.

"Yeah, I know. Like Grandpa's too." I swallow hard, missing my dad, difficult though he can be. "Finn, is this real, you and me? Or am I dreaming?"

She gives me a small, enigmatic smile. "Oh, it's real. And you're dreaming too. It's both."

"But are you real?"

"Of course I am!" she says indignantly. "That's not a very nice thing to ask."

"If you're real," I say, "what did you do today?"

Straightening her spine in a way that reminds me of myself readying for conflict, she fixes me with an austere gray stare. "Mommy and I went to the beach. To Morris Island. She told me the story about the lighthouse, the one about how there used to be a schoolhouse there and everything. How it was beautiful, painted all pretty, and you could hear the children playing from shore if the wind was right. But then the island got smaller and smaller, and soon everyone had to leave and the lighthouse was all alone." She cuddles against me, butting her head against my shoulder, and I wrap one arm around her.

"I always feel bad for the lighthouse, out there all by itself," she says, her breath gusting warm against my skin. "So whenever we go to the beach, I ask Mommy to take me to see it. And I have her tell me the story, so I can remember all about how it used to be. Because as long as someone remembers, then it isn't really gone."

At this, a shiver runs through me. When Isabel and I used to steal my dad's beer and make out on the beach at Morris Island, she always used to beg me to tell her the story of the lighthouse. She loved gazing out over the darkened water at the looming, lonely building, leaning back against my chest as I told her how the water had crept up, higher and higher, washing the sand away until only the lighthouse was left. *When you tell me the story, Max,* she'd say, *I can see it. You make it real.*

Finn turns her head toward me, about to speak. Then she jerks upright, eyes wide in the dim glow of the lamp. She tilts her head, listening.

"What is it?" I ask, but she shakes her head furiously, curls flying, one finger pressed against her lips. After a moment I hear what's disturbed her—footsteps on the stairs, coming closer.

"Oh, no," she says, scooting back under the covers. "It's Nana, checking on me. You should hide."

"Hide?" I say blankly. "Why—"

"She won't understand. She'll be frightened. You need to go." She's pushing at me now, her small hands splayed on my chest.

"But where—"

"Under the bed," she says impatiently. "I don't know. How did you get in?"

I open my mouth to tell her that I have no idea, but then the world tilts and she is gone. I have the strangest sense that time is moving, folding in on itself like one of those origami fortune-tellers that the girls used to make in middle school. Move your fingers one way, and the revealed triangle of paper would read, *You'll be rich and drive a BMW.* Again, and it would say, *He'll love you forever.* A third time, and *The devil is going to claim your soul. Too bad, so sad.*

I feel like I am in the center of the fortune-teller, some great, implacable force pushing the edges of my world together, compressing my lungs. One thick beat of my heart, and the paper moves, showing a battlefield soaked in blood, backlit by hellfire. Another, and it moves again, giving me a brief glimpse of Isabel standing in the doorway of an unfamiliar bedroom, wearing a blue tank top and black workout pants, her hair tumbling to her waist in a torrent of messy curls. Beside her stands a tall man I don't recognize, clad only in his boxers. His hair is tousled, as if he's been sleeping, but his hazel eyes are focused, his gaze sharp. Even in the dream I can sense the tension emanating from him, the coiled energy, as if he's woken expecting to take on a threat. *What is it?* Isabel says to someone I can't see, urgency clear in her voice. *Did you have a nightmare?* She crosses into the room, and I hear Finn cry, *Daddy!*

Then the scene is gone. The fortune-teller folds again, and my heart struggles to beat, straining against the immense pressure. When the weight yields, I am standing at the edge of a cane field. I can see the great house from here, but it's not one I recognize. Someone touches my hand, and I look down to see Finn beside me. Look up, and realize that Julia is on her other side.

"I've missed you," Finn says, and, smiling, she reaches out to take Julia's hand in hers. "I'm so glad I found you. I was worried I never would."

Then her other hand slides into mine, and the smile fades. "It's coming," she says.

I don't question this. I figure that I know. But on her other side, Julia says, "What's coming, Finn? What do you mean?"

Her eyes still on my face, Finn replies, "Danger."

There is a beat of silence. Then Julia says, her voice a bit too bright, "Don't worry, honey. Everything will be fine. Tell your grandpa—tell Andrew that we're safe."

Finn turns to look at her, and then she shakes her head. "He hasn't seen you in such a long time," she says sadly. "He doesn't understand."

The misery in her voice wrecks me, and I lift her up, holding her close. She is unexpectedly light in my arms, as if her bones are hollow, like a bird's. Carefully, she extends one hand and touches the aquamarine stone in Julia's necklace. "Pretty," she says, resting her head on my shoulder.

I swallow hard, feeling her warm, trusting weight settle against me. "Give your mother a kiss for me, sweetheart," I whisper into the cloud of her hair, so much like Isabel's. "Whatever comes."

Finn replies, but I can't make out the words. My arms are suddenly empty, and everything—Finn, Julia, the cane field—is retreating down a long tunnel, or maybe I'm the one who's retreating. It's impossible to tell. All I know is that with every passing second, the distance between us grows. I'm moving faster and faster, falling. I land hard, with a thump that drives the air from my body, and lie still, trying to catch my breath.

For a moment all I know is immediate sensation—a terrible sense of vertigo, the thump of my heart, the struggle to breathe. And then I become aware that someone is calling me. Summoning me.

My eyes snap open, and I see Jubah sitting across from me. She hasn't moved. The skull is still on the table, as is the cup—but the candle has burned down to little more than a stub, and the sky beyond the window is beginning to lighten. Impossible as it seems, I am still sitting in the chair, my elbows braced on the table.

"What—" I begin, but the word emerges as a harsh croak and I have to clear my throat several times before I can go on. "What happened?"

"You traveled far, Maxwell Adair. But not so far that I can't follow."

"What does that mean? You saw—what I saw? What was that? A dream? A vision?" My voice is trembling, despite my best efforts to steady it. I can still taste the ashy residue of the concoction she gave me, heavy on my tongue.

Jubah shrugs her narrow shoulders as if this is of no consequence. "The name don't matter. I see what I need to know. The day you spoke for Cuffee, I promised you what aid be in my power. So now— ask your questions, and I answer what the spirits will."

I open my mouth, shut it again, and then say, "The rebellion. Can I stop it?"

"You just one man, Maxwell Adair. The rebellion be lifted up by many, broke down by more. One man can't stand against the tide."

"So—" I say, my voice breaking, "there's nothing I can do? Nothing at all?"

"I ain't sayin' that." Her eyes are on me now, shrewd, searching. "One man can save another, eh? Only you know how to wipe your heart clean of what stains it. There be more than one way to die."

"So I shouldn't give up? I should keep trying?" The candle is guttering now and the rising sun is not yet bright enough to illuminate the hut. I strain to see her expression more clearly, but all I can make out is the intensity of those dark eyes, peering at me as if they can pierce straight through my clothes to the sinew and soul beneath.

"You do what's right," Jubah says, nodding sharply. "You a good man. Your heart beats true."

"But—" I say, afraid to ask the next question. The words build in my throat, jamming against one another so that it is hard to breathe, but somehow I manage to force a trickle of air through. "Will I ever go home?"

"Ah," she says, one finger stroking the cat's skull. "Home for you be far and far, Maxwell Adair. Where your little girl is, eh? Your little girl who got her daddy's eyes."

"Finn," I say, the word like balm in my mouth. "Is she real, then?"

"Oh, she real all right. Real as you and me. 'Cept—not yet." She palms the skull, cradling it against her chest, and I have to fight back a shudder of revulsion. "You be here an' there, eh? So does she. A traveler, that one. A one that see clear."

"A traveler? What do you mean?"

She waves her hand, dismissing this. "You want to know—can

you go home. You and the other one both. And I tell you—yes. The spirits show me true. But there will be one day for it, an' no more."

The other one—Julia. For the first time since I got here, I feel a surge of hope. "When? We'll be ready, I swear. Just tell me, and we'll be there."

"Easter Monday," she says, dark eyes on mine. "'Round midday. The way open then, and then only."

I feel my heart sink, plummeting into my stomach with a sudden, nauseating weight. "Easter Monday? But that's right in the middle of the rebellion!"

I've spoken without thinking, and Jubah's eyes narrow. Then she reaches out and pinches the candle flame between her fingers, extinguishing it as if the heat means nothing. Across the darkened space she regards me, and when she speaks, her voice is grim. "You go back the way you came when I tell you, you get your chance. But you wait—and the way close behind you. Here you stay."

Isabel

S weat-soaked and exhausted, I shower, load my gear in the car, and drive to my dad's house to pick up Finn. I find her in my old bedroom, sitting at my little white desk, drawing by the light of the gooseneck lamp. She's deep in concentration, but when I come in, she turns and waves at me before returning to work, tongue stuck out of her mouth ever so slightly, the way it always is when she's deep in thought.

"What are you drawing, baby?" I ask, willing myself to sound normal.

"Just a picture. There wasn't a red marker, so I had to use pink. It's not turning out how I wanted at all."

The petulance in her voice is genuine, and I have to force myself not to smile. "I'm sure it's beautiful. Can I see?"

She turns the drawing toward me. I lean closer, peering down. And then I get a good look at the piece of paper, and any hope of normalcy goes right out the window.

It's a picture of a man and a woman, standing in a field. The man has Max's wavy dark hair. Next to him stands the woman, short and curvy, with straight blond hair falling around her shoulders. And around the woman's neck hangs the dragonfly necklace, both wings intact, an aquamarine stone at its heart, clearly drawn and unmistakable.

I take a step backward, unable to help myself. Finn is talking to me, but I can't hear a word. "Dad," I manage, and then louder, "Dad! Come here!"

My father comes running, summoned from whatever he was doing—eating, it looks like, based on the napkin clutched in his hand—by the alarm in my voice. Mute, I hand him the drawing, and watch the shock spread across his face.

"You don't have a picture of her wearing it, do you?" I ask him, even though I already know the answer.

He shakes his head, as pale as I've ever seen him. "You know I don't. Did you show her any of those photos you took?"

"Why would I do *that*?"

White-faced, my dad kneels in front of Finn. "Sweetheart," he says with forced calm, "where did you get the idea to draw this picture?"

Finn looks from her grandfather to me, her lower lip trembling. "Did I do something bad?"

At this, I emerge from my stupor and wrap my arms around her. "Of course not, honey. Just tell us—did you see that necklace somewhere before?"

Confidence returns to Finn's face. She sits up straight, out of my embrace. "Of course I did," she says, and relief courses through me as I wait for her to offer a logical explanation. "My grandma Julia showed it to me."

My father sways, and for a moment I think he is going to pass out. "What do you mean?" he says, his voice barely above a whisper.

"Finn!" I say sharply. "That's not funny."

My daughter looks at me, confusion writ large on her features. "But she did show me, Mama. She wanted you and Grandpa to know that she's okay, and not to worry. And Daddy says to tell you—"

But whatever missive Max might have intended to pass on from the great beyond is lost in the ringing of my cellphone. I look down and, with no surprise whatsoever, see that the call is from the archaeology professor in Barbados. In what feels like slow motion, I raise the phone to my ear. "Hello?"

"Dr. Griffin?" she says, as if maybe someone else has commandeered my phone. Then again, maybe I don't sound all that much like myself.

"This is she," I say automatically. "Dr. Absolom?"

"Yes. I'm on my way to a meeting, so I'll get right to the point."

"Please," I say, looking down at Finn, whose gray eyes have gone huge in her face. My father is sitting on the bed, looking as if someone has hit him where it hurts.

Outside the window, a fat bumblebee hovers over the wisteria my mother planted when we first moved into this house. I watch its progress with rapt attention as Dr. Absolom says, "You asked me to look for the remnants of that necklace, yes?"

"I did," I say, eyes fixed on the bee. "Did you find something?"

"We did, yes. This morning, as a matter of fact. It's a fragment—a wing, I suppose you'd call it, matching the one on the other side. There's an inscription on it, all right, stamped into the metal."

All the blood leaves my head, and the image of the bee wavers, lost in a sea of gray. Dimly I am aware that my father has crossed the room and taken me by the shoulders, that Finn's face has gone paper-white, but they have no place here. All of my senses are concentrated on the voice on the other end of the line as Dr. Absolom reads the inscription off, the one I know as well as my daughter's name: *"The dream is the truth." Love always, I. & A.*

Max

Jubah's cryptic advice is the first clue to our way home I've managed to discover—and I can't wait to share it with Julia. I manage to get a message to her to meet me at Caroline Lee's tavern, the day before Good Friday. That morning, I wake early and try to distract myself in Bridgetown, although after I finally see the Cage for myself, I wish I had stayed in my room. It is much as Sarey described it—a stinking, slat-walled building with grated doors and windows located on the town's Broad Street.

When I brave the stench to peer inside, I step back quickly, convinced I've gotten a glimpse into hell. The mass of contorted figures resolves itself into a woman huddled in the corner, a man clapped in stocks, and another, little more than a girl, who presses her face against the gap between the boards, desperate for a breath of fresh air. Seeing me, she lets out a wail and holds up her chained wrists, shaking them in a plea for freedom.

I stumble away, nearly knocking over a woman balancing an entire chicken coop on her head. The contents squawk, flapping their wings in protest and sending an ammoniac reek into the air. Wiping my streaming eyes, I jump out of her path—and almost run down a huckster hawking her wares behind me.

Everywhere I look there are people walking with wooden trays balanced on their heads, holding everything from food and jewelry to clothes and toys. A tall woman in a blue turban and saffron-colored dress sways past me and I stop her, trading a few coins for a plum and a stone jar of water, hoping to ease the sick ache in my stomach. With a smile, she tucks the money into the pocket of her skirt and merges seamlessly back into the crowd, calling out, "Fruit! Drink! Best prices in town!"

The chained girl's wail still ringing in my ears, I edge toward the flagstone sidewalk and lean against a grocer's shop, peering through the window. I have to dodge out of the way to avoid being run down by an older white woman hustling out the door, berating an amber-skinned girl who trails behind her.

"I do be sorry, Miss Elizabeth," I hear the girl say as they make their way down the street toward a shop whose shingle reads APOTH-ECARY, a mocking note in her voice.

"No you're not," the woman retorts. "You've never been sorry for anything a day in your life. I can't imagine why I put up with you, as much trouble as you cause me. Go purchase me a bottle of Lancaster Black Drop. I shall be at the seamstress, buying a new bonnet; you can meet me there when you're done. Mind you don't tarry now, Polly Bell, we've places to be."

The girl nods obsequiously, but as soon as Elizabeth is out of sight, she ducks past me and makes her way to the corner, where a large woman sits perched on a tiny stool, two small children playing at her feet. "Afternoon, Bennebah," she says to the woman. "You got anything good today?"

The woman looks up, smiling. "For you, Polly Bell, I got the spe-cial things," she says, her accent stronger than any I've heard before, turning "things" to "t'ings." "But first, sit you down and have a sugar cake. You know Bennebah's sugar cake's the best."

I take a bite out of my plum as Polly Bell glances over her shoul-der, in the direction of where her mistress has disappeared. "I can't be sittin' down," she says bitterly. "Her Highness told me to fetch her some of those useless potions out the 'pothecary shop. She'll be fussed if I don't have them for her directly."

At this, Bennebah laughs. "She think she's the queen of every-thing, sure 'nough. Queen Elizabeth Fenwick, she fancies herself. Well, she's queen of that school of hers, and that's about the size of it. She'll be findin' that out, all right."

Polly's face darkens. "She's always going on 'bout the 'horrid in-stitution of slavery,'" she says in that same high, mocking voice. "Once I say to her, you think it's so horrid, Miss Elizabeth, why you own slaves, then? And she tell me not to sass her, that the problem lies with the slaves. *Lazy, insolent creatures, every one of you,* that what she say. *Why, you won't even work unless I have you beaten.* I feel like tellin' her I won't work for her no ways. But I got to eat."

Bennebah bends down, extracting a cake from a tray beneath her stool, and wraps it in paper, pausing to mark something on the sheet before handing it to Polly Bell. "You most surely do," she says. "And this won't cost you nothing. Don't you waste the paper, though. You never know when a body might need it."

When Polly glances down at the sugar cake in her hand, her eyes widen. "Really?" she says. "Good Friday? That soon?"

At Bennebah's nod, Polly smiles. "I'll spread the word, then," she says. "This come from Bussa himself?"

"Come from him and Joseph Franklyn. It can be trusted." Ben-nebah sits back. "Now you best be going, before Queen Elizabeth decides to come lookin' for you. Don't forget about the dance at River tomorrow," she says, and winks.

A grim smile lights Polly's face. "Not likely. She can look all she likes. I take my time." And she strolls off in the direction of the apoth-ecary, cake in hand. She walks right by me, and my pulse races.

By the time I look over at Bennebah again, I see that she is staring at me, her expression neutral. She nods once, sharply, as if in confir-mation, then turns away, bestowing her gap-toothed smile on a pro-spective customer.

After this encounter, which confirms that things are unfolding as the history books promised they would, I need to talk to Julia more than ever. I get to Caroline Lee's before she does and stand when she comes in, a ridiculously wide smile breaking across my face. "Hey," I say, giving her a little wave.

No sooner does she slide into her seat and give her order to the serving maid than she's looking me over, as if for damage. "Hey, yourself, Max. Are you all right? God, I was so worried."

"I'm fine," I assure her, sitting back down.

She scrutinizes me as the serving maid plunks down two glasses of lime water, along with our food—chicken for Julia, a steaming bowl of beef stew for me. "What have you been doing? Are you really okay?"

I hardly know how to begin, but I give her the basics of my living situation, then tell her all about the conversation I just witnessed and my encounter with Jubah. I look around to make sure we're not being overheard, and then turn back to Julia, satisfied. The tavern is filled with ships' captains and officers, drinking ale, eyeing the waitresses, gambling. No one so much as gives us a second glance.

And a good thing too, because at the mention of our escape, Julia's eyes light up and she lunges across the table, grabbing me by the wrist. "Home?" she says. "On Monday? Oh, Max, do you think she could be right?"

"I think it's the best chance we've got. But how it would work, I have no idea. Maybe just find our way into the cane fields where we started. *Go back the way you came*, that's what Jubah said."

She settles back in her chair, looking thoughtful. "But I didn't come through at Sweetwater. I was in the Brightmores' field. So we'd have to be separated?"

"Sounds like it. And in the middle of the rebellion? Julia, I just don't know."

She hears my hesitation and seizes on it. "What don't you know? Max, we have to do it. We have to!"

"But it's right in the midst of everything," I protest. "Right in the middle of the fighting. I can't just leave."

"Of course you can!" Her voice is rising now, agitation clear in every word. "We don't belong here. If there's the slightest chance that we can escape—that we can go home—"

"Shhh," I admonish her. "Someone will hear."

Julia blots her mouth with her napkin, pressing it to her lips as if to hold the words inside. When she looks up at me, her eyes are swimming with tears. "Don't you *want* to go home, Max?"

"Of course I do. But I have to believe that we're here for a purpose. For a reason. I can't just run away." I rub my hand over my jaw, thinking. "Maybe there's a way for me to do both—to dissuade the slaves from fighting and go home with a clear conscience. I'm going to that dance tomorrow night. I think it'll be my last chance."

Julia freezes, her glass of lime water halfway to her mouth. "You're going to sneak onto River Plantation and infiltrate one of the largest slave gatherings of the year—after they've already told you they want nothing to do with your plan? Are you nuts?"

"Maybe," I say, spearing one of the carrots floating in the stew.

"And if you fail? Or if they kill you? What then?"

I shrug, with more confidence than I feel. "Well," I say, "then I guess it's all up to you." She eyes me, openmouthed, and I laugh. "I'm kidding. Julia, they could have murdered me eight times over by now."

Julia makes a disgruntled sound and sets her glass of lime water down with a clink. "And what am I supposed to do while you're undertaking this ridiculous plan?"

"It's not ridiculous," I say heatedly. "I just don't want you to risk yourself a few days before we might get out of here for good. Right now, unless Lily decides to share what we've told her, everyone just thinks of you as the Simmonses' tutor. See if you can learn anything that will help us."

"Uh-huh." Lips set, she stabs at the toasted, buttered yam on her plate as if it's done her an injury. "I'll do that. And you—you try not to die."

Max

─────

I hear the music long before I see the dancers. Someone's beating on a kettle drum, setting the pace. Other drummers join them, and then I can hear the mournful cry of a banjo, the rhythmic shake of rattles. The moon is full, and as I draw closer to the slave village, I can see shadowy figures moving by its light. Closer still, at the edge of the yard, and I make out a circle of people, ringed around the musicians. The audience is dressed for the occasion, their usual plainclothes augmented with bead-and-shell necklaces twined around their limbs and draped from their necks. As I watch, they raise their hands above their heads and clap, hollering in time to the music.

Quietly as I can, I slip into the circle. Now I can see the dancers for myself, and for a moment my breath sticks in my throat. One of them leaps, and the other follows, winding herself effortlessly into his shadow, though they never touch.

Fascinated though I am, I step away from the circle, hearing the murmurs as heads turn toward me, hoping I was right when I told Julia that if anyone planned to kill me, they would have done it days ago. My pistol hangs heavy on my left hip, and I feel the weight of my knife where it's strapped inside my stocking. Their presence is reassuring, and I move into the darkness, seeking a familiar face.

I haven't gone far when a form separates from the shadows and materializes in front of me, blocking my way. "Master Max," a woman's voice says coldly. "What you doin' here, sir? You said your piece, and I listened. Did I not send you on your way?"

I blink, and the apparition resolves itself into Nanny Grigg. She's clad in a white linen wrap, her ears bedecked with beaded hoops, her hands planted firmly on her substantial hips. "Good evening to you too," I say, and try to smile.

She doesn't smile back. "Don't you good e'en me, sir. You got no place here. This ain't a spectacle for your amusement."

"I know it's not. I didn't come to spy on you. I came to talk to Bussa—if you'll let me."

"Bussa?" She shakes her head. "I don't know what you got in mind, but you best think again. You ain't talking to Bussa, nor no one else. Leave us be and go on home."

"I won't," I say stubbornly. "I can't."

She lets out a deep breath and opens her mouth to reply, but someone else beats her to it. "That's enough." The voice is deep, confident, and clear. Its owner steps from the shadows of a hut into the light, next to Nanny Grigg. He's broad-shouldered and thick-boned, a solid block of a man. "You want to speak to Bussa? You find him, then."

"I just want to talk," I say. "And then I'll leave, I promise."

"Umph." He looks me over, from my borrowed shoes to my pistol, and I have the distinct impression he finds me wanting. Then he nods. "Come inside. You're making a commotion out here. Nanny G., you too."

I follow Bussa into the hut, which is candlelit and full of people. As soon as they see me, all conversation stops. I look from one face to the other, recognizing only Jackey and John, from Simmons.

A short man standing by the hut's one window speaks first. "What you about, Bussa?" he says angrily. "You want to get all of us killed?"

"Hush your whining, Daniel." Bussa speaks mildly, with the thicker accent I've heard from some of the slaves—maybe just a more intense Caribbean lilt, maybe a relic of his country of origin—but his air of calm authority is clear enough. "You want him kicking up a fuss outside, letting everyone know our business?"

"It's bad enough *he* knows our business," Jackey says, glaring at me. "I told you already, he knows all about it. How else he know to come here tonight?"

My hand drops instinctively to my pistol. But before I can touch it, a man steps forward, better-dressed and lighter-skinned than the others. "Hold your tongue, Jackey," he says, each syllable clipped. "This gentleman is come among us, a stranger. As we could have taken his life, several times over, so too could he have betrayed our plans. And yet he does not speak, or raise a hand against us. If he is indeed a seer, so much the better. Nanny Grigg, did you not tell me he gave you information when you asked—where the battles will be fought, where we will suffer the greatest casualties?"

"Ha," Bussa says, a harsh exhalation. "And this does not trouble you, Franklyn?"

I can feel my eyes widen. Unless I'm mistaken, this is Joseph Pitt Washington Franklyn—a freed slave who the rebels chose to govern the country should the insurrection succeed. Though the majority of historians hold that Bussa is the undisputed leader of the rebellion, a few argue that Franklyn actually played the starring role.

The man who must be Joseph Franklyn shrugs. "I'm curious what he has to say. Appearances can be deceiving," he says, turning to me. "You see, sir, my father Joseph Franklyn was a white man. But my mother, Leah, was a slave. I was born a slave, raised as a slave. Freed, by my father's will . . . but my brothers will not claim me as their kin." His foot taps the floor, and when his gaze lifts to meet mine, I see fire in its depths.

"Yes, I am free, but that freedom is little more than an illusion. Once a white overseer came into my home against my will and made advances on one of my female relations. I defended my home and my honor. For that I was convicted—I could not give evidence against a white man—and was sentenced to six months' close imprisonment."

He leans forward, face knotted with passion. "I am not a slave, Mr. Adair—nor am I truly free. I must serve in the militia, but an officer I cannot be."

He takes one step toward me, then another. "Planters fear me, because they believe I might inspire insurgency in the hearts of slaves—and well I might! Yet they must grant me some privileges, lest I ally with the slaves and overthrow them completely." He clenches his fists, so the bones stand out beneath his skin. "And the slaves? My mother's people? They do not trust me, either, and why should they? Why should I be different from so many free men eager to prove they share nothing with the beasts who work the fields or the domestics who do their masters' bidding?" His voice is scornful, but Bussa and Nanny Grigg stiffen just the same.

Franklyn comes to a halt, breathing hard. "I am a man out of place, at home nowhere, suspect in the eyes of all. And you, sir—you seem the same. I cannot define it, but I sense it nonetheless. So this once, I will listen to you. But you'd best speak true."

I step closer, so we are eye to eye. "This is what I know. If you fight, you won't live to see freedom. It will come—but not in your lifetime." The words rise from a place far beyond me, drawn from the falling night outside and the flickering light of the candle flames. "You'll be underarmed and outnumbered. Bussa will die in battle at Bayleys. They'll name the rebellion for him. And you? You'll be executed."

Franklyn opens his mouth to reply. But before he can say a word, one of the men standing in the shadows hisses through his teeth, his eyes fixed on my face. "You talk to the spirits, then, buckra? You call them down to do your will?"

"No."

"Then what?" He pushes off the wall. "You look like the buckra, true. But what if you slip your skin, wear someone else's? Only obeah can see the future. Who you call up? Whose bones you make rise an' walk again?" Sinuous and slow, he stalks toward me, body blending in and out of the darkness. He pauses two feet away, sizing me up. "My name is Johnny Cooper," he says. "Can you tell my end?"

I wince, not wanting to answer. But I came here to be honest. "You'll die," I tell him. "They'll hang you on Trent's Hill in St. Peter, as an example to the other slaves."

He hisses again, drawing back as if burned. "I say you're a liar, except you taste of the truth. You know our plants, our medicines. Jubah say so. What else you know? Maybe you make the drink that calls the spirits, for all your skin be pale as milk."

"Is Jubah here?" I say, seized with sudden confidence. "She'll speak for me."

Another man steps forward from the shadows, giving a derisive snort. "You know the future but not this? Jubah in the Cage. They take her away the day 'fore yesterday."

"The Cage?" I remember the seething mass of humanity, the woman in irons, face pressed against the gap between the slatted boards, and suck in my breath. "For what?"

"Murder." His voice is matter-of-fact, and hoarse, as if from shouting. "An' sorcery. They say she kill Bess's baby, over at Bayleys. I am the head carpenter there; King Wiltshire is my name. Jubah, she marry my brother Joe. He tell me what happen." The man spreads his hands, and in the dim light of the candles, I can see that his fingers are scarred, knuckles swollen. "Master Edward always bothering Bess, won't leave her alone for nothin'. Takes her in the fields, in the kitchen, in her own home with the children sleeping right beside her." He spits in disgust.

I've grown accustomed to the Barbadian slave dialect's tendency toward the present tense, half the time instinctively translating it into the past tense in my head. Still, hearing Wiltshire recount the story this way—like it's happening right now, all over again—makes my blood boil. *Damn Edward Thomas*, I think. *That power-craving, rapist son of a bitch*. Part of me wishes I'd killed him that day in the field, and the hell with the consequences. I suck in a deep, steadying breath as Wiltshire goes on.

"Bess try everything to get rid of his baby growing in her. But nothin' worked. So she tell Jubah—when this babe come, she not want it to live." He flexes his big hands, balling them into fists. "So Jubah do it—but someone see her. Someone tell."

I can picture this scene all too clearly. Despite myself, I think about my own child—imaginary or no—and repress a shudder. "And Bess?"

Wiltshire eyes me, his gaze flat. "Master Edward whip Bess within an inch of her life. Then he order she put in the Cage with Jubah. The two of them likely dead before too long, less there be some kind of miracle. You got one of those to offer, buckra?"

"No," I say, ignoring the hostility in his tone. "I wish I did."

"Enough," Bussa says, slamming his hand down on the table. "Talk won't help Bess or Jubah. Only help is what we got in mind. If this plan works, we set them both free. No point thinking about what happened. That's the past."

"Ain't the past to them," Cooper mutters. "Ain't the past when they locked up in the dark, chained like animals, just waitin' to die."

Bussa shakes his head. "Ain't nothin' happening to them tomorrow or the next day, neither. White folk too busy goin' to church of a Sunday, eating themselves stupid, never noticing what's goin' on right beneath their noses."

His eyes fall on me, and he gives an angry grin. "You think you see the future? Well, the future can change. We will come out of the canes set on battle, to avenge ourselves and our ancestors. For here their bones lie, so far from our homeland."

From the darkness in the hut comes a murmur of approbation. I feel the trip wire of violence pulled taut, the trap waiting to be sprung. When Bussa speaks again, his voice is soft, but fierce. "The first night, we light the fields afire, make them watch their sugar and rum burn, everything they built on the backs of slaves. They're gonna cry, 'Water!' and beg for help. But who's gonna help them?"

One of his large hands closes on a discarded cornstalk doll that lies on the edge of a pallet. The doll's crude head disappears inside his fist, and I hear the stalks crunching, giving way. "The next night, the fighting starts. There be an army of us, thousands strong. We rise up against them and show them what we made of."

His hand opens, and the doll falls to the ground. "They can beat us an' whip us an' take our children away. They can use our women and shame our men. But inside—that be somewhere they can't see, somewhere they can't touch." His foot comes down on the doll, crushing it into the dirt, and his gaze rises to meet mine. "That second night, we show them that they may stripe our backs, but they can't break our spirits. They fall in the dirt, in the field, in the house, and the life run out of them, 'til we take this island for our own. We fight 'til they surrender. We make them cry out, 'Blood.'"

Isabel

I hear myself thank Dr. Absolom, hear myself say that this is useful information about the necklace, very useful indeed. My voice is clear and professional, not giving away the fact that I'm curled on the floor of my childhood room, shaking so hard, it's a challenge to hold the phone. It must pass muster, because Dr. Absolom goes on, saying she's sent me photos so that I can see for myself. We hang up, and I stare at the phone as if it is a portal to the great beyond, trying to gather the courage to check my email.

"Isabel?" my dad says. His hands grasp my shoulders, tight. "What's the matter?"

I don't say a word. I can't. Instead I tap the Safari icon on my phone and log into my account, feeling as if reality has somehow slid sideways.

If you'd asked me ten minutes ago, I would have told you that I'd give almost anything to get this call. Now, in its aftermath, I am terrified. *It can't be*, I think, opening the message from Dr. Absolom. *How can it? Surely there's been a mistake.*

I open the message, click on the attachment, brace myself. And then I see it—tarnished and worn, showing the marks of long interment, but unmistakable nonetheless: the missing wing from my mother's necklace, inscription and all.

Dimly I am aware that my father is still talking. I try to speak, but the words lodge in my throat. Instead I shove the phone in his direction and stumble to my feet, racing down the hall to the bathroom, where I throw up until there is nothing left in my stomach.

When I emerge, my father is sitting on the bed, clutching the phone. Finn is rubbing his back the way he does for her when she isn't feeling well. "Do you want ice water, Grandpa?" she's asking anxiously. "Does your head hurt?"

My father shakes his head, face paper-white. "I'm okay, honey," he says, patting her hand clumsily to reassure her. "Isabel—can I talk to you?"

We stand in the hallway, and he leans against the wall as if it's the only thing holding him up. "I don't understand," he keeps saying. "It's not possible, is it? There can't be another one like it—but what does it mean? It has to mean something, right?"

"I don't know what anything means anymore, Dad." I reach an arm out for Finn, who's come into the hallway after us, and pull her against my side.

"I don't understand," my father says again. "After all these years . . . does it mean she's out there, somewhere? That she might find her way home, still? Or just that they haven't found—" He stops abruptly, smoothing Finn's hair, but his meaning is clear enough. Perhaps my mother's body is buried somewhere on the grounds of Lowthers Plantation, a grisly discovery awaiting Dr. Absolom's crew.

"They'll keep digging." My voice sounds wooden, a weak facsimile of its normal self. "It's an extensive project and this is a crucial site. If she's . . . there . . . they'll find her."

My father nods jerkily. "I'm sorry," he says, backing away. "I just—I can't—I need to be alone."

He pushes my phone back into my hand and walks off without another word. I stare after him, resisting the desire to call him back.

What about me? I think, with the bitterness reminiscent of my ado-
lescence. *What about what I need?*

But what I need doesn't matter anymore, because now I have
Finn. And goddamn it, I will not fail her.

"Mommy?" Her fingers curl around mine, icy cold the way they
were when she woke from her dream of the world on fire. "Was my
drawing bad?"

"No, honey, no." I pull her close, brushing tendrils of hair behind
her ears.

"It was! It made Grandpa's face go all white, and you got mad at
me."

"I wasn't mad—"

"Nobody ever believes me. You thought I made it up, about
Daddy and Grandma Julia. But I didn't. I didn't!" She squirms out of
my arms, small face contorted with fury, white to the lips with rage.
"I hate this stupid picture," she says, and only now do I realize that
she's still holding it, balled up in her fist. "I wish I'd never drawn it. I
hate it!" And before I can stop her, she rips the picture into bits.
Pieces of white paper fall to the floor, and she stamps on them for
good measure.

"Stop," I say, alarmed. I try to grab hold of her, but it's like holding a live wire. She wriggles out of my grasp, all knees and elbows,
past any kind of soothing.

"You don't understand," she wails, scrabbling on her hands and
knees for what remains of the picture, tearing it into smaller pieces
still. "And I can't make you. I don't know what to do."

In the end I pick her up, arms and legs flailing wildly, and carry
her to the car. She's screaming now, a keening animal wail that
frightens me more than anything that's come before. I dig my keys
out of my purse with one hand, then open the backseat and buckle
her in.

The moment I get her into the car, she goes limp. The wailing
subsides into hiccupping whimpers, and by the time we pull up to
the stoplight before the Ravenel Bridge, it's stopped entirely. I glance

back and see she's asleep, bits of paper clasped tight in both small fists. Gently, I open her fingers and let the pieces flutter to the floor.

She's still sleeping when I pull up in front of our house. I carry her inside carefully, so as not to wake her. It's not as easy as it used to be—she's heavier now, her legs dangling as I navigate the stairs—but I make it without incident and lay her down on top of the quilt, next to Raggedy Ann. She looks so small lying there, fragile and incapable of the whirlwind ferocity that consumed her at my father's house.

I won't fail her, I tell myself. *I won't.* If she's right—and I don't understand—then maybe someone else will. I made myself a promise, and I'll do whatever it takes so that she is okay.

Quietly, I make my way out of her room and down the stairs. I settle myself on the living room couch, phone in hand. And then I dig the piece of paper with the therapist's contact information out of my wallet, and I dial.

Max

"They wouldn't listen to me," I tell Julia as we walk through the gardens at Simmons on Saturday evening after dinner. "I thought if I laid things out logically—with all of them together—they'd see it my way. But not so much."

"I'm sorry, Max," she says softly.

We've paused by a grove of cherry trees. I reach up and pluck a few of the fruits, handing some to Julia, who sinks onto a stone bench in the middle of the grove. "Well, that's that, then, I suppose," she says.

"What do you mean, that's that?"

"I mean," she says, meeting my eyes head-on, "the rebellion's going to happen. So, now we need to figure out how to get out of here."

I brace myself against the rough trunk of a cherry tree and say it out loud for the first time. "I'm not leaving, Julia. Lily's right. I have an obligation to stay and fight."

In an instant, Julia's on her feet in front of me with her hands on her hips and a horrified expression on her face. "No, you don't. And you won't!" she says, the certainty every bit as clear in her voice as it had been in mine.

"Really? How are you going to stop me?"

She ignores the question, plowing onward. "What makes you think you can help? You aren't a soldier, Max!"

"And you think they are?" I point down the road to the fields. "They have no fucking clue. They're going to fight with pitchforks and hoes, for Christ's sake. And be slaughtered. At least I have a musket."

Julia takes a step back, muttering something under her breath that sounds like *stubborn son of a bitch*. Then she tosses her hair back from her face and folds her arms across her chest. "Well then," she says briskly. "I'll fight with you."

Now it's my turn to stare at her, openmouthed. "Like hell you will!"

"Why? Because I'm a woman?"

"No! Because—because—"

She unfolds her arms and glowers up at me. "I'll tell you why not. Because it's a stupid thing to do, and you know it, Max Adair. And—what? You won't have me risk my life, but you'll throw yours away?"

"I'm not throwing my life away. What kind of person would I be if I just sat back and let innocent people go to their death?" My voice spirals upward, and I bite down on the inside of my cheek, hard, to stifle the flow of words. Blood floods my mouth.

Julia is glaring at me, furious. "This isn't your fight, Max. You don't belong here, any more than I do. You can't help what your ancestors did. And you don't know that you can stop a damn thing."

"Be quiet, would you?" I hiss. "Someone will hear."

"I hope they do hear! I have half a mind to tell them myself." She's pacing now, scuffing her red slippers in the dirt of the grove.

"You wouldn't," I say. "After everything—you wouldn't, Julia. If you do—they'll die anyway. At least this way, they'll go down fighting."

"And you think that's better? More honorable?" She stamps her foot, sending fallen cherries flying toward the path. "This has already happened, don't you understand? They'll lose no matter what you do! And if they don't—what gives you the right to change things? Who are you to play God?"

I wrap my fists around an overhanging tree branch, wrenching until the wood creaks. "Then why are we here?" My voice breaks on the last word, and I hang my head.

Julia touches my arm. "Max," she says, gently now. "I came here for all the wrong reasons. I was lost, looking for answers that I already had—where I come from, where I belong. But you found me. You can bring me home. And maybe that's why Robert came for you. To take me back. Maybe it's just that simple."

"That's what you think? That it has nothing to do with a higher calling—with standing up for what's right? Saving a woman and a child, standing up for defenseless people? That this is all about *you*?"

Her grip on my arm tightens. "I don't know. But the point is, you don't, either. If there's a chance we really can go home on Monday, and I make it back alone—how can I tell Isabel that you died in a battle you knew would fail? That I let you? Or that you survived, only to be hung? How will she forgive me?"

"No, Julia, how will she forgive *me*?" My voice comes out thick, but even, just the same. "If I don't do this, and I make it home . . . How can I tell her I just stood by and let this happen? That I'm no different than the rest of my family? I can't do that. I won't." I shake my head and step away, letting her hand fall.

She gives me a narrow, resigned glare. "And what about your child, then? My grandchild? You're fine with leaving her . . . or him . . . without a father?"

I shake my head. "You can't leave someone without a father who won't exist."

Julia inhales sharply. "You can't have it both ways, Max Adair," she says, sounding so much like Isabel, it almost brings a small smile to my face. "You can't stop a rebellion and save a woman, canceling your own existence out in the process—if that means you won't be there to stop it and save her in the first place."

"Maybe not," I say. "But I can try."

Julia is silent, and when I glance at her, I see that her eyes are fixed on the leaves of the cherry tree, shadowy in the gathering dusk, her expression distant. "I dreamed of her, you know," she says.

A chill runs down my spine. "Her?"

"A little girl with Izzy's curly dark hair. Gray eyes like yours. She was beautiful."

I take a step back, shock reverberating through my body. "In your dream," I say, sounding as shaken as I feel, "what did she do?"

Julia peers at me, puzzled. "It was just a dream, Max. Why does that matter?"

"Just humor me."

"Well," Julia says, "we were together—you, me, and the little girl. Here. I remember thinking she seemed so familiar. She said her name was Finn. We were standing outside by the cane. She put her hand in mine and said she'd missed me, that she was so glad to have found me at last. And then she put her other hand in yours. *It's coming*, she said. When I asked her what she meant, she answered, *Danger*."

She gives me a wry smile, but I don't return it. My knees give way and I sit down hard, right in the dirt. Julia gasps, kneeling next to me. "What's the matter, Max?" she says, one hand on my forehead, as if feeling for fever. "It was just a dream."

"No," I tell her, my voice coming from very far away. "No, it wasn't."

"What do you mean?" She sounds frightened, like she thinks I've lost my mind.

With some effort, I lift my head and search her face. "I've dreamed about her too, more than once. She looked just the same. And her name was Finn. She told me she was going to bring us home." I stumble to my feet, pulling Julia up with me. "In your dream . . . did she touch your necklace? Did she tell you it was pretty?"

Julia doesn't say a word. She doesn't have to. Her hand closes around the blue-green stone. "How—"

"I have no idea. But if she's real, Julia . . . how long have I been gone? Seven years? Eight? That's years of Isabel thinking I abandoned her—or that I'm dead." My voice breaks again and I turn away. In the distance, I can see the glow of fires burning in the slave village. I stare at them, hard, until my vision blurs and my head starts to ache.

"Goddamn it," I mutter, mostly to myself. "What a motherfucking disaster." My hands clench into fists and I hit the trunk of the nearest tree over and over, ignoring the hail of fruit that rains down around me.

Julia's hands are on my shoulders, tugging, pulling me away. "Max, stop," she says. "This isn't any good. It won't help us. It won't help *her*. Damn it, stop!"

I wheel around to face her, panting. She stands her ground, staring up at me, her lips set. "Does that change your mind?" she says at last. "If that really is your daughter—she's waiting for you. Isn't that what you want?"

"Of course it is." The knuckles of my right hand sting, and by the light of the moon, I can see silvery traces of blood. "But I also want to be someone she can be proud of, who doesn't stand by and let hundreds of innocent people be slaughtered, who doesn't leave a pregnant woman to die. I don't want her to have a father who's a coward."

"But Max—how can saving Lily and her baby be more important than raising your own child? That's its own kind of bravery, don't you understand? You've tried to make a difference. Over and over. But one man can't stop a war—Jubah told you that herself. You think it's selfish to leave? Well, I think it's selfish to stay."

I gaze over her head, into the distance at the slave fires. And then I take a deep breath and look down, into her face. "You really think Finn is real?"

We both know the answer, but Julia nods, anyhow. "I do."

"Yeah." I scoop some cherries from the ground and lob them

sidearm toward a tree at the edge of the grove. They hit one after the other and fall into the gathering darkness. "I do too."

Inside me I can feel emotion gathering like a storm. God, my little girl's face—so beautiful, so fucking trusting. So filled with belief in her ability to make things right. *I'll bring you home*, she'd said. *I'll save you and Grandma Julia both and you can't stop me.*

Who does that remind me of?

There's no noise in the grove but our breathing and the chirp of insects. But the sound inside my head is rising, a roaring insistence that is impossible to ignore.

"I want to go home," I say, half to myself.

Thunk.

"I miss Isabel. And my parents. I want to see my daughter."

Thunk.

"But I've got two centuries of blood on my hands. If I have a chance—any chance at all—to wash that clean, I've got to try. All my life I've believed my blood is dirty. That it's in my DNA. I'm sick of it!" I wheel around, crushing a handful of cherries in my fist. Juice seeps between my fingers, red as blood.

Julia is staring at me, her eyes wide. I know I should calm down, but I can't seem to manage it. Instead, I draw back my arm and hurl the dark pulp as far as I can. Juice splatters from my fingers, going everywhere. "Do you know what it's like to live that way? Like there's no way to make it right?"

These are things I've never spoken of aloud, words that have festered inside me for years. It is a relief to give voice to them at last. "This is my chance. It's all I want."

As soon as I've said it, I know it isn't entirely true. I lower my eyes, but I can still feel Julia's gaze searing through me, just like her daughter's always did. "Is it, Max?" she asks, her voice little more than a whisper. "Is that really all you want?"

Quiet as they are, the words strike me like a blow. I shake my head hard, half in negation, half to keep it from spinning. "Not everything," is all I get out before the words catch in my throat. I turn away, concealing my face, and try again. "I do want to make things right, badly. But there's one thing I want even more, and that's Isabel. Even if she can't ever forgive me. Maybe—probably—that makes me a selfish prick, but there it is."

I spin around and force myself to look at Julia. She stands still, expressionless and waiting, as I draw one deep breath, then another. Finally I knot my hands behind my head and speak. "All right," I say. "Noon. Easter Monday. I'll be in that field, like you. Because you're right—staying here is just another kind of cowardice."

A smile breaks over her face, and I hold up one hand, forestalling whatever she's about to say. "But until then, I'll fight, Julia. I'll do everything I can to save Lily, if she'll let me. I'll do my best to help the slaves. I won't give up until I leave this island, and don't bother trying to change my mind."

I drop my hands to my sides, palms falling open. My breath is rough, my chest heaving. I must look like hell, but Julia doesn't flinch. Instead she comes right up to me and pulls me into a hug, heedless of what it might look like to anyone passing by. "I'm proud of you," she whispers. "You have nothing to be ashamed of. Anyone who says otherwise—well, they'll just have to answer to me."

Max

Easter Sunday dawns all too soon.

I heave myself out of bed with an overpowering sense of dread and stand at the window, watching one family after another, dressed all in white, make their way through the crowded streets to church. Without meaning to, I find myself moving my own lips in prayer—something I haven't done since I was eight years old, kneeling beside my bed with its superhero sheets to recite Now I Lay Me Down to Sleep.

Dear God. Don't let me die. Let me hold Isabel again. Let me meet my daughter.

I don't want to be afraid—have been shoving the feeling down every time it shows its ugly face—but now fear tears through me and I let it. For one minute. Then I cast it out, jaw locked and teeth gritted, and steel myself for what lies ahead.

The countryside is quiet as I ride up to the gate at Simmons. No doubt everyone's in a food coma after the Easter meal. My pistol is shoved into my belt, along with my powder, and I've slung my cartridge box across my chest. There's no way for me to hide my musket, and so I ride with it across my legs. I tug on the reins and whoa Havoc, bringing him to a stop at the side of the road. And then I wait.

Two minutes, three, and then Julia appears, walking down the path from the great house, wearing the blue dress she'd had on that first day I saw her at Bayleys. She's carrying a large bundle that, as she gets closer, is redolent of honey, cinnamon, and roasted meat. Havoc lifts his head, sniffing hopefully.

"Ham sandwiches," Julia says by way of greeting, patting Havoc on the neck. "For you, not the horse. I thought you might be hungry."

I swing down out of the saddle. "Thanks. I'm starving, actually."

"Well," she says, "you can't very well eat it standing here. Let's get out of sight, before someone notices I'm gone and comes hunting for me."

I inhale the sandwiches, which are delicious, and show Julia how to fire the pistol, just in case. Then we ride for Sweetwater, where we sweet-talk our way past Penelope, who is concerned about her mistress's health—apparently Lily's been in bed since morning, with the Easter meal brought to her on a tray.

"Hannah, is that you?" she asks as Julia pushes the door open. Her voice comes from a tall four-poster bed that stands against the far wall, its netting pinned back. "There's no need to check on me so often, darling, I promise. I'm just resting."

Julia clears her throat. "It's not Hannah. It's us."

Momentary silence, and then Lily struggles upright against a mass of pillows. "What are you doing here? I told the two of you that I never wanted to see you again."

Julia sits down in a chair by the bed, pressing Lily's hand in her own. "You did."

"And yet, here you are." She pulls her hand free and rests it on the rise of her belly, atop the quilts. "In my bedchamber, no less."

Julia makes a small sound of distress. "Please don't get upset, Lily. It isn't good for the baby."

"And you think that your presence is guaranteed to improve my health? If that was your concern, you never would have come here today."

The best that can be said for the conversation is it deteriorates from there. We try, to no avail, to convince Lily that the rebellion will take place—not just soon, but tonight—and she should leave while she still can. Finally I say, "Well, if you won't go, do you mind if we stay to look after you? We won't be any bother, I promise."

"Suit yourself, though I fear you will be most dreadfully bored. I am not fit company for an organ-grinder's monkey at present, being much discomfited." She shifts, pressing a hand to her lower back. "You have a daughter of your own, Julia—tell me, were the final weeks of your confinement this difficult?"

I take this as my cue to leave. "What a fucking mess," I mutter under my breath on my way to the back door, earning a shocked look from a young slave in the hallway. Emerging into the humid air, I make my way to the cherry grove where I hobbled Havoc, who lifts his head from grazing and whinnies a greeting. My musket is still where I stashed it, propped in the fork of a tree. I shoulder it and lead Havoc to one of the grooms at the stables. And then I settle in to wait. And wait. And wait.

Up at the house, Hannah serves Easter leftovers for dinner. Julia eats upstairs, emerging only to report that Lily's back hurts and she doesn't have the slightest interest in eating.

"She says she's still full from lunch, but I just don't know," Julia says, looking worried. "I asked her if I should call for the midwife, but she said it was too soon."

Not overly reassured, I go upstairs to the veranda, loaded musket at my side, pistol in my belt, and watch the sun set, subsiding below the horizon in a defiant display of red and orange. The sky goes dark and I watch the stars come out one by one, pinpricks of light on a black, eternal canvas. I am still standing there twenty minutes later, peering out into the night, when I see the first blaze of fire in the canes.

Isabel

When Dr. Rossetti calls me back on Monday, she insists on meeting with me before she talks with Finn. I submit to this grudgingly, even though I haven't seen the inside of a psychologist's office since the one time my dad made me go, after my mom disappeared. I took a strong dislike to the counselor—a pudgy, bulldog-faced man who reeked of cigarettes and spent half his time trying to peer down my shirt—and had refused to keep the second appointment, or any of the ones thereafter. My dad had put up a token argument, but after a couple of minutes he'd thrown his hands up and said that if I didn't want to go, he wouldn't stand in my way—and that had been that.

Dr. Rossetti doesn't look like a bulldog, nor does she smell of cigarettes. I put her in her sixties, a tall, regal woman with nut-brown skin and silver hair that's pinned up in a complicated twist. She's wearing a sleeveless green shell and linen pants—the kind I'd wrinkle in about two seconds—and a simple pair of silver hoops. A pair of cat's-eye glasses hangs around her neck, suspended from a funky beaded chain. Her office smells pleasantly of lavender and sage and her handshake is firm, fingers gripping mine with a confidence that inspires the same in me.

"So," she says, as I settle into an overstuffed chair that threatens to swallow me whole. "Tell me about Finn."

How do you explain a life? I do my best, telling Dr. Rossetti about the disappearance of Max and my mother, about the picture Finn drew, how upset she got, how she screamed that no one believed her, no one understood. I tell her how sensitive Finn is, how perceptive. Choosing my words with delicacy, I tell her how hard it is for Finn to make friends, how she always seems to be alone.

I don't mention what Finn told me the night we made roast chicken and apple pie—how sometimes she can't tell the difference between what people are merely thinking and what they've said out loud. After all, I don't want Dr. Rossetti to think that my daughter is crazy. And certainly I don't tell her about Max's phone call, or the fact that I woke to see him standing in my room. I don't want her to think that I am crazy, either. But I do tell her about Finn's dream— the burning grass, her fear that bad men are chasing her father, that he won't escape in time.

In answer to Dr. Rossetti's questions, I say that, yes, Finn is talking about Max and her grandma much more than she used to—that I don't know why this is, but that it worries me. She asks if there's anyone in my life, romantically speaking—*Not that there needs to be,* she says, seeing a disturbed expression cross my face, *of course there doesn't. I just wondered—for Finn, you know, if there are any men who have played a role in her life, other than your father.*

I tell her about Ryan, leaving out the incident in his studio, dwelling only on his relationship with Finn—how he's always taken care of her, since the moment we met, how he's more involved in her life than the fathers of most of the kids in her class, many of whom are living right in their homes. I don't mention how we've only spoken once in the past few days, and that was on the phone—when I'd called him, despite my reservations, to let him know about the necklace. How he was polite, almost formal, saying all the right things— and how I'd wished I could reach through the phone line and shake him, shattering his reserve and bringing my best friend back to me.

How he has always been my sanctuary, my safe haven—and now he is all dead ends and sharp corners, a maze of complicated feelings that I'm struggling to navigate.

At the end of our hour together, Dr. Rossetti says she'd be happy to work with Finn, that it sounds like she's wrestling with some understandable grief and anxiety. I make an appointment for the following day, after camp, telling Finn only that she's going to talk with someone who will listen to whatever she has to say and take her seriously. Finn nods, but I can sense that her attention is only partially focused on me; she's gazing out the window of the car, head cocked to one side, as if she's tuned in to a radio station only she can hear. Since her outburst on Sunday, she's been quieter than usual, almost subdued. No matter my personal feelings about psychologists, I feel relieved that someone else is going to try to figure out what's going on with my daughter.

I fidget in the waiting room during their appointment, imagining what might be occurring behind Dr. Rossetti's closed door—if Finn is playing any of the board games I saw stacked on the bookshelf, whether she's sharing her innermost secrets or sitting in silence, swallowed up by the impossible chair, while Dr. Rossetti attempts to coax her into speech. Whether she's telling the therapist that she can read people's thoughts.

By the end of their session, I am a wreck—a condition that doesn't improve when Dr. Rossetti opens the door of her office, ushers Finn back into the waiting room, and asks if I'd mind chatting with her for a moment. Automatically, I agree, and admonish Finn not to take off for parts unknown. She sits down in the chair I've vacated, under the watchful eye of the receptionist, and picks up a worn copy of *Ranger Rick*. I examine her face for clues, but it is as serene as a Buddha's, no hint of what's transpired in the small room down the hall. She turns the page, enraptured by a story of unlikely friendship between a kitten and a gosling, and I make my way down the hall, heart thumping.

Dr. Rossetti shuts the door of her office behind me. She looks shaken, wearing an expression I know all too well. I've seen it on my own face, more than once—reflected in the window when I saw Max standing on the patio; in Barbados, when I'd slipped my mother's broken necklace around my neck, feeling the weight of it settle, cold against my skin. It's the expression of someone who's experienced the impossible.

As soon as I see Dr. Rossetti's face, I know what's happened. Part of me wants to take my daughter and run, to go home and make boxed macaroni and cheese and pretend things are normal. The rest of me knows that running is no longer an option. I sink into the ridiculous easy chair, prop my chin on my hand, and wait to hear what she has to say.

It doesn't take long. Their session had been perfectly normal, Dr. Rossetti tells me—if not terribly revelatory—until the end. Finn had sat at the low table, playing with one of the many toys scattered around the office: a ball pendulum called Newton's Cradle. Thoughtfully, she'd lifted one silver ball and let it crash into the rest, setting all five of them in motion. And then she'd said, eyes fixed on the swinging silver orbs, "It wasn't your fault, you know."

"Excuse me?" Dr. Rossetti had said, wondering if she'd misunderstood.

"The accident. What happened. It wasn't your fault. She never blamed you."

A chill had run straight down Dr. Rossetti's spine. She'd reached out, stilling the balls, and touched Finn's hand. "What accident?" she'd said.

Finn had smiled at her. "You know," she'd said, and set the balls in motion once more.

Again, Dr. Rossetti had stilled them. "Tell me what you mean, Finn," she'd said, filling her voice with a calm she did not feel.

Finn had sighed and settled back in her chair. "She was dead before she fell," she'd said. "Leaving your boots on the stairs had nothing to do with it. She didn't trip. It was never your fault." And then she'd gotten to her feet and walked out of the office.

Dr. Rossetti clears her throat and looks at me. "My grandmother," she says, her voice barely audible. "She lived with us, when I was small. Our house had two floors and we were always leaving things on the landing upstairs—books, clothes. My mother yelled at us for it all the time—she said someone would trip and fall. But we were kids, and we didn't listen. And one day, coming down the stairs—well." She presses her lips together, blots her eyes with a tissue. "My grandmother fell. She fell, and she died. And that day, the only thing on the landing was a pair of snow boots. Mine."

My mouth drops open. I think of Finn's drawing of my mother's necklace, of the times she'd claimed to talk with Max.

"Isabel, I'd like to see her again. But I need to ask—is there anything you're not telling me? I get the feeling that there's more going on here than you've chosen to share."

For a moment I consider confessing everything. Dr. Rossetti's eyes are so kind, her expression expectant—and she isn't afraid of Finn. Still, something holds me back. It's one thing to accept that my daughter may have abilities outside the norm. It's another to admit that I might be hallucinating visits from my missing boyfriend . . . or his ghost. "It's been a complicated few weeks" is all I say. "But if you think you can help Finn . . . I'll bring her back."

Dr. Rossetti gives me a long look, in which empathy and a wry acknowledgment are mingled. "I would like that," she says eventually. "And when you're ready to talk, I'm here."

Max

I blink, staring across the fields, to make sure I'm not imagining things. But no—there is a line of red sweeping steadily toward me, becoming more visible by the moment. A second later, the unmistakable scent of scorched sugar fills the air.

From my position on the veranda, I can see people emerging from their huts in the slave village, clutching torches, peering in the direction of the fires. I can hear excited voices, but I'm too far away to make out words. Instead I turn and run back into the house, bursting into Lily's room without knocking.

Lily is sitting up, her weight braced on her hands. Julia and Hannah stand beside her, Hannah with a cup of water in her hand, Julia with her palm resting on Lily's lower back. All three turn toward me, openmouthed.

"It's happening," I say, panting. "I saw it. The fires have started, and it's only a matter of time before they reach us. We have to go."

"Fires?" Hannah says.

I cross to the window and throw the shutters wide. "Can't you smell it?"

Lily sniffs, her nostrils flaring. "What's on fire?" she says sharply. "The cookhouse? What?"

"No," Julia says, her eyes on my face. "The island."

Lily gets to her feet, cradling her belly, and slides out of the four-poster bed, leaning heavily on Hannah for support. She makes her way over to the window and grips the sill. And then she gasps. "The cane fields! As far as I can see, they're burning. And I can hear screaming . . . who is screaming?"

I open my mouth to venture a guess—and then I don't have to. It's Penelope, the housekeeper, voice raised high in triumph, and Sarey, who I've never heard speak louder than a whisper. "Come on!" they are yelling. "Back here! This way!"

There is an earsplitting bang downstairs, and then the voices are in the house. Above them I hear the furious roar of the overseer. "Hoy! What do you think you're doing? Put that down, the pair of you. I've a pistol—what do you plan to do, shovel me to death? I'll see you hanged, you—"

There is an awful clunk, audible even from where we stand, and his voice cuts off. I yank the pistol from my belt and run to the top of the stairs in time to see him sink to the floor, blood flowing from his head and Penelope standing over him, still holding the shovel.

"There," she says matter-of-factly, stepping back. "That's better. I'm most terribly sorry, Master Simon, sir, but all of your carrying-on was giving me the headache something fierce."

My heart pounding so hard I'm afraid they can hear it downstairs, I melt back into the shadows and run for Lily's room in time to see her crumple to her knees, letting out an agonized wail. "It's too early," she moans. "I'm supposed to have another month."

She reaches out, groping blindly. Hannah takes her outstretched hand, grasping it in both of her own. "It be okay, missus," she says fiercely. "My sister Luce had her baby too soon, and that babe is just fine. We'll take good care of you."

"But the midwife," Lily gasps, her nails digging into Hannah's hand. "How will we send for Jubah now, with all this . . ."

Hannah lifts her head and looks first at me, then at Julia, stricken. I've taken up a position behind the door, holding the pistol. Julia is kneeling beside Lily, looking as horrified as I feel. That night in the cherry grove, I'd told her about Bess's baby, what Edward Thomas had done. "You can't have Jubah," she says, her tone gentle. "They took her away on Thursday, Lily. She's in the Cage."

At this, Lily wails even more loudly, and Hannah claps a hand over her mouth. "You got to hush, Miss Lily," she says. "We can get you out of here, but you can't be makin' noises like that."

"Max," Julia says urgently. "We have to go, don't we? It's probably safer for us out there than it is in here, even with her—like this."

I nod, my head cocked to try and hear what's going on downstairs. "From what I remember, the rebels won't harm women and children. We can get her into a carriage, maybe, and go as fast as we can."

Hannah glances up from the floor, where she's smoothing back Lily's hair. "From what you remember?" she asks, her voice hard. "What you mean by that?"

Shit. "Not now," I tell her. "The important thing is that I think we can make it."

Hannah gives me a suspicious look, but she doesn't question me further, hurrying to help her mistress as Lily crawls forward.

"Let's go," Julia says. "Max—go out and see if they're still in the house. I don't hear anything, do you?"

I shake my head, edging forward. The three of them follow me as we begin our agonizingly slow procession through the hallway and down the stairs. We creep past the dining room and toward the back door. Just as we reach it, there is a massive crash from the front of the house, and then the sound of glass shattering. I spare a glance for the dining room in time to see two men heft a huge cabinet and heave it through the front window, where it joins the couch I sat on the first day I came to Sweetwater.

"My mother's china!" Lily wails. Her voice trails off into a moan, and she doubles over, clutching her stomach. I can hear Hannah murmuring to her, making small comforting sounds, but most of my attention is for the chaos in the dining room. We're almost to the door; just a few feet more, and we'll be outside. Then we can make a run for the stables, and hopefully get the hell out of here.

The contraction must ease, because Lily straightens up again, face white, and Julia tugs on my arm. "Come on," she hisses. "We'll go out the back. We'll have a straight shot to the stables. If they haven't taken the horses, we have a chance."

"The house—" Lily says, breathing hard.

"Don't you worry none, missus." Hannah is pulling her along now, casting a frightened look over her shoulder toward the front of the house, where we can hear voices shouting and the occasional report of a pistol. "What you think Master Robert cares 'bout more? His money, or you and the babe?"

Maybe it's the fear in Hannah's voice—God knows Lily can't be listening all that clearly to her words. Either way, she looks up and gives a jerky nod. "All right," she says, and folds over her belly again, panting. There's a strange splashing sound, and I look down to see that all of us are standing in a rapidly spreading pool, Lily at its epicenter.

"Oh, no, oh, no," Julia is saying, over and over. "Oh, hell. Max—"

There's only one thing I can think to do. I pull the pistol out of my belt, thrust it into Julia's hands, and press the musket into Hannah's. "Careful," I say, kneeling on the floor next to Lily. "They're loaded."

Julia nods at me, white-faced, and sticks the pistol into the waistband of her skirt as if she's done it a hundred times. I heave Lily into my arms and get to my feet, bracing myself on the wall to keep my balance. Hannah has already edged forward, nudging the back door open with the barrel of the musket—which is nearly as big as she is. "No one back here," she reports. "Not that I can see, anyhow, 'less they hiding in the trees. Let's go."

And so we do.

"What do you see?" I whisper to Hannah, who has made her way to the corner of the house and is standing silently, regarding whatever lies beyond. The shouting is louder now, the smell of burning cane an acrid stench that fills my lungs.

"Men everywhere, and some women too. With torches and hoes and such," she whispers back. "But they're not going for the stables, not yet. They're burning the fields and the garden. Maybe we have a chance." She hazards a glance back at the three of us, places a comforting hand on her mistress's foot, and squares her small shoulders. "You ready, then? Run."

And we do.

The hundred yards between the house and the stable feel like a thousand miles. I am painfully aware of how exposed we are, out here in the open. *It's like running wind sprints on the football field,* I tell myself. *You've got plenty of practice with that.* Which is true enough—but I've never done it with a woman in labor in my arms, in the midst of an insurrection. It's dark out here, the only light coming from the flaming fields and the rebels' torches. All I can think is, *God, don't let me trip.*

Sweetwater is in chaos. Cane ash drifts through the air like snow, broken glass rains down everywhere, and above the screams of the rebels, I can hear the frantic whinnying of the horses and the howls of the plantation's dogs. Somehow we make it to the stables and I set Lily down on a bench inside. She clutches herself, rocking back and forth. Hannah kneels beside her, one hand still resting on the musket.

Julia approaches the horses—and lets out a shriek as a shadow emerges from one of the dark box stalls. Faster than I've ever seen her move, she grabs the pistol out of her waistband and points it at the figure. "We're armed," she says in a voice that trembles only a little. "Take another step, and I'll shoot you through the head."

There's the sound of a flint striking, and then a flame reveals Peter, one of the grooms, candle in hand. In his other hand, he clutches a machete. "Don't shoot," he says.

Julia doesn't lower the pistol. "What are you doing in here?" she demands.

Peter relaxes his grip on the machete. "I thought you were some of them rebels, sure," he says. "Then I heard Miss Lily carryin' on, and I think maybe I can help. You taking her safe away? To the forts?"

"If we can get her that far," I say. Lily is sobbing now, a low, desperate sound, and I am terrified that she'll give birth to the baby here in the stable if we don't escape.

"You can't take the carriage," Peter says, with a definitive shake of his head. "The road's full of soldiers and rebels, not to mention women and children running away. You gonna have to ride."

I throw a despairing glance over my shoulder at Lily. How am I ever to get her on a horse, much less keep her there?

Julia squeezes my arm. "We have to, Max. We have no choice," she says.

So the three of us saddle up the horses, and decide that Hannah will ride with Lily. I'll take the musket; Julia will keep the pistol. Peter insists on coming with us, and I don't argue—at this point, the more folks we have on our side, the better off we are.

We lead the horses outside, into the raging night, and Lily follows. In the flickering light of the candle, her face is a ghostly shade of white, her hair pasted to her cheeks with sweat. "I can ride," she insists when she sees the doubt on my face. "I'll not have this baby in a stable."

Arguing seems pointless, so I kneel and cup my hands so that Lily can step into them. I boost her into the saddle and Hannah swings up behind, reaching around her to grasp the reins. She nods at me, face grim. "I got her, Master Max."

The plantation yard is a maelstrom of bodies and flames. As I watch, one man darts forward, grabs a chunk of wood and hurls it through one of the few remaining windows. It finds its mark with a splintering crash, and he howls in triumph. Then he lifts his torch high so that the light shines full on his face, and I see who it is: Ophran, the first man I met when I arrived in Robert Adair's cane field two weeks ago. The man who thinks that maybe I fell from the sky.

He sees me too, and lets out a cry of warning. Havoc paws the ground, sending up clods of dirt, and I struggle to hold him steady. "Let us pass," I call out to Ophran, lifting the musket from its resting place in the saddle.

"Hsssst!" The sound comes from one of the men on horseback, and it brings everyone near him up sharply. Behind me I hear a distinctive, alarming click—Julia, thumbing back the hammer on her pistol. They hear it too, and freeze.

I lower the musket and raise one hand, hoping Julia can see it in the light from the torches. "We have Lily Adair with us," I say, choosing each word deliberately, so that I can be sure not to misspeak. "She's in labor. We just want to get her to the fort in Bridgetown if we can. We mean you no harm."

"Who else with you?" It's the man who hissed at us, his voice threaded with suspicion. He's on a huge bay horse, a cudgel grasped in his fist.

I sit straight in the saddle, hoping that he can't see the way I am trembling. "Myself. Lily Adair, as I said. Julia Griffith, a tutor from Simmons. Hannah, Mrs. Adair's body slave. And Peter, one of the Sweetwater grooms."

At this, the man bares his teeth. "A body slave and a groom, hmmm? They rather flee with you, like cowards, than stand up and fight?"

"I ain't a coward, Mingo," Hannah says from behind me, each word measured. "No sir, what I am is loyal." She doesn't edge her horse any closer—with Lily on it, I'm sure she doesn't dare—but the disdain in her voice is clear enough, all the same. She clears her throat, the sound every bit as menacing as the click of the hammer on Julia's pistol. "Now, you gonna step aside or we gonna have to ride you down? 'Cause either way, I plan to see my mistress safe."

This pronouncement is greeted with dumbstruck silence. I feel like cheering for Hannah—or I would, if I weren't afraid that I was going to have to shoot someone. Then Mingo laughs. "You Jubah's sister's girl," he says. "Eh? I knew your mama. You just like her, hmmm? No, you ain't no coward, sure 'nough. But you foolish, just the same."

He canters closer, the cudgel raised high, and I drop one hand to my musket. But then Ophran speaks, his voice edged with unease.

"This man, he got some kind of magic, Mingo. I told you, he land in that cane field out of nowhere. He tell Nanny G. all about what gonna happen, he tell everyone at River how they die. If he not obeah, he somethin'. You want to let him work his sorcery on you, that's your business. But if he means to ride for Bridgetown, I ain't gonna stand in his way."

Mingo squints, peering at me. I stare back, unblinking. Something in my gaze must unnerve him, because a shudder ripples through his body and he lowers the cudgel. He stands high in his stirrups, raising his voice so everyone can hear. "Let them pass."

The crowd parts as if by magic, and the five of us ride through without incident, heading for the road. I look back as the great house passes from view—just in time to see a tiny figure pull back his arm and hurl a flaming projectile through the last unbroken front window, setting the curtains aflame.

Isabel

———

Back at home that night, I stand in Finn's doorway, watching her sleep.

She lies on her side, clutching Raggedy Ann, under the watchful gaze of the oversized stuffed giraffe that Ryan gave her for her fifth birthday. At the time, the giraffe had been taller than Finn herself, which had been the subject of some low comedy, as she'd insisted on taking it everywhere with her—to the breakfast table, into the tub, even, to my eternal amusement, for a ride in Ryan's Ford F-150 pickup, a vehicle whose street cred was sorely tainted by the three-foot-long neck and wobbly head of the spotted ungulate sticking out of the open passenger-side window.

I'd laughed so hard at the sight that I'd had to sit down on the curb. Grinning, Ryan had said, "You know what they say, Iz. Long neck, long . . ." Then he'd driven away mid-sentence, Finn belted securely in the middle, one tiny arm looped over the giraffe's neck, head leaning on Ryan's shoulder in perfect trust.

Ignoring the wave of regret that breaks over me at the thought of Ryan, I tiptoe into the room to tuck Finn's quilt around her. Leaning down to turn on her Snoopy lamp, I have to fight the urge to snuggle up next to her, guard her from dangers real and imagined. I want to empower her, to teach her to be strong.

So instead I walk back into the living room, where I settle down on the couch with my laptop. Not for the first time, I wish I had a partner to share my worries with, someone else who would tuck Finn in and make her feel safe. Someone who would sit on the couch and mock a dumb romantic comedy with me until the idea that Finn possessed some sort of paranormal abilities seemed nothing short of absurd.

I shake my head, dismissing this fantasy. *I am enough*, I tell myself. *I am enough, because I have to be.* Picking up the remote, I flip through the channels until I find the most innocuous film I can imagine—*You've Got Mail*, starring a fresh-faced Meg Ryan dating all the wrong men.

That's when I hear the knock on the door.

"Who is it?" I call, alarmed.

Silence, and then a familiar voice, faintly penitent. "It's Ryan."

I'm so surprised by this development that for a moment I just sit there, stunned. I don't know who I'd expected, but after the scene at Ryan's house the other day, he isn't high up on my list of potential late-night visitors.

"Isabel?" Ryan says from the other side of the door. "Are you going to let me in?"

I yank the door open and see him standing there, a pint of Ben & Jerry's in one hand and a wrapped box in the other. "Surprise," he says.

I eye him suspiciously. "What are you doing here?"

He raises one eyebrow. "Apologizing?"

"I thought you were mad at me," I say, feeling my own eyebrows knit.

Ryan shrugs. "I was. I am. But it was my own fault as much as— Christ, Isabel, do we have to do this here? The ice cream is melting, my hand is freezing, and this box is heavier than it looks."

"Fine," I say, surrendering, and take the mysterious box from him. Inside, I set the box on the coffee table and then retrieve spoons from the kitchen for the Ben & Jerry's.

When I come back, Ryan has taken my spot on the couch and is smirking at the TV. *"You've Got Mail?* Really?" he says, taking a spoon from me.

Despite myself, I blush. "You can turn it off." I make a grab for the remote, but he snatches it up and holds it just out of my reach, grinning.

"I wouldn't dream of it," he says, knotting his hands behind his head. "By all means, let's you and me sit here and eat Phish Food and watch Meg Ryan fall in *luv.*"

It doesn't escape me that this is what I was wishing for just a few minutes ago—someone to share my couch and make fun of Meg's wide-eyed innocence, her storybook ending. In spite of this—or maybe because of it—I get defensive. "This is a perfectly good movie," I say, digging a spoon into the ice cream.

"Sure it is," Ryan says mildly. "If you're planning to go all *Mystery Science Theater* on its ass." I open my mouth to protest, and he holds up one finger, adjuring silence. "Besides, it's a little hard to take you seriously with chocolate on your nose."

He reaches out to wipe the ice cream away, which I'm sure he intends as an innocuous gesture. But when his fingers touch my skin, I freeze, remembering the feeling of his hands warm on my thighs, the rough sensation of his stubble against my bare breasts. My eyes widen, and Ryan squares his shoulders, resignation clear on his face.

"So," he says, and draws his hand back cautiously, as if he'd meant to pet a kitten but found himself face-to-face with a cobra instead.

"So what?" I say back to him, and wipe the chocolate off myself.

"I fucked up, Isabel. Okay? Can we leave it at that?"

"I don't know," I say uncertainly. "Are you going to do it again?"

This makes him laugh. It's a brief, somewhat bitter laugh, but a laugh nonetheless. "That depends," he says.

"On what?" My voice comes out every bit as wary as I feel.

"On whether you want me to," he says, and holds up one hand

when I start to argue. "You kissed me back, Iz. You know you did. We could sit here and fight about whether it was reflexive, whether you just didn't want to hurt my feelings, whatever. But I know you, and I know the difference. You could have pushed me away, but you didn't."

I sit there, mute, and stare at him. I can't think of a single thing to say, but that's okay, because he isn't done. "Anyway," he says, "that's not the point. The point is that you're mad at me. You wish I hadn't done it and you feel like I fucked up our friendship when you need me the most. Am I right?"

I still can't find my voice, and Ryan sighs. "Just nod if you agree with me, okay?"

Silently, I nod my head. He rolls his eyes at me. "So," he says, as if this is a perfectly normal, two-sided conversation, "I take it back."

With this absurdity, I finally regain the power of speech. "You can't take it back," I say, channeling *When Harry Met Sally.* "It's already out there."

Ryan rolls his eyes again. "I can't believe you just said that."

"Well, it's true," I say stubbornly. "It wasn't just the kissing, and the — the other stuff." A blush stains my cheeks, and I do my best to ignore it. "You said you stayed here because of how you . . . how you felt about me. How am I supposed to look at you the same way after that?"

Ryan mutes the movie and drops the remote back on the table. "Well," he says in as neutral a tone as he can manage, "I've kept my feelings about you to myself for seven years. I can do it some more. It's one of my strongest skills." His gaze drifts away from mine, down toward the worn green fabric of the couch. "As for moving to New York with me — that's not so crazy, is it? You'd have better job opportunities up there. And I'm the only father Finn's ever known. It might even be good for her."

"Ryan," I say, imbuing those two syllables with the full weight of my skepticism.

He looks up at me, and this time he doesn't bother to hide the pain in his eyes. "Let it go, Isabel," he says, his voice quiet, even. "I'm asking you. Please."

"But—"

"You let it go," he says, knotting his hands around one knee so tightly that the knuckles turn white, "and I swear to you that I will too. I'll never bring it up again unless you do first. I'll never touch you in anything but friendship unless you ask me to."

There is so much I want to say, so many questions I want to ask. I want to take Ryan's hands in mine and ask him to forgive me, to apologize for not being able to feel the same way he does, to do anything it takes to wipe that hurt look from his eyes. But in the end I don't have the heart. "Okay. You can take it back. It never happened."

"Thank you," he says in that same quiet voice. And then he unknots his hands and pushes the box in my direction. "Here. I got this for you."

"I kind of figured that," I say, and Ryan snorts, sounding almost like his old self.

"Just open it, would you?" he says.

So I oblige, pulling the box onto my lap and undoing the floppy red bow that's tied off center. "Ry?" I say, pulling it loose.

"Yeah?"

"Just so you know, I don't think you have a career as a professional gift-wrapper." I tear off the paper—no great challenge, given the lopsided taping job—and let it fall onto the coffee table. "Seriously, I don't understand how a guy who can build a dollhouse like that can't figure out how much wrapping paper it takes to cover a cardboard box."

Ryan balls up the discarded paper and tosses it at my head. "Fuck you, Griffin."

"Sorry, sorry," I say, doing my best to sound contrite—and then something else occurs to me. "The dollhouse," I blurt, even though bringing this up is a little too close to things I've promised not to discuss. "Can you fix it?"

His eyes slide away from mine again, focusing somewhere over my left shoulder. "Sure. It wasn't as bad as it looked."

"Good," I say, more awkward than ever. "I'm glad."

"I shouldn't have said what I did," he says, still looking anywhere but at me. "I was just mad. But . . ."

"It's okay," I tell him hurriedly. "Apology accepted. So . . . what's in here?" I shake the denuded cardboard box and an odd thumping sound issues from within.

He smiles, and his eyes refocus on my face. "A peace offering. Just open it."

I hold out a hand, and without comment he puts his Swiss Army knife into my palm. With precision, I slit the packing tape and hand the knife back to him. The box's flaps fall open, revealing new kickboxing gear—gloves, hand wraps, Thai pads, and a strike shield. They're a vibrant shade of blue—my favorite color—and clearly expensive.

I don't know what I was expecting to find inside the box—a lifetime supply of chocolate, maybe—but this is a surprise. My face must show it, because when I turn to Ryan, he chuckles. "You like them?" he says.

"For sure," I say, running my hand over the curved top of one of the Thai pads. "But Ryan—why?"

He shrugs. "I figured it'd be less clichéd than flowers. And if you want to beat me up . . . well, you might as well do it in style." He clears his throat. "Anyway, you kept bitching about how all of your gear was falling apart. I thought this would help."

"You did good," I say softly, and his eyes meet mine. I can see that other Ryan in them, the vulnerable one. He blinks, looks anywhere but at me, and I'm suddenly in dire need of a change of subject. "Can I tell you what happened today?" I ask him. I hadn't intended to share what Dr. Rossetti had said about Finn—the revelation about her grandmother, the fact that she thinks Finn is special—but desperate times call for desperate measures.

"Sure," Ryan says, and busies himself cleaning up the wrapping paper. I think he's as relieved as I am.

Max

The road is strewn with debris of every description—casks of liquor, the contents of entire storehouses of food, bookshelves, and bedsteads—and choked with people. A woman, two children, and a coterie of slaves pass us, probably also heading for the fort in Bridgetown Harbour. The children are crying, begging to know what's happening, why the fields are on fire. We're forced over to the edge of the road—and that is when I see them up ahead: a rebel contingent, many men deep, advancing toward us.

I can't tell how many there are, not for sure. By the light of the torches they carry and the burning field, I estimate their numbers to be at least fifty strong, maybe more. They see us coming—how could they not?—and I brace myself for a standoff. But instead they move aside in unison, letting all of us pass.

As we ride through the rebel lines, I can feel Havoc coiled beneath me, tension in every muscle. He wants nothing more than to run, and I would like nothing more than to let him. Instead, we take the horses through the lines at a canter—long enough for me to see the faces of the men and women who have stopped their march on the estates to let us by. Their eyes are alight with excitement, their hands tight on their weapons. Firelight glints off the head of an axe, the muzzle of a pistol. The smell of sweat, dirt, and scorched sugar emanates from them, and their clothes are ragged and torn. Still, they radiate a sense of anticipation. As soon as the last of our party makes it through, the man in front barks a command, and they set off down the road, into the heart of St. Philip.

Relief washes over me—and then Hannah calls out behind us. "Master Max. Miss Julia. Stop!"

Immediately, we rein up—and turn to see that Lily is slumped in the saddle, her breath coming in short pants. "I'm sorry," she says. "I can't go any farther. I just can't."

Desperately, I glance around at the blazing fields. Then Hannah speaks up again. "We go ten more minutes down the road, we reach Brightmore's. The mistress is one of Miss Lily's particular friends. If there ain't no problems there—or even if there is—we probably safest with Miss Alicia and Master John."

Julia's eyes flick to mine, her expression somewhere between expectancy and amazement, and I realize that winding up at the Brightmores' estate is just what we need—or what *she* needs, at least. If Jubah's right, Julia should be in the Brightmores' cane field at noon tomorrow. No matter what happens to me, she will be safe.

I try to smile at her—although it probably looks more like a grimace—and turn to Lily. "Can you ride that far?" I ask, hoping I don't sound as apprehensive as I feel.

"If I have to," she says, sounding choked. "But—hurry."

We make it to Brightmore without a hitch, directed by Hannah. None of their fields are ablaze, but the windows of the great house are all lit. As soon as we enter the yard, a crowd comes forward to meet us, despite the late hour. A tall man with a shock of dark hair and a neat beard steps in front of the others. "I am John Brightmore, owner of this estate," he says in a deep, even voice. "Identify yourselves."

"Maxwell Adair," I say, since Lily is incapable of speech. "With Mrs. Lily Adair, Mrs. Julia Griffin, and two slaves." I wince as I reduce Hannah and Peter to this description, but it seems the safest bet. "We're seeking shelter," I continue. "And a midwife. Mrs. Adair is in labor."

Before John Brightmore can reply, Lily lets out a despairing groan, which jolts him into action. "Get her down," he orders. "And take her—take her—"

There is a flurry of skirts, and then a small, blond woman appears at his elbow. "John!" she scolds. "Stand back. You're behaving like a perfect fool. Here," she says to Peter and me as we help Lily to the ground. "We'll take her up to my room, poor lamb. Dinah, send for the midwife," she says to a slave standing silently at her side. The woman next to her nods, wide-eyed, and darts off into the night.

"Now," she says with a businesslike air, "can one of you carry her?"

I bend to pick up Lily again, and the blond woman says briskly, "Follow me. Lily, darling, it's Alicia. We'll go right up to my room and get you settled. Don't you worry about a thing. Betty's a fine midwife, she's delivered all of my slaves this past year without difficulty. Why, she even delivered my own—" She stops abruptly, casting an anxious glance at her husband, and passes a hand across her mouth. Then she pats Lily's dangling hand in reassurance. "Come along," she says, leading the way into the house. Behind us, I hear John Brightmore ordering his groom to see to the horses.

Alicia keeps a patter of conversation going all the way up the stairs, mostly directed at Lily, who doesn't reply except for the occasional moan. We go down a hallway lit by sconces and into the bedroom, where, with considerable presence of mind, Alicia orders Hannah to strip the bed. At her direction, I set Lily down.

"All right, then," Alicia murmurs. "Betty will be here in just a moment, and then we'll see what's to be done. You just relax, poor dear." She steps away for a moment, comes back with a damp cloth, and wipes the sweat from Lily's face. "Mr. Adair, why don't you go downstairs?"

John Brightmore is waiting for me in the front room, standing at the window. Two glasses and a tumbler of whisky sit on a side table, and he gestures to them at my approach. "Here, man. You look as if you need it."

"Thanks," I say, filling one of the glasses. "I do."

"Your musket's there," he says, pointing his chin at the corner of the room, where the weapon leans against a tall bookshelf.

"Thank you," I say, and he nods, waiting for me to take a gulp of liquor before he speaks again. "Tell me, sir. What in hell drove you out in the midst of that insanity?"

"The rebels attacked Sweetwater." My voice is hoarse, and I swallow again in an effort to clear my throat. Then I tell him everything, ending with our flight through the rebel lines, until Lily couldn't travel anymore. "And here we are," I conclude. "Not a second too soon, as far as I'm concerned."

John Brightmore doesn't strike me as a particularly expressive man, but when I glance up at him, his eyes are wide with shock. He runs a hand over his face. "I'll say this much for you," he mutters, eyeing me. "You've balls, that's for sure."

I'm on the verge of replying when an unnerving banshee shriek echoes from upstairs. Brightmore casts an uneasy glance in its direction. "You think the woman's likely to die?" he asks in a low voice.

"I certainly hope not," I say, though his suggestion has sent a cold chill through my body. What if we've changed nothing?

He shakes himself all over, like a dog after a bath. "It's a dangerous business, childbirth. I've lost children of my own—the last one nearly took my wife along with it. Afterward, I thought Alicia would die of grief. She's not able to bear children anymore. I'd think it a blessing, did I not want an heir. Were the choice Alicia's, she would doubtless insist on attempting anew—so badly does she long for a babe of her own."

Now I understand the worried look Alicia Brightmore gave her husband. "I'm sorry," I say, realizing anew just how uncertain childbirth is in 1816, where most babies are delivered at home, without the benefit of accomplished physicians or drugs.

John Brightmore is staring through the window again, his gaze fixed on the road. "Do you have children, sir?" he says.

"I do." The words come before I know that I mean to say them. "A little girl. But I haven't seen her in quite some time."

"Really," he says, still looking out the window. "And where might she be?"

There's an edge to his tone now, a sharpness that makes me uneasy. "In South Carolina," I say warily. "With her mother."

"Indeed. And what brings you to our fair island, so far from home? You're kin to Robert, eh?"

The words are innocent enough, but I grew up in the South, land of polite doublespeak. John Brightmore doesn't trust me as far as he can throw me, my gallant rescue of Lily aside. I sit up straight, feeling the hair all over my body bristle. "I am."

He turns from the window, his features unreadable. "Is that so," he says. "For I have never heard him speak of you."

"There's no reason he should," I say, fighting for nonchalance. "We aren't close—cousins, that's all. Mrs. Adair was kind enough to take me in, just the same."

"Took you in," he muses, "and evicted you summarily, is that not so?"

"I didn't want to impose on her hospitality." What is the man after? The fucking island's on fire and Lily's in labor upstairs—why choose this moment to fixate on me?

An agonized wail echoes from the second floor, forestalling his response. One of the slaves comes running down the stairs, a pile of bloody rags in her hands. Lily's shrieks rise, then cut off abruptly, replaced by moans that send a chill up my spine. God, is this what Isabel went through? And I wasn't even there to hold her hand—

"—Adair?"

My train of thought is derailed by Brightmore, who has evidently been speaking to me for some time. "I'm sorry, what?"

He's eyeing me with great interest now, a hawk who has spied a particularly juicy mouse. "I said, what exactly is it that you do for a living, Mr. Adair?"

"I'm a botanist."

"Is that so? Are you affiliated with a university, then, or do you prefer to muck about in the dirt, collecting samples?"

The last is said with unmistakable scorn, reminding me so much of my parents' attitude toward my career that I can't help it—I snap. "Forgive me, Mr. Brightmore, but surely we ought to be more concerned about the dangers of the insurrection and Mrs. Adair's health than the details of my profession."

Brightmore's mouth twists. "Of course. My apologies," he says, but I don't believe him for a second. He lapses into silence, looking out the window again, and I study him. There's something about the man that just plain rubs me the wrong way.

"It's curious to me," he says, "that you should appear on this island, and not two weeks later a rebellion breaks out, the likes of which we have never seen. Why, the very day of your arrival, you interfered with one slave disciplining another."

He turns from the window, eyebrows raised in response to the surprise that must show on my face. "Did you think word of that incident would not reach others, Mr. Adair? Slaves talk, sir, and that girl—her mother is an infamous runaway. Perhaps that could be excused—perhaps you have not seen such brutality before. But your act of violence against Edward Thomas—how can there be a defense for that, sir, unless you are most unavoidably on the side of the slaves and their foolish acts of insurrection?"

Shit, shit, shit. I fumble for a reply that doesn't implicate me too badly—something that won't rouse his suspicions even further and stand in the way of our escape. "I'm on the side of humanity," I say finally. "It's not in my nature to stand by and watch a little girl be beaten, or a man whipped. And I don't believe it's in a man's nature to let himself be whipped or a young girl beaten. There's no correlation between my arrival and the burning of the fields. But the connection between the treatment of slaves on this island and the current state of affairs cannot be denied."

Brightmore's face reddens, and his mouth opens, framing a reply. Then he glances out the window again and his spine stiffens. "Do you see that?" Grabbing his pistol from the end table, he heads for the front door without waiting for me to answer.

It takes a moment for my eyes to adjust to the darkness after the diffuse glow of the oil lamps. When they do, though, I see the dim outline of a figure on horseback, galloping toward the great house. Following Brightmore, I round the corner to see Edward, the groom who'd stabled Havoc, in the foyer, panting. "Someone comin' down the road, sir," he says. "On a fast horse. You'd best come."

"I saw them," Brightmore says, turning so the light falls on his pistol. "Adair?"

With a dreamlike sense of unreality, I realize that I have unholstered my own gun. The metal is warm against my fingers, holding my body heat. "Right behind you," I say. He nods, apparently willing to set our conflict aside in the wake of this new development, and we go out to meet whomever is coming our way.

Edward is right—whoever it is does have a fast horse. We're outside only a minute before the rider draws up in the courtyard with a hasty salute. He is young—he can't be more than eighteen—with streaks of dirt on his face and flecks of ash on his uniform. His horse's sides are heaving. "Private Morris, sir," the man says to Brightmore, panting for breath. "They're calling up the militia. All able-bodied men must fight."

Brightmore's mouth flattens into a grim line. "So this is truly a rebellion, then."

"Indeed, sir. The slaves have ransacked Bayne and Clarke's, and laid waste to the entire store." Morris brushes at the sleeves of his jacket, eager to be off. "They've taken every implement that can do a bit of damage—hoes and pitchforks, axes and cudgels, the lot. The militia's mustering in St. Philip and Christchurch; they plan to march before dawn. Colonel Mayers is riding now to the garrison to tell Colonel Codd what's to do."

Hearing this, John Brightmore whistles through his teeth. "Hell and damnation. Where are you to go next?"

"Thicketts and Fortescue, sir. The Colonel's sent another rider to Fairy Valley, Brewsters, and Newcastle to alert whom he may. But with so many of the owners overseas, he fears we'll be shorthanded against the rebels."

At this, Brightmore spins on his heel, jaw set. He heads back to the house at a fast clip, and I follow. "We've got armaments and training on our side, lad," he calls over his shoulder. "They'll not take this island."

As we walk inside, he turns to me. "I'm tempted to call upon you to march with us—but my wife and Mrs. Adair are better served with you here." His mouth twists again and he gives me a long, slow once-over. Then he draws a deep breath and squares his shoulders. "Should you need to flee, head for the forts. Although with a woman in labor—hellfire, I don't know how far you'll get."

"I'll do my best," I tell him, and he nods. Then he takes the stairs two at a time, calling for Alicia. The next time I see him he wears his braided officer's uniform and boots, stalking out the front door with his cousin and his overseer in tow.

Outside, Brightmore throws his leg over his horse and looks down at me, his dark eyes focused on my face. "Look after them," he says, pitching his voice loud to be heard over the chaos in the yard.

"I will," I say, though it's only a partial truth. Julia and I will look after Alicia and Lily as long as we can—but unless something goes horribly wrong, I'll be well on my way back to Sweetwater before John Brightmore finds his way home.

He nods once, briskly. "I'll trust you, then. See that you do." He wheels his horse around and kicks it into motion, waving to the men behind him to follow. Together, they gallop out of the yard, a cloud of dust rising in their wake.

I head back inside, where I find Alicia sitting at the dining room table, blotting her fine-boned face with a lace handkerchief. She lifts her head and looks at me straight on, eyes red-rimmed. I search her features for echoes of Julia or Isabel, and find none—save the expression of determination in those bloodshot, tear-filled eyes. "You'll think I'm terribly foolish," she says, "but I'd rather ride out with my husband than stay behind to wait and see what happens, like a helpless child."

My reply is interrupted by an unearthly wail from upstairs, so pain-filled it hardly sounds human. Alicia Brightmore gathers up her skirts and dashes for the stairs, her slippered feet pounding the treads. I hear a door open, hear Alicia's voice rise in an exclamation, and then another one of those ungodly cries. Then Hannah runs down the stairs and throws open the doors to the linen closet. She grabs an armful of sheets and runs back up, darting a hunted look at me as she goes by.

The night passes in an agony of marking time. This waiting—for Lily and the baby to live or die, for an attack on Brightmore—is unbearable. I pace the length of the first floor, peering out the windows at the ever-encroaching line of fire snaking through the darkness. The silence is broken only by the barking of the plantation dogs and the occasional scream from upstairs, hoarser now but just as anguished. It sounds like Lily is being torn apart, and I pray that when Isabel had Finn, she had the benefit of anesthesia.

I am still pacing hours later at dawn, when Alicia comes to tell me that the baby has arrived. Exhaustion marks every line of her face, but she is smiling radiantly nonetheless. "A beautiful little girl, healthy and rosy-cheeked, thanks be to God." Her hair has come undone, hanging about her shoulders, and she twists it back up with a practiced gesture, pinning it into place. "Hannah is swaddling her now."

"And Mrs. Adair?" I ask, my heart picking up speed.

"She's exhausted, naturally, poor thing. And she did lose a lot of blood. But thank goodness Betty was able to see to her, and turn the child—it was sideways, and pressing on her spine, that is why it pained her so." Alicia purses her lips in sympathy.

"Thank God. I'm sure she's not ready for visitors . . . but will you please tell her how happy I am, and congratulate her on the birth of her daughter?"

Her lips twitch. "I will. She also gave me a message for you, sir, if you will."

"Oh?" I say, bracing myself for the onslaught. All's well that ends well, of course—but I can see all too easily how Lily might blame me for dragging her through the violent, dark countryside on horseback in the middle of a rebellion.

"She bids me apologize for her earlier indiscretion," she says, dimpling prettily despite the dark circles under her eyes, tokens of the sleepless night all of us have spent."She was very much mistaken indeed, to say that you are no gentleman. She is most grateful to you for all you have done."

My hands clench at my sides, trying to contain a sudden rush of feeling—joy for new beginnings, sure, but also incalculable regret that I couldn't be with Isabel for Finn's birth. I close my eyes, feeling the prick of tears against my lids. When I open them again, Alicia is gone. I hear her footsteps on the stairs, quick and light, and then the reedy, outraged, welcome sound of a newborn baby's cry.

Isabel

The morning after Ryan comes over, bearing peace offerings, I wake up determined to put paid to at least some of the questions swirling around in my head. I get Finn dressed, make her lunch, drive her to camp, and run a bunch of errands, all the while formulating a plan.

I have never been good at inaction. It's one reason I chose to go into field archaeology rather than museum work, arranging exhibits. When something bothers me, my first reaction is to charge directly at it, to solve the problem. Of course, some problems you can't solve—losing Max and my mom taught me that—and there's nothing to be gained by poking at the pieces of something broken, analyzing it to death. Unless I'm in the field, of course. Then it's a different story.

I drive to the gym just in time for the afternoon kickboxing and Muay Thai class, suit up in my new gear, and walk onto the mat, ready for a serious workout. This class is focused on cardio and sparring, which is exactly what I need right now. Running wind sprints the length of the gym, then hitting the mat and doing one sit-up after another, I feel my mind clear. We have a visiting instructor today, with an MMA background that incorporates tae kwon do and Muay Thai, and clearly he wants to see what we're made of. He has us do jump front kicks and roundhouse kicks across the floor, then makes us jab the air over and over, all the while critiquing our technique. By the time he lines us up in front of the heavy bags to do fifty jabs, fifty uppercuts, and then one hundred kicks of our choice, the tension has drained away.

With a thud, my fist connects with the number 6 painted on the side of the bag for accuracy. As the impact jars my body, it shakes loose the knowledge that there's nothing more I can do about Max. *Thud*, and I know that I'm doing everything I can for Finn, that I was right to take her to Dr. Rossetti. *Thud*, and I am able to stop worrying about Ryan, dismissing my lingering guilt. *Thud*, and I decide that it's up to my father to pursue the discovery of my mother's necklace with the police.

Thud, and suddenly something starts to nag at me. Something about Jennifer's story from the other day. When I was doing my research for the dig in Barbados, I came across Robert Adair's name multiple times. This made perfect sense—Robert owned a large estate and plantation, after all, along with many slaves. But Lily Adair—at the time the name had meant little to me, but now I could swear I'd seen it somewhere in the South Carolina Historical Society's archives. This strikes me as very odd, not least because back then, society was a patrimony, and women were second-class citizens at best. But on top of that, Lily died in childbirth during the slave insurrection.

At the time, I hadn't given it a second thought—but now, I can't help but wonder. What if the document I'd seen could shed some light on Jennifer's bizarre story about the Thin Place?

I finish my time on the bag and move through my sparring matches on autopilot, blocking, kicking, and punching by instinct, with the muscle memory born of practice and habit. As class winds down—which, in this case, means we get off easy with two hundred sit-ups and two hundred knuckle pushups—I become more and more excited by the idea. I call my dad and ask if he can pick Finn up from camp and give her dinner, so I can drive to the College of Charleston's Special Collections department downtown.

Finn's arrangements complete, I drive over to the library, anticipation building in my chest. I've always loved this library; the whole building is constructed around a rotunda that stretches from the first floor to the third, where Special Collections is housed. There are cozy chairs tucked between pillars that overlook the rotunda, the perfect place to hunker down with a book on a rainy day. When Finn was younger, she used to love to stand next to the railing and gaze all the way down to the first floor, watching people walk by, books clutched in their hands.

I park on a side street, feeling lucky to have found a spot so close, and make my way to the library, taking a shortcut through one of the tree-lined courtyards that houses some of the college's older buildings. The sun is brutal, and the humidity's not much better. I push open the door to the air-conditioned lobby with a sense of deep relief.

The library is quiet, the silence broken only by the hum of voices at the reference desk. I take the stairs, relishing the way my legs ache after this morning's workout. By the time I get to the third floor, my heart is pounding, and I have to take a moment to center myself. Then I walk up to the locked double glass doors of Special Collections and wave at the librarian behind the desk.

She buzzes me in, and we spend a couple of minutes chatting quietly, so as not to disturb the researchers sitting at the wooden tables, fragile documents spread out in front of them. Then I claim a table near a window display that overlooks the third-floor lobby, making sure that my phone's on vibrate. Adrenaline courses through me as I make my way to the computer near the door. My hands trembling, I type "Lily Adair" into the library's online catalog and hit "submit."

By this time, I have talked myself into believing that I imagined seeing her name. And honestly, the first few records that pop up don't look all that helpful: *Adair History and Genealogy*, compiled in the early 1920s; a record of Robert Adair's holdings in Barbados, listing Lily as his wife; her death notice in the Charleston paper. At some point an overzealous historian cataloged the contents of Max's parents' house, and the painting of Lily Adair is listed: *Portrait, Oil, commissioned from miniature.*

I scroll down farther and discover several volumes of Robert Adair's journals that were gifted to the Historical Society. Not surprisingly, Lily is mentioned extensively in these. After my conversation with Jennifer, I'm more than a little curious about these journals, but I already know what I'll find there—a portrait of a man wading deep into the land of the dead. I'm no stranger to that grief, so I keep scanning the results of my search: *Letter to Lily Adair from Robert Adair, unsent, 1816. Epitaph from gravestone of Lily Adair, commissioned by Robert Adair and placed on the Adair family property, 1816.*

While all of these are interesting enough, none of them seem likely to shed new light on my conversation with Jennifer. I'm beginning to think that my little investigation is a dead end when I see it, halfway down the third page of results: *Letter, Lily Adair to Robert Adair, April 20, 1816. Unsent. In Brightmore family collection.*

My heart starts pounding again, slamming against my ribs until it's hard for me to breathe. April 20? The insurrection took place on April 16, 1816, and, as far as I know, Lily died in childbirth almost immediately after. If the letter was unsent, it's likely that neither Robert nor any of his descendants ever saw it. What it's doing in the Brightmore collection is another mystery. I'm familiar with the Brightmore name as well—some of their descendants live in Charleston now. I know this less from my own research than from my mother's: I can remember seeing their names on her handwritten family tree, can remember the way her face lit up when she'd discovered she had some Brightmore ancestors. But why would the Brightmores have Lily's letter to Robert? Why wouldn't they have sent it on to him?

Something isn't right here, I can feel it. I fumble in my purse for a pencil, fill out the call slip to request the letter, and hand it to the librarian, who disappears to find it.

It feels like forever, but it's probably only about five minutes before the librarian emerges, carrying the letter with her, encased in an archival-safe, acid-free plastic sleeve. She sets it down in front of me with the usual admonitions—no flash photography, no photocopies, no taking it out of the room, no pens anywhere near it—and I nod at appropriate intervals to demonstrate that I am listening. I've heard all this before, but she's new and she's just doing her job, so I rein in my impatience and try to look attentive until she runs down and retreats behind the desk again.

Carefully, I pull the letter toward me and examine it. My first impression is that the writer was not well. Penned in black ink, the letters wander across the paper at an alarming slant, blurred in places by sweat, tears, or simply the pressure of the writer's hand. The penmanship is excellent, clearly that of an educated person, and each letter is formed in the flowery script typical of the early nineteenth century. Still, it's clear that something is amiss—in some places the ink is so dark, it's almost a blot, whereas in others, there's only the barest indication of the mark of a quill.

Dear Robert, the letter begins, *you are gone, and I am alone. The slaves have rebelled, and our plantation has been ransacked, the cane fields burnt to the ground and casks of rum set afire in the road. And yet—how can I not be happy? Our daughter has been born. Yes, we have a baby girl, born at the Brightmore estate, which was fortunate not to suffer such damages as we. In your absence, I named her Charlotte for my own dear mother, gone from us these five years past. I trust you will not take offense at this, and indeed I gave her your sweet sister Ellen's name as well.*

Charlotte Ellen Adair is her name. I think it most beautiful—as is she, with your gray eyes and my fair skin. She is well, despite having come into the world somewhat earlier than we anticipated, and I give thanks to God for this miracle.

I stop reading for a moment, puzzled. The baby had been born healthy, if a bit premature. Perhaps she'd gotten a fever, or something else that carried her off quickly? In those days there were no antibiotics, and medical care in the West Indies would have been even more primitive than in England. I imagine Charlotte cradled in her mother's arms, opal-skinned and tiny, with Finn's wide gray eyes, and feel a pang of sympathy for the doomed pair of them. Biting my lip, I turn my attention back to the letter.

It pains me to tell you this, Robert, but I do not fare as well as our daughter. I have had a fever for some hours since her birth, and though the midwife has done all she can to stem it, it continues unabated. I am by turns hot and cold, and my hands shake so that it is an effort to write, let alone to hold our precious Charlotte. The midwife will not say so, but I am fully sensible of the knowledge that I am unlikely to survive much longer.

Alicia Brightmore, who has been attending me in a most dedicated manner, has been doing the same for sweet Charlotte. Even fevered as I am, it pleases me to see the solicitousness with which she dotes upon our baby. You might recall that Alicia and John lost their infant daughter last year, and then a son, after which the doctor instructed her that she should not attempt to bear more children. She never complains, but I know that this wounds her deeply. What a blessing, to have her here with me.

My darling Robert, I know that you will grieve for me, but I beg you not to blame our Charlotte for my loss. She is the greatest gift I could ever imagine bestowing upon you, and if I am to relinquish my own life in the process, I will consider the price fairly paid. I do not blame you for being elsewhere during Charlotte's birth; I know you left to ensure our fortunes, and did not expect Charlotte to join us so precipitously.

Here I stop reading again, one finger resting on the clear plastic. Obviously Lily had not died giving birth to her baby, but soon after, likely from infection. Somehow she'd found the strength of will to write to her husband, absolving him from any responsibility—so why wouldn't the Brightmores have sent this letter?

Something itches at the back of my mind, a thought that won't quite materialize. The more I try to haul it free, the more elusive it becomes. I have the strangest feeling that the mysterious idea has something to do with my mother—but how can that be? Rubbing my temples in frustration, I turn back to the letter.

I have implored the Brightmores to write to you, so soon as regular packet boats resume their travels, informing you of all that has transpired here and of our sweet Charlotte's birth—and to enclose this letter, poorly penned though it may be. Alicia tells me that I must not worry—I will recover soon, and we will be together again with our daughter. But I see the truth upon her face.

Here a tremendous blot of ink mars the paper, as if Lily has upset the inkwell onto the page. I flip the plastic-covered sheet over and am relieved to see her writing begin again, though even more disordered than before.

Dearest Robert, there is something else I must tell you. Alicia insists that I should rest, but what does it matter now? Rest will not help me. I told Alicia she must not worry—that my dear Mother has been here, sitting on the side of my bed, holding my hand in hers—but this only brought tears to her eyes, though she was loath for me to see. I am not afraid. Alicia and John will see our baby safely delivered into your arms. In this I have faith. I am much obliged to them, and grateful for all they have done. How fortunate we are, to have such friends.

I must tell you, though, a secret I swore to keep—in case the knowing of it should matter. You are familiar, I trust, with the most unusual lady who joined us from the Americas a month before your departure. We have always found Julia to be most unorthodox, both in her attitudes and her opinions, but quite pleasant nonetheless.

At the mention of my mother's name, I gasp, so loudly that the other patrons look up from their work, fixing me with disapproving stares. Of course, it must be a coincidence, but it shakes me nonetheless. Hands trembling so that it's hard to hold the paper, I keep reading.

None of us know her people, nor does she have connexions of the

*sort befitting a lady. Though she has an amiable disposition, it seems
to me that there is about her always a tremendous sadness . . .*

Here another inkblot soaks the paper, and try as I might, I can't
determine whether it conceals additional observations about the
mysterious Julia. A shudder runs through me, and I have to set the
plastic-sheeted document down on the table to read the rest. This is
no easy task; what remains is written in such a shaky hand, the letters
wavering across the page, that I can barely make it out.

*I am sorry, Robert. The room trembles around me so that it is hard
to see, and it seems to me that it is growing dark, although Alicia assures me that this is not the case. I have slept and woken and slept
again, and always she is by my side, along with Hannah and the
Negro girl that has waited upon Alicia since she was a child. They
have put cold cloths upon my head to quell the fever, but still the chill
eats at my bones, so that I quake beneath the sheets as if I will never be
warm again. But then a wave of heat comes over me, unlike anything
I have ever felt. I imagine that this must be what the flames of Hell feel
like, licking away at my flesh, so that I am surprised to look down and
find my body undamaged beneath the sheet, other than by the ravages
of childbirth—but you will forgive me of speaking so crudely about
such matters. I fear that I am not myself. And I do not know how much
longer I will be able to share my thoughts with you.*

*To Julia, then: In recent weeks she has been joined by a young man
who resembles you to an alarming degree—so that if I did not know
that such a thing were impossible, the two of you being nearly of an
age, I would suspect you of the most perfidious infidelity. As it is, he
claims to be one of your relations, lately of South Carolina. Shortly
before the rebellion, they came to converse with me. They sought to
warn me of the rebellion, although to my shame, I did not take their
admonitions in the serious spirit with which they were intended. But I
must tell you this—they saved me, Robert. They knew that our house
would be set aflame. And they took me to safety, to the Brightmores,
where Charlotte was born.*

I believe Julia and Mr. Adair to be most extraordinary individuals.

Perhaps they are not people at all, but angels sent to save Charlotte. On my hope of heaven, I believe there are such beings. Or perhaps they are something else entirely—seers? Witches? Perhaps they have the Sight, as everyone believed of your grandmother. You will think I am mad in saying these things, I know . . . yet I must.

I do not seek to convict Julia and her companion with the notion, for they have been nothing but kind to me. Were it not for their intervention, I should likely have perished in the flames, and our baby with me. Still, the fact remains: They know things about us, the two of them. They say they are trying to change things—that what they know may not actually come to pass. But it scares me, Robert. It scares me for our daughter.

Here the letter ends abruptly. I can only assume that after she penned those words, Lily succumbed to her fever, entrusting it—and her child—to Alicia Brightmore. I have a moment of pure empathy for the latter . . . how awful to lose two children of her own, only to have Charlotte die on her watch as well.

Sitting back in my chair, I regard the letter. Something still doesn't add up. Something isn't right. Absently, I take out my phone, check to make sure that the flash is off, and snap a shot of the letter's second page. Then I flip the paper over and photograph the front, all the while puzzling over what I've read. *My mother's name. People who claim to know the future. A man with Robert Adair's gray eyes . . .*

I have an idea then, a wonderful, terrible idea, as ridiculous as it is impossible. Ryan would laugh me into next Tuesday, right before he dragged me to Dr. Rossetti for a complete psychological assessment. But what if I found my mother's necklace in the wreckage of that nineteenth-century plantation house because she was there—*then?*

Shaking my head, I dismiss the thought as quickly as it's come. Jennifer Adair must be getting to me, with all her talk of thin places and veils between worlds. There has to be another explanation, something valid and scientific and explainable.

In search of it, I read through the letter again. My gaze falls on one line and lingers there: *Perhaps they have the Sight, as everyone believed of your grandmother.* Staring down at Lily's uncertain handwriting, a shiver runs through me. Is she implying that people believed Robert's grandmother was some sort of clairvoyant? For just a moment Finn's drawing of Max and my mother pops into my head.

I dismiss it just as quickly, shaking my head again as if to shake the thought out of it. When this fails to work, I shake myself all over, like a dog shedding water. And then I get to my feet, ignoring the curious looks of my fellow researchers, check my phone to make sure the photographs are legible, and return the troubling letter to the librarian. I sling my purse over my shoulder and leave the Special Collections room, closing the door behind me as silently as possible.

All the way down the steep stairs to the first floor, I ponder Lily Adair's last words. The content of the letter is disturbing enough — but I still feel like I'm missing something. The certainty of this flickers at the edge of my consciousness, hovering just out of reach like the lyrics of a forgotten song or a half-remembered movie line.

You are familiar, I trust, with the most unusual lady who joined us from the Americas.

Pausing at the landing, I press my hand to the glass of the small window, eyes squeezed shut in an effort to remember. I call up the last time I saw my mother, standing at the edge of the crowd at Max's family's party, that wistful expression on her face. As if there was something she meant to say, except she never got the chance.

And then, as surely as if she's spoken to me, I know.

Max

Now that I know both Lily and the baby have survived, I feel as if an immeasurably heavy weight has been lifted from me. Still, part of me expects to vanish at any moment—how can I be here, if they are too?

Thinking about this hurts my head, and I take to pacing back and forth again, alternately scrutinizing the fields around the plantation for rebels and staring down at my hands to make sure they aren't disappearing. How will it happen, I wonder? Will I vanish piece by piece, like the Cheshire Cat, leaving only a grin behind? Or will I wink out of existence all at once, like with the *Star Trek* transporter?

I'm still pondering this when Julia comes downstairs, a bundle cradled in her arms. She looks exhausted but happy. "It's a girl," she says, folding the blanket back to reveal a red-faced infant with long, dark lashes and a puff of chestnut hair. "Lily says she's going to name her Charlotte, after her mother."

"She's alive." I touch the baby's soft cheek with my finger. "They're both alive."

"Yes, they are. You did good, Max." She smiles at me, brown eyes tilting up at the corners.

"*We* did good," I correct her. "Kick-ass, if you really want my opinion."

The two of us grin like idiots, and then I see realization break over her face. "If they're alive, though . . ." she says, "no offense, but how can you still be here?"

"I wish I knew." I raise both hands, palms up, in puzzlement.

"Do you feel any different? Strange?" The baby's fussing, screwing up its tiny face. Automatically, Julia rocks it—but her eyes are on my face, searching.

"No," I say. "But Julia—it's time."

"I know." She runs the tip of one of her index fingers over the infant's cheek, just where I'd touched. "I'll give the baby back to Lily, and then I'll go. That is, if Alicia will let me—she almost wouldn't give Charlotte up long enough to let me swaddle her, much less bring her down here. If Lily hadn't insisted Alicia stay with her, I doubt I would've managed it at all." She drops her voice, glancing up the stairs to make sure no one's within earshot. "That woman is downright hungry for this little one, if you want to know the truth. Not that I blame her—this has to be so hard for her."

"Well, maybe it's good," I say cautiously. "I mean, Robert's not here—so at least Lily will have someone to help her. She won't be alone, even if—*when*—we go."

"No," Julia says. "She won't. And you, Max—you'll be all right, heading right back into the middle of everything?"

"I will," I tell her, trying to sound reassuring. "Don't worry about me. I'll be careful. As for everyone here—I don't think the rebels are coming this way. You'll be fine. I'll leave my pistol with you, just in case, though."

She nods, but her face has gone paper-white. "Max—are you sure?"

"I am. But Julia, if I don't make it back—"

She grabs my arm, squeezing hard. "You'll make it."

I force myself to smile. "I hope so. But if I don't—tell Isabel I love her, assuming she still knows who I am. And kiss my daughter for me . . . assuming she exists."

Tears are slipping down her face, but she nods. "I'll tell her you were a stubborn son of a bitch," she manages, trying to return the smile. "Who wouldn't listen to a damn thing I said. And who was one of the bravest men I've ever met."

My mouth falls open in surprise. But before I can say a word, she turns on her heel and flees upstairs, the baby clutched in her arms.

I emerge from the gates of Brightmore into total pandemonium. The air is thick with cane ash, filled with the whinnying of horses and the howling of plantation dogs. In the distance, I see a flash of red: militia on the march, led by an officer on horseback.

Havoc shifts uneasily, ears laid flat, and I speak soothingly to him, as much for my own benefit as his. "It's okay, boy," I tell him. "Just hold on. We'll be okay."

And then I grip the horse with my knees, unstrap the musket, and canter down the road, avoiding obstacles as best I can. In the daylight, I can see the full extent of the debris—broken hogsheads of sugar, half-spilled casks of rum, bushels of corn and sweet potatoes, and even the remains of a four-poster bed. How Brightmore managed to escape this devastation is beyond me.

Ahead of me, I can see the officer of the company standing in his stirrups, shouting orders at the men behind him. I can't decipher the words, but I recognize the voice well enough. It belongs to John Rycroft Best, colonel of militia.

"Goddamn it," I mutter, tightening my grip on the reins. Best is infamous for his role in quelling the insurrection, in hunting down and killing fleeing rebels. Wherever his company is going, there will likely be a massacre.

And I'm riding straight into it.

Best stops shouting and lowers himself down onto his horse. As one, his men move forward, turning left and marching down a rutted

road. I know that I should let them go—that my business lies elsewhere, in the cane fields at Sweetwater. I promised Julia. Hell, I
promised *myself.*

Then again, Jubah didn't say I had to be back at Sweetwater right
at noon. She said *midday.* Which means that maybe I could at least
see what's going on here, even help, and still go home to Isabel and
Finn.

I draw Havoc to a halt, instinct at war with common sense. Julia
is expecting me to go to Sweetwater. If I die here, in a battle on some
anonymous plantation, how will she ever know what has happened
to me? I should do the cautious thing, the careful thing, and go
straight to Robert Adair's estate.

Then I hear the boom of a musket, and suddenly I'm running on
adrenaline. Kicking Havoc into a gallop, I race after the soldiers—
and draw up in the plantation yard, in the middle of a world gone
mad.

It seems like the entire rebel army is here, brandishing pitchforks
and what few guns they've managed to secure. "Come on!" they
shout at Best's militia, taunting. They form an irregular line, defiant
despite their ragged clothes and lack of munitions, dark skin gleaming in the blinding sun.

One of them waves a red flag, and I am close enough to see the
image pictured on it—a white woman having sex with a black man,
the ultimate inflammatory taboo in these crazy times. Beside the
flag-waver is a rebel wielding a sword, teeth bared and eyes wild. He
rushes toward one of the soldiers closest to me, and I see the man
loading his musket, ramming the ball home. He fires, and the rebel
is gone, invisible beyond the cloud of white smoke that fills the air. I
can smell him, though—the stink of perforated bowels, sharp and
pungent. The smoke clears and he lies motionless in the dirt.

For a moment, I am stunned. I have never seen a man die before.

Then the adrenaline kicks in again and I canter to the side of the
company of militia. All around me there are horrible screams, the
boom of muskets and rifles, the screeching of battle cries. A rebel

soldier falls, right in front of me. Her mouth opens and closes in an effort to speak, but no sound comes out. The tattered banner clutched in her grip seems to take a thousand years to reach the ground, so that I have an eternity to read the letters painstakingly inked on the cloth: *Happiness ever remains the endeavour.*

Grief stabs me, followed by an awful, freeing sense of abandon, and I aim at a militiaman poised to shoot an axe-wielding rebel. I feel as if I have left my body, as if someone else is raising the musket, bracing it against his arm. I have a clear shot. The world narrows until this is all it contains: the rasp of my breath, the warm metal of the gun, the red coat of the man in front of me, stretched taut as he lifts his weapon.

But as my finger squeezes the trigger, a shot booms close by, startling Havoc. He rears, throwing me to the ground, and my shot goes wild. I land hard, gripping the musket and gasping for breath. Havoc stares down at me, stomping, and with superhuman effort, I roll clear of his hooves. I jump to my feet and grab for his reins, but he gives me a white-eyed look of terror and bolts for the road, ears laid back against his head.

At least I distracted the militiaman from his target—if only temporarily. As the smoke clears, he aims again, straight for the rebel with the axe. Now I can see who it is—Jackey, his face contorted with effort, charging this way. Ten feet from us. Eight. Six.

At this distance, there is no chance that the militiaman will miss. And I have no time to load my gun.

One man can save another, Jubah had said as the candle guttered low between us in the shadows of her hut. *Only you know how to wipe your heart clean of what stains it.* Her voice echoes in my ear as I heft my musket, hoping it's heavy enough.

I have no idea what alerts the soldier to my presence. Maybe he just senses me there. Either way, he jerks around and looks up, taking in my white skin and the musket gripped in my hands. His mouth opens in wordless surprise.

Over his shoulder, I can see Jackey, eyes wide, axe raised, the three of us in a deadly freeze-frame. And then I bring the musket down on the man's head with all my strength, feeling the muscles in my arms strain and my bones jar with the impact. His knees buckle, and he drops to the dirt. Blood courses from his head, obscuring his face.

With a cold-bloodedness I do not recognize, I step over his body, pry the musket from his grip, and hold it out to Jackey. "Here." My stomach churns as I tug the cartridge box free from under the man's body, ignoring the limpness of his flesh.

Mutely, Jackey accepts the musket and box. He gives me a brief nod of thanks. And then he melts back into the rebel lines.

My hands are shaking, and sound roars back around me: The whinnying and the howling, the bang of the guns, the screams of victory and death. I look down at the man at my feet and find him gray, covered already with drifting, sifting cane ash.

Later, I will realize that is all it is. But in the moment, it looks as if the man has decomposed in front of me, rotting away in the instant it took me to hand the musket to Jackey. Bile rises in my throat.

I turn away—and come face-to-face with John Best. He doesn't say a word; he doesn't have to. It is clear that he has seen where my allegiance lies.

A triumphant yell from the rebels draws his attention away from me, and I turn to see a second group of men marching into the yard, armed with pistols and muskets. Their skin is dark, but they wear the red coats of the militia. This must be the West India Regiment, come to support the white troops. The rebels whoop with joy, brandishing their billhooks and cudgels overhead. They think these are the King's men, come to fight with them. How wrong they are.

A white man amidst the newcomers barks an order and the tallest soldier in the regiment raises his pistol. He fires it point-blank into the chest of an advancing rebel, whom I recognize with a start as King Wiltshire. Wiltshire's body jerks, and a red stain spreads across his torn shirt. He presses one hand to his chest and falls.

"Traitor!" a voice yells from the ragged rebel line, hoarse with fury. I look up to see Jackey leveling the musket I gave him. He fires, hitting the soldier in the belly, and all hell breaks loose. The rebels shriek in triumph and run for the plantation house, intending to claim it as their own, the militiamen charge, and I am caught in the middle.

Suddenly I am dodging oncoming rebels—who see only my white skin—and militiamen, who have witnessed what I did to their comrade and are doing their best to return the favor. Clutching my musket, I duck and weave my way through the plantation yard and toward open air. Sweat slicks my skin, dripping into my eyes and mouth. The salty taste is thick on my tongue, mingling with ash and the metallic tang of blood.

I stagger into clear terrain just in time to see the members of the West India Regiment bearing down on me. They thunder up the wide stone steps of the great house at a dead run and disappear inside. I hear shouting, and then the reports of guns firing at close range. The front windows splinter, sending shards of glass flying everywhere. One catches me in the leg and sticks. I reach down and pull it loose, pressing a hand against my thigh to stanch the flow of blood.

The surviving rebels flee through the broken windows, the West India Regiment in hot pursuit, and the remaining rebels in the plantation yard scatter. Some disappear into the cane field, others into the slave village. The militia charges after them, screaming.

Taking advantage of the chaos, I find a grove of low-hanging lime trees and conceal myself amongst them. I set my musket down, wipe my powder-stained hands on the grass, and inspect my body for damage. My leg is bleeding, but not too badly. I draw a deep, relieved breath, then lean back against the trunk of a tree for support, taking stock. I've lost my horse. I've killed one man, and saved another. The militia is on to me. On the bright side, I'm not dead—yet.

Isabel

harlotte Ellen. I've seen that name before, I'm sure of it. Only, it wasn't Charlotte Ellen Adair. It was something different.

Seized with conviction, I race down the rest of the stairs and into the growing darkness. It's all I can do to obey the speed limit on my way out of town, back over the bridge to Mount Pleasant. By the time I reach my dad's house, the sun has set. I wrench the front door open, drop my bag on the floor, and force myself to be quiet as I check on Finn, safely asleep in my old bedroom. My dad himself is nowhere to be seen.

Heart pounding, I speed walk through the dining room and back into the kitchen, where I grab a flashlight from the junk drawer. Clutching it in one hand, I head for the garage, where my dad stored all of my mother's papers in Rubbermaid containers, thinking that they might one day yield a clue to her disappearance.

On my way through the backyard, I pass my father, scrubbing the grill clean with a bristled brush. "Where are you going?" he calls after me.

"I'm looking for something," I yell back, and yank the garage door open, shining the flashlight into the gloom. I can make out our bicycles, the humped shape of the generator, a ton of garden tools, and finally, at the back, safe from the elements, the shelf holding my mother's research. I plunge inside, tripping over a bag of mulch in my haste.

A hand grabs my elbow and yanks me upright, so that I let out a squeak of alarm. "What the hell are you doing?" my dad says. "Have you lost your mind?"

Too excited to be offended, I shake my head. "I need to look at Mom's papers," I tell him. "I found a letter at the library today, and there's something I need to see."

The pained look on his face tells me just who I sound like, but he doesn't try to stop me. Together, we haul several of the boxes off the shelf and set them in a clear space on the floor. My dad fumbles around and comes up with a second flashlight, which he hands to me. He shines the beam of his down on the Rubbermaid containers, which are liberally festooned with spiderwebs, dust, and mouse droppings. "You're sure you want to do this?" he says.

"Absolutely," I say, and drop to my knees next to the boxes. None of them are labeled; I'd packed up these papers myself, in an effort to get them out of my dad's sight, and he'd stacked them in here. I spare a thought for my sixteen-year-old self, wishing she'd been a bit less impetuous and a lot more organized. Still, I know what I'm looking for—that handwritten family tree, the one that my mom showed me the night that she'd disappeared. Clear as if she were standing next to me, I can hear her saying, *You've always known who you are, Izzy . . . I can't go forward until I understand where I began.*

It isn't in the first box I open, full of letters and scribbled notes that tug at my heart: *Izzy—chorus auditions tonight—Don't forget!!!!!* She had forgotten, anyhow, and I'd had to run the whole way there, arriving sweaty and less than presentable, with barely enough time to catch my breath before delivering my solo. That night she'd been full of apologies, but I hadn't wanted to hear any of them. Three weeks later, she was gone.

"Not in here," I say a little too loudly, dropping the note back into the box and shoving the whole thing onto the shelf. My father doesn't reply, and I wonder if looking at all of this stuff is too difficult for him. I'm about to suggest that he go back into the house when I tug the next box open and shine the flashlight inside.

"This is it," I say to my dad, excitement coloring my voice. "I'm sure it is. I'm looking for that family tree she drew—you know, the one she was working on that night. And here—this box has all of those photocopies in it, printouts from Ancestry.com and census rolls and ship registers. See, there's her great-grandma's birth certificate, the one she was so excited to find."

Without a word, my dad picks up the box and carries it outside, where the air isn't so dusty and the light is marginally better. There's a full moon, and I can see the box clearly as he sets it down on the gravel driveway. I can see my dad's face too, set in grim lines. "Dad . . ." I say, shining my flashlight into the box, "you really don't have to stay."

He glares at me and sets his jaw. "Cut it out, Isabel. You're about as subtle as a rampaging elephant. Whatever you're going to do, just get it over with already. And then we'll put all of this junk back where it belongs."

"Fine." I crouch down, flashlight clutched in one hand, and start sifting through layers of paperwork, enough to fell an entire forest. As I get closer and closer to the bottom, I begin to worry that the family tree isn't in here, that I'll have to haul the box back into the garage and start all over again. But just as I'm about to give up, I see it: the black-inked, calligraphic flair of an "F" and the spear-point tip of an "A," peering out from beneath a yellowed copy of a 1930s phone book entry. My heart pounding, I tug the paper free and open it. Sure enough, *Family Tree* is inked across the top in my mother's most careful, elegant handwriting.

I close the box and smooth the paper out on top of it. Then I lean closer, bringing the flashlight to bear on the page, scanning it line by line. I see my name, and my mother's, and then her mother's—my grandmother Penny, whom I never knew. Back and back, one generation after another, until I see it—the name that's been nagging me all afternoon. *Charlotte Ellen Brightmore. b: April 17, 1816, d: December 14, 1886.*

Brightmore. Not Adair. Oh, God.

I go back one generation further—Charlotte's parents. In her careful calligraphy, my mother has inscribed their names: John Daniel and Alicia Marie Brightmore.

"Oh my God," I say, staring down at the words illuminated in the beam of light. "Oh my God, the Brightmores stole Lily's baby."

"What are you talking about?" my father says, shifting impatiently. "Lily who?"

"Lily Adair." I wave a hand in front of my face to drive off a moth that's hovering over the paper, drawn to the gleam of the flashlight. "You know, Max's however-many-times-great-grandfather's first wife."

My dad gives a grunt of acknowledgment, clearly wondering what any of this has to do with me, much less why it would drive me to dig through my mother's papers at nine o'clock at night. I hurry on, trying to explain. "Dad, Mom's birth family didn't just know the Adairs way back in Barbados . . . they *were* the Adairs."

He takes a step backward, folding his arms across his chest. "Come on, Isabel. You're starting to sound just as obsessed as Julia. What does any of this matter now? Haven't we dealt with enough? Give it a rest."

I shake my head. "Just listen, Dad. Today I read a letter in the archives that Lily wrote to Robert Adair when she was dying. She said some wild stuff, but I know one thing for sure. This was her baby's name, *Charlotte Ellen*—but she's listed as a Brightmore." I look up at his face, half-shadowed in the moonlight. "Robert never knew his daughter survived. The Brightmores kept her for themselves. Don't you see? If Robert hadn't lost Charlotte, maybe we'd still have Mom. Her whole history would've been different. What the Brightmores did—it changed everything."

"What are you talking about, Isabel?" my dad says roughly.

I believe Julia and Mr. Adair to be most extraordinary individuals.

A shiver runs through me, and I grip the flashlight tighter.

When you have eliminated the impossible, whatever remains, however improbable, must be the truth.

"In the letter, Dad—the one Lily wrote—she talked about a woman named Julia." I pause, my hands shaking so badly that the flashlight flickers and I set it down. "She talked about how strange Julia was, how she didn't fit in. And how she brought a man to meet Lily, a man who had the same gray eyes as her husband. She said they knew the future. What if Mom—"

My father stares at me. "What on earth are you suggesting, Isabel? Julia is *gone*. Max is *gone*. We need to accept that. Not just for us, but for Finn."

Finn. I think about my daughter, and how she knows who's on the phone before it rings. How she told me that the bad men were after Max, that we had to help him. *Perhaps they have the Sight, as everyone believed of your grandmother.* "Oh, no," I say, almost to myself. "Oh, God. Oh, no, no, no."

"Isabel!" my father says sharply. "Come back to me!"

But I'm spared any reply, because just then, the motion sensor light that borders my dad's property clicks on. In its glow, I can just make out the form of a small child with long dark hair, stepping into the woods that separate my dad's land from the Adairs'.

Finn.

Max

Now that the adrenaline rush is dying down, I realize where I must be: Lowthers Plantation, after the first major skirmish of the rebellion. History holds that it ended badly for the rebels, disheartening many of them and imbuing the white Barbadians with tremendous confidence—intelligence that I'd passed on to Nanny G., for all the good it had done. What I saw this afternoon doesn't contradict that in the slightest.

I know what comes next; the battle at Bayleys will take place at dawn. Bussa will die there. Forty rebels will be killed. Seventy will be taken prisoner.

"Goddamn it," I mutter under my breath, staring into the wreckage of the plantation yard. I'm not looking forward to crossing that yard to reach the stables. The dirt is bloodstained, the plants trampled, and the trees hacked to stumps. The rebels that have fallen lie still. I can see flies landing on them, smell the reek of death and blood.

Dimly it occurs to me that there's something I should remember about the aftermath of the battle at Lowthers, something important, but I can't seem to call it to mind. Ignoring the nausea rising in my throat, I get to my feet—and freeze. Someone is coming toward the house, riding like a demon—one person, alone. The rider's hair streams in the wind, sparking gold in the unsparing sunlight. Something about the small figure is unmistakably familiar. I edge closer, trying to see—and almost drop my gun.

Galloping toward me, reins gathered in one hand and pistol in the other, is Julia. Her eyes go wide at the carnage in the yard, and she slows, careful to skirt the bodies.

I am so shocked, I forget all about seeking cover. I step out into the yard, in plain view of the Barbados militia, the British garrison, and whatever rebels might care to put an end to me. "Julia!" I yell. "What the hell are you doing?"

She reins up sharply, her head swiveling toward my voice. Then she sees me, and a fierce grin breaks across her face. "I told you," she says. "If you fight—then so do I."

At this, all the blood drains from my face. "Jesus, Julia. Of all the stupid, thoughtless, dangerous—what are you thinking? You're supposed to be in the Brightmores' cane field, trying to get home. Do you want to get yourself killed?"

She swings down off the horse and leads it toward the grove of lime trees, hobbling it with a rag from her skirt pocket. "No," she says. "Do you? *You're* supposed to be at Sweetwater. Also, you're bleeding."

The cut on my leg throbs, and I press my fingers to it in an attempt to dull the pain. "It's not bad. How did you find me?"

She shrugs. "I saw the militia ride out—about half of them anyway. The rest went through there." She gestures at the field behind us. "So I hid until I could come looking for you. I had a feeling you wouldn't go where you were supposed to."

I'd be more indignant, but I'm trying to think what it is I ought to remember about this fight. There's something important—more important than ever, now that Julia is here. I'm sure of it. I cast my mind back desperately, but nothing comes.

"Where's Havoc?" she asks, interrupting my train of thought.

"Gone."

Julia grimaces. "See, Max, it's good that I came. You'd never make it to Sweetwater on foot, not in time, anyhow. We can take my horse. She's strong enough to carry both of us, and I'm sure if you can get back home that way, I can too."

"For Christ's sake," I mutter, ignoring this. "You could have been killed." I run my hand through my hair, breathing hard. And then I hear them, and realize what I should have remembered all along: When the battle at Lowthers was over, not all of the rebels fled. Some came back to finish what they'd started.

We are standing at ground zero of what will soon be a disaster zone.

"Shit!" I say out loud. "We have to get out of here. Come on, we have to go!"

But Julia doesn't move. She is staring at the field of cane, the grass flattened before the charge of a company of rebels. Their heads are lowered, their clothes tattered and blood-streaked, but on they come, brandishing torches and weapons, uttering ululating battle cries. They surge into the courtyard and begin to take the house apart.

The rebels haven't seen us standing at the edge of the trees yet, but any minute now, they're bound to. As one after another hurls flaming torches through the windows and a second group sets fire to the cookhouse, I feel my heart clench. "Come on!" I say, grabbing Julia's wrist. Through the smoke and flames, I can make out a figure running right toward us. I'm not in the mood to find out who or why.

After what feels like forever, Julia takes a step toward me. We haven't gone two paces, though, before she lets out a sharp sound of dismay and her body goes taut as a rope. I turn to see a soldier gripping Julia's other arm, his face as red as his coat, the other hand tight on his gun. Julia's pistol falls to the dirt.

"Hoy! Leave off, sir!" the man shouts at me. "What do you think you are doing with this woman?"

Julia is glancing between us, stunned. Then she comes to life and tries to pull away from the soldier. "Let me go!" she screams at him.

The redcoat looks baffled. "I can't do that, madam," he says, polite despite the inferno of destruction that has erupted behind him. "This man is a known Negro sympathizer. I'm afraid you must come with me, for your own safety."

I tug hard on Julia's other arm. "You heard the lady. She wants to come with me."

For a second the militiaman seems to waver. Then he raises his musket and points it at my chest. "Drop your weapon. And let her go," he says. "Or I'll shoot."

"You'll shoot us?" I say, sounding as incredulous as I feel.

"No," the man says, baring his teeth at me. "I'll shoot *you*."

For a second I try to calculate whether I'm faster than he is. But in the end I decide I can't risk it. I set the musket on the ground and stand as straight as I can, in an effort to disguise the fact that my legs have turned to water. And then I let Julia go.

Immediately, he jerks her back—but he doesn't lower the musket. Instead he glances left, then right. His finger whitens on the trigger.

The son of a bitch intends to shoot me, anyhow.

I almost go for my gun—after all, I have nothing to lose. But that's when I see Jackey, running out of the smoke, musket in hand. "Run," he mouths at me. "Go!"

Oh, sure. So the soldier can shoot me in the back? I don't think so. Ever so slightly, I shake my head.

His face a mask of concentration, Jackey raises the musket. He points the gun at the militiaman and I lunge past the soldier to grab Julia, pulling us both to the ground. One of my hands catches on her necklace. I feel it break. There is a single, bright spark as the pendant tumbles into the dust.

The soldier stares down at us, astonished. Then he wheels, musket ready, just as Jackey pulls the trigger. I cover Julia's body with mine, bracing myself for the crack of the shot. But instead, the gun clicks on an empty chamber. It has misfired.

I get to my knees, scrambling for my own gun. But before I can reach it, the soldier lifts his musket and fires. A starburst of blood spreads over Jackey's chest.

Sickened, I grab Julia's hand, lunge for my gun, and take off into the field. Behind us, the soldier is shouting, trampling the cane as he chases after us. Julia is screaming something, but between the bellows of the militiaman and the thunder of my heart, it's just noise. She screams it over and over again, though, and at last I understand.

"Finn!" she is yelling. "It's Finn!"

I jerk my head up, startled. Straight ahead, dwarfed by the towering sugarcane, is a small girl in a white nightgown, her dark hair straggling loose from its braids. And behind her, a sudden blaze of fire. Someone has set this field aflame.

My nightmare has come to life.

I didn't think it was possible for me to run faster, but I do, musket banging against my side. The noise in my ears looms louder, shrieking and ringing and howling combining to such a fever pitch, I can barely hear my own voice. "Finn!" I scream, the word tearing loose from my throat. "Finn, run!"

She takes one step toward me, then another. I see her lips form my name.

Then the ground beneath me disappears. Finn is gone, and with her the soldier, the cane, the smell of charred sugar. Julia's hand turns in mine, gripping hard. And then there is nothing but the alien, familiar falling, the descent into nothingness. The wailing and the dark.

Isabel

"Oh my God," I say. "What in the world—where does she think she's—"

The woods close around the small figure in its white nightgown, and I'm galvanized into action. I grab the flashlight off the gravel and sprint across the lawn, heading for the gap in the trees where my daughter disappeared. I'm dimly aware that my dad is following me, that he's yelling something, but I can't spare him any attention. All I can think about is the pond, deep and edged by trees, easy to stumble into. Rocks that could cut Finn's feet, animals with sharp white teeth, blackberry brambles that could catch her and scratch her. And beneath all those fears is the other. The Thin Place, waiting to suck my daughter in and take her away from me forever. *Not real*, I tell myself, *no matter what that damn letter said. Not possible.*

But I can't help the fear that shoots through me, as quicksilver and unstable as mercury. I run faster, shoving branches out of my way and flinging my body headlong through the dark, heedless of what obstacles might lie in my path.

It's been a long time since I ran through these woods in the dark, but my body hasn't forgotten the way. And a good thing too, because my mind has descended into panic. The flashlight's beam is weak and I can see only a few feet in front of me, just enough to avoid tripping over roots and blundering into bushes. As for Finn, she has vanished into the blackness. My only clue that she is still there is the racket she's making—the snapping of twigs under her feet, the crash of her small body into the brush and trees. Wherever she's headed, she's in a hurry.

A branch catches me across the cheek, narrowly missing my eye, and I duck, hand up to protect my face. The second one scrapes my palm, and I feel the slippery wetness of blood trickling down my skin. I ignore the pain, concentrating on chasing after my daughter, who has skirted the pond—thank God—and is headed for the thickets on the other side. For a moment I can see her clearly. There's mud on her small ankles and the hem of her nightgown, and her hair has come undone from its braid, threaded through with leaves that gleam silver in the light of the full moon.

"Finn!" I yell, and see her head turn toward me. She lifts one hand in a beckoning gesture—*Come on*. And then she darts into the woods again.

My father emerges from the trees behind me, panting. "Where is she?" he says, and I point the flashlight in the direction that Finn disappeared.

"Just through there. I think she's heading for the clearing," I say over my shoulder, already running after her. From the trampled undergrowth in the path of my flashlight's beam, I can tell that I am right—she's racing straight for Max's tree house.

"Finn!" I scream again, shoving my way through a stand of blackberry bushes and scraping my arm against the bark of a huge oak. I call again and again, but there is no answer. Despite myself, I can't help remembering the last time I ran through the woods like this, heedless of roots or consequences, calling Max's name. By the time I shove my way through the last set of bushes and into the clearing, my father behind me, I am convinced that it will be empty, that my daughter will be gone.

It takes my eyes a second to adjust to the spill of moonlight, bright and painful after the pitch-black of the woods. I blink, trying to clear them. Voice hoarse from screaming, breath coming harsh in my throat, I say Finn's name.

To my great relief, she answers me this time, from just a few feet away. "Mama," she says. "Mama, look."

I wipe my eyes clear of sweat and see her standing in front of the tree house, tiny in her white nightgown. "Jesus, Finn, you scared me. What got into you, running through the woods at night like this? Don't you know it's dangerous?"

"No," she says, and walking forward, takes my hand. "Mama, *look.*" She turns me toward the trees across the clearing, so that I can see two figures standing in the shadows.

My heart gives a horrible jolt, then starts racing. "Get behind me, Finn." Without waiting for her to comply, I step in front of her, blocking her from view. "Dad?" I say, but he is already beside me, shielding Finn as well.

"Who's there?" I say, imbuing my voice with a confidence I don't feel.

I am ready for almost anything—gunshots, hand-to-hand combat, attempted kidnapping. In my current state of mind, nothing seems too farfetched, and I feel my body readying itself, settling into the focused, icy calm I know I will need in order to fight. But out of the darkness comes the one thing I didn't expect.

"Don't be afraid," he says, and steps forward, into the light. "Isabel, it's me."

The man in the clearing is wearing ripped, stained clothing, and one side of his face is dark with what looks like blood. In one hand, he's clutching an old-fashioned musket, and somewhere he has lost his shoes. But it's Max, there's no doubt about it. I'd know him anywhere.

I blink, then open my eyes, but he's still there. My stomach lurches, as if the ground has fallen away. I try to speak, to move, but I can't do either one. Instead I stare at him, waiting for him to disappear, like he did in the rainstorm on my patio, that night at the foot of my bed. But he's solid as the trees behind him, and as the seconds tick by, I feel a faint, dangerous flicker of hope.

I drop Finn's hand and wrap my arms around myself, shivering in the warmth of the summer night. "Dad?" I say, hating the quaver in my voice. "Please tell me I'm not losing my mind. Tell me you see him too."

My father sucks in breath to reply. But I never have a chance to find out what he was going to say, because before he can make a sound, the second figure steps out of the shadows. Moonlight falls full on her face, illuminating her blond hair and pale skin, her almond-shaped brown eyes.

"Grandma!" Finn says, and beside me, my father falls to his knees.

Standing next to Max is my mother. She's dressed just as oddly, and looks as bedraggled. Her face is smudged with dirt. Her dress is torn.

"Julia," my father whispers, reaching out his hands to her. "Julia?"

"Andrew." Her voice breaks.

"How—" he manages. "You—I thought you were dead. Am I dreaming?"

She shakes her head, tears streaking her cheeks. "I'm so sorry." Her eyes find me, and the tears flow harder. "I'm sorry for everything."

My father gapes at her, wordless, on his knees in the dirt. Then Finn has hold of him, pulling him to his feet, and my mother is running to meet them both. She throws her arms around my father, holding tight. Together they embrace Finn, who giggles, saying, "Grandma, you're squashing me! I can't breathe!"

Over my father's shoulder, my mother meets my gaze, her eyes brimming. Surely I should be crying too. But I can't. I can't move. I can't think. Over and over again the same words ricochet through my head, a pinball careening through a machine, a rat trapped in a maze.

Not real. Not possible. Not possible. Not real.

I stare at the three of them, then back at Max. How can this be happening? Have I gone completely mad?

As if he has read my mind, Max speaks. "You're not crazy, Isabel," he says. "I know how this looks. But it's me. I swear."

His voice is low, rough, as if from smoke or shouting. But it is his.

I shake my head, clinging to myself. *Oh, God. Not possible. Not real.*

He drops the musket into the dirt. And then he lifts his hands, palms open. His lips rise in a wicked grin I thought I'd never see again. "I did tell you I'd meet you in the clearing," he says. "Sorry I'm late."

I gape at him. And then my paralysis breaks and I am running toward him, and he is holding me in his arms. He's filthy, he reeks of sweat and smoke, and the stuff on his face is definitely blood, but I don't care. I try to ask him where the hell he's been, what happened to him, but all I can get out is a single word.

"Max," I say. "Max . . . Max . . . Max . . ." I say it over and over again, until his name blurs, meaningless and indistinguishable, into the sound of my sobs.

Max

S ince that night, there have been questions on all sides, excla-
mations and raised eyebrows and unspoken suspicions. I went
to see my parents right away, Finn at my side, and nearly gave
my mother a heart attack. She pressed a hand to her chest, gasping,
her mouth opening, then closing again, and finally she flung her
arms around me and wept. "Max," she kept saying. "I knew it. Oh, I
knew it. I knew you'd come home."

My father squeezed my shoulder, his eyes suspiciously wet, and
offered me a drink. He took my musket and stashed it in his gun safe
without a word. And then we all sat down in my parents' living room,
and the explanations began.

Julia and I told the truth about what happened. I didn't expect
anyone to believe us. But when it was Isabel's turn to speak, she told
us about the phone call that she'd gotten on the dig at Lowthers, finding Julia's necklace buried in the dirt. Her dreams, and Finn's. Seeing me in the garden, in her bedroom. Reading Lily's letter.

"Wait," I said, leaning forward. "Lily died—but the baby lived?"

"I think so," Isabel said, and then she went on to explain what
she'd found on Julia's family tree. Not Charlotte Ellen Adair, after
all, but Charlotte Ellen Brightmore—our common ancestor. Horri-

fied, I remembered Julia cradling the baby, saying *that woman is downright hungry for this little one*, and had to suppress a shiver.

My eyes met Julia's, and I was sure she was thinking the same thing. "Oh, no," she said, her face turning pale. "Oh, that poor woman. After everything—" But then she'd caught herself, and forced a laugh. "Well, I suppose it's not incest, Max. Not that far back. People used to marry their first cousins, after all." At which point my mother had a coughing fit and excused herself to drown her sorrows in a glass of water.

When you've been as good as dead for eight years, it's all the mundane technicalities that trip you up. Renewing your driver's license, for instance. Reactivating your cellphone. How I convinced the State Department to consider my passport application is a mystery to me, nothing short of a miracle—and forget reopening my bank account. At one point I found myself shouting into the phone, "I understand that you can't check the credit score of a dead person. But I'm not dead, goddamn it. I'm talking to you, for Christ's sake. What do you think this is, a telegram from the Great Beyond?"

Then there are the explanations we've had to give the police in order to close our missing persons' cases. After some debate, Julia and I agree to simply say that we don't remember what happened to us. It's a weak explanation, for sure—but it sounds more plausible than the truth. There's no way the officers believe us, but there's not too much to do about it, in any case, so they accept our story, with admonitions to call them immediately if our memories should return.

Unfortunately *The Post and Courier* gets wind of what's happened and runs an article featuring the miraculous return of two amnesiac Charlestonians, one of them the son of a prominent society family. Julia and I are flooded with requests for interviews, which sucks. The last thing either of us wants is more questions we can't answer.

After a few days of feeling like I am living under a microscope, I ask my parents if they still own the house in Folly Beach. When they say yes, I pack up my things and head over there within the hour, in my old car. Thank God my parents kept it all these years, hoping one day I'd come home and drive it again. Alone in the empty beach house, I finally feel the awful tension ebb, feel my lungs fill with a tidal surge of relief.

I know I should want to spend every second with Isabel right now—but since I got back, the only two people I feel like I can be my true self with are Julia and Finn. My daughter's easy with me, showing me her frog terrarium and her prized collection of books, telling me all about the past few weeks. "No one believed me," she says, hopping up and down with excitement. "But I knew you were real. I said so to Mama and Grandpa. I knew I could bring you back—and here you are."

Finn and I have spent hours together, in which she's answered my myriad questions about school, her favorite things to do, and whether incidents like the strange dreams she had about Barbados have happened before. It takes her a while to open up about the latter, but eventually she does, telling me a series of stories that make my head spin and ending up with her visit to Dr. Rossetti. She talks about Ryan a lot, how she can't wait for me to meet him. I'm not sure how I feel about any of this—her strange experiences, her closeness with a man who is a stranger to me—but I listen in silence, stunned by my daughter's intuition, the perceptive way in which she sees the world. She's an amazing little girl, beautiful and smart, and I can hardly believe she's mine.

Isabel hovers in the background during most of these conversations, trying to give us the illusion of privacy. Her aloof demeanor puzzles me: After that first night in the clearing, whenever I get within two feet of her, she shies like a nervous pony. I can't figure out whether she's waiting to see if I'm completely insane, if I've made the whole thing up, or whether it's far simpler—that I'd never confessed the truth about seeing her mother in the woods all those years ago.

When I'd finally worked up the courage to tell her, Isabel was silent. I waited, sitting across from her at her kitchen table, my gaze drifting between her face and the view of the patio through the window over the sink—the same patio I'd stood on in my dreams, calling out to her.

"All that time?" she said finally, voice cracking. "And you never said a word?"

"I'm sorry." The words felt painfully inadequate. "I didn't know who she was. I'd been asleep, and I thought maybe I'd dreamed it. Because the alternative—that I'd seen Lily, that the two of them just disappeared—well, would you have believed that, Isabel? I mean, come on."

Isabel shook her head. "You lied to me," she said softly. "All that time, you lied."

"I did. And there's no excuse for it, I know. But once we became— what we were—I spent the whole time trying to find her again. Why do you think I majored in history, on that damn rebellion?"

Her eyes fixed on my face, searching. "That's why you wanted me to meet you in the clearing that last day, wasn't it? You were going to tell me the truth."

"I was," I admitted. "But I never got the chance."

She blinked, and for a moment I saw the bright shine of tears in her eyes. Then she pushed her chair back from the table. "I don't know what to say."

"Isabel, please." I reached across the space between us, catching hold of her hand, but she twisted her wrist, breaking my grip.

"Finn's calling me," she said.

"Can't we—"

But she'd already turned, heading for the stairs, toward the sound of Finn's voice. "We'll talk about it later, Max," she said over her shoulder, and disappeared from sight.

Isabel

"This is nuts, Isabel," Ryan said when I called to tell him the news the morning after Max and my mother came home. "I mean, listen to yourself. It doesn't add up."

"I know it's nuts," I protested. "But it's amazing too. Come on, Ry. To have both of them back? It's unbelievable."

"Oh, it's unbelievable, all right." He cleared his throat, and I got the distinct sense he had another, less polite word in mind. "So—what, you're just going to swallow their story whole? You're going to be with him again now, like nothing happened?"

"I never said that! I'm not an idiot. I have a ton of questions. But all of it—it matches up with everything that's happened, Ry. The dreams Finn and I had, he had them too. The necklace, Finn's picture—everything fits." I took a gulp of my third cup of coffee, eyes burning from lack of sleep. "Maybe . . ." I said quietly, "maybe it doesn't matter, in the end. Maybe all that matters is that they've come home."

When Ryan spoke again, the harsh edge in his voice was gone. "I'm happy you have your mother back, Iz. And Max too. I want Finn to know her father. I just don't want the two of you to get hurt, is all.

And sometimes, when things seem too good to be true . . . well, there's a reason for that."

I forced myself to remember that he was only looking out for us. "You have to meet them, Ry. Talk to both of them. Maybe you'll see a pattern I don't, be able to make sense of it in a different way. But right now, however improbable—based on the evidence at hand, this is what I believe."

Ryan muttered something incomprehensible, and then we hung up, with promises to talk later in the day, when everything had settled down. But nothing has.

Contrary to Ryan's insinuation, I haven't simply leapt back into my relationship with Max. We've spent time together every day, but we haven't been alone, other than a few minutes here and there. This doesn't feel entirely like a bad thing; I can't figure out how to act around him, how to be now that eight years have gone by. The trouble is, it hasn't been nearly as long for Max—just a few short weeks, if he and my mother are telling the truth—and I can see him getting restless, can see the way he looks at me when he thinks I'm not paying attention, as if he's trying to figure out what's going on in my head. Max is a patient person, more patient than I am, for sure. But he won't wait forever.

I will myself to get over everything, tell myself again and again that the sacrifices he made to bring my mother home outweigh the secret he kept from me. Tell myself that he is the same boy I always loved, that I should say whatever is necessary to erase the hurt, bewildered look that comes over his face whenever he reaches for me and I slip away from his touch. But I can't bring myself to do it, not yet.

Maybe the problem is me, pure and simple. Maybe something in me broke when they left, something unfixable. There's a part of me that wants nothing more than to throw my arms around him and my mother, to hold them close and tell them how much I missed them, to never, ever let them go. But every time I consider doing just that, an icy voice speaks up inside me—the voice that has kept me going all this time, that got me through the loss of both of them, through watching my father drift away, through having Finn and putting my-self through school and taking one kick after another in the ring, until I rose up, planted my feet, and gave back as good as I'd gotten.

The voice tells me to be careful, that to love unreservedly is to lose everything—and I won't survive that kind of loss a third time. That I'm no longer the girl who went to meet Max in the woods that day eight years ago, heart in her hand and everything beginning. Like it or not, I am someone else now, someone harder, colder. The question is, how much of my new identity is comprised of my de-fenses . . . and how much is simply who I have become?

I see the loss of that young girl in Max's eyes, hear it in my moth-er's voice whenever she speaks to me. I haven't missed her in a long time, not really. I considered her sacrifice the price I paid for sur-vival. But now, confronted with the return of the very people whose disappearance caused me to erect the walls around my heart, I am struggling with the choices I've made, the person I've grown up to be.

I don't like feeling this kind of uncertainty. It unsettles me, asks the question—if I am brave enough to tear down those walls, then who will I find inside them?

I'm not sure I'm ready to find out. But the thing is, I don't think Max and my mother will give me a choice. And a part of me—the most venial, petty, ugly part—hates them for making me see myself this way, making me risk everything. For coming home.

Be careful what you wish for indeed.

Isabel

W e're sitting outside, my mom and I, on one of the benches under the giant oak trees that shelter the Charleston waterfront. A few yards away, Finn is playing in the fountain, leaping through the confluence of water at the center, as giddy and carefree as any child.

My mother keeps glancing at me shyly, like she can't believe I'm really here. I can't blame her—I'm doing the same thing, in between checking on Finn and rummaging in our cooler for sandwiches. My mom packed lunch, and I was responsible for dessert—triple chocolate cake from Kaminski's, plus iced coffee with cream, sugar, and cinnamon, sloshing away in an insulated thermos I've had for years. Come to think of it, the thermos's existence probably predates my mother's disappearance, lo those many years ago.

"What type of sandwiches did you make?" I ask, for the sake of conversation. It's awkward between us, or at least I feel that way. My mother knows me so well, and yet she doesn't know me at all. I can't figure out how I ought to relate to her. After all, we're both adults now, and I haven't had a mother in a long time. Now here she is, sandwiches and all, and I am at a loss to know how to behave.

"Try one and see," my mother offers, tucking a strand of bright hair behind her ear.

I shoot her a suspicious look, and she laughs. "You look just like Andrew when you do that," she says, her voice softening. "I can't get over how beautiful you are."

Embarrassed, I unwrap one of the sandwiches and discover that they are an exotic combination of pesto, gouda, and tomato. "You have to say that," I mutter, feeling about twelve years old. "You're my mother."

My mom reaches out and lays her palm against my face. "It's the truth," she says. "When I left—it was all there in your face, the promise of what you'd look like, who you'd be. You can't imagine how it feels . . . to have been gone for a year, and come back to find you all grown up."

"I can't imagine a lot of things," I say. "Like how it felt to walk into the woods after a ghost and wind up in the nineteenth century." The words sound absurd, and I can't help but grimace. "I know what I saw . . . and what you and Max have told me . . . and then there's Finn. But it still feels like a fairy tale to me."

My mom's mouth curves up in a cryptic smile. "Try the sandwich," is all she says.

I do, and sigh with delight. "It's delicious," I say after I've swallowed. "But I hope you've packed something else for Finn. As amazing as this is, I can't imagine that I can convince her to eat it."

My mother's laughter peals across Waterfront Park, blending with the sound of children's shrieks that are emanating from the fountain. "What do you take me for?" she says. "One of those is ham and cheese, with mayonnaise, lettuce, and tomato, made on bread that doesn't have 'any of those funny seed things on the top,' like she told me the other day. I did raise a child, you know."

"Of course you did," I say, momentarily ashamed. But when I glance over at my mother, she doesn't look offended in the least. Instead, she is watching Finn splash in the fountain with a look of such tenderness, it sends a small, sharp pang through my heart. I follow her gaze and see my daughter, clad in her purple one-piece bathing suit, chatting with another little girl. Finn must feel our eyes on her, because her head turns, and she lifts one hand in a wave.

"I remember when you were that little," my mother says, startling me. "I used to take you down to Coronado Beach and make huge drip castles with you. We'd stay out there for hours, building moats and drawbridges, turrets and courtyards. I'd bring lunch, and while we ate you'd tell me stories about the people who lived in the castle. Not just the royalty, either. You'd tell me all about the maids and the people who worked in the stables. A finely honed sense of justice, even then."

I glance over at her. She's still staring straight ahead, looking at Finn, but I'm pretty sure her calm tone conceals a stronger emotion—regret, maybe? "I remember," I say quietly, cradling one of the foil-wrapped sandwiches in my hands.

"Do you?" she says, swiveling to look at me.

"Sure I do," I say, and shift uneasily on the bench. "You used to make those lemon cookies, with the icing on top. By the time we got around to eating them, they'd be all melted, but I never cared. They were my favorite."

"That they were," my mother says. "Do you still like them?"

I shrug, suddenly feeling too hot in my T-shirt and capris and wishing for a turn in the fountain myself. "I wouldn't know," I say, tracing a whorl in the green wood of the bench. "I haven't eaten them since you left."

My mother sighs. "Isabel . . ." she says.

I wait for her to continue, but she doesn't. Finally I say, "Yes?"

For a long moment she is silent. We watch Finn dash through the water arcing from the squat cylindrical columns that border the fountain, squealing with glee as the spray catches her by surprise. I've decided that my mother's going to keep whatever thought she's had to herself, and am reaching into the bag for the thermos of iced coffee, when she says, "Why are you so angry?"

My head snaps up. "What do you mean? I'm not angry."

"Yes, you are," my mother says, with the implacable calm I remember from my childhood. It's the voice she used to employ to talk me down from a temper tantrum, to help me see reason when reason had escaped me. "You're mad at me. You're mad at Max. You're even mad at that man of yours."

"What man?" I say, more bewildered than ever. "You mean Ryan? You've met him exactly once. How can you possibly know how I feel about him?" Ryan had come over to my dad's house the second day after my mom and Max returned, eaten dinner with my parents and Finn, asked all the right questions, and gone back to his house looking as if there were a thousand words roadblocked behind his lips, none of which were remotely appropriate to say. He'd been on his best behavior, though, and I can't remember snapping at him or even giving him a warning glance.

My mother shakes her head. "I wasn't born yesterday, honey. That man loves you."

"Ryan isn't mine," I say, thoroughly disconcerted.

"No?" my mother says, taking one of the sandwiches out of the cooler. "Poor thing, the way he feels is written all over his face."

"Besides," I say, entirely discomfited by the turn that this conversation has taken, "I'm not angry with Ryan. He hasn't done anything wrong."

"Whereas Max and I . . ." my mother says, leaving me to finish her sentence.

"That's complicated," I say, and take a big bite of my sandwich to forestall further discussion.

"Not really," my mother says, in that same even voice. "Max couldn't help what happened, Isabel, any more than I could. He didn't do it to hurt you. The whole time we were gone, all he did was think about getting home to you. Love like that . . . it's a rare thing. Don't just throw it away."

"I'm not throwing anything away!" I say, my temper rising along with my voice. "He's the one who lied, not me. He's the one who left.

And you know what else? None of this is your business. If Max wants to talk to me, he should do it himself."

Finn is padding toward us, dripping water on the flagstones, a quizzical expression on her face. Forcing a smile, I get to my feet and wrap her in a beach towel, then scoop her up and settle her between us on the bench, an effective barrier. My mother gives me a pointed look, but she doesn't say anything else as I unwrap Finn's sandwich and begin rubbing her hair dry. In fact, other than making cheerful conversation with Finn about the girl she met in the fountain, the fine quality of the ham-and-cheese sandwich ("No seeds. You remembered!" Finn crows, looking pleased), and the addictive nature of the chocolate cake, she doesn't talk to me at all for the remainder of the afternoon, other than to say goodbye. I have the distinct feeling that she is disappointed in me.

Max

I've been back in town for almost a week before I finally meet Ryan, during a casual afternoon at the beach. The gathering is Isabel's idea, or maybe Finn's—my daughter has been chattering about the guy since I got home, telling me how he helps her design her Halloween costume every year, how he was the one who taught her to swim. I know I shouldn't be jealous—I ought to be grateful to him, or at least appreciative, and on some level I am. Still, the more Finn talks about him, the harder it is for me to suppress the feeling that he's usurped my place in her life.

Isabel and Finn show up at my house first, the latter clutching a drawing of a castle that she's made for me. I accept it with gravity, complimenting the details of the tiny windows and the terrifying nature of the many-toothed monster rising from the moat, and Finn glows. We're in the midst of filling water bottles and debating whether it's worth lugging my parents' stash of canvas chairs the four blocks to the ocean when the doorbell rings.

"Hold that thought," I tell them, and stride down the hallway. I square my shoulders and open the front door wide, face set in a smile. But when I see who is standing on the other side, my mouth falls open and the words die on my lips.

I have never met this guy in my life, but I recognize him, sure enough. I recognize that tall, lean build, those clear hazel eyes, narrowing to a sharp focus when they find my face. This is the man from the dream or vision or whatever the hell you want to call it that I had when Jubah made me drink that noxious tea. The one wearing only his boxers.

All I can do is stand there gaping at him. Then I remember my manners and introduce myself, extending my hand. His grip is warm and firm—a simple handshake, not a dominance play or a test of strength—but I feel the caution in it, nonetheless. He is as wary of me as I am of him.

"Come in," I say, standing aside as Finn barrels past me.

"Ryan!" she says, throwing her arms around him with enough force that he has to steady himself on the doorframe.

"Ow," he says mildly, and bends to kiss the top of her head. "Hey, sweetheart. Hi, Iz."

I turn to see that Isabel has joined us in the foyer, sunscreen in hand. "Hi," she says, and an odd look passes between them. After a moment, Isabel looks down, breaking his gaze, and clears her throat.

"C'mere, Finn," she says, holding up the bottle of sunscreen. "Let's put this stuff on you before we get outside."

"Moooommmm," Finn complains, drawing out the word, but she follows Isabel into the bathroom, talking a mile a minute.

Ryan and I stand there awkwardly, waiting for them to reemerge. I do my best to make small talk, asking questions about his work. He's polite enough, but reserved, his answers clipped. "No thank you," he says when I offer him a drink, and then falls silent, hands in his pockets, shifting his weight. I think both of us are relieved when Finn skips back into the room, asking if we can take some bodyboards to the beach.

So I dig a couple of boards out of my parents' storage shed and we lug them down to the beach, in lieu of the chairs. At Finn's request, I show her a couple of basic tricks that I remember from my summers spent on Folly—nothing special, but from the look on her face, I might as well have executed a series of 360 spins. She watches me intently, trying again and again with a stubbornness that reminds me of Isabel. When she finally masters a cutback, she comes racing out of the waves and leaps into Ryan's arms, a gleeful grin on her face. "Did you see me, Ry? Did you see me? I didn't fall or anything."

He tosses her skyward, then catches her and spins, making her giggle. "You're a rock star," he pronounces. "Got your mama's coordination, for sure."

Finn wriggles out of his arms and turns to Isabel. "Did you see me, Mama?"

Isabel has been lying on a towel in her bikini, sunning herself. At the sound of Finn's voice, she props herself up on her elbows and gives a sleepy smile. "I saw, baby. You're getting good, all right."

"Will you swim with me?" she says, bouncing over to Isabel and tugging on her hand. "Please?"

"For a little while. It's getting late, see?" She digs her phone out of her beach bag to show Finn the time. "The sun'll be setting soon."

"Then come on," Finn says, pulling Isabel to her feet. I try not to stare—she's so gorgeous in that damn black bikini, and it shows way more of her than I've seen since I've come home. The two of them disappear into the water, leaving me with Ryan.

The moment they're out of earshot, he turns on me. "What do you think you're doing?" His voice is low, vicious. The guy who'd caught Finn in his arms and swung her around is gone. In his place is someone wound tight as a bowstring, his muscles so tense, I can practically feel him vibrating.

His eyes narrow, waiting for my answer, and for a split second I want to deck him—for being with Isabel and Finn when I couldn't, for thinking he has a claim on them. Taking a deep breath, I push the thought away. "I don't know what you mean."

He shoots me a look of complete disgust. "Oh, yes, you do. Where have you been the past eight years? You think you can just turn up like this and pick up where you left off?"

"I told you what happened. I know how crazy it sounds, but it's the truth."

He takes a couple of steps toward me, closing the distance between us, and it occurs to me that no matter what I do, a fight may be unavoidable—especially if he wants one this badly. "You don't know anything," he says, glaring. "How about the first word Finn ever said? Her favorite stuffed animal when she was a baby? Her blood type? Or the antibiotics she's allergic to, for God's sake? Do you know *that*?"

My eyes drift to Finn, who is laughing at something Isabel has said. As if she can feel me looking at her, she turns and smiles, then dives under an approaching wave. I focus on the spot she's gone under, looking at the blank expanse of ocean and thinking about everything I've missed, the time I can never get back again. "No," I say. "I don't."

Next to me, Ryan shifts on the sand. "Sucks, doesn't it?" He doesn't sound the least bit sorry, and when I turn to look at him again, I see satisfaction on his face, pure and simple. He's sizing me up, taking my emotional measure—and he damn sure hit the mark. It's pretty impressive, even if it is at my expense, and my estimation of him ratchets up a few notches.

"Look," I say, "I appreciate the way you've looked after the two of them all this time, I really do. From what Isabel's told me, you've been an incredible friend to her. And as far as Finn is concerned—well, I might not like it, but you've been a father to her and I'm more grateful than you can imagine. I get that you feel protective where they're concerned. In fact, I'd be disappointed if you weren't."

"I don't need your approval. Or your gratitude." He digs his feet into the sand.

"I wasn't implying that you did," I say, just as a family with a little boy passes within a few feet of us, the child scooping up shells and holding them out so his parents can see. As we watch, the father bends to pick up his son, lifting him above his head and blowing raspberries on his bare belly. The little boy's shrieks of glee resonate across the beach. "More, Daddy!" he cries, and the man tosses him high, then catches him and sets him down on the sand. He runs off, chasing a seagull, and, without looking down, the man takes the woman's hand. I feel a twinge of envy. They make it look so easy.

"I don't understand you," Ryan says, beside me. "I see how you watch them. But you left. You left Isabel, pregnant and without any-one to depend on except her dad—who didn't have the best track record, from what she tells me. Where were you when Iz sat and worried over which school to send Finn to, or whether she needed to see a shrink, or when she woke up crying because she thought there was a three-headed monster in her closet? Gone, that's where. In my book, that makes you a first-class asshole."

Yet again his arrow finds its target, and I wince in response. "What's your problem, Ryan? Do you have daddy issues, is that it?"

I don't know where this comes from—maybe it just seems like the most likely source of his hostility where I'm concerned—but the moment the words leave my mouth, I know I'm right. I glance at Ryan's face just in time to see shock transform his features. Then his expression goes blank, and he folds his arms across his chest.

"Fuck you," he says, his voice measured.

"I'm sorry," I say at once. And I am. Unlike Ryan, I have no axe to grind here. Alienating him will only make Isabel angry with me, especially if it's over something personal like this.

"Fuck your sorry. My issues are none of your goddamn business, and I'll thank you to stay out of them." He shoves his hair out of his eyes and glares at me.

I inhale, tasting the salt air on my tongue. The wind picks up again, whistling through the dunes and carrying the sound of Finn's laughter to both of us. "I didn't want to leave," I say. "It was an acci-dent. And then, once I understood—I was trapped."

Ryan makes a noise deep in his throat. It hovers somewhere be-tween exasperation and contempt. "Oh, sure. You followed a dead guy into the woods and wound up in the land of your ancestors." He grits his teeth, and I can see the effort it takes for him not to lay hands on me. His fists are clenching and unclenching at his sides, and he's gone an alarming shade of white beneath his tan.

Seeing this, I go still, like an animal that's sighted a hunter in the woods. I know without a doubt that the slightest provocation will make him swing at me. And I know too, that if he does, I will fight back with everything I have. Already I can feel it rising in me—the frustration of the past few weeks, and then the rage, to finally make it home and discover that nothing is as I thought it would be. Add to this my jealousy—however misplaced—plus my guilt about leaving Isabel and Finn, and you have a truly unsettling brew. I would love nothing more than to punch him. Quite frankly, it would be a relief.

Ryan must see this on my face, because his mouth rises in a half smile. "You want to hit me? Go ahead, do it. Swing first, and Isabel won't even be able to blame me."

I envision my fist connecting with his jaw, his head rocking back with the impact. It's a gratifying image, and for a split second I indulge myself, imagining the scene in all its particulars. And then, with regret, I shake my head. "Sorry," I say again. "I'm not going to hit you, no matter how much I may want to."

Ryan is quiet. A bad moment passes, in which I think that he's going to jump me anyway. Then he takes a deep, deliberate breath, and I feel the tension go out of him. He stretches out his arms, fingers linked, and cracks his knuckles. "Well, damn. Why the hell not?"

"Because of them," I say, and gesture out past the breakers. As if our conversation has summoned her, Isabel turns toward shore. Finn follows, and the two of them begin splashing their way in our direction. Not a moment too soon, either—on the other side of the dunes, the sun has begun to set, slipping below the line of the horizon in a burst of color. The water shimmers in the fading light, and the last of the surfers begin to paddle in from beyond the break.

I watch Finn lift her hand to point at a pelican that's swooped down, beak-first, in greedy pursuit of a fish. Just like that, time folds, and I remember another such bird, another beach, another time. I think of running through the woods only to find myself alone in a cane field, sunlight glinting from a raised machete's blade, of galloping down the road through the sifting clouds of cane ash, the baying of the dogs and the thunder of the horses' hooves loud in my ears. The salty air is suddenly alive with the acrid smell of burning cane and the iron reek of blood, thick with the sound of screams. I see the ground littered with rum and sugar, hear the roar of the guns. In the warm air of a Charleston summer, I can't help but shiver.

Ryan gives a snort of derision, for which I am paradoxically grateful. It grounds me in the here and now, banishes the unwelcome image of an island on fire. "Fair enough. You're either a time traveler or a liar, Max Adair. I'll give you one guess what I think. But Isabel believes you, for some godforsaken reason, and I guess that's all that matters."

I am getting very tired of explaining myself to him, especially because I don't seem to be getting anywhere. "She believes me because it's the truth. Ask Julia if you want. She'll tell you."

He waves a hand, dismissing this. "Whatever. My point is this: Hurt either one of them, and I'll make you wish you'd never come home." His tone is mild, but its sincerity rings clear enough.

I can't think of a suitable reply to this—or, at least, one that won't make things worse—and so I don't bother. Instead I watch as Isabel and Finn splash toward us, holding hands. Isabel's lips move—she's counting—and together they leap over one of the small waves breaking on the shore. The setting sun picks out identical sparks of red and gold from the crowns of their heads, silhouettes them against the darkening blue of the water.

My eyes fix on Finn, whose pigtails have come undone and whose bathing suit is slipping off one shoulder. And then they find Isabel, who has stopped, knee-deep in the breakers, to fix the strap of Finn's suit. Her hair spills down her back, baring her face. I can see the rise of her breasts, the swell of her hips. With sudden, stark vividness, I imagine walking into the ocean to meet her, untying the string of her bikini top so that it falls, forgotten, into the waves. I imagine the silken feel of her breasts, water-cool and heavy in my hands, and the taste of her mouth under mine.

Isabel turns her head, and for a second she looks discomfited to see me staring. Then she gives a self-conscious smile, breaking my heart all over again, and strolls toward us through the diminishing waves. Finn bounds in front of her, long-legged and gawky as a colt, pigtails bouncing.

I'm so absorbed in watching them, I've forgotten all about Ryan until he makes a small sound. It may be no more than his weight shifting in the sand, but after all that's gone before, my senses are on high alert. I have no desire to get sucker-punched, and so, reluctantly, I turn to glance at him.

I needn't have bothered. All of his attention is focused on Isabel, and on his face there is an unguarded look that explains much, made no less unnerving for its complete familiarity. In the light of the dying sun, the expression on his face mirrors nothing so much as my own feelings. What I'd mistaken for a friend's suspicion and protectiveness is, in fact, a lover's jealousy—earned or otherwise. I wonder if he's slept with Isabel, if there's more to their relationship than she's let on, and feel like punching Ryan all over again. But then I study him more closely, and think I understand.

"You love her," I say with simple finality.

I don't expect Ryan to respond. But as Isabel and Finn come up beside us he speaks, so quietly I can barely hear him over the crash of the surf. "Yeah," he says. "I do."

Isabel

The day after our beach trip, I deliver Finn to my parents' house at noon. My mother promised to show her how to weave bracelets, and Finn is all excited at the thought of making Real Jewelry. When I hear this, I have to laugh. My mom had tried to instruct me in the fine art of bracelet-making when I was Finn's age, but my inability to follow her instructions was on a par with my disinterest in the entire project, and so she'd abandoned the idea. Finn, on the other hand, is thrilled, and the moment I drop her off, she makes a beeline for the craft station that my mom's set up on the dining room table.

I stand still, watching the two of them—the blond head and the dark, bent over a tray of beads, excitedly debating the merits of this one or that—fighting the feeling of unreality that has consumed me ever since I stumbled into the clearing to find Max and my mother standing there. It comes on me in waves, like the grief I felt when I lost them. The whole thing seems impossible, like living someone else's life.

A small movement in the doorway startles me, and I glance up to see my dad standing there, a huge grin splitting his face as he regards my mom and Finn. He catches me staring and smiles even wider.

"Look at them," he says, gesturing happily. "Who would've ever thought?"

"Well, me," I say, but my heart isn't into giving him a hard time, and he knows it.

"It's a miracle, as far as I'm concerned," he says, his voice a reverent whisper. "A gift. A second chance."

"Yeah, either that or a really detailed hallucination," I mutter. He gives me a sharp look. "What, Dad? You were all set to have me see a shrink when I told you Max had called. You think this is saner than *that*? Maybe I've just lost my mind completely and you've locked me in some padded room."

"You don't really believe that." The smile has faded, and now he's examining my face with familiar skepticism.

I wilt under his scrutiny, shoulders sagging. "No. Yes. I don't know. The whole thing is so crazy, I guess I'm having a hard time accepting it."

His hand descends on my shoulder, squeezing. "You never accept anything, Isabel. You never have. You're a fighter. It's what's kept you going all of these years. If you didn't question something like this, you wouldn't be you. Just—make sure you're fighting the right things, huh?"

His advice echoes in my ears as I drive to the gym to work out, and then, on an impulse, over to Ryan's. Something passed between him and Max at the beach, I'm sure of it. Ry was quiet for the rest of the afternoon, his jaw set tight and his calm impenetrable, as if a thin sheet of glass had fallen, separating him from the rest of the world. With each passing moment, I feel him drifting away, and it fills me with an unfamiliar panic, squeezing my heart and sending my stomach into free-fall. Other than my dad and Finn, he's been the one constant in my life for the past seven and a half years. When things aren't right between us, my whole world feels askew.

And so I stop by the Sugar Bakeshop to pick up some cupcakes—double chocolate for me and the lime-curd coconut for Ry, his favorite—and head in the direction of his house. It's only after I knock repeatedly and he doesn't answer—despite the fact that his car is parked out front—that I wonder if maybe he's got a girl in there. Well, too late now. I knock again, to no avail, and am digging my phone out of my purse to call him when the door swings wide. Ryan's standing there, a tube of glue in one of his hands and a screwdriver in the other, looking thoroughly unromantically inclined. "Hey," he says, eyes widening in surprise. "What're you doing here?"

"I don't know," I say, feeling suddenly self-conscious. "I just—I missed you, I guess, and I—well, I brought cupcakes, see? Here." I thrust the box at him, and, looking amused, he accepts it, balancing the screwdriver on top.

"A peace offering?" he says, motioning for me to come in and nudging the door shut with his foot.

"I don't know," I say warily. "Do I need one?"

"Well," he drawls, setting the cupcakes on the coffee table, "I guess it depends."

"I brought your favorite," I say, feeling unaccountably nervous. "The lime coconut one. They'll only have it for another month, they said."

"Ah. So I owe you, is that what you're saying?" He's grinning now, looking up at me from under those long lashes of his, and I elbow him in the ribs.

"You always owe me, Ry." I mean it as a joke, but he sighs.

"Ain't that the truth. So. Why are you here, other than as a dessert delivery service? Not that I don't appreciate the thought," he adds, opening the box and devouring half of his cupcake in one bite.

"That is disgusting, Ryan," I say primly. "Don't you chew?"

He swallows the giant mouthful and rolls his eyes. "I was hungry."

"I can see that. What were you doing, anyhow?" I nod at the screwdriver and the tube of glue. "Fixing something?"

Ryan looks abashed. "Oh, that. Just putting the finishing touches on Finn's house. Although now—I don't know, giving it to her seems a little anticlimactic, if you know what I mean. Here, have a father!

And a grandmother! And . . . a dollhouse. Maybe I should just wait for her birthday." He sets the other half of the cupcake back in the box and wipes his mouth with his hand. "Speaking of which—how are you holding up?"

The sudden change of subject catches me off guard, and it takes me a moment to figure out how I want to reply. "I don't know, Ry. It's like I'm in a fog, trying to see clearly. It's so strange to have them both back—I feel like I have to learn how to have a mom again."

"And how to have a boyfriend too, I imagine," he says, aligning the screwdriver and the glue next to the cupcake box with precision, so that all three are perfectly parallel. He doesn't look at me.

"Max isn't my boyfriend," I retort. "He's—oh hell, I don't know what he is to me, Ryan. I can't seem to figure out how to act around him. It's like I waited so long to have him back again, now that he's here, I don't know what to do. Part of me thinks I should just be able to slip back into the way things were, but I can't do that. I don't know why."

"Of course you can't, Isabel." His voice is dry. "He's been gone for eight years. He abandoned you and your daughter. You'd have to be totally without self-esteem to jump right back into a relationship with him."

"It's not like that," I say, offended on behalf of both of us.

"Sure it is. He left you. He *lied* to you." Ryan's voice is rising, all of his jocularity gone. "How can you not see that?"

Despite my conversation with my father and all of my doubts, I find myself playing devil's advocate once again in the face of Ryan's wrath. "Come on, Ry, you met him. Does he seem like a sociopath to you?"

"No, Isabel. He seems charming, actually. A nice guy. But so what? You think that means anything? That's how sociopaths are, now that you mention it. They come off all nice and then they suck you in. The next thing you know, they're off chasing their narcissistic little dreams, leaving you to raise your kid on your own and showing up when the spirit moves them with some messed-up lie about where the hell they went."

"I told you, he didn't mean to leave. It was an accident."

"That is such bullshit, Isabel." His hands clench into fists. "The guy is gone for years. Years! And then he shows back up with this cock-and-bull story and you just swallow it whole? Are you that gullible?"

Anger flashes through me, sharp and sudden. I have to make myself take deep breaths, make myself think about what I'd say if our roles were reversed. "It's not just his story," I say, striving for calm. "It's mine too—the phone call, the necklace . . . And my mom confirmed everything he said. Do you think all of that's a lie? Like the two of them conspired to make up the same crazy story?"

Ryan braces one hand on the cracked white paint of his mantel. "I hadn't wanted to mention this to you before," he says. "But what if there was something going on between the two of them? And your mom left, out of guilt, or—who knows what. But then Max went to find her—and now, for whatever reason, they've come back. God knows what their agenda might be."

I am rendered speechless as his accusation sinks in. Then my hand rises, lightning-quick and of its own volition, to strike him across the face. He sees it coming, though, and catches my wrist. "Don't," he says, his tone icy.

Fuming, I wrench my hand free. "*You* don't, Ryan. How dare you accuse my mother of—what? Cheating on my father? Seducing a teenage boy? And then Max . . . what was he doing, then? Sleeping with me, because he couldn't have my mom? Are you nuts?"

"I could ask you the same question. You really think that's more unlikely than the idea that the two of them walked into the woods and went back in time? You're a scientist, Isabel. Come on."

His voice is heavy with scorn, and for just a moment, I hate him. Because he's right—his version of events, however twisted, is far more credible than Max and my mother's. All I have to go on, really, is my faith in both of them—that, and the bizarre events of the past few weeks. But if I let that go, I can see Ryan's side of things all too clearly. Doubt fills me, and reflexively, I lash out. "I know you have some major trust issues, Ryan, but this is low. You're just jealous."

He's started pacing, prowling the room like a caged animal. This brings him up short, though, and he stares at me. "You think I'm that petty? Like if I can't have you, no one can? *That's* what you think of me?"

"Not *no one*," I say, heedless of grammar, and feel a nasty smile spread across my face. "Just not him. And anyhow, I wasn't talking about me and Max."

Ryan's eyes narrow dangerously. "Who, then? Go ahead, psycho-analyze me, Isabel. I can't wait to hear what fascinating theories you come up with."

"Well," I say, "it's pretty clear, isn't it? You lost your parents, both of them. But I got my mother back, and Max too. You're jealous, because you want what I have."

Even as the words leave my mouth, I want to take them back, but it's too late. Ryan's face pales, and he swallows convulsively. Then he takes a step closer to me, eyes blazing in his white face. "How can you say that to me?" he hisses. "It's a lie." He steps closer still, lifting his shirt so I can see. "This scar," he says, pointing at the faded white crescent just below his ribs. "I told you it was from a knife fight I had when I was a kid. Well, it was from a knife, all right. But there wasn't much of a fight about it. An eight-year-old doesn't stand a chance against a grown man, not when he's holding him down."

My mouth opens in shock, then shuts again. I want to apologize, but there is nothing I can say. Instead I watch as Ryan's mouth quirks upward in that half smile of his, the one that's really not a smile at all. "You want to know why social services took me, Isabel? My father tried to carve me up like a Thanksgiving turkey. He was on something—meth, most likely. It made him mean as a snake, that stuff."

As long as I've known him, Ryan has never said a word about why he was placed in foster care. I never asked—I figured if and when he wanted to tell me, he would. But I never imagined he was hiding anything like this. Nor have I ever heard him sound so venomous. *I did this*, I think miserably. *This is my fault.*

"Ry," I say, taking a step in his direction, not knowing what I mean to do, just wanting to offer comfort. It doesn't matter—he won't let me anywhere near him. Eyes locked on mine, he backs up, putting the coffee table between us. The brightly colored box still sits there, looking forlorn and abandoned, my uneaten cupcake inside.

"He wanted me to do something for him—make him food, get him a pack of cigarettes, I can't remember. Whatever it was, I didn't do it fast enough. So he grabbed me by the hair and he took a kitchen knife and he opened me up. 'I'll show you who's boss,' he said. And my mother, she just stood and watched, high as a motherfucking kite." His hands are in fists again, and his voice is low, shaking. "As soon as he let go of me, I ran. Faster than I ever had in my life, dizzy and dripping blood. And when I couldn't run anymore, I crawled. I made it to a neighbor's house and she called 911. I never went back to those sorry sons of bitches again. They didn't deserve to raise a roach, let alone a child."

Silence falls, and I feel something between us—trust, maybe—shatter like broken glass. "I'm sorry," I say in desperation. "I really am. Ryan, I'm so sorry. I didn't know."

"Well, now you do. And stop looking at me that way. I didn't tell you that story so you'd feel sorry for me, Isabel. I told you so you'd understand. I don't remember loving my mother, or my father, for that matter. And you can't miss what you never had." He unclenches his fists, flexes his fingers. "But I don't care what you say to me, or how you treat me, either. I am damn well going to look after that little girl. I won't let anyone hurt her, not even you."

"I would never hurt Finn," I say, incredulous. "How can you even think that? And neither would Max. He loves her."

"Max hasn't earned being Finn's father, for any reason other than biology," he says, each word measured. "I don't know him. And neither do you, not anymore."

I want to argue with him, but on some deep level, he's right, and we both know it. Regardless of why Max vanished eight years ago, the simple fact is that he hasn't been around for any of the milestones in Finn's life—large or small—whereas Ryan has been there for all of them. One thing I can dispute, though, and I do. "Max wouldn't hurt Finn," I say stubbornly. "He would never lay a finger on her."

Ryan gives me a long look. He doesn't say a word, but then again, he doesn't have to. I know what he's thinking—that today, in this room, I have eviscerated him, and I didn't land a single punch. "I'm sorry," I say again, scrutinizing his face for forgiveness.

His mouth twists. "I believe it. And so am I. Now get out of my house, please."

"You must be joking."

"I'm completely serious. Leave, before we both say something we're going to regret. Something there's no coming back from." He thrusts the box of cupcakes at me and flings the front door wide. "Go home to your daughter, before we wreck seven years of friendship in a single afternoon. Unless that's what you want. In which case—stay here, by all means, and we can keep tearing each other down."

Put that way, how can I refuse? "I'll go," I say, with what dignity I can muster, and pick up my purse from the armchair.

"Good," is all he says in reply, and stands aside, arms folded across his chest, so I can pass. The air between us is so thick I feel like I'm choking, but neither of us speaks. He's right—there's nothing left to say.

It takes all of the willpower I have, but I don't look at him again until I've slid behind the wheel and pulled out of my parking spot onto Grove, my failed peace offering on the passenger seat beside me. He is still standing in the doorway, shoulder propped against the frame, a haunted expression on his face, watching me drive away.

Isabel

I'm deeply shaken by my conversation with Ryan on a number of levels, especially by the revelations about his family. My heart breaks for him, although he's made it clear enough that he has no interest in my sympathy. We've never argued, not like this, and I want desperately to fix things between us. There's only one thing I can think of to do, and that's to step up and stop being a coward where Max is concerned. Hard as it is, I need to quit running and confront whatever's bothering me head-on.

So I invite Max over for dinner, and after Finn has gone to bed and he's standing in the dining room, tossing his car keys from one hand to the other, I summon all of my courage and ask him to stay.

He straightens up, regarding me warily. "All right," he says at last, setting his keys down. "If that's what you want."

I nod, and for a moment we just stare at each other. An awkward silence descends. Then Max says, "The thing is . . ." just as I begin, "I guess we should . . ."

We both trail off into silence. Then he says, "You first."

"No, go ahead," I say. The truth is, I'm not sure what would've come out of my mouth if I'd kept talking. For what feels like the hundredth time, I wonder if I'm dreaming. Or maybe I never made it home from the library the day I found Lily's letter. Maybe I crashed my car and am in a coma. Maybe the stress of the past few months has done me in, and I've had an honest-to-God psychotic break. Maybe at this very moment, I'm sitting in a psych ward, dosed to the gills with Thorazine or whatever they're giving folks these days. Any of these scenarios seem more likely than time travel.

"Isabel," Max says, and from the patient tone of his voice, I guess that it isn't the first time. "Earth to Isabel. Where did you go?"

I shake my head, then rub my eyes, but he is still there—all six feet one inch of him, wavy brown hair streaked with blond the way it always is when he spends a lot of time in the sun, blond stubble glinting on his cheekbones and his jaw. I used to tease him about that, how, with his brown hair and blond beard, it looked like he'd been put together by committee. With a pang, I remember him telling me I'd pay for a comment like that, remember him rasping a day's worth of stubble against my cheeks and then down my neck to my breasts, the warmth of his mouth closing over me and the noise he'd made when I'd set my nails into his back, half pleasure, half protest. I didn't know it then, but I was already pregnant with Finn. It was one of the last times.

I don't know what expression is on my face, but it must be a fair reflection of my thoughts, because Max says my name again, this time in an entirely different tone. He reaches for me and I move back, out of his grasp. It's instinctive, the way I block kicks in the ring or duck a knife-hand strike to the head. I don't mean to do it, don't even know I have until Max's hands drop to his sides and I realize I'm standing in the living room now, the threshold between us. A hurt look flashes across his face.

"I'm sorry," I say, wrapping my hands around my upper arms.

"What are you apologizing for?" His voice is hoarse, and he clears his throat viciously. His eyes flicker toward the floor, away from mine, as if he's afraid of what I'll read in them.

"You just startled me," I say. "It wasn't personal."

He glances up at this, and I get a good look at his face. The hurt expression is gone. He laughs, a bitter sound I can't remember ever hearing from him. "Not personal, huh? Jesus, Izzy. I don't think it gets much more personal than this." His eyes are fixed on mine now, the steely gray of a winter sky. "Have I lost you, Isabel? All the rest of this . . . it's just words. I'll tell you whatever you want to know. But you tell me first—are you coming back to me, or did I lose you the moment I saw your mother walk into the woods? Because if that's the case—well, shit. I might as well go home now and spare myself the humiliation."

I suck in a sharp, startled breath. "Am I coming back to *you*? You left me, Max. I've had to raise our daughter alone. I thought you were dead," I spit, and before I know that I mean to do it, I draw back and strike him across the face. Unlike Ryan, he doesn't stop me—either because he doesn't see it coming in time, or because he thinks he deserves it. I can't tell which. "That's for letting me believe you died," I say, in case he is wondering. "And for not trusting me with the truth to begin with, you son of a bitch."

Max rubs his cheekbone, amusement drawing one side of his mouth up in a wry smile. "You do realize that this isn't entirely my fault. But by all means, keep beating me up. At least I know you care."

"Oh no you don't, Max Adair," I say, more infuriated than ever.

He raises an eyebrow in inquiry. "No I don't what?"

"Don't you dare make me laugh. I'm mad at you. Actually, mad doesn't even cover it. I'm furious. And God, I was so terrified. And I thought I was going crazy. And I . . ." My voice trails off, and I rub a hand hard across my mouth, trying to keep the words inside.

"You what, Isabel?" His voice is gentle, coaxing.

I shake my head. "Damn it, Max. How could you?"

"I'm sorry, baby," he says, palms outward as if to show me he's defenseless.

"Don't you call me baby. And don't you come one inch closer. I mean it."

The moment the words leave my lips, I realize I have made a mistake. He tilts his head, regarding me curiously, and slides a bare centimeter forward. "Oh yeah?" he says, drawing out each syllable. "What will you do?"

"I have no idea," I admit. "But I am a resourceful person, and I will come up with something good."

Max laughs. "I'd like to see that." He steps closer to me, just enough to make his intentions clear.

I frown. "Back up, Max," I warn.

A smile spreads across his face—half amusement, half challenge. "Make me," he says, and closes the distance between us. His fingertips are light on my face, tracing a careful line along my jaw. I shut my eyes, suddenly dizzy, and try to shift away from him, but he won't let me go.

"Isabel," he says, and his hand slides around to the back of my neck, gripping it, holding me still. His voice is breathless, as if he's been running. Through the warmth of his skin, I can feel his pulse pounding—or maybe it is mine. "Look at me. Please."

When I do, his grip intensifies, fingers knotting in the curls at my nape. "What's wrong?" he whispers.

Infinitesimally, I shake my head, and he exhales, making a small, pain-filled sound. I feel his breath against my face, a moment before his other hand comes up to cup my cheek. "Tell me you don't want to be with me," he says. "Tell me you don't want me anymore, and I'll leave you alone."

"I can't tell you that."

He makes a small, frustrated sound. "Then why won't you let me touch you?"

"Why do you think?" I snap at him. "You can't just . . . vanish . . . for eight years and then show up here and expect things to go back to the way they used to be."

At this, Max's eyes narrow. "So that's all it is, huh? Don't bullshit me, Izzy. You're wasting your time."

"What do you mean?"

His voice comes low, emotion roughening each syllable. "You've got everyone snowed, haven't you? Tough girl, black belt. Lead archaeologist. Charleston's excuse for Lara Croft. I can see right through you, Isabel. What are you so scared of?"

"I'm not scared," I say. It comes out quieter than I'd intended, less certain, and I lift my chin in defiance.

"Yes, you are," he says, and then he bends his head and kisses me. His mouth is rough on mine, and when I stand there, frozen, he bites my lip in demand. It hurts, but the pain is all mixed up with wanting him, the feel of his hands on me. My body remembers Max, the seamless way he'd always tangled violence and sex, all threat and promise. I think of that first time in the woods, the silvery taste of his blood in my mouth, and shudder against him. And then my hands rise, as if of their own accord, to twine around his neck. I pull him down to me and kiss him back.

He makes a noise then, deep in his throat, and his hands tighten around me.

"What are you scared of, Isabel?" he murmurs against my lips.

I shake my head in fierce negation, and he runs one hand into my hair to hold me still. "Don't you run from me, goddamn it," he says, cupping my face with the other hand. "Not me."

I open my mouth to tell him I'm not going anywhere, but then he kisses me again, and speech becomes impossible. I close my eyes and there is only Max—the familiar Christmas-tree smell of him, the unmistakable touch of his fingers as he slides his hand underneath my shirt. With my eyes shut like this, we could be anywhere, any-when. The intervening eight years slip away, and we move together as if we have never been apart. Under my hands I can feel Max shaking, a fine tremor that he makes no effort to hide.

"I thought I'd never see you again," he murmurs, his lips light on my neck. Gone is his angry tone, replaced with an unguarded tenderness that sends a bolt of guilt straight through me. "I missed you so much."

I don't say anything, and he lifts his head to look at me. "Did you miss me, Isabel?" His voice is teasing, but I know him well enough to hear the genuine question underneath. I know what he is asking: *Do you still?*

I open my mouth to reply, but no sound comes out. Max searches my face, and his eyes darken. He's backed us against the wall, has one hand in my hair and the other braced on the wall above my head. I'm pretty sure I could get away from him, but it would be a fight. "Tell me," he says, and his lips brush mine.

"Tell you what?" I say. I mean it to sound flirtatious, but it comes out antagonistic instead, and Max's body stills.

"Oh, I don't know. Why you're acting like a fox run to ground, for one thing. What you're so frightened of. Why you're with me and not, all at the same time." He pulls back so he can look down at me. "How many times have I kissed you, Isabel? Hundreds? It may have been eight years for you, but for me it's been less than a month. Do you think I can't tell when something's wrong?"

"Nothing's wrong," I say. My mouth has gone dry.

Max steps away from me and sinks down on the couch. "Why are you lying to me?" he says. "Is it because of him? Ryan?"

"Ryan and I are friends," I say, smoothing my clothes and waiting for my heart to resume its normal rhythm. I feel stupid standing up while he's sitting, but I don't trust myself on the couch next to him. Instead I sit down on the blue armchair and brace my hands on my knees, relearning how to breathe.

Max runs a hand over his face and gives me a look of profound skepticism. "Uh-huh."

"We are," I protest. "I met him just before graduate school. After you—well."

"He wants you," Max says, calmly enough. "You must know that."

I can feel a blush creeping up my cheeks. "How do you know? Did he say something?"

"He didn't have to. It's clear enough from the way he looks at you." Max sighs. "Have you slept with him, Isabel? I'm not trying to be a dick, but I need to know."

"I told you, we're friends," I say, and the blush burns hotter. I think of Ryan's confession at his house, and later, the conversation we'd had in this very room. *Let it go. I'm asking you. Please*, he'd said. And so I had. Whenever I thought about what had happened between us in his studio, my primary emotion had been relief, like I'd dodged a bullet. So then why do I feel guilty, like I'm lying to Max—or letting Ryan down? I huddle in the blue chair, trying to make sense of things. Then I get sick of huddling and give Max the full benefit of my irritation. "Why do you want to know so badly? What does it matter now? Here you are."

As soon as the words leave my mouth, I realize that this is a really shitty—not to mention inadequate—response. Clearly Max thinks so too, because he jumps to his feet and looms over me, glaring. "Answer my question."

I stand up too, fury arcing through me. "Don't talk to me like that. Don't you tell me what to do. And kindly remove yourself from my personal space."

He closes his eyes, steps back, takes one deep breath, then another. Without opening his eyes he says, "I apologize. Isabel, please. Just tell me the truth. Have you been with him, or not?"

"Not," I say, ignoring the little voice that says I'm selling Ryan short, and lying to Max—a lie of omission, but still. "All right? Is the inquisition over?"

Max's eyes flicker open. "You swear."

"What are we, five?"

"Isabel," he says, and runs a hand over his face again. "You have to understand—a few weeks ago, you were my girlfriend. I was going to ask you to marry me, even before you told me about the baby. I had a ring and everything."

"You what?"

He waves my question away, as if it doesn't signify. "I'm not trying to pressure you or make you feel guilty. What I'm trying to say is— I know it's been eight years for you, almost. Of course things have changed. But—Isabel, can you see my side at all?"

"You were going to ask me to marry you?" I say, having fixated on this.

He sighs again. "Why is that so hard for you to believe? I loved you, Isabel, for Christ's sake. I loved you every damn day I was trapped on that motherfucking island and I still do. Even if you—" His lips compress into a thin line.

"Even if I what?" I say, when it's clear he's not going to go on.

"Never mind."

"Max."

"Forget it," he says, pulling on his Vans. He doesn't say another word, but the way he ties his laces—with deft, angry movements of his fingers—is eloquent enough.

I follow him to the door. "Max, don't do this. Don't leave."

"I can't stay here," he says. "Not like this. You know what I want. I don't know how many ways I can say it."

I swallow hard. Max is right, I do know what he wants. He wants me to say that I love him, that I've never stopped loving him. That I missed him all the time he was gone, the same way he missed me. And it's true. Didn't I push Ryan away because he wasn't Max? Haven't I spent the past few months—hell, the past seven and a half years—searching for evidence that Max was still alive? Now he's in front of me, and I can't even tell him I love him. I try, but the words stick in my throat. Tears well in my eyes.

Seeing this, Max reaches out and strokes my hair. "All the time I was in Barbados, I only thought about coming home to you. How things are—it's not your fault. I know that. But it rips me up, all the same." He turns, one hand on the doorknob, and gives me a sad smile. "I love you, Isabel," he says. "But I can't be around you this way. Give me some time, and then maybe—hell, I don't know. Just give me time."

And he walks out the door.

Max

Isabel's aloofness is breaking my heart. Aside from stopping the rebellion and saving Lily, coming home to her has been my mission, what drove me forward and kept me going when there was nothing else. I've never allowed myself to think about the peace that might come afterward—and whether, in it, she might turn away from me.

Yet here we are.

Coming home to the silent beach house, I find myself prowling from room to room, pacing their perimeters as if I am measuring the distance of a cell, plotting my escape. And after my fourth circuit through the house, it occurs to me that is exactly what I'm doing.

I need to go back to Barbados, to see it the way it really is today. To anchor myself somehow, because I can't move forward until I see where I've been. All my life, the Adair family legacy has been an albatross around my neck, a deadweight of blood and obligation weighing me down. But now, having embraced it and done my best to expiate it, I need to see what I've left behind.

I want to see what is left of Sweetwater, to pay tribute to the spot at Lowthers where Jackey sacrificed himself to save me. To drive from Robert's plantation to the Brightmores', to mourn Lily as I traverse the path we took that night, drenched in ash and fire. To close my eyes and remember. To honor the slaves who died for freedom. Perhaps if things between me and Isabel were different, I wouldn't want to leave right away. But I'd still need to go. The past few weeks have changed me in ways I am only beginning to notice, much less understand.

When I mention the idea to my parents, they are vehemently against it. My mother in particular can't stand the idea of letting me get on a plane without her after losing me for so long. Gritting my teeth, I propose a family vacation. At this, she lights up and starts researching villas with ocean views. I tell her that that level of luxury is hardly necessary, that such a trip is likely to cost a fortune—but she keeps saying that money is no object, and so I go along with it to make her happy.

There's just one problem—I'm heartsick at the thought of leaving Finn.

I know she has a valid passport, but I don't fool myself into thinking it will be easy to convince Isabel to trust me with our daughter, whether my parents are there or not. Still, one thing is for sure—I plan to ask, to plead if I need to. Because as strong as the pull toward Barbados might be, the pull toward my daughter is stronger. I've lost enough time with her. I don't want to lose any more.

Isabel

inn's next appointment with Dr. Rossetti is on Friday—her first since Max and my mother have come back—and I'm more than a little nervous about what their conversation will reveal. I called Dr. Rossetti to fill her in on the basics of what's happened, but I didn't go into specifics. Certainly, I wasn't going to let her know that I'd followed my daughter into the woods and found my mother and Max standing there—much less that they'd claimed to have been trapped in the nineteenth century.

Still, I wanted to do the right thing for my daughter. I can't ask Finn to lie—or justify yanking her out of therapy when she might need it the most. And if worst comes to worst . . . well, Dr. Rossetti has her own experience with Finn to draw upon. Hopefully she'll be more inclined to consider the extraordinary than the average PhD.

Despite this promising line of thought, I wasn't about to go into too much detail over the phone. And so I simply said the situation was complicated, but my mother and Max had both returned—that Finn seemed to be dealing with it well, but that I was sure she'd have a lot to share at their next session, to say the least. At which point Dr. Rossetti had promptly asked me to come in, so that the two of us could talk.

This is how I find myself sitting in her lavender-and-sage-scented office, sunk in the same squashy chair that had threatened to engulf me the first time I visited, exchanging pleasantries and wishing that I was somewhere, anywhere else: stuck in traffic on I-26, cleaning the toilet, discussing Ryan's childhood. Anywhere would do.

Dr. Rossetti is wearing a black suit and sky-blue shell—an outfit probably meant to inspire confidence in her professionalism. Lovely as it is, it doesn't exactly convey an openness to time travel. I don't know what would make me feel better—a purple caftan, an amulet suspended from her neck, a stack of Diana Gabaldon's *Outlander* books? I sigh, deciding that nothing would improve the situation short of a hefty dose of Xanax or several shots of bourbon, and Dr. Rossetti leans forward, evidently taking this as an indication of my willingness to begin. "So," she says. "Tell me."

I squirm, feeling horribly uncomfortable. "I can't. It's a crazy story, and not necessarily all that believable—except that I believe it, which is embarrassing, and . . . oh, hell." Eyes on the teetering stack of board games in the corner, I take a deep breath. "They're both back. My dad is over the moon."

"And you?" She sounds concerned, and no small wonder. In the interest of convincing her of my sanity, I make myself meet her eyes.

"Me? I'm fine. Well, not fine, but—shouldn't we be talking about Finn? I mean, that's why I'm here, right?"

She pushes her glasses up on her nose with one blunt-nailed finger. "Of course. But you're her mother, so how you're handling these—developments, shall we say—has a direct impact on her well-being."

"Well," I say, somewhat defensively, "Finn seems fine too. No tantrums, no regression, nothing out of the ordinary—for her, anyway. It's as if she's known my mom and Max all along. She calls them Grandma and Daddy, has from the very first day. The transition's been a little too easy, if you want to know the truth."

I'd hoped that bringing up Finn's smooth adjustment to Max and my mom's reappearance would distract Dr. Rossetti, but no such luck. "How about Ryan?" she says, as if she's just been biding her time, waiting to bring him up. "We've talked about how he's been a father figure to her. Has she expressed any concern or confusion over what his role in her life ought to be, now that Max—her actual father—has returned?"

"No," I say, shifting my weight. "She hasn't said so directly, but it would be normal for her to have some confusion about it, I think. It's like you said . . . Ryan's been her dad all these years, or as good as. Now suddenly here's the real thing, and Ry's reduced to—what? A friend? I'm sure they both feel conflicted. I know he does."

It's more than I meant to say, and I bite my tongue, intending to stop the flow of words before I wind up in dangerous waters. But Dr. Rossetti's brown eyes are soft and encouraging behind her glasses, no hint of judgment on her face, and somehow I find myself going on, telling her about what happened with Ryan in his studio, our awful fight, and the afternoon that Max walked out.

"He asked me if I'd slept with Ryan," I say, "and I told him no. But I don't think he believed me." I take a deep breath, inhaling the lavender-scented air, but for once it does nothing to calm me. "This whole situation is so ridiculous. You didn't know me before all this, but I went for years without having any drama at all. I taught, I led my digs, I practiced martial arts, I did my best to be a good mom to Finn, a good daughter, a good friend. Men—they weren't really part of the picture."

I look up to see Dr. Rossetti steeple her fingers under her chin. "From what you've told me, at least one man was part of the picture. Ryan."

"Well, yes, but not like—I mean, we were friends, like I told you. There was never—at least on my side of things—ugh," I say, my voice trailing off. "Why does everything have to be so complicated?"

Dr. Rossetti touches the chain holding her glasses, letting it slip through her fingers like the beads of a rosary. "Do you feel that way? Like things are complicated?"

"It's all complicated! And none of it even makes sense," I say, struggling free of the chair's claustrophobic embrace and getting to my feet. "I waited all these years for Max to come back and now I don't want him? What the hell is wrong with me?"

"He left you," Dr. Rossetti points out. "Regardless of his reasons, he abandoned you and your daughter, knowing full well what had happened with your mother. You could have retreated into depression, or chosen to give your child up for adoption, given how young you were and the fact that you had very little family support. But you didn't, Isabel. I'm a single mother myself," she says, giving me the first glimpse into her personal life since that session with Finn weeks ago. "My children are grown now, but I remember how hard it was."

I rest one hand on her bookshelf, uncomfortable with the turn our conversation has taken. "I swore to myself that if it ever happened to me, I'd put her first. I wouldn't turn my back on her."

"Noble enough," Dr. Rossetti says, her voice gentle. "But at what cost?"

Caught off guard, I swivel to face her. "What do you mean?"

"You put Finn first, and that was admirable. No one can fault you for that. But where did that leave you? What did you give up?"

"Nothing!" I say, eyes searching her face. "What are you talking about? I went to grad school, I got my black belt, I have a great job . . . I didn't give up anything."

Dr. Rossetti doesn't reply, and silence falls between us. I can feel its weight pressing on me, so that my skin feels too tight and my breath comes short. My heart pounds in my ears, echoing the way it does before a sparring match, when the world narrows to contain me and my opponent, all my attention poised on a knife-edge of tension and decision. Finally I say, "I saw what losing my mother did to my dad. I never wanted to be that person. I never wanted one human being to matter to me so much that if I lost them, I'd lose myself too."

I straighten up. "After Max, I dated men, if you could call it that, but Finn never met any of them. Neither did my dad. Sometimes they wanted more, but I never did. I told myself that it was because I was still in love with Max, but—oh, Christ," I say, feeling a ripple of fear run through me, "what if it was because of Ryan?"

"Because of Ryan, how?" she asks, her voice careful.

"Well, because—because—" I'm stammering, something I hardly ever do. Remembering how it had felt to sit with him in my guest bedroom, his hand moving in mine in the dark, wet with my tears. How I'd pressed my lips against his palm, tasting citrus and ink and rainwater, and fought the desire to lie down next to him, safe in the warmth of his body, as if it was where I belonged. "What if it was because I wanted him?" I ask, my voice barely above a whisper. "Because I loved him?"

"Do you?" she says, so quietly that it sounds like the voice of my conscience.

"Of course I love him," I say, sounding as bewildered as I feel. "I mean, he's my best friend. He just happens to be a guy."

Dr. Rossetti nods. "And he stood by you," she points out. "Whereas Max left."

"Yes, but Max didn't mean to," I say, feeling defensive all over again.

"Whether or not he meant to, Isabel—and short of kidnapping, I'd say his motives are debatable—he's been gone for eight years. You're allowed to have a reaction to that."

Despite myself, I feel tears sting my eyes. "I feel awful. He's so disappointed in me—I can see it every time I look at him. He hasn't said so, but I know. And if Ryan—if we really—" I swallow hard, unable to frame the words. "It would devastate him. It would break his heart."

"Like he broke yours?"

I shake my head, blinking to clear my vision. "No. Not like that at all. Because what he did—he did for love."

Dr. Rossetti gives me a skeptical look over the rims of her black glasses. "I saw the article in the paper, Isabel. I know what his party line is—that he doesn't remember. But from the conversation we've had here today, I'm willing to bet that's not the truth."

"No," I say, fidgeting under the weight of that discerning gaze. "It's not. But it's a long story. Maybe one day I'll tell it to you—if there's a valid scientific explanation."

Both eyebrows quirk upward at this, but she doesn't press the issue. Instead she says, "Speaking of scientific explanations, have you given any thought to what I said about having Finn tested, regarding her—how shall I phrase this—unusual abilities? Duke's Rhine Research Center has a good reputation, as those things go. It would be a starting point, at least."

I'd thought nothing could be more awkward than talking about Max and Ryan, but this is a close second. "I'm not sure. I mean, she is who she is, right? What would I even do with the information?"

Dr. Rossetti's glasses have slipped down her nose again. She considers me over them for a long moment. And finally she says, "What you decide to do with the knowledge is up to you. Sometimes—it's better just to *know*."

Isabel

It's six-fifteen on Friday night, and Ryan is exactly where I thought he would be—still working. Work has always been a balm for him, a panacea when everything else has gone to shit, and tonight is no different.

I'd left Dr. Rossetti's office in a state of shock, driving to pick Finn up from camp and then dropping her at Max's parents' house, as promised. Try as I might, I can't remember a single thing we talked about on the way, nor much of what I'd said to Jennifer, either. Moving like an automaton, I'd gotten back in the car and started driving, with no clear idea of where I meant to go.

Without knowing I intended to do it, I'd come here, to Mage—arriving just in time to pass Ryan's co-worker Michelle on her way out. She'd smiled at me, and I'd done my best to make small talk . . . but whatever I'd said must have been more than a little bit off, because her smile had turned into a faltering sort of grimace and she'd hurried out the door, calling, "Have a good weekend!" in a doubtful sort of way as she went. I'm sure she knows about Max and my mom—everyone does, after that article that ran in the paper, hailing their reappearance as a miracle—so perhaps she'll just attribute my bizarre behavior to some kind of delayed reaction. And who knows, maybe it is.

The fog finally lifts when I make my way to Ryan's office, door open wide, the sound of blues music filtering into the hallway. Ryan is sitting at his desk, which is covered in comic books and bits of half-finished sketches, as usual. It is bewildering to me how someone with such deep-seated attention to detail prefers to work in an environment that is nothing short of chaotic. From where I stand I can see a dangerously teetering stack of graphic novels, their spines facing outward: George R.R. Martin's *A Game of Thrones*, Craig Thompson's *Blankets*, and *Daredevil: Man Without Fear*. He's holding his iPad, probably designing a new app. From the frown on his face, it isn't turning out the way he's envisioned.

I clear my throat, feeling like an intruder, and his head jerks up. For a second he just stares at me, lost in whatever place his mind wanders when he's working. Accustomed to this, I wait patiently for him to recognize me. Finally his eyes clear and he says, "Oh. It's you." He sounds less than thrilled, and I can't say I blame him.

I take an uncertain step into the room, not sure if I'm wanted. "Are you still mad?"

Ryan shrugs and sets the iPad down, switching the music off. His hair falls into his eyes, and he shoves it back, looking annoyed. "I don't know, Isabel," he says, his tone matter-of-fact. "Lately I don't seem to know how I feel about you at all."

My stomach plummets at this—it's skirting way too close to things we'd agreed not to discuss—and I can feel my face pale. I drop my head so Ryan won't notice, but when I glance up at him, he isn't even looking my way. Instead he picks up a file, examines its contents, and settles back in his chair. "Anyhow," he says with considerable nonchalance, "that's neither here nor there. What's Prince Charming doing tonight?"

"If you mean Max," I say with as much dignity as I can muster, "I have no idea. We had a—disagreement, I guess you'd call it, and he hasn't spoken to me for two days."

Ryan raises his eyebrows. "Really? Trouble in paradise?"

I've been doing my best to be conciliatory, really I have. My intention in coming to Ryan's office was to make things better between us, not to fight over the same old stuff, but his attitude is truly pissing me off. Hands on my hips, I give him the evil look I usually reserve for Finn when she's done something egregious. "Jesus. Would you stop being such an ass?"

Ryan must recognize the look, because his lips quirk into a self-deprecating grin. "I'm sorry," he says. "I'm not doing it on purpose."

"Maybe you have a natural talent for it, then," I say, my voice mild.

He winces, then takes a deep breath. "I'll stop. I promise. Tell you what, let's start over." He comes out from behind his desk—negotiating several precarious piles of books in the process—and takes a stack of paper off the couch, making room for me. "Have a seat, and tell me all your troubles."

"You don't really want to hear them," I say, sinking onto the worn couch.

"Sure I do," Ryan says, and forages in his file cabinet. "Look, I even have chocolate. And red wine. Only one glass, though, sorry."

I have to laugh as he hands me a small, unopened box of what, if its label is to be believed, contains truffles from one of Charleston's most exclusive bakeries. "Why do you have chocolate and wine in your cabinet? Are there even any files in there? No wonder your office is such a disaster."

"They're left over from that book opening we had a few months ago," Ryan says, affronted. "I'd watch out if I were you, Griffin. I'm far less likely to share my truffles and"—he tilts the bottle slightly to check the label—"Shiraz with women who insult me."

"I'll keep that in mind," I say, doing my best to sound repentant. "And I am terribly sorry for impugning your good name and sense of order, fragile as the latter may sometimes seem. Wine, please?"

Corkscrew in hand, Ryan hesitates. I eye him, puzzled. "Now what's the matter?"

He clears his throat, looking embarrassed. "Who else is still here, do you think? Did you see anyone, coming in?"

"Well, Michelle let me in, but she was on her way home. It's after six on a Friday night. Why, do you think you're going to set a bad example?"

He shrugs. "No."

"You do," I say. "You are such a Boy Scout, Ry."

"I am not," he protests, but he's smiling at me now—his real smile, not the self-conscious grin he uses to hide what he's really feeling. I've missed that smile, I realize. I want to see it again.

"Sure you are," I tease. "Next thing I know, you'll be trying to get me to buy some caramel corn."

Ryan shakes an admonitory finger at me. "I know what you're doing, Isabel. And I was never a scout of any kind. Delinquent, yes. Scout, no."

"Well, maybe you're trying to make up for it now," I say, and bat my eyelashes at him again, all innocence.

For a second Ryan just stares at me, corkscrew in hand. Then he mutters, "Oh, the hell with it," and sets the bottle of wine down on his desk. I watch as he struggles with the recalcitrant cork, which threatens to splinter.

"Need some help?" I offer, and he shoots me an evil look.

"No, no, I got it," he says, twisting the top of the corkscrew tight again.

"You sure? What kind of delinquent can't even open a wine bottle?"

"What, you think I drank Shiraz as a kid? The shit I drank came with a twist-off cap. And hush, anyhow. I'm trying to concentrate." He turns the corkscrew one more time, pushes the arms down, and this time the cork pops free. Inspecting the glass for cleanliness, he rubs the inside with his shirt—earning a disgusted sound from me—fills it halfway, and hands it over. Then, giving me a wicked grin, he tilts the bottle back and gulps. "*Salut*," he says. "So. What's the problem?"

"I don't know," I admit. "But I'm pretty sure it's me. I just . . . I can't tell him how I feel. Or maybe I'm not sure how I feel. Or— Hell, I can't explain it, Ry. It's only, I thought having Max back was everything I ever wanted. But now that he's here . . . things are different than I thought they'd be."

Ryan reclaims the glass and fills it again. "Different how?"

I bite into one of the truffles to give myself time to think. "It's crazy. I mean, for him it's only been a couple of weeks. But for me, it's been eight years. I've grown up, and he hasn't. Or maybe he has," I amend, thinking of everything Max went through after he followed Robert Adair into the woods, "but he doesn't know me anymore. It's like he only sees the person I used to be."

"I don't think that's true," Ryan says after a moment of contemplation. "Much as it pains me to say it, I think he sees you for who you are."

"Well, maybe then I'm not a good person anymore," I say tiredly, and hold out my hand for the glass.

"Is that what you really think?" His tone is gentle.

"I don't know. Maybe." I take a big gulp of wine, trying to summon some bravado.

"Well, then you're crazy," Ryan says, with such finality, it makes me giggle. I glance over at him, and just as quickly look away. The tenderness on his face threatens to undo me completely. I know I don't deserve it.

"I've missed that sound," he says, and takes the glass from my hand. His fingers brush mine, square-nailed and warm, as familiar to me as my own.

"I've missed *you*," I blurt, before I can think too much about what I'm saying. "I've been a shitty friend to you, Ry. I'm really sorry."

"Apology accepted," Ryan says without hesitation. He refills our glass and drinks the contents down in one long swallow, then pours out the last of the bottle and hands the glass back to me.

Our eyes meet, and in that moment I feel like I see Ryan, really see him, for the first time in a long while. He's been my best friend for so long, a father to my daughter. Even now, when he has every right to read me the riot act or object to hearing me work through my feelings about Max, he's putting me first. He loves me, without reservation or complication, and for the first time I take to heart what that means.

I take a deep breath for courage, inhaling his scent of Ivory soap and pencil shavings, mixed now with the heady aroma of the wine. And then I lean forward, setting our wineglass on the floor, and turn toward him.

Startled, Ryan says, "What?"

But I don't answer. Instead I lean across the space between our bodies and kiss him, tasting the tartness of the wine and the rich dark chocolate of the truffles. He kisses me back, exploring my mouth, letting me have his. And then he pulls away.

"Stop, Isabel," he says, and when I don't, he puts his hands on my upper arms, holding me still. "It's the wine," he says, his expression rueful. "It isn't you."

I brush his hair back from his face. His eyes are wide, the pupils dilated. "Ryan," I say softly.

"Yeah?" he says, loosening his grip. He lets me go, but I can still feel the places where his fingers pressed against my skin.

"I'm not drunk. Are you?"

"No."

"Then what's wrong?" I ask, and he shakes his head.

"This isn't a good idea. In fact, I'm pretty sure it's a terrible one."

With one finger, I trace the shape of his face, outlining his cheekbones, drifting over the blond stubble on his cheeks and chin, a softer plush than I'd imagined. He allows this, his eyes fixed on mine. He's waiting—for me to say the right thing, for me to ruin this. I try to muster a logical train of thought, a way to contradict him, but the wine has stolen my ability to think clearly—perhaps I am drunk, after all?—and in the end I just regard him, mute. He seems to take this as confirmation, because his body tenses, and I feel him shift, readying himself to stand up.

Through the haze of the wine, somehow I find the words to make him stay. "You remember when you told me you'd never bring up how you felt about me again, never touch me in anything but friendship, unless I asked?"

Ryan freezes. Then he settles back on the couch, his expression cautious. "Sure I do," he says. He lifts one hand and wraps it around mine where it touches his face. His fingers are warm, his eyes steady on mine.

"Well," I say, "I'm asking."

Ryan stares at me harder. He blinks, once, twice. "What did you say?"

"You said I could ask. This is me asking." I try to sound sure of myself, like the seductress I imagine this moment requires, but my voice shakes, giving me away.

"Are you sure?" Ryan says, and his voice is hoarse. "You're sure, Isabel?"

Right now, I don't feel sure of anything. But I know if I admit this to Ryan, he will walk away. And I know that when I am with him I feel safe, as if the world is a place that makes sense. I am tired of feeling afraid and confused, tired of doubting myself at every turn. So I lift my other hand to cup his face, and I kiss him again. I trail my nails lightly down his neck, and he shudders.

"Isabel," he says against my lips. His voice is wary. "I don't know."

He is trying to give both of us an out—I know this. Trying to salvage our friendship. If I were a better person, I would take it. I'd make some excuse, blame it on the Shiraz. And looking into his eyes from an inch away, I seriously consider doing that very thing. But in the end I am so sick of thinking, of analyzing everything to death, worrying about the repercussions of this and the implications of that. I want the oblivion that Ryan can give me, no matter how temporary, want to lose myself in him. And so I kiss him again, tugging at his bottom lip with my teeth.

He makes an eager noise then, low in his throat, and pulls me tight against him. One hand still gripping mine, he traces my lips with his tongue. His mouth closes on mine, and then he lifts my shirt and pulls it over my head. He feels for the clasp on my bra and un-hooks it, letting it fall to the floor. Then he leans back and simply looks at me.

The air is cold on my bare skin, and I have to fight the instinct to cover myself. It takes everything I have to hold still, not to snatch my shirt up off the floor. And maybe Ryan knows this, because he says, in reverential tones, "Jesus. You are so beautiful."

A blush rises, burning hot in my cheeks. "You don't have to say that."

Ryan snorts, sounding like his normal self. "What, you think I'm saying it out of some misguided sense of obligation? God, Izzy. For a brilliant woman, you can be so damn oblivious sometimes." He drops his head, brushing his lips over my breasts with a light touch that makes me shiver. "I thought I'd told you how I feel about you. But just in case there's any confusion, let me make myself clear."

He looks up at me then, and the expression on his face makes me shiver all over again. The Boy Scout who wondered if we'd set a bad example for drinking wine at Mage after hours is gone. There is love in his face, sure, and that disarming tenderness. But more than any-thing else there is desire, strong enough that it gives me pause. Ryan is offering me his whole self, heart and body both. More than any-thing he could put into words, the way he's looking at me right now tells me how much this means to him. And I have a moment to wonder if I am making an awful mistake.

"What are you doing?" I say, more to myself than to him.

Ryan circles one of my nipples with his fingertip, and then his tongue. The moan that rises in my throat muffles his reply, but I can still hear him clearly enough. "Answering you," he says, against my skin. "If you're sure this is what you want."

He lifts his head, and we regard each other for what feels like an interminable moment. It's probably only a few seconds, but in that time I consider so many things. I think about Max, how I waited so long for him to come home, how he will never forgive me for this. I think about Ryan, and how unless I am willing to give him what he's offering me—everything—I should put on my clothes and walk away. To do anything else would be cruel. I think of what it would be like to leave Charleston, to take Finn and move to New York, to build a new life. I see Max's face, hear him asking me what I'm afraid of.

And then I look at Ryan, who is waiting for my answer. His face is calm enough, but I'm sure he's as nervous as I am. Sure enough, I place my palm against his chest and feel his heart racing. "Isabel?" he says, and in his voice I hear both hopefulness and fear.

I should probably leave. But instead I tighten my fingers on the fabric of his shirt, yank it off over his head. "Get up," I say.

"Excuse me?" Ryan says, affecting a bewildered look. "Are you kicking me out of my own office? Half-naked? Is this some kind of object lesson?"

"No," I say, the wine making me bold. "But you have to get up." I push at him, and he complies, albeit reluctantly.

"Wow, you're bossy," he says, staring down at me. He's wearing my favorite jeans, the ones I got him at a thrift store in Asheville. Ryan works out, has for as long as I've known him—he says it's so he can keep up with me—and I've seen him with his shirt off a thousand times. Still, I've never looked at him like this, like someone who might be mine. I let my eyes travel over him, let myself really take him in—the way his jeans hang from his hips, the line of dirty-blond hair that rises from his belt buckle toward the flat planes of his stomach. My eyes pause on the crescent-shaped scar just below his ribs, then drift upward.

Ryan stands stock-still, allowing this scrutiny. He doesn't move, doesn't make a joke or even a sound. And when I finally meet his eyes, I understand why.

What I see there gives me pause. The bewildered look is gone. Gone too are the hopefulness and the fear. What I see in his eyes is lust, pure and simple, a raw wanting that rouses an answering echo in my own body.

There is a small part of me that still believes this is wrong. A part of me that worries that I am using him. *Leave*, I tell myself viciously, one more time. *Go now, before you do something unforgivable.*

But in the end, I do no such thing. The confusion of the past few weeks, the feeling that my world is spinning out of control—I would do almost anything to make it go away. So I give myself to the dizzying current of the wine, to the pull of Ryan's eyes. Slowly, as if I am moving underwater, I reach out and run my fingers over that trail of dirty-blond hair. I trace the shape of him through the worn blue jeans, hear his sharp intake of breath. He presses himself into my palm, making a hungry sound that resonates in the silence of the empty office. Desire pools in my belly, aching and unexpected.

Before I can lose my nerve, I lie back on the couch and shimmy out of my skirt, so I'm only in my underwear. They're plain blue cotton panties—the best that can be said about them is that at least they are bikini-cut—but from the way Ryan's eyes widen, I might as well have on a black lace thong. He steps toward me, but I shake my head.

"Shut the door," I say. "Just in case. And then come here."

Isabel

I think about stopping a thousand times. When Ryan clicks the lock on his office door and comes to me without hesitation, kneeling next to the couch and taking my face in his hands. When my fingers go to the buckle of his belt and he slides his hand over mine, stilling me, saying, "No games, Isabel, just tell me. Yes?" When I nod, wordless, and he tugs my underwear off and drops it to the carpet, his eyes fixed on mine with a sort of animal wariness, as if he expects me to haul off and slap him.

I think about it when we are both naked on the worn old couch where we've spent so many hours, eating lunch side by side and talking about everything from old *Twilight Zone* episodes to the sorry state of affairs in the Middle East. When Ryan's mouth is on mine, and he is making small eager noises, stiff against my belly, hands twined in my hair. When I slip my hands between us, cupping him, stroking, and he sucks in his breath and pulls away, just enough so I can see his face. His eyes are wide, the pupils swallowing everything but a thin line of hazel. I can feel him trembling against me, feel the deep breath he draws in an effort to steady himself.

"What's the matter?" I whisper, reaching up to brush his hair out of his eyes.

Ryan stares down at me, wearing an unreadable expression, and shakes his head. His muscles tense, as if it's all he can do not to jump off the couch and run out the door, leaving this whole complicated situation behind him. I see the thought pass through his eyes, feel it in the way he shifts his weight to his palms, lightly balanced, like a cat poised to jump. Then he takes another deep breath and smiles down at me, a crooked grin that holds very little humor. "I suppose it's too much to ask for you to just close your eyes and think of England, huh?"

For a moment I just look up at him, confused. And then I understand. The last time I saw this look on his face, we were in my living room, and he was asking me to let him stay the night, to watch over me and Finn because we were the closest thing to family he had. *Don't make me go,* he'd said, and I hadn't—but he'd gotten angry all the same, because I'd seen too far inside.

Moved by the desire to keep him safe—even if it's from himself—I put my arms around him, holding him close. "It's okay," I whisper, and feel him give way suddenly, all the tension rushing out of his body.

"I'm sorry," he says, dropping his head so that his face is buried in my hair. "I don't know what happened. I didn't mean to—I wanted it to be simple."

"You do know." My voice is even. "You just don't want to say."

Ryan gives a startled laugh and lifts his head. "Fair enough," he says. "I don't."

I sigh, exasperation and tenderness warring for the upper hand. "You don't have to hide, Ryan. Just tell me the truth. I won't laugh, or run away." As soon as I hear myself say this, I know it's true. I could have gotten up and left Ryan here, if this had just been an act of lust. As mean and hypocritical as it would have been, I could have done it. But this conversation has changed things. He's my friend, and he's suffering—that much is clear. I could no more walk out on him now than I could pick up a gun and shoot Finn.

His eyes flicker away from mine, and he rolls onto his side, slipping between my body and the back of the couch, pulling me to face him. He slides a knee between my legs, but it's not sexual—this is the only way we can fit, unless one of us wants to stand up. I wait to feel strange, embarrassed, but somehow I don't. This new, self-conscious version of Ryan is far less threatening than the one who stood by the side of the couch, shirtless and silent, heat in his eyes—or the one who told me I looked beautiful, just before I felt his mouth against the skin of my bare breasts.

"It's not that," he says, shifting his weight. "I just—shit, this is hard to say."

"Just say it, Ryan. How bad can it be?"

I feel his muscles tense again, the fine blond hair on his chest and belly prickling against my skin, and put a hand on his arm. "Trust me," I say, and with that he looks directly at me, challenge clear in his gaze.

"Fine. If you must know—I've never done this before."

I was prepared for him to say many things, but this was not one of them. My shock must be visible, because he laughs. "My God, Isabel. The look on your face."

"You've never had sex?" My voice emerges as a croak. "What about all your girlfriends? Pam? Lisa? Genevieve? What did you do with them? Play Parcheesi?"

His body shakes where it touches mine, but this time it's with laughter. "Oh, sure, I've had sex. Plenty of it. Since I was fourteen, with my foster mom's daughter."

"Nice, Ry," I say, before I can help myself, and he shrugs, the familiar arrogant, distant look transforming his features into something I recognize.

"You wanted the truth. I've gotten a little better at it since then, I hope, but the basic idea's the same."

He's grinning at me now, on safer ground, and I want to slap him. "What are you talking about, then?"

The smile fades, replaced by an assessing, serious expression. "Well," he says, his hands on my back now, pulling me closer. "I've had sex, like I said." He presses his lips to my hair, then lower, trailing down my neck to my collarbone. I can feel his breath, warm on my skin. "But what I haven't done," he says, lifting himself up on his elbow so he can look me in the eyes, "what I haven't done is had sex with someone I love."

His last sentence hangs in the air, echoing in the silence of the deserted building. The illusion that has enabled me to feel comfortable about lying naked on a couch with Ryan evaporates, and my heart starts to pound. I am suddenly aware of the press of his hands, callused and sure, and the growing weight of him, trapped between our bodies. Just like that, the energy between us alchemizes, quicksilver and dangerous, and now I am the one who wants to run. But I promised him I wouldn't, and so I just lie there, frozen, letting his words sink in. My mouth opens, then shuts again. Try as I might, I can't think of a single thing to say.

"Breathe, Isabel," he says wryly, and only then do I realize that I have stopped. I take in a lungful of air, feeling light-headed.

Ryan skims one hand over my hair, the corner of his mouth quirking up again in that self-deprecating half smile. "You remember," he says, letting his palm come to rest on my hip, "what I told you, years ago—when you grow up how I did, you either decide that having feelings is too expensive, or you learn how to hide them?"

I thaw enough to nod. "I remember."

"So," he goes on, his voice musing, "I did a little bit of both. I learned how to hide, all right. Anger, fear, hatred, you name it. If it would get me in trouble, I hid it and I hid it well. But love—I never had to hide that."

"Why not?" I ask, though I'm pretty sure I know the answer.

He runs a finger down the groove of my backbone, his touch meditative. "Love—it turned out to be too expensive," he says. "I didn't decide not to—not on purpose. It just happened. Somewhere along the way, I realized that if I disappeared, the only person who would mind was my foster mom, and that was because her check would stop coming. I had no ties, no one who cared if something happened to me—and vice versa." His gaze turns inward, focused somewhere in the past. "I knew that should hurt, or frighten me, at least. But instead I felt . . . nothing. Or—that's not exactly true. I felt free, like I could make any choice I wanted, and no one could say a goddamn thing about it. And a little bit sad, if I'm being honest, but not for the way I'd become—for the way I could have been, if things were different."

Filled with distress, I open my mouth to speak, but he puts a finger to my lips. "Let me finish. If I stop, I don't think I can start again."

Reluctantly I stay silent, and he goes on. "I lived like that for years, and I thought I was happy. That I had everything I needed. But then I met you and Finn. And I saw—Isabel, you'd lost people too. Your mom. Max. But you didn't shut down like I did. You didn't close everyone out. You were braver, better. And I started to think, maybe what I'd seen as strength all these years . . . how I stood on my own, how I never looked back . . . maybe it was just cowardice, when you got right down to it. Maybe love wasn't a weakness I couldn't afford." His hand tightens where it rests on my hip, and his voice falls lower still. "I started thinking . . . maybe it could save me."

His eyes meet mine, and they are filled with raw pain that sends a visceral echo through me. My heart clenches, and despite my best efforts, I feel the sting of tears. One spills over and makes its way down my cheek. He wipes it away.

"Don't," he says. "Don't cry for me, Isabel. If you do—I'll fall apart. And that I know I can't afford."

I swallow hard, trying to dissolve the lump in my throat. "I'm not brave, Ryan. I'm not. Without Max, I never would have made it through losing my mom. And I never would have made it through losing Max . . . without you."

"But that's the thing, don't you understand? You didn't have to let me into your life, Isabel. Or into Finn's. But you did. You opened the door wide. And me . . . I came in." He's looking straight at me now, and the last three words are a whisper, lit with wonder. He cups one of my breasts, thumb brushing over the nipple, so that it rises in response to his touch.

"I came in," he says again, "and before I knew it, there I was at Thanksgiving and Christmas. There I was, being a father to your little girl. I didn't mean for it to happen, God knows I didn't. But one day I woke up and I realized . . . I cared about both of you, more than I cared about myself. And it scared the living hell out of me. I thought I'd forgotten how." He drops his head and closes his mouth on my breast, his tongue flicking over my nipple. I can feel the rush of wetness between my legs, feel him stir against my belly, and he presses closer, sliding his thigh deeper between mine.

When he speaks again, his voice is rough. "I tried to stop loving you, Isabel. Tried everything I knew. But you knew me too well by then, and I couldn't take it back. And Finn . . ." He shakes his head, his hair brushing my cheek. "She cut me wide the fuck open, trusting me like she did. We'd take walks and she'd hold out her hand to me at street corners, not even looking, just expecting I'd be there to take it. To protect her. The three of us would go places together, and everyone assumed I was her father. Your—your husband." The last word gets stuck, and he clears his throat savagely, with a sound like tearing cloth.

"I should have told you how I felt long ago. It wasn't right, what I did. It felt like lying. But for the first time I could remember, I had a family," he says, his voice colorless. "And I didn't want to give that up. But it wasn't real, Isabel, because at night I didn't go home to you. I went out with Pam, or Lisa, or whoever, and then we'd go back to my house and just fuck. I'm sorry," he says as I wince, "but it's true. It's not like the sex was bad, or there was anything wrong with them. It was me. I'd changed."

"How?" I tilt my head back to see him more clearly, and just like that, his lips find mine. He opens my mouth with his, making me take more of him, so that I gasp and move against him, hard, pressing him into the back of the couch. He bites my lower lip in admonition and pulls away.

"Before, fucking would have been enough," he says, breathless. "It was all I knew, all I thought I wanted. But then I met you, and I wanted more."

He rolls over, taking me with him. "I wanted you," he says, and moves against me, so that I arch my hips in instinctive response. "And not just for this. I wanted—things I thought I gave up on long ago. But you . . . you wanted him. Years later, you still wanted him. And I didn't know what to do."

I don't want to talk about Max, not now. And I start to say just that, but Ryan isn't done. He draws back, propping himself up on his forearms, holding himself above me so that our bodies barely touch. One of his hands grips the fabric of the couch, so tightly that his knuckles are white. "I want to make love to you," he says, "more than I can remember ever wanting anything. And that makes me think I shouldn't, because it matters too much, and what if I—" He swallows hard.

"What if you what?" I say, reaching up to touch his face.

His eyes meet mine with what feels like an effort, and the words come tumbling out. "I keep thinking, what if I mess this up some-how, and you never give me another chance? And then I think that having feelings is a bitch, and what if it isn't worth it? Except how could it not be, because when I'm with you and Finn, I feel alive. Like a whole person. I don't want to give that up." He digs his fingers harder into the fabric, and I hear something rip. "Before, I wasn't living, is the thing. I was still just surviving. Survivors make it through the day, but they don't have room for love. And I—"

He sits up abruptly, sliding away from me. His head turns and his eyes center on the black-and-white photo of the abandoned farm-house on the wall, with its broken windows and yawning emptiness where the door ought to be. For the first time, it occurs to me that maybe he chose that photo to remind him of where he came

from—of who he thinks he really is, no matter how many scholarships he's won or how many times Finn's told him she loves him.

Guilt stabs through me, sharp and painful. If I'd really been a
good friend, I think, I would have asked questions about his past, if
only to show I cared. The worst he could have done is refused to
answer. As it is, our friendship has existed in an eerie no-man's-land,
bordered by his silence on the subject of his upbringing and my re-
fusal to share my real self with him, my willingness to allow him to
take a boyfriend's place in my life.

Ryan watches me glance at the photo, then back at him, sees me
put two and two together, and his mouth compresses to a thin line.
"Jesus," he mutters. "This is ridiculous. Say something, Isabel. Tell
me what you want. Because I'm halfway to running out that door, no
matter how much I want to be inside you. And I do, believe me."

He turns his head, and his eyes fix on mine, burning. With that,
his masks fall, and I can see that he's telling me the truth. He's
afraid—of what I'll say or do, of the price he'll pay for honesty. But
despite that, he's still here with me—because he believes that if I can
be brave enough to confront my demons, he can damn well do the
same. The irony, of course, is that I haven't been brave at all—but if
Ryan can show this much courage, then I won't do any less.

I get off the couch and kneel in front of him on the faded wool
carpet, resting my hands on his thighs. This close, I can see the way
his blond eyelashes darken to brown at the tips, the way his irises are
rimmed with a clear, bright circle of gold. "You think I'm brave," I
say. "But I'm not, I told you that before. When Max left—sure, I let
you into my life, but that was *safe*, Ryan. You were my friend, you
took care of Finn. It didn't cost me anything—not the way this is cost-
ing you."

He stares down at me, motionless. I can see how much he wants
me to make this right, to help him make sense of it. There's fear on
his face, and hope, and watchfulness—but he lets me see it. He
doesn't turn away. And so I tell him what I wouldn't say to my mother,

what I wouldn't tell Max. "You said that what we had—our family of three, you, me, and Finn—that it wasn't real. But I always thought it was, Ryan. And if it wasn't—well, then I'm to blame as much as you. Because having you here, with us, it meant I didn't have to look anywhere else."

He blinks in surprise. "What do you mean?"

"You said it yourself—you went everywhere with us, you were there for every Christmas, every birthday. You picked Finn up from school when my dad and I couldn't. You held her hand that time she stepped on a broken bottle and I was out of town, all the time the doctor was stitching her up. You know all of her favorite movies, and every Halloween costume she's ever worn. Hell, you made the costumes half of the years, because you knew anything crafty gives me the heebie-jeebies. You played dolls with her and had tea parties with those tiny animals she loved—what were they again?"

"Calico Critters," he says, rolling his eyes. "God, I hated them. Koalas and rabbits and God knows what else, with their cutesy overalls and gingham dresses and creepy black eyes. The craftsmanship was terrible."

"But that's my point, Ryan. You know all that stuff. You're even the one who made the monster spray for under her bed. I bet no one ever did anything like that for you."

He shakes his head, and his eyes drift back in the direction of the photo. "I had to look it up online. Man, some of those parenting websites are moronic, but I didn't know what else to do. She was so scared. I couldn't take it."

The floor is hard beneath the thin layer of carpet, and my knees are beginning to ache, but I don't dare move. "See, Ry," I say, "no one had to teach you how to love Finn. You gave her your whole self, from the beginning. And me—I could've handled things so much better. All this time, I've only done what's safe. Getting my black belt, not really dating anyone—I told myself that all of it was to protect Finn. So that I could look after her, in case whatever got Max and my mom wanted her too. You know what, though? As long as I kept looking backward, grieving for Max, I never had to move on. And if I didn't, no one would be able to hurt me again."

Ryan looks bewildered. "But isn't that what you're supposed to do for the people you love?" he asks. "Protect them from what might hurt them? Take care of them?"

"Sometimes," I say, choosing each word carefully. "But other times you wind up protecting them from all the wrong things." I meet his gaze, make myself go on. "The other day, when Max and I had that big fight—he asked me what I was so scared of. And I got mad, because I didn't want to admit that I was afraid of anything. But deep down, I know better. And I'm ashamed, because you—you've had so much less, Ry. And you've lost so much more. But here you are, telling me how you feel, even though you're afraid you'll lose the people you love most in the world. If you ask me, you're the brave one."

Ryan stares down at me like he's never seen me before. "Isabel—" he begins, but I don't let him finish. Instead, before I can lose my courage, I move my hand from his thigh and wrap my fingers around him, feeling the velvety softness of his skin, feeling him grow under my touch. He takes a sharp breath, inhaling between his teeth, but doesn't pull away—not then and not when I close my mouth over him. One of his hands comes down on the back of my head, heavy, his fingers knotting in my hair. I can hear him breathing, a fast, staccato pattern. He tastes like the sea, like salt and hidden things.

This is the final moment when I panic, wonder if we are indeed making a terrible mistake. Because just as surely as I know that Max will never forgive me for sleeping with Ryan, I also know that if I shut Ryan out after this—if I turn around and go back to Max—he will never trust me again. Oh, he won't stop being my friend, at least to the best of his abilities, or loving Finn. He'll tell me that he understands. But he will never be honest with me about his feelings, not the way he was tonight. He'll slam that door closed between us, and it will be a cold day in hell before I can pry it open.

Suddenly desperate to make the right decision—or to be worthy of the choice I've made, to really be here, with him—I lift my face and let my eyes travel over his body. My gaze drifts upward, over his stomach with its trail of dirty-blond hair, his ribs with their crescent-shaped scar, the expanse of his chest, tanned from the afternoon we spent on the beach. His head is flung back, his lips parted, but his half-shut eyes train on me, their focus sharpening. "What?" he says. "Is something wrong?"

I think of him saying, *Maybe love wasn't a weakness I couldn't afford. Maybe it could save me.* And I know I cannot abandon him now, or go back on my promise. Instead, I curl my fingers around him and slide them down his length—slow at first, then faster, my tongue tracing a sinuous path in their wake. He makes a deep, helpless noise, and I feel that tug of desire again, spreading hot and unpredictable through my blood.

One of Ryan's hands is still twined in my hair. The other covers mine, and he moves our hands together in a relentless, unmistakable rhythm. "Isabel, I can't think," he says, and in his voice I hear what I didn't realize I was waiting for—the loss of his hard-won control. "And pretty soon I won't be able to stop. Please tell me what you want."

"Don't go," I say without hesitation. "That's what I want. Stay here, Ryan. Make love to me."

He hauls me back up onto the couch and lets his weight settle onto me with something like a sob. And then he is kissing me, his mouth fierce on mine, the length of him hard against my thigh. He reaches over the edge of the couch and fumbles one-handed on the floor, rummaging in his jeans for his wallet. I hear the crinkle of a foil packet, and then he tears it with his teeth, on his knees between my legs.

"You're sure," he says one last time, his voice uneven.

I don't trust myself to speak. Instead I nod, my gaze fixed on his, and pull him down to me. I fight the urge to close my eyes, determined to keep my promise—to really be here, with him. Not to run, or to pretend. To be the person that both of us deserve.

And so I watch as he kisses his way down my body, as his tongue finds me, searching, and I cry out. I watch as his eyes darken, as he rears back and lifts my hips in his hands. As he hesitates for just an instant at the moment of decision, until I take him in my hands and guide him inside, filling me, and he says, "Oh my God," with a reverence I've never heard from him before, devoid of mocking wit. "You're okay?" he says, his voice husky, and when I nod, he starts to move, taking me with him.

I watch as he murmurs my name, making breathless, hungry sounds, stroking my tongue with his. As he circles his hips, slow, to make this last, and I rise to meet him, urging him onward, wanting more.

"Harder," I demand, and watch as he rises up, his eyes wild, and obliges, pulling away and then slamming into me with a violence that rouses the same in me. As I rake my nails down his back and he sets his teeth into my neck, his hands under me, pulling me tight against him, rocking me. Tipping me over the edge so that I lose myself, splintering into a thousand pieces. And feeling my release, lets himself go, coming apart in my arms. I hold him, both of us shuddering and slick with sweat, and hear him whisper, so low that it could have been no more than my imagination, "Whatever happens now . . . thank you."

Max

I'm in the back bedroom, stuffing clothes in a duffel bag, when I hear Isabel's car pull up outside. Her headlights sweep the driveway, the motor cuts off, and she knocks, calling my name.

"Come in," I yell, and hear the door creak, the way it has since my parents bought the place when I was twelve. Every summer my dad attacked it with WD-40, but the effects only ever lasted about a week. Salt water is hell on metal. Still, I make up my mind to oil the hinges tomorrow—not that I'll be around that long to benefit from the results.

"Max?" It's a question this time, as if she thinks someone else might be lurking in the master bedroom. Who, I can't begin to imagine.

"Back here," I say, and a few seconds later she materializes in the doorway, wearing a black tank top and shorts, long hair spilling down the way I've always loved. It takes everything I have not to throw my arms around her, but one look at her face and I know she's not here for that.

"Hey, Max," she says, voice tentative. "Is this a good time? I wanted to talk."

"I figured as much," I say, fighting to keep my voice even. Some emotion must bleed through anyhow, because she winces and looks away.

"I wish things were different," she says, almost to herself. "I never expected this."

"That makes two of us," I say, sitting down on the edge of the bed. I can smell her familiar scent from here, lavender and vanilla, sweat and salt. If I don't do something, I'll wind up kissing her, and judging by her face, that wouldn't do either of us any good.

"I came here to tell you," she begins. Then she catches sight of my expression and her face crumples. "Oh, Max," she says, sounding as sad as I've ever heard her. "I'm so sorry. About everything."

"Don't be sorry," I say. "Just tell me, whatever it is. The suspense is getting old."

I expected this to piss her off, and it does. But the anger that flashes across her face is mixed with something else, unfamiliar but unmistakable all the same: guilt. My stomach plummets, and I know what she's going to say before the words leave her mouth. I want to tell her not to bother, but I'm too late. She's already speaking, my hurt and rage tinder to her flame. "I slept with Ryan," she says, each syllable falling into the silence of the room like a stone.

You'd think knowing what was coming would ease the pain of hearing it. As it turns out, this isn't the case. I'm on my feet before I know it, crossing the room, looming over her in the way she has always hated. "When?" I snarl.

To her credit, Isabel doesn't flinch. She stands her ground, adjusting her stance so subtly that I might not notice if I hadn't spent the last two weeks with fighting men. "Tonight," she says, lifting her chin. And then she waits—for what, I can't imagine.

No sooner does the question cross my mind than I realize my hands are balled at my sides, tight with the need to hit something, anything. I turn and slam my fist into the wall next to the doorframe, hard as I can. The punch lands in between studs, but it still hurts like a son of a bitch. Horsehair plaster flies everywhere, dusting our clothes, and Isabel stares, mouth open wide. "Why are you *doing* this to me?" I say, low and savage. "Are you punishing me for leaving? For not telling you the truth?"

She takes a step back, face pale. Whatever reaction she expected, this isn't it, and I have a moment to wonder if maybe the time I've spent in the nineteenth century has devolved me somehow. Would the old Max have taken this in stride, hurt and anger notwithstanding, or would he have responded with violence, like this?

I close my eyes, trying to find my way back to the earlier version of myself, but this doesn't help. Now I can feel the gun in my hand, see the militiaman in front of me, eyes wide in shock as I raise the musket high and bring it down with all my force. Blood blooms in the darkness behind my eyelids, seeping from his head the way it did that morning. I watch him fall, collapsing to his knees, then face-first into the dirt, and feel something inside me break all over again.

My eyes are closed, but something—maybe a stir in the air— alerts me to the fact that Isabel has moved. Seized with a sudden fear that she means to comfort me, I open my eyes and take one step back, then another. If she puts her hands on me, there's no telling what I'll do—fall at her feet and beg her to take me back, grab her and try to make her mine, all over again. "Don't touch me," I say. "Not now." And I brush past her onto the balcony, where I stand, trying to catch my breath.

I hear Isabel's footsteps on the wooden decking before she speaks, and brace myself, gripping the rail. My left hand throbs with a dull, bruising pain, in sync with my heart. "I'm sorry," she says again. "I know you'll find this hard to believe, but I still—"

"Don't you dare say you love me," I say without turning. "I swear to God, Isabel, if you say that to me, I'll lose it completely. And I don't think either one of us wants to see what that looks like."

She is silent for a moment. "Fine," she says, her voice empty. "I won't. I suppose you know that your hand is bleeding?"

I glance down. Sure enough, all four of my knuckles are split, and blood is pouring over them in a steady stream. Wearily, I regard them, and then shrug. "I don't give a fuck," I say, sounding as exhausted as I feel.

Isabel gives an exasperated sigh. "To answer your earlier question," she says, "and at the risk of sounding extraordinarily selfish — I'm not doing anything to you, at least not on purpose. I'm doing it for me."

"You're right," I say, taking in deep lungfuls of air in an effort to maintain a modicum of control over myself. "It does sound extraordinarily selfish, especially from where I'm standing. Although I'm sure Ryan thinks your motives are more than altruistic. This is so fucked up," I say, slamming my damaged hand down on the railing. Isabel winces, but I don't care. The pain clarifies things somehow, brings my feelings into focus. "And if you don't mind, I don't want to hear why you did it. As long as you intend to do it again, I don't think it matters."

Isabel doesn't say anything, but her silence is answer enough. Swearing under my breath, I turn around and head for the bathroom, where I run my mangled hand under cold water and splash some on my face. Glancing in the mirror, I'm disconcerted to see that I look exactly like I feel: pissed off and shell-shocked. My eyes are gray smudges, and my face is pale, hectic spots of color burning high on my cheeks. I stare at myself for another second, then give up and walk out into the bedroom.

Isabel is standing next to the bed, looking at the duffel bag, which I guess she missed on her first pass-through. "Going somewhere?" she says, her gaze as level as any of the guns I faced in the battle at Lowthers Plantation, and just as dangerous.

I cross to the bed and yank on the bag's zipper, not wanting her to see what lies on top: photos of the two of us, smiling on the front porch of my parents' house, sprawled out on a towel at the beach. "Well," I say, turning to face her. "As a matter of fact, yes."

Isabel

"Max, no," I say, in desperation. "You don't have to leave."

He yanks the zipper of the duffel bag so hard I think it will break. "Yes, I do. I can't fall out of love with you here. Everything just reminds me of us. Besides," he says, looking down at the floor, "I don't fit here anymore. It isn't my home."

I can't dispute this, but that doesn't mean it hurts any less. "Where are you going?" I say, hating the way my voice trembles.

He sighs, sinking onto the bed next to the bag. "Back. I'm going back."

"No," I say, horrified anew. "Max, you can't."

"I have to." He drops the bag on the floor with a thud. "Not . . . in time. I don't mean that. I don't even know if I could. And besides, there's nothing for me there, either."

"But then—"

"To Barbados," he says patiently, as if he's explaining something to a small child. "I need to see it, Isabel. The way it is today. I need to make peace with what happened, and this is the only way."

Fear seizes me, and I force it back, make myself speak rationally. "When were you planning on telling me, Max? If I hadn't shown up, would you have taken off without saying a word?"

He shakes his head. "Of course not, Isabel. I—*we*—only just decided. My parents are coming too. Of course I was going to talk to you about it. We haven't exactly been getting along. But I wouldn't have just left."

"You're packing *now*," I point out.

"Yeah, but—" He shrugs helplessly. "I needed to feel like I was doing something, you know? I can't just stay here and tread water while everything falls apart."

My heart twists, and before I know it, I'm sitting next to him, gripping his hands in mine. "You don't have to leave, Max. I was just there. I can tell you whatever you want to know. Ask me anything."

He turns our hands over, loosening my grip so that my palm lies open in his. With infinite tenderness, he traces my lifeline. "Why do you want me here so badly, Isabel? And don't say it's because you love me," he adds as I open my mouth.

The gentleness of his touch disarms me. I look down and see that traces of his blood line my palm now, staining my skin. Seeing me notice, Max gives me a small, sad smile, and I know he's done this on purpose. He is marking me the only way I'll allow it, claiming me for the moment, however impermanent. My eyes well with tears, and I force the words to come.

"I spent eight years wondering if you were dead, Max. Eight years praying that you weren't. After my mother, losing you was the worst thing I could imagine. Maybe it was worse, even, because after she left, you saved me." My voice sticks in my throat, but I push on. "People said you left because you didn't want the baby, but I never believed it. I knew you wouldn't do that. What was the alternative, though? That you'd died? I didn't want to believe that, either. Getting you back was like a miracle. It was all I ever wanted."

"Except that it wasn't," he points out, his hand motionless in mine.

"It was," I insist. "It's only . . . when I lost you . . . I never wanted to feel like that again. So I just stopped—caring, growing, everything. I spent so much time looking backward—looking for you—that I didn't realize how much I'd changed. I don't think I wanted to. But when you came back . . . it was like time started moving again."

"Ironic," he says, his thumb moving absently over my hand, as if he doesn't realize he's doing it. "So you really hadn't been with Ryan before?"

I shake my head, and he snorts. "I said I didn't want to know. And I don't. But your timing sucks."

I glare at him. "Really? You disappear for eight years, and *I* have bad timing?"

Max laughs, short and bitter. "Well," he says, "maybe you're not the only one. But Isabel, I can't stay here. You must see that."

"What about Finn? You only just met her," I counter, suddenly fierce. "Does she mean so little to you that you'll turn around and leave her again?"

A pained look passes across his face. "Of course not."

"But you'll do it anyway." I let go of his hands and wrap my arms around myself, trying to stop my teeth from chattering. This kind of cold emanates from the inside out, though, and all I succeed in doing is holding myself still, so my shivering doesn't show.

Max is shaking his head, hands braced on his thighs. "I won't," he says quietly, his eyes on the floor. "I won't leave her."

"Well, what do you propose? Astral projection? I guess it's not that far out of the realm of possibility—you've done it before—but I don't think it's all that reliable as a form of communication, you know? Not to mention, it'll be hell on wheels at parent-teacher conferences. *Hey, Mrs. Marcy, you haven't met him before, but this is Finn's father, the hologram.* Call me crazy, but I don't think it'll go over too well—"

Max's hand descends on my shoulder, a warm, reassuring weight. "Isabel," he says. "Stop for a second, okay?"

His gray eyes meet mine without guile, letting me look him over.

But what I see doesn't make me feel any better, and I leap to my feet. "No," I say in horror. "Just—no."

A small smile lifts his lips, then fades away as quickly as it came. "I wondered if you could still do that. Read my mind, that is."

"You can't take her," I say, my throat tightening. "She barely knows you."

"She knows me," Max says. "And you do too. I'd take good care of her."

"You can't," I repeat. "And why would you want to? Go on some misguided mission to find yourself, fine. But don't drag Finn into it. She's been through enough."

His eyes narrow and I can tell he's gearing up for round two. But then he sighs and pats the bed next to him. "Sit, Isabel."

"I'm not a dog!"

Max rolls his eyes. "I'm sorry, okay? Please sit down. I won't bite, I promise."

Eyeing him warily, I settle onto the quilt. "What?"

The sun is setting, and darkness gathers in the corners of the room. Max leans over to flip on the bedside lamp. He lost so much weight in Barbados, and his cheekbones stand out sharp beneath his tanned skin. There are circles under his eyes, blue shading to gray, but still, he is beautiful to me. I wonder what it would have been like for us to have a hundred nights like this, or a thousand. Images unspool in my mind like a movie: Max kneeling on the forest floor that first time, asking what I wanted. Making love in the tree house, the smell of pine all around and the rain coming down. Sitting in my room, geometry homework spread out between us, me asking Max about a theorem and stopping him with a kiss every time he tried to explain.

Sitting here in the growing silence, I find the words to voice what he wouldn't let me say before. "I do still love you. I always will. We're just different people now."

Max bows his head. Then he turns to me, slowly, giving me every chance to pull away. But I don't move. Instead I keep my eyes on his as he leans closer, as his hands rise to cradle my face. His lips come down on mine with none of the fierceness of the last time we were together. In his touch I feel the weight of everything he has lost. "Please," he whispers against my mouth. "She's my daughter. Please trust me."

Isabel

My cell rings the next morning, startling me so that I slosh coffee onto the kitchen table. I rescue the phone from the puddle right before it goes to voicemail and answer without looking at the caller ID.

"Hey, Isabel. You're alive, after all."

Oh, God, Ryan. After Max's announcement and his request to take our daughter out of the country, I haven't allowed myself a second to think about what happened in Ryan's office. I'd driven home, fallen into bed, and only woken up when Jennifer rang the doorbell an hour ago, delivering Finn.

"Me? What about you?" I counter, operating on the premise that the best defense is a good offense. My heart pounds, and I clutch the phone so tightly it creaks in protest.

He clears his throat. "Fair enough. It's just—when you didn't call . . . and you didn't pick up at first . . . I thought maybe you were avoiding me."

"I'm not," I say. "Really. I dropped my phone in a puddle of coffee."

He laughs, a short, surprised sound. "That better be true, Griffin, or you're the worst liar in the world."

"Oh, it's true," I assure him. "Want to come over and see?"

There's a pause, and I wonder if I've overstepped. But then he says, "I'll be there in five minutes."

The three of us end up spending the day together, Finn's presence effectively foiling any awkward discussions that might ensue. We make it all the way through dinner and a movie, then bath and bedtime, before Ryan finally lets his façade crumble.

We're sitting on opposite sides of the couch. Beer in hand, Ryan is ostensibly relaxed. But the fingers of his other hand beat an unrelenting rhythm on his thigh and he is very studiously not looking at me.

"You're nervous," I say at last, stating the obvious.

"I am not." He shifts restlessly, stretching out his legs and propping his feet on the coffee table. It's meant to look casual, and maybe under other circumstances he could've pulled it off. As it is, his left foot nudges a pile of books, which promptly cascades to the floor with a crash. Ryan grabs for them and misses, succeeding only in slamming his fingers between Cheryl Strayed's *Wild* and the collected works of Arthur Conan Doyle. He yelps and swears so colorfully that I can't help but giggle.

"Fucking heavy cryptic addict son of a bitch," he concludes, slightly muffled by the fingers he's stuck in his mouth.

"It's not Sherlock's fault," I protest. Ryan shoots me a resentful look and sets his beer on the coffee table. He looks so grim, I start giggling all over again.

Ry glares, unamused. "It's not funny."

"I'm sorry," I say, doing my best to sound repentant. "Of course it's not."

Getting down on his hands and knees, he restacks the books in the middle of the table. I can't help but notice that he goes out of his way to place them in size order, aligning the spines precisely, and it sets me off again. Ryan scowls. "Quit it, would you?"

I clap a hand over my mouth to stifle my laughter, but it doesn't really work. Glancing over at me again, he sighs. "What is so goddamn funny?"

"You," I say, lowering my hand. "And your obsessive-compulsive disorder."

"What? I don't have—"

"You do too," I say, and point at the books, so neatly stacked that they could be photographed for *House Beautiful*.

Ryan glances down at the books, and then his mouth quirks up at the corner, the way it does when he's trying not to laugh. "Well," he concedes, "maybe just a little."

"Uh-huh. And you're not nervous, either."

For a moment, his body stills, and I think he's going to deny it again. But then his eyes meet mine, and in them I see both challenge and invitation. Quick as a cat, he boosts himself back onto the couch and sprawls out with his head in my lap. Eyes closed, he says, "Calm me down, then."

The sudden warm weight of him startles me. I stare down at him, at the sweep of his long lashes, dark at the roots and gold-blond at the tips, at his mouth, set in deliberate nonchalance. Tentatively at first, then more confidently, I run my fingers through his hair. It's thicker than Max's, but soft. I let the strands run through my fingers—light blond, darker gold, and brown, all mixed together.

Ryan makes a low, contented noise, almost a purr, and I feel his whole body relax. "I like that," he says unnecessarily. One of his hands rises and comes to rest on my thigh, fingers spread wide. He takes a deep breath, lets it out slow, and I feel the last of the tension leave his body.

"Better than Xanax," I say, without thinking. "Do all your girl-friends do this?"

His eyes flicker open and flash to mine. On his face there is a curious look—somewhere between surprise, alarm, and dismay. He doesn't say a word, but then again, he doesn't have to.

"Sorry," I say hastily. "I didn't mean—"

Ryan shifts in my lap, propping himself up on his elbows. "You can imply whatever you want."

I study him, puzzled. "Then what's wrong?"

He leans back and looks me full in the face, bracing himself as if for impact. His hand tightens on my thigh until it hurts, but I don't move. "What?" I say again.

He regards me, assessing how honest he wants to be. "My mother used to do that when I was little, to help me sleep. She'd sit on my bed and sing to me—and run her fingers through my hair." His voice is a whisper. "It was the only time I felt safe."

My heart twists. "Ry—" I say, but he interrupts me.

"After what happened," he says, forcing his gaze back to mine, "I didn't want anyone to touch me like that. It made me feel . . . I don't know." He shakes his head viciously, as if he's trying to shake the memory out of it. "But with you, I want things to be different. I know I can be a defensive ass. That's easy. This . . . this is hard."

I don't ask what he means. I don't have to. Instead I run my hand through his hair again, intending comfort, but he catches my wrist mid-gesture and presses his face into my palm. "I notice you don't deny that I'm an ass," he says, and I feel him smile against my skin.

"In all fairness, you're not usually an ass to me," I say. "Just recently."

"I know. I'm sorry. I don't mean to be." He shrugs. "Max coming back, worrying about Finn—it stirs up things I've managed to avoid for a long time, things I thought I'd put behind me. Obviously, I was wrong." Passing headlights sweep through the room, and he blinks, rolling onto his back. "I don't like to think about this shit, much less talk about it," he says to the ceiling. "Every time I tell you something, I live it through again."

"So don't. You don't have to tell me everything if it makes you feel awful."

He shakes his head again. "You deserve to know," he says. "Plus, I think maybe it's like poison. If I let it out, then maybe—maybe it will finally leave me alone." His jaw sets in determination, as if he can erase his childhood through force of will.

Acting on the instinct that has guided me through a hundred sparring matches, that told me Max was still alive even when everyone around me said he couldn't possibly be, I lean down and kiss him. Gentle at first, a mere brush of lips. But then Ryan makes a hungry sound, pushing himself up on one elbow and knotting his other hand in my hair, and his tongue slides along the seam of my mouth. I catch his lower lip between my teeth and he chuckles, low in his throat.

"Oh, it's like that?" His voice is huskier than usual, and when his teeth graze my neck, I shiver. He rises up, pulling me with him so that I'm sitting in his lap, one leg on either side of his hips. One of his hands cups my breast, teasing until I cry out. And then he pulls away.

"Ask me," he says.

Dazed, I blink down at him. "Ask you what?"

"Anything." His hands are steady where they rest on my hips, but I can feel the pounding of his heart, a rapid rhythm that belies his calm tone. Still, he meets my eyes and doesn't look away. "Anything you want to know, Isabel," he says. "Any part of my past. Go ahead and ask. It's yours." He lets go of me, and his hands fall open at his sides, palms up in invitation.

A thousand questions come to my mind then—about whether Ryan ever misses his mother, whether he's considered searching for her, whether he knows if his parents are still alive. Where, exactly, he grew up, and whether he ever drives past the place he used to live, wondering about the lives of the people inside. I open my mouth to ask, and instead wreck the moment by saying, "Why now?"

He stares at me, puzzled. "What do you mean?"

"I've known you for almost eight years, Ryan. In all that time, you've never shared any of this with me—not that I blame you. Not five minutes ago, you were telling me how much you hate talking about this stuff. And now suddenly you've become an open book?" I shake my head and slide off his lap to sit on the couch. "I don't buy it."

Ryan turns his head to look at me. "I told you," he says. "If you're going to be with me, like this, you deserve to know. The hell with that—as my closest friend, you have the right. And it's probably good for me to talk about it. That's what all the shrinks said anyway. If I would just talk it through, eventually it would go away."

I regard him for a moment, considering, and irritation flashes across his features. He runs a hand through his hair in frustration, a familiar gesture. "I'm offering you the truth, Isabel, whatever you want to know. What possible motive could I have? Unless—" His eyes spring wide, and then narrow, fixed on my face. "Oh," he says, cold as winter. "I get it now."

Bewildered by this transformation, I reach for him, but he ducks away, so that my fingers barely brush his shirt. "If all of this was too ugly for you, Isabel, you should have said."

"What are you talking about?"

"You know exactly what I'm talking about," he says, getting to his feet. "I should have known. You never asked me any questions. Anyone else who had the slightest clue about my childhood, they'd pry. Maybe it's some sort of morbid curiosity, the way people stop for a car wreck even though they don't really want to see. I have no idea. But you—you never said anything. I deluded myself into thinking that it was because you respected my privacy. But now I understand."

I'm on my feet now too, staring at him in complete bewilderment. "I did respect your privacy," I say. "I mean, I do. I figured you'd tell me when you were ready."

"Bullshit." He spits the word at me. "Spare me, Isabel. You don't have to make excuses. I'll just go."

"Wait. If all of *what* is too ugly?" I say, but I am talking to his back. He's turned away from me and is heading toward the front door, his stride determined. At my question, though, he turns, face white to the lips.

"Me, Isabel," he says, stabbing a finger at his chest. "Who I really am. When you said *Don't tell me*, you really meant it, huh? What an idiot I am, thinking you wanted to hear—" His voice rises, and he breaks off, maybe because he's thinking of Finn, maybe for another reason entirely. "Never mind," he says viciously, his hand on the doorknob. "I'm leaving. You can go back to living in your perfect little world, where everyone comes back from the great beyond and reality doesn't exist."

He turns the knob, and for a moment I just sit there, frozen, trying to figure out how the tables have turned so quickly. And then I leap to my feet. "Stop, Ry."

Ryan ignores me, pulling the door open as if I haven't said a word. He walks through and shuts it behind him. A moment later, I hear the engine of his Forerunner turn over, then rev. I brush the white linen curtains aside just in time to see his taillights disappear down the street, fading into darkness.

Isabel

In the wake of Ryan's dramatic exit, I am first taken aback, then distraught, and finally exasperated. I keep thinking he'll come back, but he doesn't—story of my life. I'm beginning to realize that he is more fucked up than I ever imagined. Underneath that impassive façade is a world of hurt, and more defense mechanisms than the Cold War. I love him, of course I do, and he's been there for me—and Finn—a hundred times over. But God, this new version of Ryan is a tremendous pain in the ass.

Even in his pissed-off state, though, Ryan didn't slam the door, so hopefully Finn's still asleep. I have to remind myself not to stomp as I make my way up the stairs to check on her. But when I push open her bedroom door I'm relieved to see her lying on her side, quilts thrown off as usual, her pale profile just visible in the dim glow of her night-light.

For a moment I stand there, resisting the urge to lie down next to her and close my eyes. But then I stiffen my spine and close her door, heading for the kitchen. I empty the dishwasher and wipe down the counters, trying to keep myself from worrying about Ryan.

It doesn't work. I picture him driving aimlessly around Charleston, maybe heading to Folly Beach, grabbing a few beers at Loggerheads, and then what? Picking a fight with Max? In his current state of mind, I wouldn't put it past him. And Max—what would he do?

I pick up my cellphone, then put it down again. *They're grown men*, I tell myself. *Grown men.* And I march myself into the bathroom, where I turn the hot water on as high as it will go and step into the shower, willing the steam to clear my head.

I don't quite know how I sense I'm no longer alone. Maybe it's instinct or years of training, because I can't see anything but steam, or hear much, for that matter. I'd locked the front and back door and all the windows before getting in the shower, out of pure habit, so I don't understand how this can be the case. But as surely as if someone's touched me on the shoulder, I know that I'm no longer by myself in the bathroom.

A cautious person would turn off the water, look around for a weapon—my razor?—but after everything that's transpired, I have no more caution left in me. Instead I grab the shower curtain and yank it aside—and suck in a deep breath, part relief, part confusion and dismay.

Ryan is standing on the bath mat, outlined by the rising steam. When he sees me, naked and streaming water, his eyes go wide and he says, "Jesus." It sounds like a prayer.

I am so stunned, I don't think to turn the water off or grab a towel to cover myself. Instead I say, "What are you doing here?" It comes out as a neat blend of shock and hostility. My heart is going like a trip-hammer, and it's hard for me to breathe.

Ryan's mouth opens, but no sound comes out. Finally he manages, "I used my key. I came to apologize." He swallows, hard, and tries again. "I called your name. I did, Isabel. I didn't mean to end up standing here like some creepy stalker."

"And yet here you are," I say, imbuing my voice with as much sarcasm as I can manage. My heart's finally starting to slow, and I reach for the faucet in an effort to wrest back some control. Ryan's already seen all of me there is to see, but this is different.

Moving like a sleepwalker, he flips the door lock and comes forward, to the lip of the shower. One of his hands covers mine. "Don't," he says. "Don't turn it off." He steps into the water, clothes and all, pulling the curtain shut behind him.

"What are you doing?" I say, my voice a squeak. "Have you lost your mind?"

This earns me a low, rueful chuckle. "Quite possibly. But you know what? For once, I don't think I care." He backs me up against the wall of the shower, pinning my hands above my head in one of his. "Tell me if you want me to stop," he says, and drops his head, licking the water off my breasts with slow, deliberate strokes of his tongue.

Desire rises in me then, unbidden but fierce and sharp nonetheless. I wrench one of my hands free, get a fistful of his hair, and lift his face to meet mine. What I see there doesn't help. He's looking at me as if I am the only person in the world, as if nothing else matters and I am all he wants.

"I thought you came here to apologize," I say, forcing the words through my throat, which has suddenly narrowed to a pinhole.

"I did. I am." He runs his free hand down my side, then lower, cupping my ass with an easy possessiveness that takes me aback. I gasp and he takes this as an invitation to pull me tight against him. "If you'll have me," he says, his breath warm on my neck.

It's hard to think, much less to reconcile this version of Ryan with all the others, but I manage. "This is your idea of an apology?" I say. "Sneaking into the bathroom when I'm in the shower? And then climbing into the tub and . . . and . . ."

"You don't like it?" he says, his free hand flat against my belly, drifting lower.

"That's not what I meant!" I say, doing my best to sound indignant. "And you're still wearing all of your clothes, which is weird, not to mention unfair."

He makes an amused sound, deep in his throat. "Oh? Well, that's easily remedied." Stepping back from me, he pulls his T-shirt over his head and drops it onto the bathroom floor, where it lands with a splat. His shorts and boxers follow after a bit of creative maneuvering, and then it's just the two of us, naked in my shower—a turn of events that, just a week ago, would have seemed like an impossibility.

Ryan stands there, the water coming down on his head and chest, looking suddenly shy. I can see other marks on him now—round ones that look like cigarette burns; thinner, white ones that look like they were made by some kind of cord. Most of them are on his thighs, I realize, where they wouldn't show. A wave of protectiveness comes over me. I want to take care of him, to keep him safe, the way he's done for me all of these years. The feeling blends with my memory of him on the couch in his office, moving in me slowly at first, then faster, me digging my nails into his back, him setting his teeth into my neck, until we lost ourselves in a dizzying rush. The two merge, twining into a feeling so intense, it overwhelms me. I stand there, staring at him, speechless.

"What?" he says suspiciously. "Why are you looking at me like that?"

I know this tone all too well, and find my voice in an attempt to avert disaster. "You're beautiful," I say, and take a step closer to him, so that our bodies are pressed together. I can feel him stir, restless, against my belly, smell the salt on his skin.

His arms come around me automatically, but he shakes his head, staring at me, puzzled. "I'm not."

"Nothing about you is ugly, Ryan. Not the way you look, not your past. Or if it is, it's not your fault. What I'm trying to say is—it's all of you that I want. Before . . . you didn't have to leave. If you'd stayed, I would have told you that."

Ryan is still staring at me, but now the look on his face has shifted to incredulity. "You mean that?" he says, fingers gentle on my face.

"I do."

He drops to his knees then, looking up at me. It's a penitent position, one I never thought Ryan, with all of his pride, would be willing to take. "I'm sorry," he says. "I'm trying, Isabel. I'm trying as hard as I know how."

"I know you are," I tell him. "I'm not perfect, either, not by a long shot. But maybe . . . maybe we could figure it out together?"

The water is loud enough that I can't hear the sound Ryan makes clearly. It's somewhere between a growl and a sob, that much I know, and he is still making it when he pushes my legs apart and closes his mouth on me. The vibration sweeps through my body, blending with the warmth of his tongue and the pressure of his fingers. We move together, his tongue deep inside me, his stubble rough on my thighs. From far away I can hear the small noises I am making, but helpless to stop them, I knot my fingers in his hair and close my eyes.

Dimly I'm aware that my water heater, having behaved thus far, has finally come to the end of its resources, but I can't seem to care. Ryan laughs, a rumble that courses through me, and steers us out of the cold spray. My legs tremble and he braces me, urging me forward until I come apart, my cries drowned in the fall of the water.

It takes a moment to open my eyes. When I do, he has shut the shower off and is standing in front of me, waiting. He takes my face in his hands and kisses me, deliberate and slow, so I can taste myself. "I want you," he says, his voice hoarse. "Tell me where."

I have never brought a man to this house, never had to take into account the fact that Finn's room is right next to mine. But my bedroom door does lock, so this is where I lead Ryan, both of us wrapped in towels, tiptoeing past Finn's door like a pair of thieves. It strikes me as hysterically funny—but when I turn to say as much to Ryan, he has locked the door and is standing naked in the middle of my room.

"Come here," he says, in a tone that brooks no disagreement.

"But—" I protest, out of sheer obstinacy.

"Here," he says again, as commanding as I've ever heard him.

"But I—"

Ryan sighs. "Look," he says, "whether or not I was willing to admit it to you before, I *was* nervous. I've been nervous all day about what I was going to say and whether you would want to have anything to do with me and what I would do if you told me to take a hike. I was nervous when I knocked over those goddamned books.

And then I screwed everything up, right in the middle of—well, you know. You were right, okay?"

"But—" I begin, and he holds up a peremptory finger.

"I drove halfway to Folly Beach before I pulled myself together. Believe it or not, I did have a big apology planned. But I did *not* expect to find you naked in the shower." He glares at me as if I'd planned the whole thing. "Not that I'm complaining. Christ, I've never seen anything so hot in my entire life. But let me say that I'm just a little bit on edge." He runs a hand through his wet hair, which obligingly stands on end as if to make his point. "Now, I want you, Isabel. And I'm pretty sure you want me too. Yes?"

Struck dumb, I can only nod.

"So," he concludes, still in that same logical voice, "drop that damn towel and come here. Right now."

And so I let the towel fall.

Isabel

ying there afterward, the bedroom quiet except for the gurgle of my lavender diffuser, Ryan strokes my hair. "What are you thinking?" he says.

My head is on his chest, so I have to twist to see his face. "Isn't that the girl's line?" I say, half-joking.

He shrugs. "Not necessarily. Although I will admit I've never wanted to ask it . . . before. Is that a tacky thing to say?"

I can't help but smile. "Probably. But it works in my favor, so I can't complain."

"Uh-huh." He shifts under me, knotting his fingers behind his head. "Is there a reason you're avoiding the question?"

"I'm not! Jesus, you're a persistent bastard, Ry. Has anyone told you that before?"

"Plenty of times," he says, his voice guarded. "Although not necessarily in the bedroom. And you still haven't answered me."

I slide off his chest and lie on my side, facing him. He mirrors me, a quizzical look on his face. "What?" he asks. "Trying to figure out how to let me down easy?"

His tone is lighthearted, but I'm sure the intention beneath it is anything but. A shiver runs through me, not just because we're lying here naked, sweat cooling on our skin. I reach down and grab the blanket, pulling it up to our waists. "I'm sure *that* one's the girl's line," I say, fluffing my pillow, which is somewhat the worse for wear.

Ryan regards me, his hazel eyes darkening. "I think I've just proved," he says, exasperation creeping into his voice, "that it's not. Would you please talk to me?"

I reach out and rest my hand on his arm. He stiffens under my touch but allows it, clearly waiting for me to speak. "Don't freak out," I say finally. "I wasn't going to say that all of this was a cosmic mistake and kick you out, or anything like that. I only—I need to tell you something about Max."

This galvanizes him, in a way that I didn't expect. His eyes narrow and he sits up, the blanket pooling at his waist. "Did you sleep with him?" he says immediately.

I sit up myself, completely irritated. "Why is that all either of you wants to know? Do you think I go around leaping into bed with people at the slightest provocation?"

Despite himself, Ryan's lips twitch. "Um . . ." he says, surveying our naked selves, the rumpled sheets, and the towels, crumpled into ignominious heaps on the floor.

"Shut up!" I say, swatting him on the shoulder. "I've known you for almost eight years, for one thing. For another, I wouldn't exactly call what happened in the shower a 'slight provocation.' And I seem to recall that you wouldn't take no for an answer."

"Fair enough," Ryan says. "But you still haven't answered my question."

I get to my feet. "No, I didn't sleep with Max," I hiss, opening my dresser and pulling out the first thing I encounter—a pair of workout pants that have clearly seen better days. "For God's sake, Ryan. I went to his house to tell him about us."

I yank a hot pink tank top over my head and emerge to find him looking at me like I am a strange new species of animal. "Really?" he says, in an entirely different tone. "What about us?"

"What do you think?" I say, trying not to blush and failing miserably.

Comprehension is dawning on Ryan's face. "Is that why you didn't call me after last night? Because you drove out to Folly to talk to him?"

"I couldn't just—not say anything. Or pretend it hadn't happened," I say, tugging my tank top straight. "What . . . are you saying I shouldn't have done it? That I should have waited for him to find out some other way?"

Slowly, Ryan shakes his head. "No. Not at all. I—you've got guts, you know that? More than most people. So what happened?"

I sink down onto the bed next to him. "It didn't go well."

"No?" Ryan says, his fingers pleating the material of the blanket.

I shake my head, remembering the way Max had slammed his fist into the wall, sinking it to the wrist, blood and plaster spraying everywhere. "Not at all. Which was bad enough. But then—he was packing. He told me he couldn't stay in Charleston anymore . . . that he couldn't fall out of love with me here. I tried to stop him, but he wouldn't listen to me."

"What about Finn?" Ryan says quietly. "He'll just leave her behind . . . again? And let us pick up the pieces?"

"Not exactly," I mumble. This is the hard part. I'd almost rather tell him Max was deserting Finn than explain what he wants to do. But there's no getting around it, so I lift my chin and look at Ry, who is staring straight back at me, his gaze flat and challenging.

"Not exactly *what*?" he says. "What precisely does that slippery son of a bitch have in mind?"

"I'll tell you," I say, the words coming slowly. "But when I do—could you promise me that you'll listen until I'm done? And that you'll consider it with an open mind?"

Ryan regards me for a long moment. And then he says, "I promise, Isabel. But first, come here, would you?"

He holds out his arms, and, eyeing him carefully, I crawl toward him. Without wisecracks or innuendos, he settles me against the curve of his body and puts his arm around me, drawing the blanket over us both. And then he says, "Okay. Go on."

So I do. True to his word, Ryan doesn't say a thing until I'm finished. He doesn't so much as move a muscle. At last I wind down and sit there, waiting.

"Well," Ryan says after a moment, "what did you tell him?"

He sounds so reasonable, I don't quite trust it. I dart a sideways glance at him and see him looking back at me evenly. "I promised to have an open mind, right? Well, this is me, having one. Let's see how long it lasts. I'll do my best, I promise you that."

"Okay," I say, and feel myself start to shake. It comes over me, sudden as a fever, and there doesn't seem to be anything I can do to stop.

Leaning against Ryan like I am, there's no way for me to hide it. Eyes narrowed, he takes me by the shoulders. "Isabel, what did you say to him?"

"Well," I say, "first I said no. A lot. And then—he begged."

Ryan clears his throat, an innocent sound that manages to be menacing nonetheless. "He begged you? How?"

I'm not a liar, but there is nothing in my moral lexicon that makes me believe I need to tell Ryan about that kiss. That was between me and Max, and to make it otherwise would be to betray what we once shared. Somehow, I make the shaking stop. And then I look Ryan in the eye and say, "He asked me to trust him."

Ryan makes the throat-clearing sound again, and this time there is no mistaking the warning in it. "And did you?"

Slowly, I shake my head. "I told him I had to think about it. But Ry—as much as I don't want to, as much as it scares the hell out of me—I think I might let her go. It's only for a month, and Max's parents are going too."

Next to me, Ryan is completely motionless. Finally he says, sounding as bitter as I've ever heard him, "If you've already decided, why does it even matter what I think?"

"It matters to me," I say, turning toward him and resting my head in the hollow of his shoulder. "If you're dead set against it, Ryan, I'll say no."

He jerks back, surprised. "You would do that for me?"

As carefully as if I were dealing with a spooked horse, I bring my body full against him, one of my legs over his and a hand on his chest to hold him still. Ryan isn't fooled. He shifts under me uneasily, a question forming on his lips, and I speak before he can ask it. "I love you, Ry. And I can see that if you're not okay with this, letting Max take Finn now might break something in you. Yes, I have a certain loyalty to him—he is Finn's father—but he can come back to Charleston and she'll still be here, probably in the same emotional shape in which he left her. I can't say the same about you, not with any degree of certainty. So you tell me, Ry, whether you can live with Max taking Finn to Barbados this summer. And if you can't—I'll tell him no."

Ryan makes a strangled sort of sound, and when I look up at him, I'm shocked to see tears running down his cheeks. He scrubs at them, hard, but they keep coming. "Goddamn it," he mutters, wiping at his eyes. "I didn't want to do this."

I have never seen Ryan cry, not once in nearly eight years, not even when his dog Bella was hit by a car in front of both of us and died in the street in his arms. I'd sobbed then, kneeling beside them in the road, the taillights of the hit-and-run driver vanishing around the corner as Bella took her last breath. But Ryan had gotten to his feet, dry-eyed and white-lipped, Bella cradled in his arms, and carried her to the backyard without a word. He'd dug the grave himself, buried her with her favorite blanket and a new rawhide bone, and then walked back into the house, muddy shoes and all, and gone straight to take a shower. When he'd come out, his eyes were red-rimmed and his face pale, but his voice didn't shake when he asked me if he could borrow my dad's chisel to carve a marker for her. I'd tried to hold him, to offer comfort, but he'd sat as stiff and unyielding as a statue in my embrace, and after a moment I'd let him go.

"Ry?" I say now, sitting up to see him more clearly. He turns away from me, but just as I couldn't disguise my trembling from him earlier, there is no way for him to hide this from me now. I put my palm against his cheek, slick with tears, and turn his face back to mine.

In a last-ditch effort at self-possession—or maybe to pretend, like a child, that if he can't see me, I can't see him—he closes his eyes. Tears glint on his long lashes. "Go away, Isabel," he says, his voice choked. "I can feel you staring. Stop, all right?"

"This is my bedroom," I point out gently. "And I'm not going anywhere. It's all right, Ry. It's okay. You can cry if you want to."

His eyes open then, finding mine. The expression in them is so raw it makes me catch my breath. "Why would you do that?" he says. "Why would you tell him no, just because letting him take her would make me unhappy?"

With my index finger, I trace the path of his tears, erasing them one by one. "I told you, Ry. Do you need me to say it again?"

One of his hands rises, fingers intertwining with mine. He leans his face into my palm like a cat and takes one deep breath, then another. "Because you love me."

"Of course I do," I say, like anything else is unthinkable.

For a long moment, Ryan is silent. Finally he says, "I trust you, Isabel. If you think Finn will be safe with Max, okay. I have faith in you."

"Really?" I say in surprise, and he gives a small, humorless laugh.

"Yes, really. Is that so hard to believe? Last night," he says, rolling onto his back, "you told me that sometimes, when you love someone, you want so much to keep them safe that you wind up saving them from all the wrong things. If you think it's right, if you think we should, then let her go."

The moon shines through my half-open curtains, bathing both of us in its light. I look down at him, at his eyelashes still matted with tears and his hair, spiked and wild from the shower and our earlier exertions. At the easy way he's sprawled on my bed, his skin golden-brown against the sheets. At the way he's gazing at me, eyes half-shut, with a heady blend of want and conviction.

"Thank you," I say impulsively, and his eyebrows knit.

"For what?"

I shrug, trying to keep the rising tide of emotion at bay. "For everything, Ry. For paying it forward that day at Metto. For sticking by us all these years. For loving Finn. And for trusting me. I know it doesn't come easily to you."

He shakes his head. "No. But—worth it, maybe?"

"I hope so."

Ryan turns onto his side, propping himself up on one elbow. "In the interest of trust, can I tell you something, Iz? Fair warning, it might make you pretty mad."

"Oh, no." Wrapping my arms around my knees for support, I look over at him. His expression is serene, but I know him well enough to tell that he is worried. "What did you do? Don't tell me you made it to Folly Beach, after all, and punched Max. Or that you were so pissed off that you keyed my car. Or that you hacked into my email—"

"Zero for three, Griffin. I took the job at Marvel." His tone is matter-of-fact, but his eyes flicker down toward the sheets, unable to meet mine.

For a second I think that I've misheard him. Then reality sinks in, and my eyes go wide. "You *what*?"

"You heard me." The first hint of defensiveness has crept into his voice. "I should've told you, I know that. But there it is."

"Damn right you should have! How could you do all—all *this* and never say a word? What was your plan? Have your fun and then get the hell out of Dodge?"

His head snaps up, and he glares at me. "Calm down, Isabel. It's not like that."

"Calm down? Of all the asshole things to do—you let me say I *loved* you—" Too furious to speak, I slide toward the edge of the bed, but he grabs my wrist. I twist and turn, trying to get free, but for all my training, Ryan has me by fifty pounds. "Let me go!" I hiss, but he shakes his head.

"I know it's fucked up. But damn it, Isabel, how was I supposed to know you were going to show up in my office and kiss me like you did? How could I know this was going to happen?" He runs his free hand through his hair, voice rising. "That first time—in my studio—you pushed me away. You told me I'd never be right for you, because I wasn't Max. What was I supposed to do? Sit around mooning after you forever? Watch you rebuild your life with him? Sit by while he did everything I used to do with you—bike rides and dinners and Finn's school projects—like I was some kind of placeholder until the real thing came along?"

His words feel like tiny knives, embedding deep in my chest. Ignoring the pain that spreads through me, the guilt at how, every time I turn around, I'm hurting someone else, I turn my wrist in his grip, feeling the small bones grate. "You should have told me," I say again.

He loosens his grasp and I yank my hand free, rubbing the places where his fingers dug into my skin. "I know that. But I—I just—"

"You just *what*? Didn't have the guts to be honest with me? Saw a chance to get me into bed and figured it was now or never?" The words emerge scathing, each syllable sharp-edged, and I have the momentary satisfaction of seeing him flinch.

"No! Not at all. I just—I don't want to lose you, okay?" His eyes find mine again, searching my face for understanding. "Not a lot of things scare me anymore, Isabel, but that—it's one of them. When I'm with you, I'm *better*. All the bullshit falls away and I see who I'm supposed to be. And when Max came back . . . I thought . . ." He shakes his head again, violently this time. "I'd almost forgotten what it was like, to be empty that way. To live like half a person, going through the motions, like nothing mattered. When he came back, and I had to start doing it again—there was no way in hell I could stay here. It would have wrecked me. And so I took the job."

I am staring at him, openmouthed. "You—" I begin, but he interrupts me.

"I'm not using you, or trying to have some kind of messed-up fling before I leave town. I love you, don't you get it? I wouldn't treat you that way."

"Then what are you doing?" I say, hating the vulnerability in my voice.

Ryan looks down at his hands, fisted in the sheets. For a moment he is silent. Then he speaks, sounding less self-assured than I've ever heard him. "I asked you this before, and it didn't go so well. I wasn't brave enough to tell you the truth, and I don't think it would've made a difference if I had. But maybe now . . ."

His voice trails off. He lets go of the sheets and reaches cautiously to take my hand in his. I can feel his fingers trembling. "Will you come with me, Isabel? I know it's a little crazy. I know your mom just came home, and Max too. I know. But I'll help, any way I can. We can put your house on the market, or we can find a tenant. I already looked into some great schools up there, and there are so many options for Finn—way better than here." He takes a deep breath, then forges on before I can say a word. "I know how important your career is to you—I would never ask you to compromise that—but I'm sure you could find something amazing in the city. I've been doing some research, and there're a couple of openings that look like real possibilities . . . one at Columbia, the other at the Museum of Natural History. I bet there's tons of great martial arts gyms too."

"But what about Max?" I object, my mind spinning. "Finn only now got him back, and vice versa. How could I justify taking her away?"

Ryan refrains from pointing out the obvious—that Max is most likely about to take Finn away from almost everyone she knows, and I've justified that fine. "He could visit, as often as he wants. She could come down here. You could work out a formal custody arrangement—whatever makes the most sense. I won't be obnoxious about it, Isabel, I promise. I was jealous and I'm sorry. But I'll be good. You'll see."

His hand turns in mine, squeezing hard, compelling a response— but none comes. I sit, silent as a stone, weighing the events of the past forty-eight hours. And I know the time for fooling myself is over. It's time to decide—what do I really want?

Taking my silence for dissent, Ryan peers anxiously into my face. "I think it could work, Isabel, I really do. I want you with me, more than anything. You make everything all right for me, you and Finn. And I'd like to think—that is, I hope—"

He's still talking, but I don't hear a word. His voice fades into the background, and instead I see everything that's happened over the past eight years, all of my choices, playing out before me like a movie. I see Max vanish into the woods, see me vanish into myself. See me raising Finn, frightened of the ways in which she is different, terrified that someone will steal her away. See day after day of working and training, stuffing one accomplishment after another into the gaping hole that Max and my mother left behind. See my grief binding me, tighter and tighter, until it became all that was holding me together, leaving no room for anything else.

And then I see Ryan walking up to me that day in Metto with his black suit and his messy hair, see him building the honeysuckle arbor and making dioramas with Finn and driving to my house in a torrential downpour the night the oak tree caught on fire. I see him juggling peaches to make Finn laugh, see the shy, proud look on his face when he showed me the dollhouse he'd made for her. See him standing shirtless by the couch in his office, staring down at me like I am all he wants, hear him saying that he loves me, asking me if I am sure.

"Isabel?" he says now, fingers tight on mine. "You look—well, never mind. I know it's a lot to take in. And I know I should've told you before about taking the job. I don't blame you for being mad at me. I'll leave, okay?" He pushes the sheets back, realizes he is naked, and covers himself again with a grimace, clearly calculating the least humiliating way to make his escape. "But think about it, would you? You don't have to decide right away. I can show you the list of schools, the jobs I found—"

Before he can go through the whole litany again, I find my voice. It's hoarse and uneven, but it comes, and I am grateful. "Stop, Ry. I don't have to think about it."

Ryan's eyes widen, and I see panic flash across his face. "Don't just say no, Isabel. Please."

"I'm not saying no."

"Then what are you saying? I don't understand."

His grip intensifies further, hurting my hand, but I don't pull away. "I'm saying yes, Ry," I tell him, and feel the last of my uncertainty evanesce, leaving behind an unmistakable sense of peace. "Yes, we'll come with you."

The panicked expression fades from his face, replaced by disbelief. "Really? You're not just saying that? Seriously, Isabel, you will?"

I nod, and, nakedness forgotten, he leans forward and wraps his arms around me. "Thank God," he mutters into my hair—the closest I've ever gotten to hearing Ryan pray. He pulls back and looks at me, smiling. I watch as his eyes well with tears again and he lets them spill, and it's only when his hand rises to my face and his fingers trace my lips, wet, that I realize I'm crying too—for everything that both of us have lost, for the promise of everything that lies ahead.

Max

F inn and I stand hand in hand in front of an engraved plaque at Bayleys Plantation. It's hot out here—at least ninety-five degrees—and her fingers are slippery in mine, but neither of us wants to let go.

"Read it to me, Daddy," she says, her voice hushed as if we are in a cathedral.

I glance at her, cheeks flushed pink from the heat, one of her curls escaping from its plait. She insisted on wearing a sundress instead of her usual tank top and shorts, out of respect, and I didn't argue. There are no graves for Bussa and Nanny Grigg, for Jackey and all the rest of them. This marker is the closest thing to a tribute to their sacrifice.

"Okay," I say, and clear my throat. "It says: 'That bussoe, the ranger, King Wiltshire, the carpenter, Dick Bailey, the mason, Johnny, the standard bearer, and Johnny Cooper, a cooper, were the principal instigators of the Insurrection at Bayleys . . . that he had read the papers that gave the intelligence that they were free.' That's a quote from one of the slaves at the River Plantation. And below it, there's another quote from a slave at Simmons, see?"

"Read me that one," Finn says. "Please?" She's more than capable of reading these inscriptions herself, but I understand why she wants me to do it: There's something ceremonial about honoring the fallen slaves by speaking these words aloud.

"'That Nanny Grig, a Negro woman at Simmons, who said she could read . . . told them that they were all damned fools to work, for that she would not, as freedom they were sure to get . . . and the only way to get it was to fight for it, otherwise they would not get it.'" That sounds exactly like her, feisty attitude and all. I remember her asking me if I was an obeah man, if I was going to spirit her up into the sky and fly us both away.

She kneels, tracing the last few lines with her finger. "'Unveiled by the Right Hon—Honour'—What's that word, Daddy?"

"Honourable," I tell her. "'The Right Honourable Owen S. Arthur, M.P., Prime Minister.' Kind of like our president."

"'On August 1, 2003,'" Finn continues. "'In com-mem-or-ation of those who fought and died in their struggle for freedom.'" She glances up at me, head cocked. "What does that mean? Commemoration?"

"It means to recognize them," I say, my voice husky. "To show that the prime minister and the citizens of Barbados realize how badly the slaves were treated and that they gave everything, including their lives, to be free."

Finn considers this, her gray eyes intent on my face. Then she breaks a spray of bright pink bougainvillea blossoms off the bush that overhangs the plaque. Carefully, she places it at the base of the rock, an offering and homage. "They were brave," she says at last. "Weren't they?"

"Yeah, they were."

"And so were you." She stands and wraps her arms around my waist, peering up at me. I rest my hand on the top of her head, letting the warmth of her hair sink into my palm, and close my eyes. "I love you, Daddy," she says, hugging me tighter.

I open my eyes then, breathing in deep. "I love you too," I tell her, and she nods.

"I know that," she says, leaning her head against my side. "I've always known."

The two of us stand there, enveloped in a quiet solidarity that surpasses the need for words, and for the first time since I stepped into the clearing in my parents' woods, I feel like I've come home.

Acknowledgments

When I set out to write this book, the first thing I realized was how much I didn't know. For educating me in the finer points of field archaeology, thanks are due to Jonathan Schleier, executive director of Wilmington, North Carolina's Public Archaeology Corps, and Eleanora Reber, associate professor of archaeology and chair of the anthropology department at the University of North Carolina Wilmington. Both were incredibly generous with their time and expertise. Any errors in the manuscript are, of course, my own.

As little as I knew about field archaeology, I knew even less about life in Barbados circa 1816. I am indebted to the scholarly work of Hilary McD. Beckles, Stephanie Bergman, Kenneth M. Bilby, Charlotte J. Frisbie, Jerome S. Handler, Elsie Clews Parsons, Robert Morris, John R. Rickford, Karl Watson, and Pedro L.V. Welch for a wealth of historical information. Andrea Stuart's *Sugar in the Blood: A Family's Story of Slavery and Empire* proved an invaluable resource, as did Kathleen Catford's *"Barbadiana": A Collection of Poems in Barbadian Dialect 1931–42*, Geraldine Lane's *Tracing Ancestors in Barbados: A Practical Guide*, Matthew Parker's *The Sugar Barons: Family, Corruption, Empire, and War in the West Indies*, Gelien Matthews's *Caribbean Slave Revolts and the British Abolitionist Move-*

ment, Hilary McD. Beckles's *Natural Rebels: A Social History of Enslaved Black Women in Barbados*, Jerome S. Handler's *A Guide to Source Materials for the Study of Barbados History, 1627–1834*, Warren Alleyne and Henry Fraser's *The Barbados–Carolina Connection*, and many more volumes too numerous to list here.

I am grateful to the Bridgetown public library for allowing me access to the 1816 archives of *The Barbados Mercury and Bridge-Town Gazette* — on microfilm, no less — as well as to Harriet Pierce, the fabulous librarian at The Barbados Museum and Historical Society's Shilstone Memorial Library.

Thank you, of course, to my amazing agent, Felicia Eth, who fearlessly navigates the world of publishing on my behalf. I'd be lost without you. To Linda Marrow, the manuscript's first editor — you are missed! — and to the indefatigable, phenomenal Elana Seplow-Jolley, who leapt into the breach without hesitation and helped to shape every page of this book. Thanks, too, to Jennifer Rodriguez and her incredible production team. You've transformed my imaginary friends from a dream into reality (of a sort), and I am grateful for you every day.

To Anne Firmender, who listened to me talk about the plot endlessly before I'd written a word (*Wherever* did *Max go when he disappeared in the woods that day?*), accompanied me to Barbados and Charleston (okay, so maybe that wasn't so much of a hardship), read multiple drafts, acted as head cheerleader, and generally helped me maintain my sanity. If you weren't in my life, I'd be — well, never mind. I shudder to think about it. To my parents, Lois and Michael Colin, who gave me the gifts of time, unconditional love and support, and valued critical feedback . . . I don't know how I got so lucky. Thank you. To Neil Horne, for giving me the time and space to write, helping me work out tricky plot points, serving as all-around website guru, reading early drafts, fortifying me with endless rounds of PCJ, putting up with my gigantic piles of paper, and being patient with me as I disappeared into my head for the thousandth time. You, sir, are a saint. To Tracy Wilkes, my designated "historical reader," for making it all the way through the first draft, never letting me get away with anything, and being the best second mother a girl could have. I owe you one. Or several. To Lucas, for his compassion and thoughtfulness, and for inspiring me to create Finn. To Jessica Smith, Mitzy Jonkheer, Jessica Christensen, LaToia Brown, and Sarah Carpenter, for their friendship. To the Wildacres Residency Program, for a beautiful and quiet space in which to write. And to Matt Carvin, for making me laugh, making me think, and never letting me forget the time I pirouetted gracefully through the air and landed cross-legged at the bottom of a flight of stairs. In a dress. May Hookman preserve you.

About the Author

Emily Colin's debut novel, *The Memory Thief*, was a *New York Times* bestseller and a Target Emerging Authors Pick. Her diverse life experience includes organizing a Coney Island tattoo and piercing show, hauling fish at the Dolphin Research Center in the Florida Keys, roaming New York City as an itinerant teenage violinist, helping launch two small publishing companies, and serving as the associate director of DREAMS of Wilmington, a nonprofit dedicated to immersing youth in need in the arts. Originally from Brooklyn, she lives in Wilmington, North Carolina, with her family.

About the Type

This book was set in Electra, a typeface designed for Linotype by renowned type designer W. A. Dwiggins (1880–1956). Electra is a fluid typeface, avoiding the contrasts of thick and thin strokes that are prevalent in most modern typefaces.